Praise for *Amber to Ashes*

"Titillating, thrilling, and poetic, Gail McHugh brings on the feels with every word."

—Katy Evans, *New York Times* bestselling author of *Manwhore*

"Impeccable writing with a flawless delivery, *Amber to Ashes* is Gail McHugh at her absolute finest, weaving both unforgettable characters and a captivating plot together in a story you won't soon forget."

—K. Bromberg, *New York Times* bestselling
author of the Driven series

"*Amber to Ashes* is a gritty and consuming masterpiece. Every emotion possible is poured out on the pages, and I'm quite certain I will never be the same after reading it."

—A. L. Jackson, *New York Times* bestselling
author of *Take This Regret*

"A beautifully gritty, gripping tale that will melt your panties off on one page and have you clutching your chest with anxiety on the next. Gail McHugh's words are pure, molten fire, and *Amber to Ashes* certainly brings the heat."

—S. L. Jennings, *New York Times* bestselling author of *Taint*

"Highly addicting, heart-wrenching, pulse-racing perfection. . . . *Amber to Ashes* is an epic twister tale of turmoil, grief, pain, and guilt, perfectly fused with breathtaking passion. Gail McHugh's flawless writing will leave you no choice but to be consumed by every poetic word."

—Tillie Cole, *USA Today* bestselling author of *Raze*

"Raw, powerful, and lyrical. Get ready to be seduced by Gail McHugh's brilliant, dark tale. *Amber to Ashes* is 6+ stars!"

—Mia Asher, bestselling author of *Arsen*

"Gritty, raw, real, and tragically beautiful, *Amber to Ashes* is a story that reached into the darkest corners of my heart and mind. I'm left as wrecked as her characters and just as in love. Yet another stunning story by McHugh."

—Mandi Beck, author of the Caged Love series

"Gail McHugh owns me with every word she's penned in this book. *Amber to Ashes* is inarguably one of her greatest works yet."

—Gretchen de la O, author of *Prototype*

ALSO BY GAIL McHUGH

Collide

Pulse

AMBER

to

ASHES

⤜ *Part One in the Torn Hearts Series* ⤛

GAIL McHUGH

ATRIA PAPERBACK
New York ✦ London ✦ Toronto ✦ Sydney ✦ New Delhi

ATRIA PAPERBACK
An Imprint of Simon & Schuster, Inc.
1230 Avenue of the Americas
New York, NY 10020

First Atria Paperback edition June 2015

ATRIA PAPERBACK and colophon are trademarks of Simon & Schuster, Inc.

For information about special discounts for bulk purchases, please contact Simon & Schuster Special Sales at 1-866-506-1949 or business@simonandschuster.com.

The Simon & Schuster Speakers Bureau can bring authors to your live event. For more information or to book an event contact the Simon & Schuster Speakers Bureau at 1-866-248-3049 or visit our website at www.simonspeakers.com.

Interior design by Dana Sloan

Manufactured in the United States of America

10 9 8 7 6 5 4 3 2 1

Library of Congress Cataloging-in-Publication Data has been applied for.

ISBN 978-1-4767-6601-0
ISBN 978-1-4767-6604-1 (ebook)

The two most important days in your life are the day you were born and the day you find out why.

—MARK TWAIN

PROLOGUE

Amber

I FELL FOR THE two loves of my life when I was nineteen. Yes, two. Plural. More than one.

Immoral? Maybe. I say undeniable. Uncontained. Some say I'm wrong to feel this way about two men. Most call me a whore, a skank, or the town slut.

I don't care.

Simply put ... they each took a piece of what I wanted to give. No one will ever understand the addiction they pulled me into, both men the needle to my next hit. My dizzying high. They were as opposite as fire and ice, yet I ached for them equally.

Needed them the same way.

One was my rock. My strength. My first real ... obsession.

The other was my passion, my burn.

They owned my mind and all its thoughts, every pulse that thrummed through my body, and every inch of my shattered soul.

A crack of lightning in my dark sky, they were a raging storm I never saw coming, an unforeseen heartbreak on the edge of a dangerous cliff.

Little did I know that by the time I turned twenty, the death of one of them was going to steal them both away from my life.

His murderer?

Me ...

CHAPTER 1

Amber

Four Months Earlier

A WHIFF OF FAST food hits me as I scan Hadley University's student dining hall. Juiced-up jocks, bad boys, and uppity sorority girls to my left, creepy loners, hipsters, and random misfits to my right. Every type of personality is present and accounted for, each huddled at their socially segregated tables.

Cliques.

Whoever said college wasn't filled with them must've been smoking crack.

I can do this. I can do this. I can do this, I chant in my head, having not a speck of faith that I can. But what the hell is faith anyway? One huge misconception if you ask me. Either way, college has to be a better experience than the twelve years of mental tedium of public school.

At least I hope to God it is.

Inhaling, exhaling, right foot in front of the left, I start for an empty table—right before I feel myself . . . falling?

Kill. Me. Now.

Attention so focused on making it to that damned empty table,

2

I fail to notice a duffel bag in my path. Falling forward—momentum picking up—books and papers fly from my hands as my heart flies from my chest.

With nothing to grab, I face-plant onto something that feels like concrete, my knees buried between two jean-clad, muscular thighs. The chair Concrete's sitting in screeches sideways across the laminate floor as laughter erupts, exploding in my ears like grenades. Mortified, I wrap my fingers around his firm shoulders, my nose inches from his.

My "savior" flashes me a heart-stopping smile as he curls his arms around my waist, absorbing our impact. My breath falters, catching like a snagged sweater on a rusty nail.

Embarrassment hijacks my body as my gaze falls upon a pair of tattoo-sleeved arms. Streaks of orange fire, shaded skulls, and what appears to be Chinese writing twine their way over every inch of thickly roped muscle, from his biceps down to his wrists. My attention travels back north. A blast of jet-black hair, spiked up messily above the most striking *I can fuck you into oblivion* blue eyes I've ever seen, nearly stops my heart.

In those eyes, I see amusement. I also see trouble, a healthy dose of rebellion, and pure, unadulterated sex. I tighten my grip around his shoulders as his smile widens. There's a heavy air of arrogance in his smile, and something screams at me to run—that this dude's going to be my undoing—but I can't. I'm stuck, Super-Glued by my thoughts to his lap. His features are disarming, perfectly . . . imperfect. Lush, sculpted lips. Hard, chiseled jaw. He's a perfect composite of every piece of gorgeous, drop-my-panties-now-and-hold-on-for-dear-life male specimen I've ever come across.

God help me.

A lone dimple dots his kissable cheek. "Have you decided to be my lunch? If so, I *fully* approve of the meal."

"*Excuse* me?" I try to ignore his clean smell of soap and woodsy cologne. *Woodsy?* Did I just describe cologne as woodsy? Whatever it is, it's making me high. *He's* making me high. "What's *that* supposed to mean?"

He chuckles, and the realization of just how moronic my question was makes me want to crawl under the table and die.

"It means you're in my lap and you look good enough to eat." He runs his callused hands up and down my arms. I tremble, his touch lighting me up from head to toe. "Actually," he continues, "'eat' is *nowhere* near the correct word. 'Devour' is more like it."

An aggravated huff electrocutes the air, making me whip my head around. Some porcelain-looking blonde is clearly annoyed by our exchange. I narrow my eyes right back at her and bring my attention back to the dude whose lap is holding my body captive.

"Oh, *really?*" Though it comes out snarky, it's the only thing I can think of.

"Yes, really," he answers, his voice a low rasp. He flicks his pale blue eyes to my mouth, dragging his bottom lip between his teeth. "'Devour' is a better term for what I'd do to you."

Although we're surrounded by laughing spectators, an unexpected urge to taste his lips tickles deep within my belly.

Wait. What the hell am I thinking?

Control. He's stripped it from me, and I need to take it back.

Despite my inner whore's protest at not becoming a permanent fixture in his lap, I attempt to compose myself as I get to my feet. I smooth my hands through my wavy black hair, and with steely resolve I straighten my spine with every intention of walking away without further handicapping my brain.

My efforts mean shit when he stands, his smile spreading into a crooked grin. His eyes hold steady on mine, and the sexual intent behind them not only sends a hard punch of desire crackling through my body but also vacuums the air right out of my lungs.

At this, I mentally berate myself.

I'm so not one of *those* girls. A guy's good looks have never left me a gooey puddle of idiotic hormones. Well, with the exception of right now. But either way, Christ, my traitor body does a flip-flop as I take in the whole length of him.

This guy's a beast, standing a good foot taller than my five-foot-three frame. I feel like a speck—a tiny, little speck. To make matters worse, while I thought his lickable tattoos only graced his arms, I find I'm so very wrong. On the right side of his neck, peeking up from his plain black T-shirt, are the delicious horns of what appears to be the devil himself.

I was right. It's an omen. He's the devil, and I'm in a heavenish hell.

In an attempt to yank myself from my absurd reaction to him, I decide now is the perfect time to pick up my belongings and get the hell out of . . . well, get the hell out of hell.

"So, what time should I pick you up tonight?" he asks as I drop to my knees and reach for my English Lit book. "I'm thinking somewhere around seven. Go home and take a nap. You'll need your energy. I'm *definitely* keeping you up late."

I glare at him, my jaw nearly hitting the floor. I'm no stranger to one-night stands, and usually a guy this arrogant would have me on my back in a nanosecond, but for some strange reason, one I may never understand, all this one's doing is pissing me off. "Are you for real?"

A smirk hits his face. "When I looked in the mirror this morning, I was as real as they come."

He kneels and hands me my sociology book. I yank it from his grip. Great. Another smirk that has my resolve coming close to taking a hike.

We both rise, and amusement once again flashes in his eyes. His unfairly gorgeous face is way too close to mine. Close enough that I can feel his minty breath feathering over my cheek.

"Were you born conceited or did you just morph into an asshole over time?"

He cups his chin, his brows dipped in mock thought. "I *think* I was born this way, but I could be wrong. You'd have to ask my mother about that if ya want the honest story behind how I turned out this way." He smiles, clearly getting off on my reaction to his straightforwardness. "Any more questions for me? I'm finding your curiosity cute as all hell."

I snort, amazed that I'm still a willing participant in this conversation. "Figures. Honestly, I don't give a shit that you find _anything_ I do cute." I pause, tilting my head. "Thanks for catching me, but seriously, can you just go away?"

Laughter riots from his chest. "Whoa, killer, I'm simply trying to lend you my services. And what's happening between us is sexual tension at its finest. It's good—healthier than a cold glass of milk. Just go with it."

Oh. My. God. This is getting worse by the minute.

"_Services?_ Do you take pride in being a male whore? Oh, wait." I bounce my palm against my forehead, feigning stupidity. "How could you not? You have a dick that shoots orgasmic flames into a girl. Am I right?"

Laughter sounds from the group around the table as he smirks again, this one cockier than its predecessor. "Yeah. You're definitely in need of my . . . _services._ A good lay will brighten your pretty little ass right up." He tosses me a wink, offering me his hand. "Oh, I'm Ryder Ashcroft, by the way."

Exasperated, I don't take Ryder Ashcroft's hand. Nope. The only thing I take is an unsteady breath right before I smack him clear across his pretty face, the pain searing my hand worth every bit as I watch Pretty Boy's eyes go wide. An atom bomb of laughter explodes from all directions, adding to my absolute enjoyment of the payback's-a-bitch moment.

I barely have time to catalogue the look on Ryder's face when I hear him mumble, "Fuck. That was brilliant," half a heartbeat before his mouth is _devouring_ mine.

Stunned, I gasp, my traitor lips parting as his sinfully delicious kiss absorbs the uninvited moan that jumps from my throat.

Some douche yells, "Go for it, dude!"

A girl squeaks, "He's officially lost his mind!"

I also catch several whistling catcalls.

A split second before I slam my hands against Ryder's chest, I feel his soft tongue—which I now know has a piercing in it, a barbell to be exact—languidly caress over mine. Oh Jesus. It sends a full, down-to-the-bone shiver up my spine. I unclog my brain from its temporary high and push Ryder back a few feet, leaving us both panting.

His eyes, intense with lust and shock, darken and lock on mine, another one of his infamous smirks twitching the corners of his lips as he studies me.

With a huff and a flip of the bird in his direction, I swipe the back of my hand across my lips, gather the rest of my books, and head toward the stupid table I'd originally tried to sit at before I'd fallen into his lap. As soon as I take my first step, I feel a large hand touch my shoulder. With every intention of knocking homeboy out, I spin around, my gaze snagging wide green eyes that do *not* belong to the previous offender.

What the? Is every male in this building on growth hormones? This guy's just as big as Ryder Ass-Croft, if not bigger.

Hands held up in surrender, my schedule in their possession, he flashes me a cautious yet impish smile. "You forgot this." He places the paper on top of my books, and throws his thumb over his shoulder, motioning to Ryder. "Don't mind him."

"Don't *mind* him?" I parrot, flicking my eyes in Ryder's direction, who's now sitting at his rowdy table.

Blondie, who *seemed* annoyed earlier, is in his lap, consoling him, her arm wrapped around his neck as she whispers some shit in his ear. Ryder glances at me, a megawatt smile splitting his conceited lips.

Annoyed, embarrassed, and beyond sexually frustrated, I grit my teeth and turn on my heel. "He's an asshole."

"That *asshole's* my best friend."

I whip around, but Asshole's buddy chucks his two cents into the tension-wired air before I can.

"Still, there's *no* disputing his assholeness. It defines brutal, some of the worst shit out there." His emerald eyes light up in amusement, a grin hugging his lips as he rests a forearm on a metal post. "I also think his mother breast-fed him longer than what's deemed socially appropriate, so that *could* be the culprit to his problem."

I raise a brow, watching as the dude before me chuckles at his joke.

"My name's Brock Cunningham. I was bottle-fed, so I'm *nothing* like my friend, and I might be wrong, but you *look* like you could use some help." Somewhat cautiously, Brock reaches for the mountainous stack of books and papers that are slipping from my grasp.

With little resistance, I allow him to take half the pile.

"Cunningham, huh?" Anger waning some, I make my way toward a table and decide that sitting with a group of geeky debate team members suits me. "As in Richie Cunningham?"

"Richie?" Confusion peppers his voice.

"Yeah, Richie Cunningham from *Happy Days*." I claim a seat next to a freak wearing Coke-bottle eyeglasses, drop my half of the stack of books on the table, and watch Brock pull out a chair across from me. "It's only the best sitcom from the seventies," I continue. "You have to have seen it."

Expression bewildered, he scratches his jaw. The sun dripping in through the windows catches his eyes, their flecks of gold shimmering like diamonds. I see a twinkle of mischievousness in their mossy green depths that feels familiar, but I can't quite place it.

I freeze, only just now realizing how sickeningly good-looking Asshole's best friend is.

To be honest, he's equally as good-looking as Asshole, but in a different way. The angles of his face aren't as hard and defined; they're softer, less intimidating. His hair's lighter, its blond-caramel blend reminding me of cream soda. I lick my lips, my fingers tingling to test if the wavy strands feel as soft as they look. His boyish smile makes my heart thump erratically, and I find myself getting lost in the cute, confused look planted on his face.

"Now you have me curious," he says. "I have no idea who Richie Cunningham is, or *Happy Days*." He shrugs, his smile broadening. "You gotta give me *something*."

I can't believe I'm about to go there.

I clear my throat, gather my nerve, and do just that.

I go there.

I sing the show's theme song, trying to hit the notes without shattering the windows. Forget about the nomads sitting at the table, who are now looking at me like *I'm* the freak; a chuckle escapes Brock's throat, and I want to find the nearest bridge and jump right off it.

"Although you have a beautiful voice," Brock points out, "I can't say I've ever heard that song before."

"You're seriously deprived, Cunningham. You are aware of this, right?"

I adamantly believe this. It's my generation's loss that they didn't grow up watching Mr. and Mrs. Cunningham raise the perfect family. *Happy Days* was exactly that.

Happy days.

Days when parents didn't get high, craving their next hit more than they craved a hug from their child. Days when that child wasn't left scared, hungry, and alone without a whisper of heat to keep her warm when winter gripped the city. Days when innocent eyes didn't witness bloodshed in the home where they were supposed to feel safe, unharmed, loved.

I steal myself away from my dark, shadowy past as Brock clasps his hands behind his neck. "I might be deprived because I haven't watched this show you're talking about, but I felt deprived before you sang that . . . weird melody."

"*Weird?*" A frown crinkles my forehead. "It's so not even close to being weird."

"Sure as shit it's weird." Brock crosses his arms, his gaze locked on mine. "Still, you made me like it *more* than I should."

His flirtatious stare makes me swallow hard. What the hell's wrong with me today? I'm convinced the Frappuccino I inhaled earlier was laced with some kind of date-rape drug, because this is the second time in ten minutes that the opposite sex has made me feel high.

I draw in a calming breath and attempt to divert the conversation. "So, uh . . . why did you feel deprived before I sang my 'weird' melody?"

The tiniest of smiles tugs his lips. "That's because I don't know the name of the beautiful girl who sings weird songs on introduction." He shrugs, his pectoral muscles bulging beneath his polo shirt. "It's impossible not to feel deprived without that information. Wouldn't you agree, Miss . . . ?"

Oh, he's good.

I release the breath I'm holding, my nerves cracking my response into a whisper. "Ber."

"*Ber?*" He spikes an incredulous brow, his smile widening. "No doubt that's a . . . different name, but I'm digging it."

"No, wait!" Mortified, my words come out rushed. "It's not Ber."

Brock cups his chin, his smile ridiculously cute as he studies me. "Are you trying to confuse me, beautiful girl whose name's *not* Ber? If that's your intent, it's working."

Seriously, someone just put me in the ground now, ending this embarrassing moment. "No. I'm not trying to confuse you, I—"

"You're nervous around me, then." He wets his lips, the act nearly stopping my heart. "I'm right, aren't I?"

"*No,*" I retort, praying to every God in existence that he can't see the lie I'm miserably failing at trying to hide. "I'm not *nervous* around you."

"Yes, you are, but it's sexy as fuck, so it's all good." Brock leans forward, fastening his eyes to mine. "So what's your real name . . . *Ber?*"

I sigh, another whisper clogging my throat. "Amber. Amber Moretti."

"Amber," he repeats, tasting my name on his tongue. I like the way he says it. "Well, Am . . . *ber*, I know my asshole friend might've dampened your day, but I plan to make up for his lack of couth, if you'd let me."

Hooked.

Yeah. I feel like a helpless fish out of water, hooked by a hungry angler. At the same time, I feel like a giddy schoolgirl as a spark of excitement bubbles in my stomach, and to be honest, it makes my skin crawl.

Just like faith, love is another misconception held by those who believe in fairy tales. Fairy tales don't exist; neither do knights on white horses. In my honest opinion, every book princess in history was a stupid, naïve twit.

I can't deny that I want to be touched by love so I can feel something . . . anything. But the reality of what love ultimately ends up like screams loudly in my ears, its warning seeded deep within my numb, hollow heart. I open my mouth to tell Brock Cunningham he can take his white horse and fake suit of armor and ride off into the sunset with some other dumb chick who will fall for his future lies and bullshit promises, but he speaks before the words hit my jaded lips.

"Besides, I think it'd be cool watching reruns of *Happy Days* with you."

I snap my mouth shut as he casts me a shy smile, his green eyes zoned in on mine with nothing but warmth behind them. "That is," he adds, "if you promise to sing that weird melody while we get amped up on too many Red Bulls and nauseate ourselves with disgusting amounts of popcorn." The smile drops from his lips, sincerity replacing it. "But you also have to tell me the secrets those gorgeous eyes are attempting to hide from the world."

It's here, on the first day of my freshman year of college, that I'm aware a fork in the road of my life has reared its ugly head.

Part of me wants to hoist myself up onto Brock Cunningham's white horse, wrap my hesitant arms around his suit of armor, and maybe, just *maybe*, start to feel something. But the other part wants to jet, running as far away from him as humanly possible.

I mull it over and decide that I'm up for playing the role of a naïve princess, but I'm not about to make Prince Charming's battle an easy one. "You talk a good game," I say. "But it's going to take a lot more than a few pickup lines to get into my head."

He crosses his arms. "A challenge?"

"Yes, a challenge," I toss back, my face devoid of emotion. I'm sure that alone will scare him off. Emotionless girls aren't appealing to guys. They want sugary sweet; I'm piss and vinegar.

He watches me carefully, his face anything but emotionless. Intrigue lines his forehead, debate hindering his response.

Yep. He's outta here.

"Challenge accepted," he says, shocking me some.

Actually, he comes close to shocking me right out of my seat. I thought for sure he was a runner.

"But you have to tell me a few things before I let you fuck up my head," he says.

"Fuck up *your* head?" I scoff, deciding this is a failed effort at being swoony. The wounded guy who needs to be fixed. Most chicks fall for that fluff.

"Yeah, fuck up my head. You girls seem to think we're the only ones capable of doing it, but it's a fifty-fifty playing field."

I'm convinced he's handing me bullshit. Still, I go with it. "Okay, so your heart's been broken. Whose hasn't been?"

"Has *yours*?" His eyes soften. "I'm not sure, but something's telling me that it has, or some kind of shit's happened to you to stop you from ever opening up. It's one or the other."

Who is this guy? A mind reader?

The truth is my parents' wicked excuse of a marriage left me chained, bound to the anger that's blossomed over the years. Their union—or lack thereof—poisoned me, soiling my spirit. It made me a hater of love, never once allowing anyone to step into what's left of my world.

But that doesn't mean my heart *hasn't* been shattered. It's been hacked to pieces in ways the average person can't fathom. Trembling on a blood-soaked carpet, I cried more tears than most people purge over a lifetime.

Still, I'm sure my past isn't stamped across my forehead. I've hidden it well, masking it under a bravado most take years to master. Well, up until this point, I thought I did a good job of hiding it. "That question's a no-go," I say, firm on not letting him in on too much. "You can ask me anything else, but nothing that has to do with what my heart has or hasn't been through."

"That's cool for now." Brock leans back, brushing a hand through his hair. "Can I get your favorite color, then?"

Simple enough. "Green."

"Florida or Montana?" he continues.

"I can't stand the beach, and cowboys don't do a thing for me, so neither."

"Well, young lady," he says, deepening what I already consider a Southern drawl, "I don't own a ranch, but I'd take a spicy little snow bunny over fake implants *any* day."

His response strikes me as odd, but I can't help but laugh. He doesn't fit the mold. I like it.

"Flowers or chocolates?"

"Are you aiming for clichéd?"

"Mental note taken." He nods, acting as if he's writing this down. "Spiked heels or dirty sneakers?"

I look down at my three-year-old, seen-better-days Chucks. "Uh, sneakers." The answer should be obvious considering I'm also sporting Walmart-brand jeans and a faded vintage Nirvana T-shirt.

Brock studies me a moment. "That's the response I was hoping for. I dig different."

I feel red paint my cheeks in a flush as his gaze stays locked on mine.

As if sensing my nervousness, he clears his throat. "First number that pops into your head?"

"Sixteen."

"Beer or hard liquor?"

I roll my eyes. "*Duh* . . . both."

He chuckles. "A Perfect Circle or Coldplay?"

"Polar opposites. They're both awesome bands. Plus, that's like choosing your favorite book boyfriend. You can't."

"Agreed, but I have *no* idea what a book boyfriend is. You've sparked my curiosity, though."

I smile, not even about to go into detail of their importance to the hordes of women who compare them to every male on earth. "We need a full day for that topic."

"Got ya." He laughs, rubbing his hands together. "Vanilla, chocolate, or strawberry?"

"All three combined into one *magnificent* flavor."

"A walk in the park or a day spent riding on the back of a motorcycle?"

"Have you heard of Deuce West?"

He gives me a confused look.

I smile again. "Definitely a day spent on the back of a motorcycle."

"Very cool," he replies. "Summer or winter?"

"Winter. I hate the heat."

"Christmas or Thanksgiving?"

"I'll take a turkey over a fat man wearing red *any* day." That garners me a smile.

"Favorite sexual position?"

Sneaky. I like. I almost spill that any position—in any public or private place—is just fine by me, but I stick to innocence and widen my eyes.

"I figured I'd try," he admits with a smirk. "Favorite food?"

"Sushi."

He crinkles his nose.

"For real?" I ask, rocked that any human in their right mind wouldn't want to consume it every day. "You don't like sushi?"

"I only like certain . . . *female* things raw." He wiggles his brows.

"Hardy-har-har," I tease, giving him a look that tells him I know exactly what he's referring to.

Pussy—not money—is the root of all evil.

"You're quick." He swings his chair around to my side of the table, straddles it, and rests his forearms on the back as he stares at me with laser-like precision. "Football or baseball?"

"Baseball all the way. Football sucks."

His eyes widen, a frown dragging down his mouth. He looks like a lost, lonely puppy.

"What's wrong?" I'm somewhat disturbed by the sudden change in his demeanor. "Are you an overwired, crazed football fanatic or something?"

"Captain."

"*Huh?*" Now it's my eyes that are wide. "Oh God. Not a jock. *Please* don't tell me you're a jock."

Considering he's sporting a polo shirt and Dockers, he doesn't dress like a jock. He looks preppy and unjuiced by steroids. Okay, so he's built like a jock—broad, sculpted shoulders, pumped yet lean forearms. I crane my neck and peek at his stomach, confirming that under his polo shirt exists a six-pack slab of raw muscle. Still, he could've gained his glorious physique by lifting weights, lifting tiny girls with fake implants, or lifting cars on impulse.

But, Jesus, not a jock.

Brock nods, a dot of a grin hinting at his lips. "I'm the university's football captain. Does that kill any hope I'd had?"

"It comes close to it." I nervously pick at the edge of my schedule. "Really close. Like borderline-walk-away-now close."

Curiosity slants his brows. "And why is that?"

"It just is. But whatever. I can deal with it if you give me enough reasons to." My thoughts travel back to the night I all but sold my virginity on a muddy high school football field to a dick named Josh Stevenson. I was fourteen and wanted beer. He was seventeen and had a fake ID.

A deal was struck.

Thank God the whole, sickening ordeal lasted less than five minutes. I guess I'd expected him to treat me like the whore I'd acted like, and that's exactly what happened. By the next morning the rest of his teammates knew what we'd done, making sure to call me the appropriate names every time they saw me.

In a small fishing community just outside of Rivers Edge, North Carolina, I was the new girl known as the slut who'd fucked the captain of the football team for beer. I can't recall if it was the second or third town I'd lived in by that point—I just know it as the one where my hatred of jocks, and my self-loathing for what I was morphing into, began.

I shift, uncomfortable with Brock looking at me like he's trying to figure me out. "What?"

"I'm just happy you're willing to tolerate me and my . . . jockiness." He slides me a grin. "And I *will* give you enough reasons to deal with it."

I sense that he wants to say something more, possibly deeper, but I don't push.

"Okay, so you're stuck alone on a deserted island," he continues, "and you can only have two things other than water. What are they?"

"That's easy. Twizzlers and my journal," I answer, wishing I had both right now. Mainly the Twizzlers. They're one of my many crutches. My nervous, go-to addiction. Any flavor—the almighty Twizzler owns me.

"Twizzlers?" He looks at me like I'm the worst kind of crazy. "The squiggly licorice candy? Out of anything in the world, that's what you'd go with?"

"You're quick," I smart back, shooting him my best amused expression. "Very quick, Cunningham."

A hint of inner debate settles across his face, but soon confidence replaces it. "Well, since we're two *quick* young adults, and we're both in mutual agreement that Ryder's the asshole of the goddamn universe, I'm wondering how soon I can get you to go out on a date with me?"

"You have to work harder for an actual date." Though my words come out with conviction, even I can hear the doubt behind them. My conscience is bugging, asking what the hell's wrong with me. "Again, it's going to take work on your part."

Brock nods, extending his hand to me. After a beat, I take it, not sure where he's going with this.

Eyes on mine, he gently circles his thumb over my knuckles. "I'm gonna work my ass off to get you to go out on a date with me. But I'm warning you now, no matter *what* I have to do, I *will* get into your beautiful head, Amber-*Ber*." He cracks a smile. "More than I already have. You'll see."

Before I can blink, he brings my hand to his lips and plants a soft kiss on it. I shiver in the best way possible, his light stubble causing my flesh to pop with goose bumps. He smiles, but without another word, he rises and walks clear across the dining hall and out the doors.

With my pulse knocking around like a Ping-Pong ball, I'm left not only speechless but wondering if Brock Cunningham can do what no one else has ever managed.

Slide past every defense I've created.

CHAPTER 2

Amber

"Y ou need intro to Biology, Miss Moretti," the woman in the registrar's office informs me.

"I didn't think I needed that class," I say, frustration knotting my chest. "If I have to take it, it'll put me behind a whole semester."

"Your academic program calls for it. I'm not sure what else to tell you." She shoves her glasses up the thin bridge of her nose, eyeing the impatient, growing line of students behind me. "Make an appointment with an academic advisor if need be, but there's nothing more I can do for you."

Beyond annoyed, I hitch my satchel over my shoulder and turn, running headlong into the god of arrogance himself.

Ryder Ashcroft.

Though I'm struck stupid by the sharp planes of his face, the hint of stubble dusting his jaw, and the smirk he's wearing, I roll my eyes toward the heavens and attempt to brush past him. When I do, he moves in tandem with me, blocking my path. A second attempt at an exit on my part, followed by a second blocking on his, and I feel myself starting to fume.

"Seriously, Ryder? What's your problem?"

"You're my problem." His smirk pulls higher. "It's been a few days since we've seen each other. Did ya miss me?"

"No," I say in all honesty. Can I deny that the last forty-eight hours consisted of me repeatedly hitting the replay button on our kiss, or that I have a gnawing urge to tunnel my fingers through his thick, dark hair? Nope. I can't deny any of that. But still, I haven't *missed* him.

"You're lying," he says, finally letting me past him.

"And you're annoying."

He follows me out of the office and down the crowded hall. "I may be, but you're gorgeous *and* annoying. That's one helluva lethal blend."

I stop and spin on him, my eyes saucers. "*I'm* annoying?"

"Yeah. You fucking drive me crazy." He shrugs, tucking his hands into the pockets of his jeans. "Nuts out of my mind."

I blink, completely taken aback. "*I* drive *you* crazy? How is that even possible?"

He grins and steps closer, his chest nearly pressed to mine. I draw in a sharp breath, my pulse thudding as I try to ignore the bolt of energy between us.

"It's *very* possible, and there you go again with your cute questions." He reaches for a strand of my hair, leans down, and sniffs it before whispering, "Mm. Raspberry."

"Wh . . . what?" I stammer. Lost to the sound of blood speeding through my veins, the buzz of the loud conversations throughout the hall goes mute.

"Your shampoo." He twirls my hair between his fingers, and steps back, his gaze slowly moving over me. "It smells like raspberries. I like it. It's just a little piece of you that drives me nuts. Never mind your pissed-off pouty lips or badass sexy attitude. I won't go into what either of those things do to me, but I'm sure ya have an idea. You were sitting in my lap the other day. I'm positive you . . . *felt* what that did to me."

There's no doubt my body reacts to him in disturbing yet delicious stages. My heart comes close to stopping, arrested by the sound of his deep, raspy voice. Then my breathing picks up from the heated look in his translucent blue eyes. And last, but certainly not least, my head shits visions of animalistic, sheet-clawing fucking as he runs his pierced tongue over his lips.

"Did you say something?" I ask, honestly trying to remember.

"Your shampoo," he says, somewhat puzzled. "It smells like raspberries." A smile crinkles his eyes. "I . . . lost ya after that, didn't I?"

Yes. He. Did.

Somewhere between him mentioning the smell of my hair and some shit about my eyes, I fell into a woodsy-cologned-Ryder-induced fog, my head warped in a matter of seconds. Hating that he knows how much he gets to me, I smile wryly. "Look, I'm sure you have *hordes* of girls who willingly spread-eagle for you on your command, but it's not happening with me, buddy."

"It's Ryder," he deadpans. "And believe me, we *will* happen."

"I know your name." I sigh. "And we *won't* happen."

With a chuckle, Ryder trails me as I try to locate the hall that'll lead me to my bullshit Intro to Biology class.

"Besides," I go on, shouldering my way through the crush of students, "I'm sure the blonde who *so eagerly* replaced my spot in your lap will slice your balls off—machete-style—once she finds out you're trying to hook up with me."

"Blondie *watched* me kiss you, and my balls are still intact, so if that doesn't tell you she's a hit-and-run kind of thing, I'm not sure what will."

I mentally slap myself. He has me slightly irritated and beyond sexually frustrated, and because of that, I failed to remember that mammoth detail.

"And was that . . . *jealousy* in your tone?" he adds, *his* tone beyond wiseass.

I stop outside of the classroom, turn around, and find Ryder with his hand cupped behind his ear.

"Mm, yes. Yes. It's jealousy." He closes his eyes, thick, dark lashes and all, and lets out a deep, slow, tantalizing groan.

I come close to swallowing my tongue as I envision that groan snarled against my ear while he thoroughly fucks me from behind.

He opens his eyes, pinning them to my lips. "And such a *sweet, sweet* sound it is, coming from that pretty mouth of yours."

"It's *not* jealousy," I insist. And it's not. It's . . . it's . . . Shit, I don't know what the hell it is, but I know it's not jealousy. My fingers go stark white as I clutch the leather strap of my satchel. "You *wish* it were jealousy."

He snags his bottom lip between his teeth and shakes his head as he slowly walks backward into the throng. "It's jealousy," he calls out. "But I'm okay with you not wanting to admit it. It only adds to your cuteness, so it's all good."

I roll my eyes, a mental *ugh!* shooting through my head.

"And you never answered my question," he adds.

"What question?" With my hand poised over the doorknob, I pull my brows together. I know the last five minutes spent with him has me feeling like I just stumbled out of a psychiatric ward, but I don't remember him asking me anything that I haven't answered.

"What's the name that belongs to the gorgeous face?"

I dig a hand into my hip. "You didn't ask me that."

"But . . . I just did." He sends me a panty-dropping smile, continuing his backward pursuit down the hall. "Did I not?" He scratches at his jaw, mock confusion pinching his forehead. "I mean, I could *very* well be wrong about my assumption, it's been a long day, but I swear to the good Lord above that I asked ya."

This dude honestly finds himself entertaining. I guess some perverse part of me does too.

"Brock didn't tell you my name?" I find that hard to believe. Guys talk, and considering they're *best buds*, I have no doubt I was mentioned. "I'm sure you asked him what it was."

"Ah, very, very true. And had I *seen* or *spoken* with him since the other day, I would've, but I haven't. *Hence* the motivation behind me asking you."

I blow out a breath, knowing this is a losing battle. "Amber."

He halts, a slow smile curling his mouth. "Mm, it all makes perfect sense now."

"What does?"

"The reason your parents named you Amber."

I stare at him, having no clue what he means.

"The color of your eyes, beautiful girl." He pitches me a wink, a genuine smile hinting at his lips. "And try not to take some of the shit I say too personally. It's just . . . who I am." His smile falls away, a sinfully delicious smirk replacing it as a group of students brush past him. "But have no fear, sweets, you'll eventually get used to, and quite possibly fall in love with, all of my fucked-up personalities. *Every. Single. One. Of. Them.* If I have to annoy you every goddamn day, which, if I were you, I wouldn't doubt my ability in doing just that, I will. Believe me, I will. By the time I'm done with you, I guarantee I'm gonna be the first thing that pops into that pretty head of yours when ya wake up in the morning, and the last image floating through it before you close those hypnotizing eyes at night." A shrug, this one following the reappearance of his smile. "Just giving ya the appropriate fair warning you deserve."

He turns around and, with a wave from over his shoulder, vanishes around a corner.

As I walk into the classroom, my breath hijacked by his statement, it occurs to me that Ryder Ashcroft—with all the annoying, sexually frustrating traits he doesn't want me to take too personally— just may be correct about one thing. Maybe my parents did name me Amber because of my eyes.

Still, how can you ask your dead loved ones questions?

That's right . . . you can't.

CHAPTER 3

Amber

I TRY NOT TO choke on the balmy August air as I step out of my car. It's the kind of heat that's dense, a thick, wet towel suffocating my body. In less than a second, I'm soaked in sweat, drenched from head to toe. Over the past week, though I've secured a waitressing job, and classes are going relatively well, with each passing day, I've nourished my growing hatred for Maryland by feeding on my ache for Washington. I miss living there. Even if that's where my crippling past began, it was never humid, and the air wasn't rife with the smell of crabs.

I swipe a palm across my sticky neck, and with memories of a stolen childhood corroding my irreparable mind, I slam my car door shut and make my way across the student parking lot. Eager to get into the air-conditioned building, I haul ass and take the stairs two at a time, knocking into exhausted shoulders and lazy arms carrying books. Though I hand out the appropriate apologies, I'm shot evil glares by gangs of students who seem to be just as pissed off at the rising mercury as I am.

I swing open the doors and my skin jumps awake, frosty air coating every inch of my body like a lover's kiss, as I head toward the library. By the time I walk into the quiet, two-story space, I've cooled down and am ready to get some much-needed studying done.

After setting my belongings on a table, I head for an aisle and trail my fingers along wrinkled leather spines lining old-world-style mahogany shelves. My eyes devour rows of books, my nose pulling in their familiar scent which, no matter where my barbed-wire thoughts are, has always managed calm my spirit, bringing it some sense of normalcy amid the ghost playing hopscotch with my past. Even if just a little bit.

I locate a revised edition of John Milton's *Paradise Lost* and flip through the pages. Landing on the battle between the faithful angels and Satan's forces, I read over the words, instantly taken and somewhat disturbed by what's unfolding on the pages. Engrossed, I feel a hand brush my hair away from my neck, and I jump, my breath leaving me in a hard rush.

"Shh," Brock says, holding a finger over his lips. "You're in a library, Miss Moretti." He pauses, seduction rolling off him in electrifying currents as he rests a hand on the shelf just above my shoulder. "Though I love the way you sounded when you . . . gasped."

"I didn't gasp," I answer quietly with an abashed smile.

"You gasped, but I'm not complaining."

I swallow, unable to ignore the air instantly charged with chemistry. "What are you doing here? I didn't think *jocks* frequented libraries."

"Ah, you're incorrect. We frequent them when we know beautiful girls who'd pick Twizzlers over any survival tool while stuck on a deserted island are here." With a lazy smile, he fishes a pack of Twizzlers from his back pocket. His emerald eyes go dark, almost hunter, as he grazes the pack against my lips. "You look pretty today."

"So do you," I breathe, sexually restless. My palms, pressed to the books, go damp, my heart thwacking as he continues to brush the pack in soft, slow strokes along my lips.

He brings his face within inches of mine. "I've never been called pretty, but since it's coming from you, maybe I should take it as a compliment."

"You should." Emboldened, I wrap my fingers around his wrist to aid in his seduction. The heat from his skin billows up my arms, down my back, and between my legs. "Compliments from me are a good thing."

"I like good," he says, his eyes locked on my lips.

The plangent clearing of a library monitor's throat distracts us from each other. Hands digging into her thick hips, she shoots us a classic stink-eye, her scowl twisting her usually pleasant features.

Brock takes an easy step back, his face impassive as he nods in her direction. "Mrs. Anderson. I was just helping Amber find"—he smoothly glances at John Milton's creation in my hand—"*Paradise Lost*."

"Mr. Cunningham . . ." She sighs with annoyance, moving a rod of curly hair away from her forehead. "The library is for research and studying. *Nothing more*."

"We were about to do some *serious* research," he mutters, ducking his head to conceal a smile.

I don't conceal shit. I burst out laughing—the deep, can-barely-catch-a-breath kind. God, it feels good. It's been forever since I laughed like this.

My unacceptable reaction garners me another stink-eye from Mrs. Anderson but also rewards me with a shocked yet impressed look from Brock.

I grab Brock's hand, dragging him toward my table as I bat apologetic lashes at the less-than-thrilled librarian. "*Pardonnez-nous. Brock est une influence mauvaise, peut-être, mais j'ai l'intention de le briser de cette. Nous allons aller avant, et faire un peut de recherche véritable. Merci.*"

Now she just looks all-out confused. I'd be lying if I said Brock looks any different.

"Did you just speak . . . *French?*" Brock probes as we claim a seat at my table. "And what the hell did you say?"

"Yes, I did." I smile and pluck a notebook from my satchel. "I said something about you being a bad influence and how I plan on straightening you out. How'd you guess it was French?"

Chuckling, he shakes his head. "I'm familiar with the word *merci*, but that's where my *jock* brain ends in its understanding of the language."

I laugh, enjoying his sense of humor.

"But I'll be honest, my need to see your French-speaking mouth consume Twizzlers has magnified." He grins one of those killer grins, leans back, and crosses his arms. "It's definitely sexy."

"*Sexy?* I never thought of it like that. I always thought it added to my hidden geek factor."

"Well, start thinking it, because it is, and *nothing* about you screams geek. Even if it did, you'd be one fucking sexy geek." He swipes the Twizzlers from the table, opens the pack, and hands me one. "Get eating. This *jock's* dying over here."

I smile, convinced we've officially established an ongoing joke. Taking a small bite, I watch him watching me, carnal satisfaction blooming in his eyes.

"Where'd you learn to speak French?" he asks.

From one of the crazy foster homes I landed in. If I messed up a lesson, dinner was withheld from me that night. "I took it in high school," I say, not ready to open that casket. "How'd you know I was here?"

"I saw you in the parking lot, and I followed you."

"So you're *stalking* me?"

"If you wanna get technical, yes." He cracks a sinful smile. "Are you cool with my dementedness?"

"Can't say that I am," I lie, unwilling to admit that part of me is.

"Can't say that I'm willing to stop," he clips, his mouth curved wryly. "And keep chewing, Amber-*Ber*. I'm thoroughly enjoying the show."

Unsure of how to react to him, I smile like an idiot, my deft wit vanishing with every slick comeback he tosses my way. I want to kick him in his teeth for beating me at my own game, making me work harder at what usually comes naturally to my warped ego . . .

manipulating a conversation. But, God, I can't kick him. Aside from his teeth being perfectly white, their ghostly shimmer as straight as a stick figure's dick, he's too adorable, too inwardly twisted to inflict physical pain upon. Jock or not, and wiseass or not, this good boy's as bad as they come. I can see it, smell its deliciously dirty presence. My intuition tells me he's aware of it, and that I'll soon be introduced to the inner workings of what makes him hard.

Continuing to smile like a virginal imp, I obey and take another bite from my Twizzler, all the while wondering how long it'll take him to show me where his inner demons *really* lie.

"So do you have any exciting plans this afternoon?" he asks, entertained curiosity on his face.

"Maybe," I lie again. Well, if you consider studying until your eyes are about to bleed exciting, then maybe it's not a lie.

"Wait, did I just hear you say that you're stopping by the field to watch me practice?"

"Uh, nope." I laugh. "That must've been the little schizophrenic man in your head."

"*Nothing* on my body is little. Let's get that out of the way right now." His eyes sparkle with mirth as I sigh. "But, no. I definitely heard *you* say it. Besides, I know you wanna see me in my uniform. You're curious. I can tell."

"Oh, can you?" I ask dryly.

"Yes, ma'am. Sweat. Raging hormones. Me coming close to murdering someone. There's a certain amount of appeal to it. Don't lie."

There *is* a small amount of appeal to it. Though I'd gladly choose a double root canal over an afternoon spent watching any kind of agonizingly boring action on a football field, I can't deny that I wonder—just a little—what Brock's already-fine ass looks like in those tight pants. However, considering it's close to a billion degrees outside, the idea loses its attraction real fast.

"I have to study," I say, snatching a second Twizzler from the pack.

He pitches his head to the side, his green, seawater eyes intense. "I guess I need to tempt ya a little more, then."

"You think you've tempted me at *all?*" I balk, amused by his confidence.

He shrugs, rubbing a hand over the back of his neck. "Well, I hope my gift of Twizzlers has."

His gaze, pinned to my lips, and the boyish grin lifting his cracks my resistance, unlacing me with a sweet yet petrifying anxiety. The inescapable truth is . . . I think I like it.

I rest my elbows on the table, my hands folded beneath my chin. "And how do you plan on tempting me more than you *think* you already have?"

Brock stands, and I have to crank my head back to look up at him. "That's easy." He touches his knuckles to my cheek, my breath kidnapped by the shadow of promise in his eyes. "I'll watch every episode of *Happy Days* with you, and I'll always be the guy who brings you Twizzlers."

As Brock walks away, yet again without saying another word, my empty heart teeters between curiosity and absolute fear over something I've rarely experienced.

Human warmth.

Though I've craved it, I've been dehydrated of it, a desert thirsty for even the smallest trickle of water from a passing storm. Sure, I've received warmth in small doses, but it usually came from someone who had thwarted reasons behind showing it to me at all, including my parents.

The people who were supposed to put me before anything.

The people who were supposed to give up their breaths so I could take an easy one.

The people who were supposed to choose my smiles over a dirty needle.

After they died, I shot through a series of homes where warmth, love, and being recognized as an actual person was dangled in front of me like a meaty bone to a hungry dog.

A scrap of day-old food to a soul seeking nourishment.

Inside those homes, I was physically beaten, mentally raped, and inwardly stripped down to nothing but stagnant memories of a life that I'd sought to escape. Still, no matter how stagnant my memories of my parents were, they became the only place my mind desperately clung to in the middle of the chaos that had replaced what I had thought was evil.

What I had eventually wanted back.

It's funny how our minds execute many purposes, the two main contenders of our psyches conflicting beyond confliction. One side teaches us that it's our grand escape, while the other preps us to play the role it never wanted: our worst enemy.

It wasn't until I was placed in the caring arms of my most recent foster parents, Cathy and Mark, that I experienced any sense of feeling wanted or loved. Any sense of feeling . . . human.

But their safety net came too late, unable to save me from my ancient habits. I continue to disconnect, self-destructing one man at a time, using sex as a brain detox. Sex is and will always be where I find control, a hidden shelter keeping me benign from the cancer that will forever disease the dark, frayed edges of my thoughts. Starting at the age of fourteen, I've abused, loved, craved, and hated sex in ways most people can't fathom. It'd rock their skulls. I've given it away without feeling a morsel of anything for the person on the receiving end and, many times, accepted it from those I knew couldn't stomach me.

With the fear of possibly experiencing something real, true, and healthy eating through my bones, I head out of the library, fully aware that the only world I've ever known may become disrupted by the beautiful chaos of a boy who promised me more in two seconds than anyone ever has.

Such a bittersweet, twisted paradox . . .

CHAPTER 4

Amber

WITH MY FINGERS curled around the fence surrounding the football field, the sounds of helmets crushing against helmets, deep guttural grunts, and what could honestly pass as bones snapping in two cut through my ears. Feeling bad for the guy at the bottom of the pile, I squint my eyes and watch a herd of sweaty athletes peel off each other.

To my surprise, the guy on the bottom of the pile is the one and only Twizzler-giving captain: Brock Cunningham.

As if unaffected by the elephant's worth of weight that just crawled off him, and with the football secured between his thick forearm and broad chest, Brock stands. Pulling off his helmet and wearing a proper *fuck you* smirk aimed in the direction of the herd, he tosses the ball to the quarterback and drags a hand through his hair. Dripping with sweat, its usual dirty-blond color is now grizzly bear brown.

I bite my lip, my fingers aching to touch, grip, and tug on it. Preferably during wild sex.

"Fuck off, Cunningham," a beefy-looking lineman growls. "I'm coming for you, pussy."

"That's if your fat ass can *catch* me," Brock notes, shoving his helmet back onto his head.

30

Beefman snarls some shit, flips Brock off, and—in true caveman style—beats on his chest. I roll my eyes, praying to Buddha, Allah, Jehovah, hell, every God in existence, that Brock makes the dude look like a dick.

"Come at me, fucker," Brock taunts as they get back into position. "Hey, I have an idea. Imagine your mother's lips are wrapped around my cock while you're trying to catch up to me. Maybe that'll help ya some."

The whole team, except for Brock's target, rocks with laughter. After another growl from Beefman and a series of numbers yelled out by the quarterback, Brock's off and running, zigzagging down the field as he dodges Beefman and his pack.

With serious NFL precision, the quarterback Hail-Marys the ball down the field. I stop breathing, watching as gravity carries the spinning bullet through the sticky air. Brock stops, whirls around, and the ball nails him in the chest. With little to no effort, he catches it. A split second before a duo of amped-up whatchamacallits reach him—neither of whom are Beefman—Brock turns and takes off again, howling his way into the end zone for an *in your face, fucker* touchdown.

The air rips with excited squeals from cheerleaders who are also in the midst of practice. Unable to contain my own enthusiasm, I follow suit, squealing in a less gag-worthy way than the team's little groupies. I'm behind the fence where Brock scored his *in your face, fucker* touchdown, so it shouldn't come as a surprise that my ridiculous squeal catches his attention. But it does, my heart screeching to a stop as he jogs his fine ass toward me. He pulls off his helmet, the mother ship of sexy grins landing on his lips.

"Ah, she came," he says triumphantly. He drops his helmet and threads his fingers through the fence separating the bleachers from the field, resting them over mine. "So?"

"So?" I stare into his smiling eyes as I mentally tell my fingers to chill out despite his touch.

"So what'd ya think?"

"I think it's hot as hell."

"I already know you think *I'm* hot as hell," he points out, smacking his lips together.

I shake my head, my need to kiss those lips increasing with each uneven breath I take.

Inching his face closer to the fence, his grin broadens. "Get your mind off my pecs and *try* to concentrate on the play that just took place. I know it's difficult, but I know you got it in ya."

"It's actually closer to impossible, but I'll make an *honest*-to-God attempt." I let out a pseudo-dreamy sigh.

Brock chuckles, his face showing his amusement.

"In all seriousness, it was great," I continue. "Between you and the quarterback, it was a kick-ass play."

"Thank you, Twizzler girl." He taps my nose. "Me and Ryder are good like that."

"*Ryder's* the quarterback?" I hear the shock in my voice as my attention shoots to the sideline.

Though he's surrounded by a flock of *please pay attention to me and I'll be the next to suck you off* cheerleaders, Ryder still manages to catch my gaze from across the field. I look away, unnerved yet enthralled by everything about him. I'm not sure why I react that way around him. Maybe it's because he reminds me too much of myself.

We're both broken whores.

Still, I can't help but inwardly laugh at the way some chicks have no shame in demonstrating their whoriness to him, let alone the world. I'm a silent whore, a different breed, the shocking kind. I'm the whore a dude can safely bring home to his mother without fearing that she'll suspect I'm swallowing her baby boy's seed better than the best of them.

"I didn't know he played anything but the role of an arrogant bastard."

"I'm arrogant," Brock says with a shrug.

"True." I nod, tapping *his* nose. "But you're arrogant in a different way."

"Shit. You think I'm arrogant?" Brock asks, concern edging his eyes.

"*You* even just said you're arrogant." I giggle, a little confused. "Are you trying to prove to me that you indeed *do* have a little schizophrenic man living in that arrogant head of yours?"

He grins. "I'm really *not* arrogant, but I *just* may have a little man talking to me in my head."

"I'd be shocked if you didn't."

"Wanna know what he's telling me now?" he whispers.

"I can't deny that I'm somewhat fearful about what he's telling you, but you *both* have piqued my curiosity. Shoot."

"He's insisting you watch the rest of my practice, wait a few minutes while I hop in the shower, and then take a drive with me."

"Tsk, tsk. No dates yet, Cunningham. You're halfway up that ladder but not quite to the top."

Several of his teammates call to him from across the field. Without tearing his eyes from mine, Brock holds up a finger, signaling them to wait. "It's not a date. It's just a ride, Amber."

"A ride can turn into a date."

"And a dance can turn into a kiss," he counters. "A kiss can turn into relationship. A rich asshole can turn into a poor bastard. Get where I'm going with this, beautiful?"

I drop my hands to my side. "Yeah, I get where you're going with it. But still, I told you that you're going to have to work hard to get into my head."

"Then give me the *chance* to work hard," he implores, his eyes intense as his teammates kick it up a notch, chanting his name in loud unison.

I look off to the rowdy crew, my eyes landing on Ryder. With his elbows resting on his knees, he's sitting on the bench watching me and Brock like a hungry hawk scouring his next kill. I stare at him a long moment, our gazes locked in some kind of showdown. I bring my attention back to Brock and gnaw at my lip, my unhealthy fear of falling in love settling on the conveyer belt of distrust circling my frozen heart.

"Get your fingers back up here." Brock flexes his on the fence, an easy smile spreading across his lips. "Come on. I promise I won't bite."

After a second of debate, I bring my fingers to the fence. I have to remind myself to breathe as he touches his fingers to mine, slowly intertwining them together.

"Something about you feels . . . right, natural," he says, his voice soft and calming. "I can't explain it. I just know that you're different in a good way, and I like it. I *want* different in my life. You have no idea how much I fucking need it." He shrugs and studies my face, reading me in a disturbing way. "My heart's no less bulletproof than yours. Believe me. But if you feel like you have nothing, then you have nothing to lose, right? Give yourself a shot at being my . . . different." He looks at the ground then back at me, his breath unsteady, somewhat nervous. "Take a ride with me after practice, Amber."

I've never been confronted by so many messy emotions all at once. On top of that, I've never once been struck speechless. Words, feelings, memories, instinct, fear, longing, adrenaline, want, and anxiety all digging their razor-sharp claws into my brain. My wretched past has always been mine to keep hidden from the world, and whether or not he knows it, Brock's asking me to expose the wreckage of my life to him. He'll ask questions and expect answers. When I can't answer them, he won't think I'm different in a good way. He'll just realize I truly am a freak, a freak he'll wish he'd never tried to figure out.

Still, despite everything inside me screaming for me to run, to flee faster than I ever have, as I stare into Brock's eyes I feel like a magnet's grounding me to this spot, to this moment, this very second in time. An internal clock's ticking, the crashing sound of its pendulum tocking through my ears and reminding me that I'm running out of seconds, minutes, hours, days, weeks, months, and years.

We're each given only so much life, and I have yet to live a speck of anything that resembles one.

Running on empty and having absolutely nothing to lose, I nod. "Okay."

"*Yeah?*" Brock asks, his expression a mixture of shock and uncertainty.

Another nod.

"Thank you." A slow smile tilts his mouth, his gentle voice a caress. "You know if I weren't behind this fence, I'd kiss you, right?"

I quirk a brow. "You know I may or may not let you, right?"

He taps my nose again and picks up his helmet. "I think you're gonna be the ride of my life."

"That's possible," I call as I make my way toward the bleachers. Rounding the track, I watch Brock jog over to his teammates with a smile worth a million Polaroids.

Nerves a scattered mess, I'm pretty sure the sun is melting the flesh from my bones as I climb the bleachers, finding a spot under an overhang. It offers little reprieve from the heat but will do for now. Considering I won't get much in the way of studying done for the remainder of the day, I retrieve *Paradise Lost* from my satchel. Before I can read three words, I hear giggling along with footsteps traipsing their way toward me. I raise my eyes, noticing one of the cheerleaders headed in my direction is the chick who hijacked my spot in Ryder's lap the day he decided to . . . *devour* me.

"Great," I mumble, positive she's about to start with me. Though Ryder said she was a hit-and-go type of thing, girls can go all *Carrie* over shit like this.

With a perfect button nose, waist-long chardonnay-hued hair, and full lips any girl would kill to have, the chick could seriously be a supermodel. "Amber?" she says in a Tinker Bell voice, extending a perfectly manicured hand to me. "I'm Hailey Jacobs. I've heard . . . *a lot* about you."

I take her hand, convinced she's up to something. I can hear it in her overly sweet tone, see it in the way her periwinkle eyes are slightly narrowed, and feel it in the way she's gripping my hand a little too tightly.

"Well, hi there, Hailey Jacobs." My tone is sugar, spice, and everything nice multiplied by a thousand. "I haven't heard a *thing* about you. Odd."

Her eyes narrow further. She's onto me as much as I am her. She turns and quietly dismisses her redheaded friend, who's as equally snotty and uppity-looking. Hailey's accessory casts me a shark's smile, all teeth, letting me know she's also hungry for my blood. On a huff, she turns on her heel, swinging her dainty little ass back down to her crew of jock-worshipping followers.

Hailey brings her curious gaze back to me, a fake-as-they-come smile plastered across her glossy lips. "So you're dating Brock Cunningham?"

"Not that it's any of *your* business, but I'm taking a ride with him after practice."

A shadow of a pout darkens her face, just enough to let me know they must have some kind of past. "Brock's *not* what he appears to be on the outside." She snaps her bubblegum inches from my nose. "He wears an overcoat of some of the best charm out there to hide what lies beneath his . . . *front*. You'll soon learn what that is. But he knows how to fuck for hours like a pro, and something tells me that's exactly what you want. You *ooze* slut."

She drags her attention out to the field, where Brock's hauling his duffel bag over his shoulder, heading toward the locker rooms. She rolls her snake eyes back to me, a sneer curling her lips. "He'll definitely take you for a *ride*, that's for sure. And once he's finished with you, he'll toss you aside just like the rest."

"You mean, he'll toss me aside just like he did *you*," I grit out, my mind warped by this bitch's audacity. "That's what you're talking about, right? 'Cause something about *you* leaks bitter ex-girlfriend.

A bitter ex-girlfriend who's going *Fatal Attraction* because she lost a freak who can fuck like a pro."

A muscle twitches in her jaw, a clear indication that I've pissed the bitch off.

I continue, not quite finished. "Let me tell you something, Hailey Jacobs. I'm glad Brock knows how to fuck like a pro, because otherwise I'd get bored and toss *him* aside. Just to be safe, I plan on teaching him a few fresh tricks that you probably couldn't think of. So while you're chucking your sparkly pom-poms from one end of the field to the next, just know that I *will* be fucking the captain of the football team in ways he's never been fucked before. I doubt that'll garner me a toss aside."

Eyes wider than tires, her dot of a nose scrunches up as she surges to her feet. "Fuck you!"

Trying to contain my laughter, I give an unaffected shrug, my eyes pinned to my book. "I go both ways, sweetie. Actually have been told I lick a memorable pussy. Just give me a time and a place."

Though I have *yet* to swing to the other side—I like to keep my options open, thank you—that bit of made-up information works its charm. Speechless, Hailey whips around on an aggravated heel and bolts down the stairs without a backward glance. As I watch her join her cult, I can't help but acknowledge that today is turning out to be far more exciting than I'd pictured.

• • •

"Okay, you have to answer two questions for me," I say as Brock and I drive west on I-68.

"Anything."

"The first is where are we going?"

"That's a secret."

"Hey," I pout, "you said you'd answer *anything*."

"I changed my mind." With a smile, he rests his hand on the nape of my neck, massaging my skin. It takes everything in me to keep my eyes from fluttering closed. "What's your second question?"

I clear my throat, trying to regain my bearings. "How does a guy who's twenty-one—"

"Twenty-two," he corrects. "Soon to be twenty-three."

I sigh. "Whatever. How does a guy your age afford a brand-new Hummer? One that's pretty decked out, no less."

He shrugs. "My parents are two of the most well-known defense attorneys in Maryland. They share the wealth with their kids."

"You have siblings?"

"I do." He turns onto Route 219. "An older sister."

"Aww, you're the baby in the family."

"No 'awws' required. It was hell growing up with her." Grinning, he pitches me a sidelong glance. "Between her monthly visitor and fighting over the phone and bathroom, I nearly lost my fucking mind before I hit puberty."

I giggle, seeing his point.

After a moment, I relax my head against the window, watching the scenery melt into nothing but lush green. Thin ribbons of blue sky cut through an array of trees against a mountainous backdrop. For a brief second, a sense of peace runs through me, something I'm not used to. Before I can settle into the foreign feeling, my attention jolts from the rare beauty when guitar chords from a song I haven't heard in years begin to strum from the speakers.

I clear my throat, my body instantly plagued with unwelcomed memories. "Is this the radio or your personal playlist?" I ask, hearing the shakiness in my voice.

Brock holds up his phone. "It's my playlist from Spotify." He gives me a reluctant smile. "Go ahead, just say it."

"Say what?" I question, confused.

"That I'm weird for listening to Ray LaMontagne."

"No, it's not that at all. I love him. I grew up listening to all his songs." The haunting words of "Lesson Learned" reverberate in my ears, Ray's smoky voice as familiar as a cozy sweater. "My ... my father used to play this for me on his guitar."

"On his *guitar?*" Brock turns down a barren gravel road, and I already know the question perched on the tip of his tongue. "Is he a musician?"

Shit. I should've kept my mouth shut. Still, I had to ask. Ray LaMontagne isn't an artist many in my generation find appealing. Just another reason my age bracket sucks. They wouldn't know a good piece of music if it hit them on their heads.

Though he's unaware of it, Brock Cunningham's managed to sneak his way into my heart just from being *different*, in a good way.

"So come on. We're in the middle of nowhere." I gesture to, well, absolutely nothing. There's nothing but nature around us. Pouting my lips for effect, some of the most disturbed horror film scenes spring through my mind as I attempt to change the subject away from my father. "Please tell me where you're taking me."

Diversion accomplished, Brock grins and points at a colossal sign saying: DEEP CREEK LAKE.

Duh. "A lake?"

"Not just a lake." He stops the vehicle in front of the most breathtaking, God-touched creation I've ever seen. "It's the largest, deepest lake in the state of Maryland."

"It's amazing." I jump from the Hummer and with my arms spread wide, I spin in a circle, breathing in the fresh air. I come to a stop, my brow spiked in curiosity. "Do you have fishing poles with you?"

"Why, you fish?" Brock slips from the vehicle. "If ya do, I'm pretty fucking sure you're the coolest girl I've *ever* met."

I take a graceful bow. "Well, then consider me the coolest fucking girl you've ever met. Fishing is one of my better addictions."

"No shit, Miss Moretti," he says with a smile as he opens the trunk and produces not only a cooler but two fishing poles.

"Would you stop calling me Miss Moretti?" I roll my eyes, getting annoyed with the whole Christian Grey thing. "And do you always carry a cooler with you?"

After he closes the trunk and sets everything on the ground, amusement glides along his face as he leans against the back passenger door. "No, but I had a feeling that a *certain* beautiful girl would show up to my practice. I also had a feeling that a *certain* beautiful girl would take a ride with me to the lake after practice. This here boy came prepared."

I shake my head, a smile lifting my lips.

"And you don't like when I call you Miss Moretti?"

I shrug and lean against the vehicle too. "Maybe if I were close to retirement I would."

"It's settled, then." He sidles up next to me, lightly jerking his hip against mine. "I'll kill calling you Miss Moretti, but I'm all for nicknames, especially for cool, beautiful girls who have a fishing addiction."

"Are you?" My voice comes out thin, gauzy. I turn to look at him. Jesus. He's as beautiful as they get, an eye-orgasm-worthy blend of rough and rugged, hard and soft.

Another jerk of his hip against mine, his breath curling over my neck as he dips his head to my ear. "I am," he says, candy-shop seduction melting from his voice, the look in his eyes breaking down my battlements as a slow smile works his lips. "And I've decided my nickname for you will be . . . Ber."

"*Ber?*" My breath falters as he steps in front of me, resting his hands on top of the Hummer. "Now you're just being a wiseass."

"Why? Besides never forgetting the cute embarrassment on your face when you said it, I think it fits you. I loved it the day we met, so I'm simply making it permanent." His smile widens, the fire in his eyes imprisoning me. "It'll be our private little joke. You might not like it now, but I'm gonna make you ache to be called it."

"You think so, huh?" Every cell in my body rebels, exploding into a fight for self-control. It's not working, the merciless work of art before me making the battle in vain. He's stripping away my defenses, not only buckling my knees, but also the promise I made to myself to never fall. "I wouldn't be so sure if I were you."

"I wouldn't be so *unsure* . . . Ber."

Brock's smile collapses into something so indescribably male, fierce, and primal, I want to bare every inch of myself to him—emotional scars included. His gaze is undecided on where to settle, skidding between my lips and eyes. Along with mine, his breath hitches as he leans down, stroking the side of my nose with his. My back's pressed to the hot vehicle as I attempt to think, but I can't. My thoughts are chained, frozen in this moment. Want quakes between my thighs, its strength growing as Brock barely touches his lips to mine.

But that's all he gives me.

Before I know it, his lips are suddenly at my ear, his whisper teasing my senses. "Are you ready to get your fishing on, *Ber?*"

Disappointment kicks through me as he slowly backs away, stacking the fishing gear on top of the cooler. I give an unaffected smile as I try to quell the shaking that's taken over my body. Heart stuck in my throat and unable to do otherwise, I simply nod.

Brock watches me intently, his eyes creased in amusement with every step we take toward a graying, old wooden pier. I move to the edge and look out over the water. It's huge, its ending nowhere in sight. Miles upon miles of nothing but pristine lake, filled with small boats, families in canoes, and people fishing for as far as my eyes can see. Though we're surrounded by life in every sense of the word, we're in our own world, tucked away in a private cove.

I take a deep breath, relishing the sun on my skin as Brock sets everything up. Nevertheless, it's sweltering out, so I do what I deem necessary to avoid succumbing to a slow, heat-induced death. I kick off my Chucks and slip my T-shirt over my head, leaving me in only a bra and red cotton shorts.

From behind me, Brock roughly clears his throat.

I turn and find him staring, wide-eyed, his mouth parted. "Stop. A bra is the *same* as a bikini top. Besides, the little schizophrenic *woman* inside of my head is telling me you've seen your share of bras."

He smiles and reaches into the cooler for two beers. "Want one?"

"You're going to serve alcohol to an underaged girl?" I take the ice-cold Heineken and slide it against my neck, enjoying the temporary chill it brings to my flesh. "Such a *bad, bad* boy."

"How old are you?" he asks, his eyes playfully narrowed.

"Nineteen, *soon* to be twenty." With no luck, I attempt to twist off the cap.

Brock takes the bottle and de-caps it with an opener. However, he doesn't hand it back. Instead, he takes a long gulp, emptying half its contents.

"What the heck?" I snatch the bottle from him. "Not cool. I just deducted a point."

He turns and jogs toward the Hummer, calling over his shoulder, "Well, you *are* underage, my beautiful Ber. But it's all good. I've got a few million points left."

"Wiseass," I mumble, watching him open the driver's-side door. I enjoy the view when he leans in to flip on the stereo, his cargo-short-covered ass in my line of sight as The Script's "Broken Arrow" pelts from the speakers.

Brock leaves the door open and jogs back to the pier. "We needed music."

I nod in agreement.

"You like The Script?" He unbuttons his shirt, his smirk letting me know he's about to torture *me* with his bare skin.

A second then third sporadic nod, a nervous swallow greasing my throat as he peels the material from his body. The dick's beating me. I may have to reconsider not flawing his gorgeous teeth. Left only in his cargo shorts and Nike Free Runs, Brock smiles, and *I'm* the one who's staring now. I'm also pretty sure my mouth is hanging open, drool possibly involved in this embarrassing, mathematical turn of arrogant equations.

His chest is cut, layered with slabs of lean muscle from the hollow of his glorious neck down to the delectable V between his hips. He has the kind of chest I can lick without getting my tongue twisted up in wiry hair. Not that he doesn't have any, but he has just the right amount of hair a girl such as myself can appreciate while she rubs oil or chocolate all over it. As he turns, reaching for a fishing pole, my eyes land on a tattoo covering the top half of his right bicep. Barbed wire encases a heart, a skull's evil, flaming eyes peeking out from the bleeding organ.

He attempts to hand me the fishing pole. "Good. So do I."

"So do you what?" I ask, my attention still on his chest.

He tucks his finger underneath my chin, lifting my gaze to his. I exhale the breath I'm well aware I'm holding.

"I also like The Script," he says with a knowing smile. "And stop. It's just a chest. The little schizophrenic man in my head's telling me you've seen *your* share of them."

"I wasn't staring," I blurt, yanking the pole from him.

"Whatever you say." He laughs and squats next to the tackle box.

I sigh, hating that he caught me ogling.

He peers up at me, dangling a helpless worm between his fingers. "You might love fishing, but are you willing to get your hands dirty for it?"

"Everything has to die, right?" I take the slimy worm and hook it onto its awaiting electric chair.

An impressed grin shadows his lips. "Yeah. You're definitely the coolest girl I've ever met."

With the worm swinging in misery, I bat my lashes, deposit myself on the edge of the pier, and dip my bare feet into the cool water. After removing his sneakers, Brock sits next to me, also dipping his feet in the water. A pleasurable chill runs along my spine when I feel his bare flesh against my ribs.

"I can tell you're not from around here," he says, breaking me from the stupidity that seems to have made a cozy nest within my brain.

I cast my line into the water. "How so?"

"You have a West Coast accent."

"I'm not from the West Coast, and I *definitely* don't have an accent."

"I'm pretty *positive* you're from the West Coast, and you sure as fuck have an accent." He casts his prisoner into the lake, a lazy smile on his face. "But don't be embarrassed by it. It's a part of your sexiness."

"I'm not embarrassed," I scoff. "*You're* the one with a Southern twang."

He throws his head back and laughs. "Maryland's far from Southern, but if you say so, I'm nothing but a Southern boy for you, Miss Ber."

"Oh my God. Would you stop with the whole 'miss' thing?" I giggle, knowing this dude, this beast of a competitor, just might shake my faith in all I've ever believed in.

"For now I will, but I'm not making any long-term promises on that one." He grins, and I shake my head. "So what's the deal with you and *Happy Days*? I did a little research, and no one I know grew up running home to watch that shit."

Do I choose honesty and tell him that between the ages of four and eight, when my parents were looking to score their next fix, they'd leave me unattended for hours on end with nothing but a bag of Doritos and VHS tapes of *Happy Days* to keep me occupied, or do I go with the classic lie?

"My parents worked a lot, and the babysitter had a thing for Henry Winkler." I shrug, trying to downplay the only good memories I have of being left alone. "She was a bit of an outcast in the social department."

He smiles, suspicion glimmering in his eyes. "Right."

"Why are you looking at me like that?"

"Because *you* were the one who had the crush on Henry Winkler. Not the babysitter. Nice try."

I might've grown up with Henry keeping me entertained, but that's about as far as my noncrush went. "Are you nuts?" I ask over a laugh, positive he lost his mind long before I stumbled into the picture.

"I'm as close to crazy as they get, darlin'. But come on," he urges, lightly elbowing my ribs. "You like that I'm a little out there. Admit it."

"I'll do no such thing." And I won't.

Though he looks as though he belongs on the cover of a magazine, has a cute sense of humor, and is trying hard as hell to get into my panties, Brock has another thing coming if he thinks I'll admit to anything this early on. If ever. It's as if he's trying to open me up and read the torn pages of my heart. To be honest, I don't like it. I've already reduced myself to acting like an excited ball of anxiety around him, and I have no intention of letting the situation get out of hand.

Well, at least not the mental part. I'm all for the physical, though.

"I can't figure you out," he says, searching my face.

"What do you mean?"

"Never mind." He looks out at the water, his expression distant.

"No. Tell me," I press, nudging his arm.

He brings his attention back to me, a million questions floating behind his eyes. "From you not giving me your number, to making it close to impossible to get you to go out on a date with me . . ." A pause, a shake of his head. "I don't know. I just can't figure you out."

"Why are you trying to figure me out?" I ask, my concentration turning to the light tug on my line.

"You're like a jigsaw puzzle." He shrugs, his voice soft. "One that's in desperate need of being put together."

I swallow, my heart rioting in protest. "I don't *need* your pity, and besides, maybe I don't *want* to be put together."

Another lie.

I think I want to be put together, but I'm pretty damn sure no one can accomplish that without losing their sanity along the way.

He licks his lips and stares at me a long moment. "I'm usually not a pity-giving dude, believe that, but something's telling me you might be worth it. What if I leave you no choice?"

"*Huh?*" Thrown by his response, I pull my attention from what I'm sure is a fish murdering the worm on my hook. "I don't understand."

"Ah, sure you do. You heard what I said, Ber. What if I leave you no other choice but to let me put you back together?" He shrugs again, his eyes alight with challenge. "I'm all for nicknames and figuring out people who I think need something more in their lives. Especially ones who I'm pretty fucking sure stepped into mine for a reason."

Though his declaration comes out as a soft whisper, the conviction in it torches my ears. I clutch the fishing pole tighter and stare at him, my heart pounding as my mind replays his words. I don't say anything. I can't. Instead, I look at the water, wishing I weren't so handicapped about opening up to others.

"You *deny* having an accent," Brock says, reeling in his line a little, "but seriously, which West Coast state are you from?"

Persistent—I can't deny I like it . . . sometimes. I sigh. "Washington."

"I knew it." A triumphant smile stretches his lips. "So why Maryland? Did your parents insist on Hadley U?"

The question flares old wounds, opening the levee guarding my memories. "My parents are dead," I say flatly, my attention honed in on a canoe pulling up to a dock. I watch a couple stumble out, their laughter thundering over the sound of ducks fighting for their next meal.

"That blows," Brock notes without a hint of solemnness.

"What? You're *not* gonna go into the whole *sorry for your loss, I understand what you're going through, and if you need someone to talk to I'm here* spiel?" I bite my lip, realizing what a bitch I sound like.

Shock jumps over Brock's face, but he sobers. "To answer your first example: Yeah. I'm sorry you lost them, but I told you I'm not a pity-giving dude, and that *seems* to be what you want. You're closing yourself off to me; I can feel it. I sensed it the moment we met. So fuck pity, right?"

I open my mouth to speak but snap it shut. I can't form a coherent thought. Nothing's there. I'm blank.

He continues. "To answer your second example: No. I'm not gonna say I understand what you're going through because I don't. I've never had anyone close to me die, but I know I will one day. When that happens, then we can live bitterly ever after."

Wide-eyed, I just stare, swallow, and listen to the rest of what he says.

"And to answer your third and final example, my beautiful, mysterious Ber, who I *will* eventually piece back together no matter *what* the hell I have to do: I have ears, and if you ever decide you wanna talk, I'll listen. I'll listen to everything you need to get out. But for now, the only thing these ears wanna hear from your pretty lips is my name being called out while I fuck away *every* bad pent-up memory and twisted shit you've ever seen right out of your mind. Cool?"

I'm sure I just fell in love for the first time in my life. I nod. Jesus, the only thing I can do is nod.

"Cool," he repeats, reeling in and recasting his line. He looks at me, his eyes soft with curiosity. "So do you live here with extended family?"

Like the first time we met, in those clear peridot pools of warmth, I see something familiar yet unfamiliar. All the same, I feel as if we've met in a different space and time. Somewhere along the ragged edges of my sweetest dreams and darkest nightmares, I've talked with this boy. He's told me his secrets, and I, mine.

Still, I'm nervous about revealing too much in fear that I'll scare him off. I'm sure it's not often that he comes across a girl who watched her parents rot away into nothing but pale flesh covering bones under their heroin addiction. Add that spectacular picture to the same girl witnessing her father take out her mother with one bullet reserved for the back of her skull, and the second reserved for his mouth, and you've got yourself a chick no sane parent would approve of their son dating.

Murder-suicide makes for some great evening news. It also scares most decent families away from the one who was left in the aftermath of its destruction.

Nauseated, I decide to let Brock in on just enough that he no longer feels like I'm trying to push him away. "Can I just give you a summed-up version of my past so we can talk about something else?"

"Absolutely." He nods.

I pull in a shaky breath. This is the first time I'm about to spill my story, even a little bit, to someone I barely know. "I live here by myself and don't have any extended family members who I speak to. They ditched my parents after I was born, so I never met them, only know what they look like from old photos my mother showed me. My foster parents were set on me going to Hadley because they both graduated from there. They live in Florida now, and out of the three or so foster parents I've gone through, they're the best I've come across. I still have a relationship with them."

The curiosity in Brock's eyes thickens.

I'm aware I've already said too much, but the sutured scars have ripped wide open, and there's no turning back. Might as well keep going. "I have foster parents because my . . . my father shot and killed my mother, then turned the gun on himself in front of me when I was eight."

Brock's face clouds over with the shock I've come to know.

I brush it off, hoping to push him away from the subject for good. "Six therapists in three different states, spread over the course of eleven years of intense counseling, couldn't get me to talk. Neither could those three or so sets of foster parents, including my latest. Before them, the others couldn't take my mood swings, depression, or anger issues, so they handed me back to the state. Cathy and Mark were the only ones who held on to me."

Looking at the water, I think about how much Cathy and Mark have done for me. How much they've endured with me over the last two years. A knot of emotion wraps around my heart. Though I'm what most would consider a walking tragedy, a complete mental mess, I owe any sense of normalcy I've had to them.

I sigh and bring my eyes back to Brock's. "Fake friends at several schools talked behind my back and eventually ditched me the second I had a meltdown. I mean, shit. Even my last remaining living grandparent ditched me. Her great excuse when the state of Washington's Child Protective Services contacted her to notify her of her son's suicide?" Though there's nothing funny about what she told them, I can't help but let out a light laugh. "She couldn't *fathom* taking care of a grandchild who she never considered hers to begin with." I blow out a puff of air, a shrug lifting my shoulder. "I guess I'm unlovable. So, please, don't try to get me to talk about any of this again because . . . I won't. Cool?"

I feel completely naked, exposed. I'm no longer looking at him, but I can sense Brock's eyes on me, heavy, suffocating. I wonder how many judgmental thoughts are pelting around in his mind. I'm pretty sure he's thinking about how fast he can shuffle me back into his Hummer and as far away from his life as possible.

Silence mantles the air for the longest minute of my life before Brock breaks the tension. "Is it okay if I say I'm sorry?" he asks, his words soft, hesitant. "Or are you gonna rip into me if I do?"

More silence while I study his face. It could just be me, but he seems genuinely concerned I might hack him to death.

"If it matters at all," he continues, "I really want to say I'm sorry that happened to you and your family, Amber."

Feeling like the queen of bitches, I see nothing but sincere remorse, not a shred of judgment, behind his eyes. "I'm sorry for jumping down your throat. I just—"

"No. Please don't apologize," he states through a whisper. "That's some pretty heavy shit."

"It is, but I'm good." Yet another lie. I'm not good. I'm sure I'll never be. Either way, I'm finished talking about my shit-stained past. "So you and Hailey Jacobs had something?"

A grin quirks the side of his mouth. "Quick change of subject."

"Well, she approached me while I was waiting for you to finish up practice." I shrug, trying to play it cool despite desperately wanting to know their story. "She made it seem like you two have some kind of past. One I'm positive didn't end on a good note."

Anger flashes across his face, washing his expression into something that disturbs yet intrigues me. "What the *hell* did she tell you?"

A hard tug on my line pulls my attention away from him, my gaze flitting to the water. "I don't know. Some shit about you appearing to be the way you want everyone to think you are. That it's all an act and, within time, I'll see you for who you really are." A second tug, this one violent. I jump to my feet and attempt to reel in whatever's on the other end.

Brock hops up and positions himself behind me. Large hands seeking mine, his chest is pressed tight to my back, his chiseled jaw cushioned against my cheek, as he aids my fight with what I'm sure is Jaws. Though I'm trying hard to concentrate on the task at hand, every nerve ending fires, heat simmering in my bones as we continue to brawl with nature. A second goes by, and the line snaps, sending us both flailing backward onto the pier with a thud loud enough to shake the wooden structure.

Staring up at the cloudless sky, lying *on top* of Brock's chest, I giggle. He bursts out laughing, the sound heaven to my ears as I take in the unexpected moment. Still giggling, I attempt to get off him, but with viperous speed, Brock stops me by resting his palms on the flat of my stomach, gently tugging me back down onto him.

"No," he whispers, his nose buried in my hair. "I want to stay like this for a minute. I'm digging the way you feel in my arms."

The drowsy cadence of his voice slips through me, centering deep within my belly. I swallow, acutely aware of his soft fingertips dragging up my bare rib cage, our breathing turning into lyrical notes of want punching from our lungs as I digest his words.

"Turn over," he says, his tone soft but authoritative. "I want to see your beautiful face."

Not an ounce of rebellion runs through me as I obey his request, adjusting my body to his. Chest to chest, his gaze devours me, stroking between my eyes and lips. Brock's hands find my cheeks, his touch causing a delicious fog to overrun my mind, their warmth expelling every fear I had about opening my heart to him. My entire being focuses on the way he's staring at me, his dark rain forest eyes dominant with urgency to taste my lips, but still patient as he waits for permission. Sparks whisk through my nerves as I melt into the sensation of his fingers sinking into my hair, their adept movements eliciting a violent tremble deep within my core. I nearly go liquid as he lifts his knee, wedging it between my legs.

"I'm gonna kiss you, Ber." His words come out as a husky whisper as he lifts his head, pulling my face a breath away from his. "And it's gonna be a kiss you won't soon forget. It's gonna be a kiss I want burned into your fucking memory whether or not we get together. One that'll make you hate every other kiss from anyone else after me. You'll have no other choice but to think of *this* kiss when another dude gets his lucky chance. Cool?"

Nervous, I nod, my pulse thudding in anticipation as our gazes connect with a sizzle right before he brings his lips up to mine. The kiss starts off soft and slow, a sinuous trail of desire testing limits and exploring unknown turf. Brock's lips are silk, the taste of his tongue tinged with mint and beer.

I love the parallel between the two.

A primitive groan rocks from his throat as he pulls me tighter to him, one hand caressing my nape, the other buried in my hair. My nipples awaken, my heart stuttering like a worn-out engine. Ecstasy floods me, washing away the world around us. I barely register the hum of boats, birds, and people as the intensity of our want explodes, unleashing a string of harder strokes from our tongues. Brock moves his hands down my rib cage, his thumbs kneading the sides of my breasts along their journey. His touch is gasoline to my fire, fueling the maelstrom inside me as a soft symphony of moans fall past my lips. My head's dizzy, my body high from his touch, its rapture for him already an addict.

"You taste so sweet," he growls, nipping at my lip as his hands find their way back to my cheeks. The sticky air stirs with the sound of our heavy breathing as he pulls me closer, tighter against his chest. He licks into my mouth, his kiss reverent, skillful, one I'm sure will hold its weight against future contenders. "So fucking sweet."

"You don't taste too bad yourself," I purr, twining my fingers through his hair.

He smiles against my mouth. "Do I taste better than . . . Twizzlers?"

"Now you're pushing it, buddy," I playfully warn. Brock chuckles as I move my lips to his jaw, teasing my tongue over his stubble. "And I want to *keep* tasting you, but you still haven't answered my question."

"What question?" he probes, dusting additional mind-fucking kisses along my neck as he settles his hands on my waist and squeezes. "Seeing that I'm preoccupied with something insanely delicious right now, something I plan on repeating as often as possible, I don't recall you asking a question."

I shiver, close to trembling in the midday heat. God, this feels so good. *He* feels so good.

"Hailey," I remind him, smiling angelically. "You two had something?"

He rests his head on the pier, a shadow of aggravation passing over his face. "You sure know how to kill a mood, eh?"

"That's not fair." I frown. "I asked the question before we wound up in this position."

With a grin, one I'm sure he's wearing in an attempt to distract me, he cups my cheeks. "We *barely* had something."

"Define 'barely,' because nothing about the way she acted made it seem like you two were a 'barely' kind of thing."

Grin holding steady, he fishes his iPhone from his pocket and taps on it. After a second, his eyes light up with mischief. "Barely. It says here that it's an adverb. It also says 'hardly' or 'scarcely.' People use it to say that someone or something only has a specified small size, age, length, etc." He draws up a brow. "Just to make things *very*, *very* clear, I'm small in neither size, girth, nor length. *At. All.*"

Giggling, I yank the phone from him. "Did you seriously just look up the definition?" I glance down at his phone. Yep. The wiseass looked it up.

A megawatt smile twists his mouth. "You said 'define barely,' no?"

I set his phone on the pier, and with a mock scowl, it's me who cups his cheeks. "Yes, I did, but I'm being serious, Brock. She was . . . weird about you. I'm gonna ask the questions, and you're not allowed to do *anything* but answer. Got it?"

With a wink, he salutes me. "Yes, Miss Ber."

I roll my eyes, knowing I better get used to his formal nickname. "How long did you two date?"

"We never dated," he whispers, leaning up and slowly kissing my lips.

I pull back to look him in his eyes, mine narrowed. "You're trying to seduce me."

"Is it working?" He drags his lips to the hollow of my neck, letting them linger there. "Because if not, I *can* do better."

It *is* working, my body screaming to pull down my shorts, yank his off, and take a long test-drive on what he *claims* isn't small in size, girth, or length. However, I'm not about to let him know my thoughts, so I do what's necessary to get the answers I seek.

I give him a proper mash to his forehead with my palm, an innocent shrug following suit.

With eyes as wide as balloons, he laughs. "Holy shit of all fucking
shits. I'm making you *mine*. You know this, right?"

"Yeah, we'll see about that."

He grins, tightening his hold around my waist.

"Now you say you never dated, so you two just . . . *fucked?*" I ask.

"Mm. Blunt. This here Southern boy likes." He nods, his lips
twitching in amusement. "Correct. We fucked. She was a classic booty
call. The *I'm drunk and feel like getting laid* hookup. The mutual this-
is-going-nowhere fling."

"Mm-hmm," I hum, eyeing him suspiciously. "So I'm assuming
that's why you don't care that Ryder's hitting that now?"

It's his turn to shrug. "Ryder can do what he wants. I'm completely
cool with him tapping my seconds. Sharing *is* caring. And besides,
what are friends for, right?"

"Mm-hmm," I hum again, watching him carefully. There's a gleam
in those green eyes that I can't quite decipher, something that's telling
me there's more behind his statement.

Brock leans up and brushes his mouth against mine. "Do you
have any more questions for me?" He snags my lower lip between his
teeth, gently sucking. "Or am I still under interrogation?"

"You're still under interrogation," I confirm, trying to catch my
breath, the ache between my legs threatening to explode as he threads
his hands through my hair.

"Well, there's no denying you're a sexy detective." He smirks.
"Continue on, my little vixen."

"You have secrets." I lift my face away from his, going with my
intuition. "And I think they're the kind that can hurt me."

"We all have secrets," he whispers, bringing my lips back down to his.

He stares at me long and hard before kissing me deep, each stroke
of his tongue unraveling everything I've ever known myself to be.

Without breaking the rhythm of our kiss, Brock cocoons me in his embrace, gently rolling me onto my back.

A shocked gasp fights past my throat as he hooks his arms under my knees, drawing my legs up around his waist. Scarlet heat covers me from head to toe, perspiration dripping between my breasts as Brock pulls back, slowly eye-fucking every inch of my body.

"And none of my secrets will ever hurt you." He kisses the slope of my neck, his words muffled against my sweat-slickened skin. "I promise you that. Swear it on my life." Hands cradling my head, he brings his gaze back to mine, his expression serious as his thumbs make a pass over my lips. "You're gonna be mine, do you hear me? No matter what I have to do, I want you to be my girl." He kisses my nose, cheeks, and forehead. "I won't take no for an answer, and whether or not you want me to, I'm gonna find your pieces so I can put you back together."

His promise steals my breath as he crashes his mouth to mine. My lips part on a moan, and I grip his shoulders, my nails clawing into his golden flesh as I writhe beneath him, ignoring the pain of the splintery wood at my back. Our flavors fuse together, an intoxicating blend of beer and urgency. I kiss him hard, his sweet, musky scent invading my nostrils like a potent aphrodisiac.

And just like that, the loud ringing of his phone jolts our attention away from each other.

Brock swipes it from the pier, glances at it, and, with frustration hardening his jaw, he groans. "I have to take this." He swathes my lips in a quick kiss and stands. "I'll be right back."

I nod and push up onto my elbows, trying to cool myself down. Try as I might, I can't escape my body's need to fuck. On a sigh, I get to my feet and attempt to eavesdrop on Brock's conversation. Not only has his voice disintegrated to a heated whisper, but he's walking toward the Hummer. After a while, annoyance grabs me tight. Before I allow it to talk me into hitchhiking home, Brock pockets his phone and saunters over to me.

"I apologize." He cups my cheeks. "I was waiting on an important call."

"Secrets," I mumble, looking at the pier below us.

"No," he says softly. Lifting my chin with a gentle finger, he presses his forehead to mine, his eyes imploring. "Prior commitments. That's all."

Seeing pure sincerity in his expression and feeling somewhat embarrassed that I actually said that to him, I nod. "Okay. Do you have to get out of here or something?"

"I do." He sighs, wariness all over his face. Sliding his fingertips down my arms, he pulls in a slow breath. Tingles scatter along my skin as he brings my hands to his chest and rests them over his heart. "I know my prior commitments kind of fucked up our day, but I'm hoping you'll give me another shot at proving I'm really not an asshole."

"I don't think you're an asshole." I've dealt with my share of assholes over the years and, as of now, thankfully he hasn't earned that title.

"No?" he says, somewhat shocked.

I smile as he lifts my hands to his lips. "No."

"So since you *don't* think I'm an asshole," he says, still holding my hands to his lips, "I'm wondering if you'll let me take you out on an *official* date." He pauses, his eyes gleaming pure mischief. "I mean, considering we came close to showing each other the way we *really* feel about being together—right here on a public pier, no less—I'm thinking we can get something to eat or some shit. But, hey, it's up to you. No pressure, Ber."

I shake my head, my smile spreading. "I know *I've* said it a few times today, but has anyone *else* ever told you that you're a wiseass?"

"Never once," he deadpans.

"Well, then I'm happy I'm your first."

Expression softening, Brock kisses my right then left hand. "You wanna know what I hope for?" he whispers, winding his arms around my waist.

"Sure," I all but stutter, my concentration split between his warm fingers caressing the small of my back and the primal look in his eyes.

"I hope that you'll become my first for a lot of things." He dips his head, barely touching his lips to mine.

I shiver, my mind wiped clear of everything but the here and now. With his lips still teasing mine, Brock continues to seduce each of my senses in ways I never imagined possible.

"I hope that I become everything you need in your life." He kisses my cheek, his grip tightening around my waist. "I hope there never comes a time when you think I'm an asshole. I hope that at least once a day, even if only for a second, I can make you smile." He pulls back, and stares into my eyes, his voice a soft hum of promise. "I hope that nothing I ever do makes you cry, and most of all, I hope that some part of you eventually trusts me enough to let me into your heart. *Really* let me into it."

From the depths of my shattered soul, I feel his words drift over me like a warm blanket on the coldest of nights. Still, an anxiety so powerful against commitment of any kind blossoms to life within my gut, reminding me where this could lead.

Where this could ultimately end.

Yet above everything, I can't deny he's jolted something loose inside me, cracked a few codes. I take a nervous breath, unable to ignore the voice in my head telling me he's already captured a tiny piece of my heart. It's whispering to me that he's about to hold my hand, guiding me with care along a fork in a road I never intended to walk.

I just hope my warped past and the ghosts who still visit me don't make either of us stumble down it . . .

Praying that I don't mess up my chance at something resembling happiness, I flatten my palms against Brock's chest, push up on my tiptoes, and seal my lips over his, dipping my tongue inside his mouth for a kiss I know *neither* of us will soon forget.

CHAPTER 5

Ryder

I'D KNOW THAT ass anywhere.

Sitting in my car in front of a diner in Laurel, I whip off my sunglasses and, with a chuckle, relax into the scene unfolding across the road. I'm fairly certain there is a God, and he loves me today.

Amber Moretti, clad in jean shorts that barely cover her perfect ass, is leaning over the opened hood of her shitty Honda Civic. Smoke's billowing from the engine, mixing through a hint of a breeze. Unknowingly giving a peep show to not only me but several male commuters, Amber swipes a frustrated hand across her forehead—which is no doubt dripping with sweat.

It's hot as hell.

That is, the weather. But I can't deny Amber, who's now furiously kicking the tires of her shitty car, isn't adding to the sweat gathering on my neck. I smile a little while I wait for the air conditioner to cool down my car. Her rich ebony hair's piled on top of her head, allowing me an unobstructed view of her tits. Her gorgeous tits, which are also most likely sweaty under her barely there pink wifebeater. I lick my lips and imagine sucking on them.

"Down, boy," I mutter to my dick, which is currently demanding Amber's attention.

I have a couple of options. I can let Amber suffer in the Indian summer heat, which has my balls stuck to the side of my leg, while she waits for someone to pick her up—probably Brock or a fat tow-truck driver named Harley who'll definitely try to fuck her.

Though it'd be a shitty thing to do, I really don't need any company.

My stomach's full from having an early dinner with some married chick, Layla. I fucked her on the new carpets I installed throughout her mansion while her lawyer husband won a case against some degenerate. After a few mediocre fucks, we got hungry and came here. I paid the bill; she slipped me her number and took off in her Mercedes. No strings attached—just my type. I might call her. Either way, it's been a pretty decent day, and adding Amber to the mix could flip the script on it.

My other option includes getting Amber into my vehicle by turning on my charm, which seems to throw her into a frenzy. The charm I've been graced with comes naturally under circumstances such as this, but convincing her won't be easy. Besides my not having seen her since the day she visited Brock at practice nearly a week ago, as usual, Amber will fight our sexual attraction. But the air-conditioning and my concern for a damsel in distress should do the trick.

Deciding on the second option, I rip out of the parking lot, my dick twitching in anticipation as I wait at a stoplight. What can I say? She gets me going.

Amber's sitting on top of the trunk, a towel spread under her ass. Her elbows are resting on her knees, her hands clasping her hair, which has fallen from the security of its messy bun.

Fuck. She looks even hotter with her hair completely down.

I cross the busy two-lane road and slow my car to a crawl, stopping beside hers. Rolling her eyes, Amber lets out a scornful laugh, seemingly annoyed I just might turn out to be her fucking hero.

That's right, baby, laugh it up. I'm about to make your day so much more interesting.

"Well, well, well," I bark, my voice pitching over the speeding vehicles clogging the road as I step out of my car. "What do we have here?"

That earns me another eye roll.

I've gained points.

Many.

"God, not you. I'm being punished for something today. That's obvious." She sighs, trying to sound like she's genuinely disturbed.

I can't help but smile at her lame attempt. "Come on, momma, why you gotta be like that?"

She plows her sticky hair away from her shoulder.

Christ. My teeth ache to bite that shoulder during sex, my ears crave the little pant that would follow, and my tongue tingles to lick the painful but equally pleasurable wound I'd leave.

Amber's huff breaks me from my dick-induced thoughts. "What do you want, Ryder?"

I raise a brow. "To help, of course."

She tears her eyes from mine. "I don't need your help. Believe me, I don't."

I cluck my tongue in what I'm sure she'll find an annoying tsk and make my way toward her. She shoots me a third eye roll.

I smirk by default. Planting my hands on the trunk on either side of her waist, I give her a wide smile. Though she rears back and her gorgeous lips curl over her teeth, her eyes tell a different story.

She wants me.

Bad.

"Are you *trying* to get smacked again?" she inquires.

"Are you *trying* to dehydrate to death?" I counter. "And I wouldn't mind getting smacked again by you. It's been, what? Close to three weeks since I had that privilege?"

She narrows those storytelling eyes. "Can you back up and give me my space?" Her tone's reached the level of sexual frustration I'm aiming for.

I reward her with another smirk for being a good student. "Can you give me a kiss?"

Another sigh. "You never stop, do you?"

"I've never been known to," I point out, wondering if I should just pull down my jeans, whip out my dick, and show her exactly what she'll be missing if she keeps hanging with Brock instead of me. However, I'm in a gentlemanly mood today, so I decide to tempt her with my original plan. Cold air and my company. I cross my arms, step back, and give her the space she's lied about needing. "Is Brock coming to get you?"

"No. Why would you assume I called him for help?"

"You two have been hanging out. Why wouldn't I?"

"We just started hanging out. I'm not bothering him with my shit yet." She slides off the trunk. After tossing the towel into her car and retrieving her purse, she slams the door. "I'm going to call a tow service."

"You trust Harley?" I fish a cigarette out from behind my ear, light it, and take a long drag. "That might not be a good idea."

Her face goes all kinds of cute with confusion. "Who's Harley?"

"Never mind." She looks at me suspiciously, causing my dick to jerk in response. "Why would you pay for a tow when I can drive you back to your dorm?"

"Because I don't *wanna* get in a car with you." She scoffs.

I'm convinced she's lying ... again. I debate calling her out on it. I do.

"I'm not buying your shit, Moretti, so stop with the fucking dramatics. They're already getting old."

Her eyes go wide. Damn. This is getting good.

"You know you'd rather be in a car with me over some stranger." I flick my cigarette to the ground and stub it out with the tip of my work boot.

She scowls, but it's barely noticeable. "Technically you *are* a stranger."

I step into her face, eliciting a little gasp from her as I look down into her eyes. "Nah, we've kissed already," I whisper, twisting my lips into a grin. "I'm past the stranger-danger level."

She swallows nervously, and it takes everything in me to not bury my hands in her hair, tilt her beautiful face to the side, and plant my mouth over her racing pulse.

Instead I turn, heading toward my Mustang. "Besides"—I open the door, get in, and roll down the passenger-side window—"believe it or not, your chances of survival are a *helluva* lot better with me than with Harley. Get in the damn car."

She grimaces, stares hard at me for a minute, then looks off toward the road. With vigor, she bites her lip, and I can't help but wonder if she's going to chew it right the fuck off. I wait and watch. Wait and watch and wait and watch some more.

When she doesn't make a move, I rev the engine, startling her. I almost laugh but manage to keep my expression placid as I stare at her gorgeous, undecided face. With an expectant eye roll, she begrudgingly swings open the door, climbs in, slams it, and crosses her arms.

She's officially in the spider's parlor. I mentally pat myself on the back.

"To. My. Dorm." Insistency clings to each word as she rolls up the window. She plops her feet onto the dash, closes her eyes, and releases a soft, frustrated sigh.

I concentrate on the way she slowly moves the tips of her fingers over her forehead, removing the perspiration from her milky skin. What I wouldn't give to shove those fingers in my mouth. I'd gratefully lick, suck, and swallow every bit of her sweat off them. My eyes shift to her nipples, which have hardened in the cooler air.

Christ. She had a better chance with Harley.

I can't contain the groan that rumbles from my throat as I clutch the steering wheel tighter. It catches her attention.

"*Nowhere* else, Ryder."

"Your wish is my command." The lie flows from my mouth as easily as taking a piss. I'm not bringing her back to her dorm. No way in fucking hell. I didn't work as hard as I did to spend less than thirty minutes with her. I want—no, I *need* more time with her.

Because of me, shit's been tense the last few times we've been around each other. I have to right it, show her I'm not the total dick she thinks I am. My brain, the one I can always count on, conjures up a killer idea. I obediently follow it. Instead of making a left out of the parking lot in the direction of the campus, I drive straight across the highway, right back into the diner parking lot.

Exorcist-style, Amber twists her head around. "What are you doing?" she asks, her eyes bleeding frustration. "I said to my dorm and nowhere else."

I shrug. "I've suddenly become . . . starving."

"My ass," she hisses.

"Is absolutely spectacular," I finish, reaching for her purse.

She gasps, and I hop out of the car with it tight in my grip. Considering I'm more than positive her purse houses her cell, I've left her no other option but to follow me into the diner. I give myself another mental pat on the back.

She jumps from the car, shock visible in every pissed-off line and plane of her face. I'm quite aware I'm the source of it. Still, I want to pull her into me and kiss her anger away.

"Give me my purse!" she demands, trying to rip it from my hold.

My arm shoots up, hovering the flimsy piece of knotted rainbow cloth over her tiny yet athletic frame. "Give me a kiss."

She cracks a mirthless smirk. "What? You're not just going to *force* one on me?" She snorts and crosses her arms. "Looks like you're losing your touch."

My brows jump to my hairline. "Is that a serious comment?" She knows I'm not beyond it. Considering our brief history, I find her statement brazen. It doesn't surprise me that this also turns me on.

Still dangling her purse over her head, I step closer, forcing her back against my car. "Because if that's what you want, you know I can deliver, and deliver *very* well."

She angrily digs her hands into her hips. They're the kind of hips that have just the right amount of meat on them. The kind a dude like me can grip while pounding into her sweet pussy.

I laugh silently to myself and try to maintain a serious expression. "Answer the question, Amber. A guy can only hold out for so long under pressure such as this. Is that what you want? You want me to kiss you?"

"No. That's not what I want." She sighs, nervously flicking her eyes to my lips. Christ, the girl really has no clue how badly she needs to sharpen her lying skills. "Just give me my purse so I can call a tow."

I bring my hand to my chin and rub it. The move is an attempt to *appear* to look like I'm seriously pondering her suggestion. It lasts less than a second. "Yeah. I'm not feeling it, Moretti."

She sighs again.

I turn toward the diner doors, crooking my finger over my shoulder. "Come on. I'll give it back after you let me feed you."

"I'm not hungry," she says as she follows closely behind me.

I know this because I hear her irritated footsteps pouncing up the stairs. I also hear her let out a string of curses, a huff, and another sigh as I open the door. Trying to *finally* act like the gentleman my mother raised, I sweep a hand across the threshold, gesturing for her to go in. I'm beginning to think the only thing she loves doing while around me is rolling her eyes, since she does it again as she walks past. It's all good, though. It's her eyes—not her face, ass, or tits—that nearly mutilated my heart the first time she looked at me.

Yeah. My head was pretty much fucked sideways from that point on.

"Two?" the cheery blonde hostess asks with a confused smile. She sat me and Layla earlier, and by the looks of it, she clearly remembers me.

"Unfortunately," Amber pipes up. "Asshole here's holding me hostage."

Sweet Jesus. Every time I'm around this girl, I see why Brock's dead set on officially making her his. Though she's completely oblivious to it, and a little off her rocker, there's nothing about her that isn't truly phenomenal. She's a spitfire. My match in every way possible.

The hostess, now appearing further confused and somewhat concerned, leads us toward a booth in the back corner. After Blondie drops two menus on the table and announces that our waitress will be with us shortly, Amber slides in against the wall and rests her legs on the cushioned seat. Frustration's leaking from her pores. I can almost hear her mentally cursing me out.

"You're not gonna *talk* to me?" I make sure I sound offended.

Silence.

"That really hurts, Amber," I add, this time including my best frown.

More silence.

I chuckle, loving how fucking cute she is when she's pissed. "I bet by the time I drop you off, not *only* will I have struck up some kind of conversation with you, but I'll get you to tell me what color panties you're wearing."

She scoffs.

At least I got her to make some kind of noise.

I shrug. "Whatever. You'll see. I'm good at shit like this."

She ignores my statement.

Deciding to prove my point, I pull a dollar from my pocket, feed it into the minijukebox hanging from the wall, and hit F5 for a little Florida Georgia Line. Though I also dig it, chicks can't help but melt when they hear this song.

After a few moments . . .

"You listen to them?" Amber asks, tapping her finger against the table to the beat.

"You talked. I win," I inform her with my eyes locked on hers from over the menu, well aware that I sound like a child. "Now tell me, are they red or pink? Lace or satin?" She goes to speak, but I cut her off.

"Wait, let me guess. I'm thinking black lace? Mm. Fuck yeah, black lace." I close my eyes, a vivid, filthy picture involving spiked heels, body paint, and a video cam flashing in my mind. "Brock, such a lucky bastard. I hope he's taking care of all of that."

She rolls her eyes. "Is that all you do, Ryder? Think about sex?"

"As many times in a day as you roll your eyes, Amber," I deadpan, lifting a dark brow. I can tell she's fighting the urge to roll those pretty eyes.

She shakes her head. "Just so you know, when we *do* get around to it—and we *will*—I'm sure Brock will know what to do with all of this." She sweeps a vogue-style hand across her body.

I stiffen—or maybe my dick does. I can't be too sure at this point. Considering I already knew Brock hasn't sampled everything she has to offer, it's pretty safe to say she's jarred my head a little something more than I'm used to.

"*Also*," she continues, lifting her own brow, "good luck finding out what color panties I'm wearing."

I frown. This time it's an honest-to-God frown.

"Now can you answer my original question?" she asks.

Blank. It's me shaking my head this time. "What was the original question?"

"Florida Georgia Line," she reminds me. "You like them? I never pictured a guy like you listening to their music."

I clear my throat, attempting to rid my mind of several filthy thoughts. "Yeah, I like them. 'Cruise' is one of my favorite songs."

"It's one of my favorites too." She shrugs. "Again, I just never pictured you listening to them."

"There's a lot you don't know about me." I drop my eyes back down to the menu.

"Ryder," she says softly after a moment.

I jerk my head up for two reasons. One: in the short time we've known each other, I've never heard Amber say *anything* softly, let alone my name. Two: the sound of this new voice makes me feel strangely re-laxed, comforted. Jesus. In a split second, she's managed to twist me up.

What the fuck? Usually her voice evokes some kind of frustration in me, which then morphs into an uncontrollable urge to throw her onto the closest surface and fuck her until her legs only know how to function while wrapped around my head, shoulders, or waist.

"Amber," I reply, my eyes pinned on hers.

She looks at the table then back up at me, her voice remaining soft. "There's a lot I don't know about you because every time you're around me, you wind up acting like a certified prick." She gnaws on her thumbnail. "Is it an act?"

"Why would you think it's an *act*?" My tone comes out harsher than intended, causing her to flinch. My stomach tightens with guilt as I gaze into the eyes of a broken, fallen angel.

Christ. What the hell is wrong with me?

I know what happened to her parents. Though it took some hard convincing, I got Brock to give me the details after he hung out with her at the lake. That shit rocked my head, so I can only imagine what it's done to hers.

Still, a pissed-off Amber Moretti is as hot as they come. Call me an asshole, but since the moment her tight little ass fell into my lap, it's been pretty simple. I get off on pissing her off.

But I'm not *all* douche. Sure, some of my reasoning for fucking with her is sexual, but the other is an attempt at eliciting an *actual* smile from the girl. Her whiskey-colored eyes alone are amazing, and ninety percent of the time, they're drenched in pain. The emptiness beyond them is a mirror of what lies beneath her hardened front—bottomless, polluted torment. It nearly kills me, and had I known the source of her pain, I wouldn't have laid my shit on as thick as I did.

I wet my lips, trying to buy myself some time. I need to figure out how to respond. "I'm sorry," I mumble, dragging a hand across my face.

"You should be," she asserts. "Admit it's an act, and I'll forgive you."

I lean back and seriously think about her request. It *is* all an act, and though I don't want her pissed at me, I have *no* intention of admitting a damn thing. "There's not a second that goes by that I'm not thinking about you," I hear myself say. In an instant, my throat seizes up, and I want to slam my head into the fucking wall.

Lips mashed together, Amber's shocked attention wanders over my face. She remains silent, which causes my suddenly fried brain to continue spilling the truth.

"I didn't know how to handle you," I say, remembering the second I set eyes on her.

I knew she was cut from a different cloth from all the rest. I felt it in my bones, in the hollow of my chest. Completely rocked, I felt it in the way my lungs burned, making it hard as fuck to breathe. I don't believe in premonitions and stupid shit like that, but I saw it all the day she fell into my lap. I saw her not only in my bed but as a permanent fixture in my life. I saw her wrapped in my arms after a long day, felt her lips on mine before I kissed her. It was as if I knew she was supposed to be mine. But I fucked it up, and the only place she wound up, other than hanging out with Brock, was in every waking thought I've had ever since.

I shrug. "To be honest, I'm still not sure how to handle you."

"Why do you feel like you have to *handle* me?" she whispers, pain evident in her confused expression.

"I don't know," I mutter, wishing I did. "Look, I shouldn't have said anything. I'm an asshole, and I'm sorry."

"Don't apologize, Ryder. Not about your feelings." With a sigh, she pitches her head to the side, her sympathetic gaze and tone burning a hole in my skull. "They are what they are. But stop feeling like you have to *handle* me, okay? Brock told me that you know what's up with me, but I'm only human. A fucked-up human with a fucked-up past, but still, you get what I mean."

I nod, wanting to unfuck her spirit, open it up, and release the girl I know resides beneath the steel she's wrapped around her heart. She slides a hand through her thick mane and gives me a small smile. Sweet Christ, her smile is the most goddamned beautiful thing I've ever seen. Pure fucking candy to each and every single one of my senses.

"So tell me something about yourself that I don't know," she says, her voice light and airy.

For good measure, I check her eyes for any signs of drug or alcohol use. "It was my fault you tripped," I confess, inwardly telling myself to shut the fuck up already.

What is this? Spill-your-secrets day? Show-and-tell? I toss another dollar into the jukebox, this time going with "Bleeding Out" by Imagine Dragons since that's what I seem to be doing. Though I'm not shocked, because I knew she had it in her, this girl has me bleeding out everything I had no intention of ever revealing to her.

Her brows pull together. "What do you mean?"

"When you walked into the cafeteria the first day of the semester," I say, remembering how I got her in my lap. I chuckle to myself. I had to do it.

"It's called a dining hall," she corrects, "but how was it your fault I tripped?"

"Who the *hell* calls it a dining hall?"

"The *intelligent* people do." A smart-ass smile wavers the corner of her mouth.

I lift a brow. "Are you saying I'm *not* intelligent?"

"Maybe," she answers with a giggle.

God, now I really want to bury myself inside her.

"But, seriously, it's not called a cafeteria in college," she says.

I rest my elbows on the table, a grin sliding across my face. "If you want to get technical, no, it's not. But *only* when I'm ninety, need Viagra, and my teeth have fallen out will I ever call anywhere I eat a dining hall."

She purses her lips in thought. "It does sound kind of . . ."

"Senior citizen-ish."

Nodding, she giggles again. "Okay, you win. Now, getting back to the whole *cafeteria* thing and me tripping"—her eyes narrow slightly—"what exactly do you mean?"

"It was my duffel bag you tripped over," I state simply, trying to conceal a smile.

"Big deal." She shrugs. "It could've been anyone's duffel bag."

"True." I lean over the table, no longer concealing my smile. It's huge, like the Cheshire cat on crack. "But I purposely tossed mine in front of you when I saw ya walk into the . . . *dining hall*."

A long second passes, and her face drops. I stiffen, preparing for one of her infamous slaps.

Another second passes, but this time I'm rewarded with laughter pealing from her gorgeous mouth. "Such a prick."

Her hand darts out to cup my chin. She gives it a soft, reprimanding shake that not only makes my fucking chest burn from her touch, but has my heart negotiating its next goddamn beat. She must notice the look in my eyes, because as though my flesh singes her fingers, she quickly removes them.

She clears her throat. "You *made* me fall, Ryder."

I send her an unpretentious smile. "Did I *not* catch you, Amber?"

"You did," she says with an agreeing smile to match mine.

"Were you *harmed*?" I press.

"Not physically," she returns, her smile melting into a sexy smirk. "I won't get into the *mental* part, though."

Before I can question the depth of the mental anguish I may have caused her that day, our waitress finally decides to come take our orders. Considering I used sudden starvation as an excuse for coming here, I go full throttle and order a double cheeseburger platter. I complement it with a vanilla shake. Amber declines anything edible, sticking with water.

While waiting for the food, I study Amber closely. I watch the way, every few minutes, she nervously tucks a strand of hair behind her *right* ear. Never the left. I watch the way her eyes, caramel and waxy honey in color, curiously move around the diner when a new customer comes in. As vibrant in color as they are, they're lifeless, a murky, barren filter to a past that holds her hostage. I watch the way her tongue darts out, wetting her lips in increments, starting with the bottom and then circling up to the top. I watch the way her expression, every so often, suddenly goes distant as though crumbling under the septic wreckage of what's left of her universe.

As a mountain of emotions pile up in my heart, I watch her flip through the music selection on the jukebox. I'm half tempted to stretch out my arm and touch her face, but I know I can't. She's off-limits. My best friend's soon-to-be-kind-of-already girl . . . the ultimate forbidden fruit. Still, I need another taste of her, the urge stronger than ever before. A pull so deep within my gut, I feel as if I'm about to lose my fucking mind. Instead, I continue to watch her, trying to relish the short time I have left.

I rest my forearms on the table, my need to learn anything about her heavy in my chest. "It's your turn to tell me something about yourself."

I capture her gaze, and though she smiles, her eyes cloud over in hesitation. "Like what?"

"Anything." I shrug. "Everyone has a fetish—uh, I mean a . . . thing."

She hikes up a brow. "A thing, huh?"

"Yeah." I grin. "What's your thing, Amber?"

"If I did have a thing, why would I tell you?"

"Because I wanna know."

"Not good enough."

"Because I *really* wanna know?"

"Nope." She laughs, crossing her arms. "Not working."

"*No?*" I slide across the booth, the king of all smirks tilting my mouth. "Do I need to cause a scene to get ya to give me something?"

"God, no!" she gasps, giggling.

"Mm, now you definitely have me convinced that I gotta make a big deal outta this."

"I like Twizzlers," she blurts, panic rising in her eyes as I get to the edge of the booth. "That's my thing. Does that work for you?"

"Nah, momma. I already know you like Twizzlers." I stand and rest my palms on the table, her cute nervousness awakening my cock. "I need deeper than Twizzlers."

"Ryder, sit down," she hastily whispers, curling a jumpy hand around my wrist. She gives it a tug, unsuccessfully moving me. "You're impossible."

"I'm curious," I counter as I straighten and look around the diner. "Now give me something before my curiosity embarrasses the both of us."

"This is nuts." Her eyes dart between me and the busy restaurant. Still, she's smiling, so I must be doing something right. "I'm boring. There's really nothing to tell."

"Excuse me, everyone," I announce, grabbing the attention of several patrons. I'm not looking at her, but I hear Amber inhale a sharp breath. I also feel her tug on my wrist again. "I'm sorry for interrupting your dining experience, but I'm *desperately* trying to get this fine-looking peach to give me a little information about herself. But no matter how hard I try, and believe me, I've tried, she won't cave to my request."

"*Peach?*" Amber asks, a nervous smile twitching her lips as she glances at me, then the curious spectators, then back to me.

"Yeah." I drop my voice, every syllable a slow burn. "A *sweet . . . juicy . . . ripe* peach."

She swallows, her breath faltering. Yup, I'm definitely doing something fucking right.

"Whatever. Fine. This *peach* has a sick, slightly twisted, unhealthy crush on Jared Leto."

"Jared's not gonna do it." I chuckle. "Dig deeper, Moretti."

"I love thunderstorms," she tries, getting closer but not quite there.

"*Deeper.*" I drag out the word. "I know you can do better."

"I hate the smell of cheesecake. It nauseates me."

I blink. "Cheesecake's doing better?"

"Well? I really don't know what you're after, Ryder." Confusion twists her beautiful features. "I'm not some kind of *enigma.*"

"Ah, but you are. You just don't know it." I shoot her a wink.

"It all depends," an older woman speaks up, shoveling a bite of apple pie into her mouth. "What kind of information do you want her to tell you?"

I glance at the woman before crouching down in front of Amber. Resting an elbow on the table, I hold Amber's gaze. Her eyes soften, a storm of curiosity thundering behind them as she searches my face.

"I want to know what makes her tick, what gets her going. I want to know what she dreams about, what she fears." Still staring at her, I take a deep breath, hoping my tactics don't scare her away. "I want to know her quirks, her weird little habits. I want to know what she looks like when she wakes up in the morning and who she's thinking about when she goes to sleep. I want to know her favorite color, cereal, and band." I pause, losing myself in everything that makes up this girl, this . . . gorgeous mystery. "I want to know *anything* she's willing to tell me."

"Dean, why don't you want to know things like that about me?" a less-than-thrilled voice squeaks.

I ignore Dean's answer as Amber looks at me as if understanding my need to get inside her head. "I . . ." she starts, then pauses, her voice conflicted. Her fingers nervously rip at the edge of a napkin as she shrugs. "I write."

"Like, you're writing a *book?*" I slide back into the booth, true curiosity taking over.

"No," she says with a half smile. "But I could. That's for sure." I see memories moving behind her eyes, her expression once again somewhere distant. "I . . . write in a journal. My thoughts, how my day went, what I ate. Dumb shit like that." She shrugs again. "It's stupid, but I started keeping one the day after my parents died."

Confused, I tilt my head. "Why do you think it's stupid?"

Her fingers continue their assault on the napkin. "I don't know. It just is. Most of the foster parents I wound up with thought it was, so it must be, right?"

"Wait. *What?*" I hope I misunderstood her. When she doesn't immediately respond, I feel my jaw set in anger, fury slicing through my chest. I stare at her, trying hard as fuck to tame my sudden need to find out who those people were, show up at their houses, and beat them to a bloody death. "They told you it was stupid to write in a journal?"

"Yeah. Well, all except for Cathy and Mark. They encouraged it, but the rest of them thought it was childish."

Sick bastards. Now I'm determined to find out a few addresses. "What do *you* think about writing?"

"I just told you what I thought about it," she says, her tone edgy.

Here's where the average person might back off and tread the rough waters in a raging sea. I'm nowhere close to average. I'm beginning to see that Amber needs a hard kick in her ass to get her talking. *Really* talking.

"You told me what those assholes thought about it, not what *you* think about it." I cross my arms. "I'm calling your bluff."

Challenge knifes her eyes. "What the hell's that supposed to mean?"

"It means that's twice today I'm *not* buying your shit."

Her luscious, pink bow of a mouth drops open.

I try not to picture it wrapped around my cock as I go in for the kill. "It means that you have a brain and can think for yourself. You don't *seem* to have a problem voicing your opinion, so I'm finding it hard to believe you honestly think that writing in a journal is stupid. You said you started writing down your thoughts the day after your parents died. There's a reason for that. There's *still* a reason you use it as a way to dump out everything diseasing that pretty head of yours."

I pause, watching the fight deflate from her shoulders. At this, I lean across the table, making sure my tone holds the gentleness I know she needs to hear. "It means that I want you to admit that you know you *need* to write. Admit that at this point in your life, it's the *only* way you're surviving what happened."

"The paper listens to me better than any therapist ever has," she whispers, pain spilling across her face. "There's no . . . no . . . right or wrong about how I feel on any given day." Her attention's focused on the shredded napkin in her trembling hands, her lips beginning to quiver as her eyes threaten tears.

My heart takes a nosedive, nearly gutting me wide open as the realization that she's never spoken to anyone about this hits me. Hard. It's been hours since I smoked a bowl and days since I killed a few shots of tequila, yet I feel drunk, completely fucking high. I may not be in her every waking thought the way she is mine, but right now, Amber's giving me something greater than that . . . She's allowing me to enter her empty heart, guiding me through her bent past.

Maybe, just maybe, she'll let me be a small part of her future.

She moves her eyes to mine, her voice lost, broken. "It *is* a lifeline for me. I write without the fear of being judged. Without feeling like a freak who was birthed from a fucked-up three-ring circus. I can turn that hideous day into whatever I want without being told I'm irrational or that I need to find a way to move past what happened. I can write for a minute, or I can write for hours. There's no uppity asshole watching a clock, making sure I'm not taking up too much of his time. *I* get to choose how many breaths I waste on my parents' lack of being able to handle . . . life." She lets out a sad laugh, wiping tears from her cheeks with a tiny piece of what remains of her napkin. "But who am

I to judge what they could handle, right? I don't handle *anything* the way society says I should."

"Fuck society and what they think," I say, the response automatic.

That earns me a hint of a smile. Yeah, there she is. The soft girl, beaming as bright as the sun, who I know exists under a blackened sky of a past she had no control over.

Amber swings her misty eyes to the waitress, who I'd failed to notice has approached the table.

"You two need anything else?" The woman swipes her pomegranate bangs away from her forehead as she sets my burger in front of me.

I glance at Amber, and she shakes her head. I unwillingly bring my attention back to the waitress. "Nah, we're good. Thanks."

Red drops the check, and I stare at the burger. If I take even a small bite, I'm gonna hurl. "I need you to eat some of this."

Amber looks at me as if I'm fucking crazy.

I let out a groan. "I lied about being hungry."

A microsmile follows an eye roll. "Why am I not shocked?"

"I don't know. Why aren't you?" I ask in all seriousness.

"*Hello?* Sarcasm."

"Never heard of it." I chuckle, cutting the burger in half. I push the plate to the middle of the table. "Eat."

With little reluctance, she picks up her half. After smothering it in what I'm sure's nearly an entire bottle of ketchup, she takes a bite. I decide that I like watching Amber eat. I like it a lot. I like watching her glossy lips move as she chews, her eyes fluttering closed as though she hasn't eaten in days. I like the way she rolls her tongue over the corner of her mouth, sensually swiping away a small dot of ketchup. I like the way she feels sitting in front of me while she eats half my burger.

Great. I've turned into a freak with a fetish for watching Amber Moretti ingest food . . .

What I don't like is the control she has over me. The unrelenting steel hand she has wrapped around both my dick and heart. She doesn't know it, but she owns me, and I don't even exist in her world. Christ. In less than thirty minutes, she's disarmed me, fucking breaking down every molecule of who I've been for a while.

Only one girl was able to do that, and she shattered me, twisting my head in ways it's never been twisted. Thus the reason I turned into what Amber would call a "certified prick."

My story?

Boy meets girl, boy does what he has to do to get the girl, and the two fall in love. Fucking blissful.

The ending?

Boy walks in on his girl fucking the overaged, beer-belly-sporting father of a few kids she babysits for. Fucking hideous.

Messy break up for the boy and girl, and an even messier divorce for the cheating husband and his unsuspecting wife.

"You haven't touched your half," Amber points out, breaking my thoughts from a day I can't forget fast enough. She continues, her voice flavored somewhere between stern and playful. "The *least* you can do, since you lied about being hungry to get me here and then put me under the spotlight in front of the whole diner, is take one tiny bite." She shoves the remaining piece of her half into her mouth and sends me a smile.

Despite my stomach's protest, I grin, pick up my disgustingly greasy half, and take a bite.

Amber sends me another smile before chugging back a sip of water. "Brothers, sisters, both, or only child?"

"Younger sister," I answer, my heart caving in on itself. "She's eight."

"Does she drive you bat-shit crazy or something? Your whole demeanor just changed." She sets down her glass. "In her defense, that's a messy age for a girl. You're just starting to become aware of your looks, these weird . . . *things* happening to your body, and how the world around you judges you based on your outer shell." She shrugs. "At least that's the way it feels. You're trying to figure out where you fit in and who'll accept you. Boys start clogging up your thoughts, which only further fucks the situation." She playfully wags a finger at me. "It's a confusing time for her, so be nice, big brother."

I cringe, thinking about the cesspool of shit Casey's going through on top of everything Amber pointed out. "Nah. Actually, she's the coolest little girl around. I'd kill for her."

Amber's smile shifts to confusion. "Then why the look of disgust?"

"She has cancer. Acute lymphocytic leukemia, to be exact." Just saying it makes me feel as though I'm about to puke.

Amber's shoulders fall, her lips parting. "My God," she whispers, "I'm so sorry, Ryder. Is she—"

"They're not sure." I already know the question.

Death. Though plenty think they are, no one's immune to it. Every breath we take is one step further from our birth . . . one step closer to our ultimate dismissal. The Reaper comes for each of us, and when he shows up, he lacks prejudice. But fuck if he should be allowed to steal the life of an eight-year-old girl who deserves everything under the stars. An eight-year-old girl who's owned me since the second she stepped into my world.

The thought of losing her staggers me a second, a lump knotting my throat. "I mean, she's hanging in there. She's a fighter. Still, she has her days, and when she does, they're some of our worst."

Amber stays quiet for a few minutes, her expression crusted in sadness. "How are your parents handling it?"

"My father doesn't handle shit." I throw my arm over the back of the booth, wishing the asshole was here so I could beat him into a long coma. Since that's unlikely, I hope the Reaper's already paid the dick a visit. "He took off before Casey was born. It's just me, my sister, my grandmother, and my mother. I do what I can to help them out."

A hesitant smile moves across Amber's lips. "You sound like you're a great brother and a kick-ass son and grandson."

"Yeah. They dig me as much as I do them."

"I bet," she says softly. Her eyes are a pool of sincerity, the understanding behind them only reinforcing what I already knew . . .

With a killer personality—one I'm sure she has no idea she possesses—and a gorgeous mouth that spits out words like a filthy trucker, Amber was placed on this earth to multiply with me. She's the kind of girl who'll make it impossible to not fall hard and fast for, offering no apologies as she slowly turns you into the man you never thought you were capable of being. The kind of girl who'll let you see her shadows, but will always keep you guessing every time she reveals a new layer of herself, a new path through the maze of her heart. The kind of girl who'll have you begging on your knees, questioning your sanity, faith, and reason for continuing to live if you were to ever lose her.

Still, Brock's like a brother to me, my best friend since we were kids. My head's fucked, warring a battle I'm sure it's gonna lose. When I'm around Amber, every line I'm not supposed to cross becomes zigzagged, blurring the direction of my moral compass. She blinds me to what I know is wrong, provoking what I'm sure is inevitable. I'm about to commit the sin of all sins: I'm gonna steal Brock's girl right out from beneath him without giving it a second thought.

Dangerous territory at its motherfucking finest.

"You ready to go?" I ask, trying to dismiss my thoughts.

"Sure." Amber scoots out of the booth, stretching her arms above her head. Her back bows as a sleepy yawn leaves her lips. Fuck. What I'd do to wake up holding her. "Do you think you can give me my purse? I need to use the restroom before we leave."

"Yeah, sorry." I hand it to her, realizing how fucking psychotic I must've seemed taking it to begin with. "I'll meet you up front."

Amber nods and traipses toward the bathroom, her ass catching the attention of every guy in the diner. Lethal possessiveness hits me, but I kill it fast, knowing I have no right to react. If I did, I'd gladly knock a few skulls around. On a heavy sigh, I swipe my keys from the table and head to the cashier to pay the bill.

After a few minutes, Amber reemerges, her eyes meeting mine. "You know what?"

"No. But I heard he's a pretty cool cat," I deadpan, shoving my change into my pocket. "Do you know him?"

She giggles, a smile crossing her face. "I'm happy you held me hostage today."

I open the diner door for her and step out into the early evening heat, shocked at her confession. "You are?"

"Yeah." She stops and looks up at me, her hand poised over her forehead to block the sun. "Yeah, Ryder, I really am." Her smile widens. "It's good to know there's more to you than an arrogant prick who thinks about sex all day long."

I chuckle as she bounds down the stairs and over to my car. "Well, I'm happy I've gained your approval, but I can't say I'll ever stop constantly thinking about sex." I unlock the passenger-side door. "At least not while you're around."

"It can't be all *that* difficult," she says coolly, sliding into the seat. "Can it?"

Yup. Off her fucking rocker.

"You have no clue." I close the door and round the car, her giggle music to my ears as I get in and start the engine. "Not a fucking clue."

"Willpower, dude." She pulls down the visor, whips a small plastic tube from her purse, and coats her puckered lips with strawberry-scented gloss.

My nostrils flare, my dick reacting to the sweet smell the way any dick would—fully alert and hungry for what it needs, it all but demands a rental spot inside Amber's warehouse. I'm convinced she's trying to kill me as she smacks her lips together. It's either that, or she knows she's a walking aphrodisiac to the entire male species, using it to her advantage any chance she gets.

"Willpower's free," she continues. "Utilize your willpower, Ryder. Dig deep, *really, really deep*, and utilize it."

I'm about to utilize the backseat if she continues to fuck with me. "What do you think about politics?"

"*Huh?*" She tosses the gloss back into her purse. "How did we go from you thinking about sex around the clock to politics?"

"I'm utilizing my willpower." I groan, pulling onto the highway. "Humor me."

"Okay. Politics." She nods, drawing up a serious brow as she tries to hide a smile. "What's your stance on ObamaCare?"

"Hell no. I don't talk politics. It gets people too riled up."

"Now you have me feeling like I'm nuts, and that's hard to do. Kudos."

I swing her a sideways glance, enjoying the way her forehead's pinched in confusion. "What's your major?"

"Psychology."

"No shit. A psychologist?"

"No shit." She shrugs. "I figure someone as fucked up as I am can help others who are equally fucked up better than someone who's never been fucked up at all."

"Well, fuck, Moretti, I think that's a pretty fucking good way at looking at things that are fucked up."

"I agree." She laughs. "What's your major?"

"This year I'll complete my MBA in banking and financing."

"*Really?*" Shock widens her eyes.

Considering very few spots on my body aren't inked, and my tongue is pierced, I'm not bothered by her reaction. To be honest, I'm used to it. Most people can't picture me sporting a suit, let alone handling their retirement funds. "Yup." A cheesy smile teeters on my mouth. "Your friendly local banker."

"Very impressive," she appraises. "So what've you been doing in the meantime for cash? You're not working at Burger King with a ride like this."

Black cherry in color, chrome Bullitt staggered rims, and holding a 427 big block under her hood, other than my mother, sister, and grandmother, I live and breathe for my sixty-eight Mustang Fastback. "My grandfather gave it to me before he died." I swallow, remembering the only man who served as a father in my life. "I've restored it over the last two years."

"I'm sorry," Amber whispers, noticeably uncomfortable. "I keep bringing up sore topics. I completely suck."

"Stop." Instinctively, I raise my hand, my knuckles throbbing to touch her cheek, the nonasshole part of me aching to comfort her. But I drop it to the steering wheel and grin. "He was a cool cat. *Almost* as cool as me."

Amber gives me a small smile. "You two were close. That's good."

"Yeah." I nod. "We were really close." Damn, I miss that old man.

Our lives are not our own. They never are. From birth canal to casket, we're on lease. A contractual agreement with a threatening hand that hovers above our heads from the second we blink our eyes open. A constant scream that reminds us it can fuck us at any moment—

Ding. Time's up, asshole.

"But no, getting back to your question," I continue, the cherry-flavored scent of my grandfather's cigars unwinding from my memories, "I've never flipped a burger to earn a buck." I glance in Amber's direction. "I work as a part-time foreman at one of Baltimore's largest construction companies," I say, honestly trying to sound like I'm telling the truth.

I hate lying to her, but that part of my life isn't up for discussion. Still, it's not *all* a lie. It's just that sweating my dick off in the summer and feeling my balls turn into icicles during the winter's not how I earn my living. At least, not a good portion of it.

Among other things I do that aren't legal—one I have no intention of *ever* letting Amber know about—I run a thriving off-campus "homework agency." Well, that's the name I've given it.

Cutting to the chase: my IQ borders on genius, and I know how to hammer out quite a few Ben Franklins from a ton of degenerates who don't give a rat's ass about studying. For a passing grade, from freshmen to upperclassmen, they'll pay, no matter the cost. When new meat shows up at my apartment for my services, it's safe to say the shock on their faces is *also* something I've gotten used to. They never expected Ryder Ashcroft to actually have a brain. *Dumb fucks.*

"So you build houses?"

"I build everything."

"Everything?" She lifts a brow. "Like big buildings?"

"Huge."

"How . . . *huge?*" Her tone's suddenly sharp with huskiness, the coy look on her face telling me what she really wants to know.

I grin and almost find myself speechless, but nothing's about to stop me from stepping onto the ride. "Badass huge." I flick my gaze to her lips, visions of the tip of my cock sliding between them bulldozing through my head. "All other buildings pale in comparison to its . . . size."

"But do you know how to *use* the building?" She looks me up and down, her eyes landing on my dick before returning to mine.

I'm about to pull over, yank her from the car, and fuck her on top of the hood, adding exhibitionism to my list of twisted sexual desires.

"That's the real question, Ryder. Do you know how to use that building in the way it was built for?"

"I've never had an unhappy visitor, if that tells you anything." I continue to play the game she started, determined to fuck with her as much as she's fucking with me. "It's actually pretty sad, because once they stepped into my building, they never wanted to bother with any of the . . . *smaller* ones. My building spoiled them, ruining them for all the rest."

"You know what they say about boys with huge buildings, right?" Her delivery's all vixen, her stare eating me alive.

Sweet Jesus. The girl has me shifting in my seat, my balls screaming for release as I try to pay attention to the road. Dying for a smoke, I reach for the glove compartment and unintentionally graze her leg. She jerks away the silky, olive-toned masterpiece, her expression sliding from heated to nervous in a nanosecond.

I clear my throat. "I was just trying to get my cigarettes from—"

"They say boys with huge buildings lack . . . *willpower.*" She opens the glove compartment, shakes her head, and plucks out the pack, tossing it to me.

I catch it. "You think I touched you on *purpose?*"

Another shake of her head. "It's a good thing you didn't major in acting, Ryder."

I fish a Zippo from my pocket, spark up a cigarette, and take a deep drag. Blowing out the smoke, a smirk crawls over my mouth. "Let me tell you something, peach," I say, my voice a raspy whisper. The midday traffic comes to a dead stop. I seize the opportunity and lean over the center console, my eyes pinned on hers. "When I touch you, *really . . . fucking . . .* touch you, there won't be a shuddered breath from your pretty little mouth or a goose bump on your entire gorgeous body that *won't* know it was done on purpose. You feel what I'm saying?"

She blinks once, twice, three times. "*Arrogant* much?"

"*Provoke* much?" I toss back, amused by her sudden nervousness.

"I didn't *provoke* anything." Though her cheeks are rosy red and she's flexing her fingers around her purse, her expression is dead serious.

I haven't smoked a bowl since this morning, so I rule out being high. I also know I didn't *imagine* what just happened, so I'm forced to come to the only logical conclusion: Amber's one hot psychiatric ward escapee, and I've fucked with her delusional head. Bad.

"Are you all right?" Traffic moves, and I shift into first gear, easing onto the exit ramp. "You seem . . . flustered."

She lets out a laugh, trying but failing to hide her frustration. "I'm not flustered."

"Right." My smirk's front and center as I glance at her. "I apologize for misinterpreting your body language."

She swipes an anxious hand across her flushed cheek. "Oh my God."

"That's what they all say."

"What?" she clips. "That's what who says?"

"The women who've experienced the fine architecture of my huge . . . *building*."

Her mouth drops right the fuck open. Considering I'm as hard as they come, can barely focus on the road, and she started the torment that's driving us both crazy, I have no intention of stopping. She's making it too easy, and payback's my bitch.

"Actually, they pant or scream it," I say. "That usually depends on what I'm doing to them, though. I'm a pussy kind of guy. I can lick it from the second the sun rises to the second it sets. So if I'm indulging in that, that's *usually* when they're panting."

I pitch her a wink as she presses her lips into a hard line, her eyes bugging out of her head.

I flick my cigarette out the window. "Now, if I'm in the middle of fucking, it's not until I get them to the very edge, slow down *just* enough to make them feel like they're about to lose it, and then really hammer the message home so that they begin screaming out for both me and the good Lord above." I stop the car in front of the student dorms, a slow smile curling my mouth as I kill the engine. "Again, it all depends on what my hands, tongue, and building are doing that determines how they sound."

Amber stares at me, her knee furiously ticking up and down while I wait for her to acknowledge the picture I've painted for her. Nothing. She's mute, her eyes boring into mine.

I feel compelled to say something, so I go with the first thing that pops into my mind. "What color panties are you wearing?"

"Pink," she answers through a shaky whisper, her breathing sporadic.

"Matching bra?"

She nods, her teeth attacking her bottom lip.

Jesus. I have no clue where I'm going with this, but I'm not about to stop. "Have you thought about our kiss?"

Another nod.

"The way I tasted?"

"Yes," she breathes.

"How many times?"

"I don't know."

"Yes, you do." My hand goes to the nape of her neck, and I gently guide her beautiful face within inches of mine. "How many times have you thought about it?"

"Why are you doing this to me, Ryder?"

"You started it, and not for nothing, I couldn't stop if I wanted." My rough breathing mirrors hers, my self-control slipping with each silent minute passing by. "Now answer the fucking question, Amber. How many times have you thought about it?"

She trembles, confusion and want glazing her eyes. "I . . . I haven't stopped thinking about it."

"Then kiss me," I whisper gruffly, unwilling to take it from her this time. I've already pulled the asshole card. I can't do it again. Besides, I want it to come from her. Need it. "If you haven't stopped thinking about it, then kiss me like you know you want to."

"Go to hell," she half hisses, half moans as I fist her hair.

My lips graze her soft cheek, my head dizzy from her sweet raspberry scent.

"You're not even *thinking* about Brock."

I pull back a fraction, my gaze digging into hers. "Are *you*? 'Cause that's not what I'm getting here. Nah, I'm not getting that at all."

She swallows. "What do you want me to say, Ryder? You want me to tell you that I want you? That I've pictured fucking you?"

I manage a smirk. "Yeah, we can start with that."

"Fine! I've pictured fucking you a million different ways. I've pictured what it'd be like to ride your cock until neither of us could take it anymore. Pictured what it'd feel like to suck on it until my cheeks hurt." Her eyes narrow. "But you wanna know something else?"

I'm positive I've never been this fucking hard, and I want her to kiss me now more than I did before, but I'm not sure I want to know what she's about to say.

"I think you're spitting game," she continues, not waiting for my response, "and I'm sick enough that I kind of like it. I like being dirty. *Real* dirty. But not dirty enough to screw over your friend, because I actually like him. *He* has something to offer me, and you don't. You're nowhere *close* to relationship material." Rebellion's bold in her tone, but her eyes kill the delivery by showing a flash of remorse.

Fuck not pulling the asshole card. It's officially pulled.

I crash my lips to Amber's, and our tongues collide, exploding into a kiss charged with lust and anger. She moans, pulls her knees onto the seat, and all but crawls over the console. Furiously matching my strokes, her body hums as she sinks her fingers into my hair, gripping it tighter than I am hers.

"You think I have nothing to offer you?" I growl, growing harder by the second. I nip and suck every exposed piece of skin—her collarbone, shoulder, neck, jaw, ear. Shit, if her tits were out, they'd be in my mouth. She moans again, her breathing clipped, her heart pounding as she unleashes her pent-up sexual anguish.

"Is that what you think, Amber? I have nothing to offer you?"

"Yes," she answers through a pant, digging her nails into my skull as she straddles my lap.

God help us both. I'm about to take her right here in my car. Lips still plastered to mine, she reaches to the side and yanks up on the seat recliner, sending us flying back. She dives in for more, her kiss frantic, nearly begging me to pound the ever-loving shit out of her. Hard and fast, I lick into her mouth, my cock twitching as I rough my hands under her tank top, squeezing her ribs.

She moans, rocking her hips in rhythm with our rushed breathing. "The only thing you have to offer me is a good lay, and I can find that anywhere."

"You think so?" I snarl, kneading my thumbs under her bra. I brush a hardened nipple. *Christ.* "Are you sure about that?"

"I'm positive," she hisses over another moan as she works the fly of my jeans.

I pull my hands from under her tank top, grip her waist, and tear my mouth from hers. "Then why the *fuck* are you still kissing me?"

Realization twists her face a split second before she rears back. She looks at me, hungry for more, and just when I think she's going to kiss me again, she smacks the very same cheek she smacked the day we met.

A smirk dusts my lips. "You have *no* idea how hard you make me when you do that. Here." I tap the cheek she has yet to assault. "Go at it, peach. Smack this one if I piss ya off that much."

"You're an asshole!" She pushes open the door and stumbles out, her knees coming close to kissing the pavement before she rights herself.

I sit up and shake my head, not even attempting to try to understand where her thoughts are at as she storms toward what I assume is her building.

Purseless.

I yank her purse from the seat, roll down the window, and punch the horn a few times. "Hey, Moretti!" I catch not only her attention as she whirls around, but several other students'. I dangle the thing in the air. "You forgot this."

Breathing heavily, she's rooted in her spot.

I grin, step from the car, and lean against the hood, cheerfully swinging the strap around my finger. "Well? Do you want it back or not?"

"You drive me nuts, Ryder!" She throws her arms out to the side. "Fucking nuts!"

I chuckle, completely convinced the girl's lost her shit. "Good!"

"Good?" she parrots, her eyes as wide as basketballs. "Good? You think this is *good?*"

"Did I stutter?" Acting like two certified idiots has officially gained us a large crowd who's curiously watching us. Amused, I resume acting like an idiot, well aware that I might have to transport us both to the nearest psychiatric ward by the time we're finished. "And who's the one driving who nuts, Amber?" Eyes still pinned on hers, I point at my hardened cock. "I didn't do this on my own. You're a fucking tease."

I let jaw hits the ground. "*What?*"

"You heard me." I smirk, testing just how far I can bring her. "You're the queen of cock teasing. Take a bow for the crowd, peach."

She looks around, and with a smirk of her own, she does just that. She takes a bow, straightens, and gives everyone the finger. "The show's over, assholes. Time to go away."

Yup. She's my missing half.

As the crowd disperses—eye rolls, whispers, and laughter hot on their heels—I dig my free hand into my pocket, the other still taunting her with the purse. "You comin' to get this, or what? Since I have nothing but a good lay to offer you, I promise I won't attack that gorgeous body of yours."

Amber lets out a frustrated sigh, her feet furiously pounding the sidewalk as she makes her way toward me. She steps into my face, snatches the purse, and stares into my eyes, her breathing labored as she licks her lips. Before I can blink, think, or say a word, she throws a fast arm around my neck and pulls me down to her mouth, slowly skirting her glorious tongue against mine as she fists my hair.

Fuck. Me. Now.

Her little moan causes my blood to shift into fifth gear, my heart speeding faster than that of a teenage boy about to get laid.

But it only lasts a second.

Without warning Amber spins, shoots up the stairs, and disappears into the building. I'm left with not only the reality that I *will* be jerking off the minute I get back to my apartment, but a clusterfuck of thoughts racing through my brain.

The first: I wonder if Amber realizes I won our bet. Despite *how* I achieved it, I got her to admit the color of her panties. Sex has no rules, and if it did, I'd break every fucking one of them.

The second: She initiated that last kiss, and considering she didn't smack either of my dimples afterward, I've moved up a notch somewhere in her beautiful, psychotic head.

The third: I'm in deeper horse shit than I'd originally thought I was.

Still, whether it was because of the few hours we spent talking, opening up to each other in ways I'm positive neither of us expected, or the last few minutes we spent physically and mentally ripping each other apart, I have a feeling I'm about to dig my own grave with this girl.

Again, God help us both . . .

CHAPTER 6

Amber

WITH SWEAT DOTTING my upper lip and my heart trying to beat its way out of my chest, I jet down the hall, fumbling with the keys to my room as I try to figure out what the hell just came over me.

"Temporary insanity," I mumble as I unlock my dorm door. I close it and press my back to the frame, my weakened, sex-starved body trembling. "That's what it was." I pull in a shuddered breath, drop my purse, and try to get myself to believe the excuse I've come up with.

No, it's not an excuse. It's a fact. I've been tested harder than this. God knows I have. Ryder doesn't control any part of me.

Not one bit.

I move across the room and glance at myself in the mirror, my once-normal legs—now turned jellied—barely holding me upright. "That's all it was," I reinforce, staring at my reflection. "Temporary Ryder-induced insanity."

Simple.

There's no denying my physical attraction to him. From the second I landed in his lap, I knew he was a potent force. One that could effortlessly set my world aflame, incinerating it to ashes with each flicker of my helpless heart. Ryder's an all-consuming vortex made up of nothing but pure, primal, fierce, mind-fucking alpha male. There's not a girl on campus who doesn't chew her lip, clench her thighs, or giggle like a stupid twit when he's within a hundred feet of her.

Still, my participation in all of the above acts—and then some— has nothing to do with the fact that Ryder's the owner of a quick-witted personality I could get used to. A personality I could so easily trip, stumble, and fall for. It has nothing to do with the fact that when I spoke, he genuinely listened to everything I said. I saw it in his eyes. The way their light steel blue melted into cobalt, hanging on every word I spilled. It definitely doesn't have to do with the fact that there's a lot more to Ryder than sexual god—like tendencies and a kissable face. He actually has a heart. A heart that cares for a sister with cancer, a grandmother, and a single mother. A heart that adored a grandfa-ther who's no longer in his life. And it definitely doesn't have anything to do with the fact that I just listed a slew of reasons why Ryder Ass-hole Ashcroft possesses *more* than enough ideal characteristics to be considered "relationship material."

"No," I whisper, shaking my head. "Not him."

He's too dangerous, sexy, and toxic for me. We're mismatched. Two jagged pieces of glass that'll never fit. He's a cocky, outspo-ken bastard; I'm a closed-off, delusional bitch. He walks, talks, and breathes sex; I use it in whatever disturbing way I deem necessary. He loves and cares for his family; I loathe mine for what they did to me. Though I've used sex to fuck away the ghosts torturing every anxiety-driven breath I take, I'm not a cheater, and I don't intend to become one. Brock and I aren't official in the Merriam-Webster sense, but I've made a connection with him, and it's one I'm unwilling to break.

Brock!

I swing my eyes toward the digital clock. Five thirty. Forty-five minutes. Forty-five short minutes until I have to meet him at the main entrance for our first official date.

My heart sinks, buckling my knees as I grip my hair. "Shit!"

I zip over to the closet, pluck out a red linen skirt and white button-up blouse, and toss the duo onto my bed, my nerves rioting as I swipe my toiletries from my dresser. Breaking a record, I'm in and out of the communal bathrooms within ten minutes, having showered, shaved, and moisturized all of the necessary body parts for the evening.

By the time I'm in front of the mirrored closet and doing my makeup, my nerves are no closer to decompressed. As I brush the last bit of mascara over my lashes, I can literally recall only one time in my life when I felt as undone as I do right now. Considering that was the moment my parents took their final breaths, it's pretty safe to say I'm a complete mess.

Still, no matter what surprises today's given me, I'm determined to clear my head of any and all disturbances.

One very dangerous disturbance in particular.

One with blue eyes that see into my soul, reading beyond the fortress I've built around my heart.

One who kisses like he's literally fucking me, making me feel like I'm about to orgasm by that simple act alone.

One who doesn't care who he has to step on, best friend included, to make me his.

For the rest of the evening, no matter how many times Ryder tries to sneak into my skull, Brock Cunningham *will* own every emotion flying through my head.

Done.

I stand and shimmy my skirt over my less-than-flattering hips, button my blouse around my more-than-generous C cups, and slip on a pair of fuck-me-now red stilettos. A scowl anchors my face when I glimpse myself in the mirror. No matter how much effort I dump into my appearance, I'll forever be uncomfortable in my skin. No amount of paint on my face or fancy clothing will ever change that.

I make myself cringe.

My practically mute roommate walks into the room and yanks me from my scattered thoughts. As usual, she pays me no mind as she rummages through her drawers. I sigh, instantly uncomfortable. I'm not quite sure why her lack of conversation bothers me, but it does. We've literally spoken less than twenty words since the semester started a few weeks ago.

Other than knowing the chick's name—Madeline—I know more about aliens overtaking the universe than I do about the girl whom I'll be rooming with the next few months.

I made a decent attempt to talk to her the day my foster parents dropped me off. After unpacking, I tried the normal "Where'd you grow up, and what's your major?" questions. Instead of answering, she stared at me as if I had a dick protruding from my forehead.

And I'm the one deemed to have mental issues?

I brush off my recurring urge to put in a request for a new roommate, grab my purse, and slide it over my shoulder.

As I make my way for the door, Madeline the mute says, "Nice hit."

I stop dead in my tracks and turn around. "*Huh?*"

"I saw you smack Ryder Ashcroft a few weeks ago." A cheeky smile appears on her lips, her dark-as-sin brown irises sparkling with mirth. "You were the first girl to ever do that to him. Well, that I know of. Either way, he deserves to be put in his place. Though completely merited—considering he's sex on a chocolate-covered dildo—that boy thinks *way* too much of himself."

I'm shocked that the mute knows how to form coherent sentences and that she actually seems pretty . . . cool. A slow smirk climbs over my face. "Good. I'm happy I was his first. I devirginized him." Little does she know, my hand's fucked up his dimples twice.

Madeline giggles and claims a seat at her desk, flipping open and turning on her laptop.

I decide the conversation's come to an end and check my watch. Ten minutes. I breathe deep, continuing my journey toward the door. "Nice . . . *talking* with you."

"You're going out with Brock Cunningham, aren't you?"

Not the response I expected. I halt and turn around, the slight chastising tone in her voice piquing my interest. "Kind of. Why?" Though her back's facing me, I see her shaking her head in quick little jolts.

"I've seen you two around campus. I can't say that he's not right up there with Ryder as far as sex appeal goes. He's *definitely* a fine-looking specimen, but you should really, *really* think twice about making him anything long-term."

I suddenly feel like I'm being reprimanded by a nun. "Who are you, my *mother?*"

She shrugs. "Just a concerned citizen."

Is this chick for real? She's spoken fuck-all words to me, and now she's my relationship mentor?

"And your need to play the concerned citizen card stems from what, dear roommate of mine who's decided now's the perfect time to exhibit her skills in speaking English?" Sarcasm drips from each word like melting icicles. "Do tell."

"He's a drug dealer," she says matter-of-factly as she stands and faces me. "Though preppy in his looks, Grecian god–like in his build, and as cordially sweet as they come, Brock Cunningham's a chameleon. Wits outwitting the best of them, he races more cocaine in and out of the DC metropolitan area than NASCAR drivers complete laps."

My heart stops, my breathing following suit.

As my purse slides from my shoulder, she continues to clog my head. "They all do."

"Who's 'they'?" My voice comes out grainy, like sandpaper rubbing against sandpaper.

With guarded eyes, she tosses her crimson hair over her shoulder. "Ryder; my boyfriend, Lee; and a few local dirtbags Brock's got on his payroll."

Other than Ryder's name, I heard the word "boyfriend." Okay, she's lost me so much that for a split second I find myself scrambling to form a sentence. But in true Gemini form, I never fail to word-vomit my thoughts.

I pick up my purse, a wicked *you're a walking contradiction* smile rearing its ugly head across my lips. "Your boyfriend's on his payroll, huh?"

"Yeah." Her brow lifts in slow hesitation. "Why?"

"*Why?*" I laugh, tapping my chin in mock thought. "Let's see. Could it be because you're saying *I* should think twice about someone who deals, but *you* shouldn't?"

"Lee sells it for Brock but doesn't actually *run* the whole ring. That's the point." Her ridiculous defense comes out in fast, clipped strokes. "There's a difference. A *big* difference."

No longer interested in this bullshit conversation, I swing open the door, convinced the girl I'm rooming with is going to drive me nuts. Borderline psychotic. If there's one thing I hate, it's how easily humans throw rocks—no, boulders—against the same glass houses they reside in.

Can I deny my mind is spinning, whirling like an amusement park ride? No. Absolutely not. The captain of the football team, who's completely unaware that he's already dipped his way into my shallow soul, has managed to lump himself into the ilk of slimy bastards who turned my parents into what they were, what they died as.

He's an addict's dream, dragging unsuspecting victims off to never-never land.

Yet as I make my way down the stairs, I can't stop my feet from moving. I try, but I can't. I push open the doors, the late August sun showing no mercy as curiosity about who Brock Cunningham *really* is seizes every cell in my body. Desperation nearly blinds me as I scan the student parking lot for Brock's Hummer, snagging it before I can take another nervous breath. Though my movements appear unperturbed, my pulse's thumping like an angry fist against a punching bag. I hear the vehicle's locks unclick, their sound mimicking that of a cocked shotgun.

Bang, bang, bang goes my heart as Brock gets out, but I open the passenger-side door, preventing his intention of doing it for me. I slide in, my senses vibrating from the effusion of expensive leather and masculine cologne sweetening the air. Every nervous tic inside me comes to a complete stop as Brock ducks back in, our gazes connecting with an instant sizzle. Though it feels like an eternity's swept by, it's only a few seconds before a warm smile steals his lips, the deep sea green of his eyes dizzying my head the same way they did the first time I saw him.

That's all it takes. A single look. A single heart-stopping, breath-thieving look from him and my mind changes scripts, deciding that things between us, in our current state, are too perfect, that my questions will only bring what we're becoming—a fucked-up duo—to an abrupt end, leaving me to wonder what could've been.

Regret: the universe's way of keeping each of us a slave to its brutality. Holding our hand in its poisonous grip, regret's toxicity is the last visitor remaining by our side as we lie on our deathbeds.

Though I yearn to unearth every mystery this man's trying hard to conceal, the world around me disappears, taking with it any and all questions I had but a few seconds ago. I don't want to meet Brock's demons, the skeletons he's holding captive in a trunk of buried secrets. I have no desire to acquaint myself with them. Not now. Maybe never.

But I have to. I opened myself up to him, and he lied to me, keeping the biggest piece of himself hidden beneath a petrifying camouflage. That makes me want to run, flee, fly away from him and his world. However, as a lethal blend of curiosity and nervousness shifts through my limbs, I can't move. Something more powerful than I'll ever be keeps me planted to the seat.

"Hey, pretty girl," Brock says, backing out of the parking space. His deep baritone curls through my stomach, every tendon a live wire as he rests his hand on my thigh. The subtle act causes my blood to thrash though my veins, my breath caught in my throat as his fingers flirt along the edge of my skirt.

"Hey," I reply with a fake smile, attempting to hide the anxiety cording my spine. Heated, confused, and beyond pissed off, I try to concentrate on the lick of air-conditioning tickling my skin instead of the hypnotizing warmth of Brock's touch.

He pitches me a salacious grin, his gaze bouncing between me and the road as he makes a right out of the university parking lot. "You clean up well, Miss Moretti."

I pretend to find something of interest in the passing neighborhood. "Is that your version of a killer pickup line?"

"You're already sitting next to me." He chuckles, his fingers trailing a path down my knee, then back up my thigh again. "I could be wrong, and forgive me if I am, but I'd say we're past killer pickup lines, no?"

"True," I say flatly, "but we're not past the part where you forgot to tell me you're self-employed. You know? The whole coke-selling business you own."

He pulls to the side of the road, shock shadowing his features. "Amber—"

"How could you *keep* something like that from me?" I hold back my need to punch him by looking out the window.

"Please listen to me," he whispers. Cupping my chin, he brings my gaze back to his. "What was I supposed to say? 'Hi, my name's Brock Cunningham. I'm nothing like my friend, but I sell coke for a living'?"

"Yeah." Tears prick my eyes, but I fight them back. I may not have shared my body with him, and I'm not in love with him, but I've allowed him to glimpse into the dark window of my past. I've given that to very few people. I'm not about to hand him my tears. "Yeah, Brock, you could've."

"And you would've walked away," he remarks, his voice barely audible.

"You don't know that for sure." And neither do I. The only thing I do know is this hurts more than it should.

"You're right," he concedes with a sigh as he leans over the center console and glides his thumb across my lips. "But I wasn't about to risk that happening. I wouldn't have been able to let you walk away, Amber. I just . . . I just wouldn't have let it happen. The second I laid eyes on you, I knew you were broken, knew I could . . . fix you. Let me show you who I am under all of this. I'm sorry I lied. It'll never fucking happen again. Never. But I need you to give me a chance."

The gentle caress in his plea makes me want to console him, hold him in my arms until it hurts. He keeps saying he wants to fix me, but I'm starting to realize we both have scars we're hiding from the world. I'm just not sure how deep his run or who delivered the wounds. Still, I have questions I need answered.

"Would you have told me?" I ask, my nerves settling some.

He nods and slides his hand to my nape. "I knew I had to. I also knew Madeline would eventually say something, but I just didn't know how or when to bring it up."

"Why?"

"Well, it's not *exactly* something you mention over a cup of coffee." Fingers playing into my hair; a small grin trips the corner of his mouth. "Wouldn't you agree?"

"Yes, but that's not what I mean," I say through a sigh. "Why do you sell it?"

A brick wall slips over his face as he sits back in his seat, staring straight ahead. "I'm sorry, Ber, but I can't go there with you." He scrubs a palm over his jaw, his gaze dimming as he shakes his head. "We all have a dark corner in our mind that we refuse to revisit. One that—if for whatever reasons we do—will mentally kill us all over again, bringing us right back into that moment of loneliness and pain, the entire fucking thing eating at our very existence." He swings his attention to me, his expression eerily devoid of emotion as he cups my cheeks. "This is *my* dark corner, my . . . suicide cliff. Again, I can't do it. I *won't* do it."

"I don't understand," I whisper, hurt sidling up my throat. "You sell cocaine, Brock. You *have* to go there with me."

"I *can't*," he reiterates, resolve tightening his tone.

"Oh my God, this is bullshit." My pulse jerks, betrayal knifing my heart as I curl my fingers around his wrists, praying my words will release the demons he's harboring. "I've opened up to you, Brock. You might not think it's much, but it *is*. I've been dumped into a recycling bin of nothing but mistrust, born into this world unloved by most around me, my parents included. You have no *idea* how much I've let you in on, believe me. I'm not asking you for something *major*. I just need an explanation, a damn shadow of hope that'll let me know I *can* trust you."

Though his guard falters a bit, he keeps up his front, the moment fleeting as his brows pinch in confusion. "*Why?*" he asks, his voice hard, unyielding. "Why is it so fucking important to you? I'm a dealer, Amber. There's nothing more to it. Just leave it at that."

"No. I will *not* just leave it at that," I toss back, my tone mirroring that of a bratty child as I tighten my grip around his wrists. "And if you wanna know *why* it's so important to me, it's because *you're* starting to become important to me. Consider yourself lucky, asshole, because that's a rarity on my end." Air crackling with tension, we glare at each other, our inner demons surfacing as an edge of mortification jumps through my chest. Unable to believe I spilled my feelings to him, I shake my head, my words falling from my lips in the form of a whisper. "I'm going to ask you one more time, and if you don't answer, I'm getting out of this car and you'll never see me again. Why do you sell it?"

I watch a swallow tumble through his throat but a disturbing placidity takes over as he leans back, rushing a hand through his hair. "I'm the reason my kid brother went missing."

"*What?*" I breathe, shocked, completely confused. "You said you had an older sister. Jesus, Brock, you told me you never had anyone close to you die."

"She's the only sibling I have *left*, Amber, and we don't know if he's . . ," He pauses, a muscle working in his jaw as he stares straight ahead.

Silent, I wait for him to continue, my heart pounding.

"They never found his body, so we're trying to hold on to that." He pauses again, almost as if summoning up the courage to keep talking. "His name was Brandon, and he was ten years old when he was taken from our front porch while he waited for me to get there to let him in." He clutches the steering wheel and looks at me, pain and anger melting across his face. "Even though my mother had reminded me all goddamn week, I forgot. While the kid was going through who knows what, the piece of shit I was—that I still fucking am—was getting my cock sucked in the back of my car behind the high school."

He lets out a scornful laugh, the air electrocuting with the sound of his fist hitting the dashboard. I jump, my body shaking as much as his. My heart's bleeding out for him. I bring my hand to his cheek, hoping my touch can calm him.

Brock grabs my wrist, holding my quivering hand against his face. "I was a seventeen-year-old asshole who was blowing a nut in some chick's mouth while my brother was probably wondering if he was going to die." He releases my wrist and lifts his hands to my face, cupping my cheeks. "After that, my family lost control over everything. If my father isn't fucking his newest secretary, my mother hasn't consumed a fifth of gin before breakfast, or anyone's said a word to each other all month, something's off.

"But Debby and John Cunningham are monster lawyers, so we all have to look and act perfect. What the world sees is nothing but a mirage, one huge fucking lie. They see a family whose younger son was kidnapped but stayed strong despite it. They don't see the breakdown. It doesn't exist to them."

Still holding my face, Brock continues, his voice a low hum of anguish. "They see a daughter who followed in their parents' footsteps, becoming a Harvard-bred prosecutor. They don't see that she's addicted to trying to fix everyone around her. That when she can't, she slips into a depression that lasts for weeks, sometimes months. They see the remaining son, the one responsible for the whole fucking thing, who went to college on a football scholarship most would kill for. They see him as the university's captain. They don't see that his parents forced him to play football since he was a kid or that he sells drugs because it's the only thing he's been able to control since the day his brother was taken.

"It's my control, Ber," he whispers, lightly touching his lips to mine. "I *have* to do it. It keeps my world in check. It makes me feel normal, successful. I feel needed, like there's more to me than my fuckups." He tilts my head and moves his mouth to my jaw. "People want what I supply them. It gives me a sense of control and a purpose. It might be fucked up, but my need for control is a part of me. A *huge* part."

I slowly pull back and stare at Brock's pained face, my thoughts whiplashed as I try to process everything. I feel as if I've been hit with a sledgehammer, and to be honest, I'm not sure how to handle it. I've always been at the receiving end of help, never the one giving it. Though I'm in school to assist others with their problems, here and now, I'm not mentally equipped to aid Brock through this nightmare, nor do I think I'll be any time soon.

Yet, as I gaze into the mossy eyes of this beautiful black-winged angel, I can't ignore a pull so overbearingly strong within my soul telling me otherwise. It's screaming out to me that the emptiness in my heart can only be filled by him and vice versa. That we need each other to complete some kind of turbulent cycle of coming together broken, ultimately ending it by becoming whole as one.

I know these disjointed thoughts go against my better judgment, against everything I've known to be messed up in my life, but I think

I'm about to blindly jump into the depths of hell. I just hope the flames surrounding Brock Cunningham don't burn me.

"Do I scare you, Ber?" Brock moves a piece of hair away from my shoulder. "If I do, that wasn't my intention."

"No," I whisper, realizing I'm not experiencing fear. I know fear. Touched its poisonous thorns, heard its wicked screams, seen its malicious face. "You don't scare me. You . . . intrigue me."

"*Intrigue?*" He gives a weak chuckle, resting his lips against my forehead. "That's a new one."

I nod, my breathing spiking as Brock slides his lips to my temple, down the curve of my face, and to the corner of my mouth. "You know I'm not gonna hurt you, right? Nothing I'm involved in will ever hurt you."

"But *you* can get hurt, and if I wind up . . ." I trail off, getting way ahead of myself. Other than my parents, I've never loved anyone. Love is the mighty evil fall, and I refuse to willingly jump off its ledge of destruction into a cesspool of nothing but hurt and pain. For in that cesspool are vultures lying in wait to eat me alive.

"If you what?" Brock probes, his hands finding the back of my neck.

"Nothing."

"Say it. If you wind up falling in love with me." A grin softens his face as he dusts his lips against mine. "Let me correct that. *When* you fall in love with me."

"'When'?" My question comes out breathlessly, my eyes nearly fluttering closed as he continues, brushing his lips along my jaw.

"Yeah, when," he murmurs, curling his fingers into my hair. "Because even though you *think* you won't, you will. I'll make it impossible for you not to, but I have a feeling you're gonna do the same fucking thing to me. So we'll be even. Good?"

"Good," I say, my heart rioting, wondering if he'll be the first to crack it open.

With a slow smile, Brock captures my bottom lip between his

teeth, gently sucking as he continues. "Nothing's gonna happen to me. I've been playing this game for a few years. Besides playing it *very* well, I know the ins and outs of it. Everyone working under me does too. No one in my circle's a fool."

Ryder hijacks my thoughts, pushing through every crevice of my skull. I hadn't expected him to say anything about being a part of this setup, but considering how much we spilled today, a small part of me can't help but feel the same slice of betrayal it's feeling for Brock.

Either way, I got schooled by two guys.

Big-time.

One fit the drug-dealer stereotype in every sense of the word. Tattoos, a proper piercing, and an *I don't give a fuck* bad-boy persona.

The other?

A true enigma. The all-American boy gone bad. Really bad.

I'm aware both illusionists could be toxic to my mental state and heart. Doing what I do best, I disconnect, shoving Ryder out of my head. "I watch television. Dealers and their crews get taken down all the time."

Brock chuckles again, this one full-bodied. "I'm not going down, and if I do, it's gonna make national news."

"Is that an attempt at making me feel better?" I cock a brow, still in awe that I'm having this conversation. I'd be lying if I said my mind's not warring with the fact that I'm on a date with a dealer. "If it is, it's not working."

He kisses my forehead, a smirk plastered to his lips as he leans back and checks the side-view mirror. "Don't worry your pretty little self, all right?"

"Uh, okay?"

"And I need you to promise me something," he says, his voice serious as he eases onto the road.

I stare at him, waiting for him to go on.

"I want you. I think I've made that very clear." He brings his hand to my cheek, sliding his thumb under my chin. "But if you're going to be with me, you can't ask questions about anything I do. You'll be a part of *my* life, but you'll never be a part of *that* life."

I blink and face him. "Don't get me wrong, it's obvious you're setting boundaries. I'm not stupid. But for the simple fact that I don't take orders well from others—even though I'm disturbingly turned on by your dominance—I need you to elaborate some."

"You're turned on by this?" he asks with a lazy grin, his playfulness making a resurgence.

I sigh, unwilling to admit just *how* much I'm turned on. "Get to the point."

"You have no clue how *disturbingly* kinky I can get." He smoothes his palm up my leg, his fingers toying with the hem of my skirt. "Just preparing you."

I sigh again, but I really want to moan. "Point, Cunningham. Make. It. Now."

"Right." He shoves a hand through his hair, his grin disappearing. "I pick up once a month from my guy. Sometimes I'm gone for a few hours, sometimes I'm gone a few days. You can't come with me."

"Why?" I cross my arms, feeling like a child.

He glances at me. "Do you *really* need to ask why?"

"You're the one who made it sound like it's not dangerous."

"I never said it wasn't dangerous, Ber. There's nothing about it that's *not* dangerous. What I said was that I know how to maneuver around the assholes I deal with." Flicking on his blinker, he squeezes my thigh. "And the assholes I deal with are assholes you'll *never* be anywhere around. Ever. It's not gonna happen."

A few silent minutes go by before the need to test him strikes me. "Is it dangerous enough that you have to . . . carry a gun?"

He kicks me another glance, this one sharp. "No questions, baby. Remember what I said. None."

I swallow hard, the effort twisting my throat. He's said all I need to know. All I'm sure he's ever going to let me in on.

"You good?" he asks, his voice soft.

I nod. Despite everything dumped in my lap in the last fifteen minutes, I think I am.

"Cool." He lifts his hand and twirls my hair between his fingers. "So are you curious where I'm taking you?"

"A little." Through several texts during the week, he's dropped hints here and there—some shit about visiting a time warp—but I'm still not sure where we're going.

"A *little?*"

"Yeah, a little."

The corner of his mouth lifts in a grin. "I thought I told you, *nothing* about me is little."

"Ah, that's right." I giggle, tension disappearing from my shoulders. "Forgive me."

"All's forgiven."

The second the words fall from his mouth, we pull into the parking lot of a top-notch condominium complex in downtown Annapolis. Reserved for those who possess enough cash for such accommodations as living on the bay, it's an area I'll never be able to afford. At least not until I'm finished with school.

"Your place?" I ask.

"Yup," Brock answers.

I had no clue this was our destination for the evening, and for this, I'm feeling overdressed. Considering the topics covered in the last twenty minutes, it's only now I realize Brock's wearing low-hung jeans and a graphic T-shirt. Brock plays a gentleman, stepping from the vehicle and opening my door. With my hand in his, my heels hit the asphalt, my eyes taking in the painted purple sky and setting sun. A warm breeze hugs my skin, the smell of fresh seafood invading my nose as Brock leads me toward an elevator. My heart pounds over the laughter from drunken partygoers flocking the downtown area.

"You look nervous," Brock says, his face cool and collected. He pushes the button for the fifteenth floor. "Do I scare you?"

"You asked me that already. And I told you no."

He brings his knuckles to my cheek. "I think you're lying."

"And, as usual, I think you're a wiseass," I retort, relishing in the caress of his knuckles stroking down my collarbone. "A wiseass who has no right talking about lying."

My stomach twists with guilt. I almost raped his best friend today. Who's the bigger liar?

Brock leans into my ear, his lips flirting with it. "You got me there. I did lie. And I apologized for it. If I have to pay penance to you for my shitty lie every single day, I will. Never put *anything* past me. Besides, I'm sure I could conjure up quite a few . . . *intriguing ways to make you* enjoy my apology." With a smirk, he grips my waist, his words a soft whisper. "Do you have any secrets, my mysterious, beautiful Ber?"

I attempt to ignore the sexual potency he exudes. The sexual potency I want nothing more than to absorb into my skin. Our conversation from the lake sparks through my head. "It's human nature to lie. We pick it up before we can even walk. Still, none of my lies or secrets will ever . . . *hurt* you."

Brock pulls me flush to his chest and nips my ear, the delicious sting causing my thighs to involuntarily clench. "Ah, I see. Now you have me wondering just how sweet your lies will taste on my tongue."

Air punches from my lungs, my heart evaporating into a mist of crimson as the elevator doors part, breaking me from the ridiculous trance he so effortlessly put me under. He smiles, reaches for my hand, and guides me down the hall to his unit.

I glimpse a blade of light creeping from the kitchen as I step into his dimly lit condo. Still, I can easily make out claret-red walls, shadows slapping across polished maple floors as I scan the impressive space. It's filled with what appears to be black leather couches and large mahogany furniture. Either he had a longtime girlfriend who spread her flair for design all over the place, or he hired someone to do it. Needless to say, the lavishness in which he lives nearly drops me.

"Welcome to *mi casa*." His gaze slides from mine as he flips on a lamp. "Go ahead and make yourself comfortable while I prepare dinner."

Convinced he was ordering takeout, I cock a shocked brow. "You cook?"

"These hands," he says, lifting both, "possess *many* talents. Cooking's the most minor of them all. Stick around long enough, and I bet your body will agree."

I shake my head. "You're extremely sure of yourself."

"In more ways than you could ever imagine," he answers, an edge of playfulness in his tone as he takes my purse. Along with his keys and a knot of cash, he drops it onto a bar dripping with black granite. "In all seriousness, you're hungry, right?"

I nod and walk over to a set of French doors, my eyes exploring a balcony overlooking the bay. "Depends. What are you cooking?"

"With the help of this here handy microwave and Orville Redenbacher, the popcorn I promised you when my 'killer pickup lines' won you over the day we met."

I turn and, sure as shit, he's pulled out a bag. "You're kidding me."

A chuckle barrels from his chest as he tosses the bag into the microwave. Flashing his pearly whites, he moves toward the refrigerator, pulls out a six-pack of Red Bull, and sets it on the island. "Do I look like I'm kidding, my mysterious Ber?"

I roll my eyes. "Why the need for a nickname?"

Cool amusement hits his face as he leans against the counter, his arms crossed. "Because it's our secret joke, and you're my ... pet."

"Your *pet*?"

"Yes. My *pet*." Seduction laces his low growl. He steps in front of me, a soft smile sliding across his mouth. "Is that okay with you?" Before I can answer, he dips his head to my ear and whispers, "I handle my pets with special care, always making sure their needs come first."

He moves his lips to my jaw, his hands finding my waist. "Their pleasure is what brings mine. I fucking drown in it. Their soft moans." He licks the contour of my jaw, a deep groan rumbling from his chest. "The way their bodies tremble." He pulls me closer, his hardening erection pressed to my stomach. "The sweat glistening on their skin. Their sweet scent before, during, and especially after I place my stamp on them." He backs me against the opposite counter, his lips landing on mine. "I'll do anything to see them reach their . . . happy place."

Delicious heat coils through me, my heart thwacking uncontrollably. Though my eyes slipped closed somewhere around "glistening skin," I feel Brock's smirk.

He grips my waist harder. "Do you like being in that happy place?"

"Yes," I whisper, opening my eyes.

"Yeah? Because I can bring you there over and over and over again." His voice is a low, primal baritone, causing my pulse to spike as his fingers play with the waistband of my skirt. "I don't need much time to refuel. I also give extra treats to my pets who are good and do what I want them to."

"Is that so?" I clutch the cool granite behind me, trying to exercise the control he's stripping me of. "What kind of treats?"

"Ah, I can't divulge that information." A grin tweaks his mouth, his eyes flashing mirth. "You need—no, strike that—you *will* experience it firsthand."

Beeeeeeeeep . . .

I almost mistake the sound of the microwave for the flatlining of my heart.

As though he didn't have his fingers halfway to my "happy place," wasn't seducing me like a pro, and didn't nearly have me hopping onto the counter—legs spread and ready for treats—Brock takes a measured step back, his grin holding steady. I pull in a pissed-off breath as he retrieves the popcorn from the microwave and pours it into a bowl. He watches me intently, his eyes crinkling in amusement.

"Open your mouth," he says, nearing me again. "I want to give you something." Though his voice is a whisper, the beautiful command in it stabs my ears.

Hands clutching the counter tighter, I stare into his eyes, my heart going nuts as I instinctively obey him.

With a triumphant smile, he places a piece of popcorn onto my tongue. "Does that taste good?"

"*Mm-hmm.*" I nod and chew. "You *are* talented. You've mastered the art of popcorn making. I foresee doing anything you want for those treats of yours. *Anything.*" I swipe my tongue across my lips for effect.

I get the reaction I'm aiming for.

Expression flaring with need, Brock watches me close my eyes in mock pleasure. When I open them, his gaze devours mine, stroking between my breasts and mouth. I flip him a wink, turn around, and traipse into the living room, leaving *him* hanging this time.

I'm also a pro. He just doesn't know it yet.

I can't help but giggle when I hear him groan. I deposit myself onto the couch, my own triumphant smile spreading as Brock wanders into the room like a lost, lonely child. Holding the bowl of popcorn, he grins and positions himself in front of me. I nearly lose my breath as he leans over me, stretches his arm, and rests his hand on the back of the couch just above my shoulder.

Oh God. His lips are within kissing distance. If I move an inch, I'll hit the mark.

Like a true Southern belle, I bat my lashes and stare at him. "You have to give me your secret recipe. I mean, honestly, you're going places with it, and I feel the absolute need to be included in your success."

He cocks his head to the side, his grin broadening. "I'm all for partnerships."

"So it's a deal, then?" I try to concentrate on the smell of the buttery popcorn instead of his musky cologne. "I must warn you. I'd require fifty percent if we were to enter into a partnership."

He raises a brow, his hand staking claim on the nape of my neck. "Fifty percent's not cheap. But it's me who must warn you, I'll make you work *very* hard for that half."

"How . . . *hard?*" A spark of excitement blooms in my stomach as I watch his eyes catch my innuendo.

"You have *no* fucking idea how hard."

"Oh, but I think I do." With a husky laugh, my gaze falls to his arousal beneath his jeans.

"Open," he says, staring at my lips.

The heated cadence in his voice pulls me further into his spell, extinguishing my good friend mutiny. I once again obey his words. What the hell? Talk about the power of sexual deprivation. It's been close to three months for me, and my body's about to go bat-shit crazy if it doesn't get what it needs to maintain a sense of normalcy.

Exquisite warmth slides up my spine as Brock places another piece of popcorn on my tongue. Our gazes lock, flames flickering in our showdown, but before either of us can take an uneven breath, the sound of Brock's cell phone slices through the air. His movements still, his body straightening.

"This is a joke, right?" I ask, honestly pissed off.

Brock sighs, a frown pinching his forehead. "I have to get it." He touches my cheek, sets the bowl on the coffee table, and turns.

Dumbfounded, I watch him move across the living room to snatch the stupid phone off the kitchen counter. Anger punches me in the gut, my blood boiling. I'm about to yank the phone away from him, jet out to the balcony, and toss the fucking thing into the bay. I've decided the plan's brilliant and go to act on it; however, my attention lands on an unopened DVD box set. The first season of *Happy Days* essentially saves Brock's cell from a watery death.

Time warp. Now his texts make sense.

I can't help but smile as I stand and pluck the several discs containing the only good memories I've experienced from the towering entertainment center. Brock's kept his word.

Popcorn, Red Bulls, and Mrs. Cunningham.

Charmer.

I can't say I'll keep mine. There's no way I'm singing for him again. Impatient, I glance around and locate the remote, deciding to open up the box and pop in the first episode. Just as I reclaim my seat on the couch, and *Happy Days'* infamous "weird" melody streams from the speakers, Brock once again graces me with his presence.

With his hand buried in his hair, he casts me a hesitant smile. "I'm sorry." He sits next to me, sliding his arm across the back of the couch. "I was waiting on a call."

"Apparently." I lean forward for a piece of popcorn and toss it into my mouth, my concentration aimed at the television and not his beautiful face. On a sigh, I lean back, accepting that if I continue to see him, the constant interruptions are something I'll have to learn to tolerate.

Silence stretches for a few seconds before Brock lets out a light chuckle.

"What?"

He twirls a piece of my hair. My shoulders go slack, every muscle in my body relaxing.

"The first episode was always my favorite," he says.

"Wait." My attention floats between him and the television. "I just opened the DVD. How's it always been your favorite if you've never seen the show?"

A guilty smirk lifts his lips as he leans in and whispers, "Did you honestly think I grew up with the last name Cunningham and had *no* idea the show existed?"

I feel dizzy, thrown off-kilter by the sweet warmth of his breath. I rake my eyes over him.

His smirk turns into a boyish smile. "With the exception of the first one, which I actually liked, my mother made all of us kids suffer through every episode."

"You bastard," I huff, playfully swatting his arm. "You lied to me... again. Maybe *my* nickname for *you* needs to be Pinocchio?"

"Maybe it does. But *that* lie got you to sing for me in public." Amusement lights up his face. "It also has you sitting next to me now, so it's a lie I'll never regret telling. When I want something badly enough, I'll do whatever I have to do to get it. It usually works in my favor."

"A little high on ourselves, are we?"

"No," he whispers, his expression striking hot with want.

His eyes shift to my lips, and he slides his thumb across my mouth. Other than the pounding of my heart, I'm positive every organ in me has ceased functioning properly.

"There was a tiny piece of popcorn hanging out on the corner of your lip."

"Oh," is all I manage. I watch him suck the minuscule piece of popcorn off his thumb. I'm suddenly jealous of both his thumb and Orville Redenbacher's creation.

He stares at me a long moment. "Are you mad at me?"

"I am, but I think you know how to seduce me into forgiving you."

His grin drips sex. "Do you like when I seduce you?"

"Yes, to a point."

"I do too," he whispers, lifting his knuckles to my cheek. The featherlight touch sends goose bumps along my skin. "You're very reactive to me. But I want your forgiveness without having to seduce it out of you."

"Then you should stop touching me."

He drops his hand, his grin widening. My attention flits to the screen. It's the part where Richie finds out Potsie's fixed him up with Mary Lou.

I bring my eyes back to Brock's, a weak smile on my lips. "*Happy Days* has helped a little in the forgiveness department."

"I thought it might." He studies me another long moment. "There's more behind why you like the show as much as you do, isn't there?"

"No."

"I think you're telling me another lie." He lifts his hand again, this time massaging the back of my neck. I shiver. "Whatever it is, why are you hiding it from me, Ber? Do you not trust me with it?"

"I do, or will eventually. I'm not sure." I take a breath, a shrug tugging my shoulder. "But we're all allowed to keep pieces of our pasts to ourselves. If not, what would there be to run after?" *Or in my case, run from?*

"You think that's why I'm coming after you? Because you're keeping pieces of yourself from me?"

I shrug again. "I don't know why you're coming after me."

I honestly don't. The only thing remotely appealing about me, other than being able to spit my fucked-up past onto paper faster than a writer smoking crack, is that I can fuck, suck, and swallow better than most porn stars. I'm convinced Hugh Hefner would promptly acquire me as his next barely legal wife if he saw me in action.

"I thought it was obvious why I'm coming after you," Brock says, his voice soft. "You think I intrigue you, but it's really the opposite."

"Right." I nod. "My *unseen* pieces."

"No," he whispers, sliding his hand to my chin. "The beautiful ones you're unaware you've *already* shown me."

It's my turn to stare at him a long moment. Before I can think of a remark psychotic enough to let him know I'm not a mental mess he needs in his life—no matter how clotted up his is—Brock curls his hand around mine and stands me up with him. I pull in a staggering breath, my eyes pinned on his lips.

"You know I'm gonna decode you, right?" He moves a lock of hair off my shoulder. "I hope you do."

I bring my eyes to his, my words shaky. "You think you can?"

"I know I can. No matter how hard you make the ride, I'm not getting off, so stop trying." He drags his hand down my waist. "I'm a fighter, and I won't rest easy until I know I'm securely in that heart of yours. You're a challenge. Nothing short of trying to solve a Rubik's Cube in the dark. I like that about you." He searches my face, his hold tightening as he presses his lips to my forehead. "I think we're alike in more ways than either of us realizes. That by itself is gonna make us work. Just let it happen."

He takes me in a second before leading me toward the balcony, my heart thumping with every step. A sticky breeze hits my skin as he pushes open the French doors. The cloudless sky—pregnant with a full harvest moon—casts a silver glow on the harbor below us. Small waves rip against the docks as Brock gestures to a rattan chair. I sit, my body taut with a nervous energy I'm starting to realize comes from being around him.

"You need to learn to relax." Brock pitches me a playful look as he sinks into a chair on the other side of a marble table. "You think too much."

"Why are you always trying to read me?"

He leans forward, resting his elbows on his knees. "You make it impossible not to."

I prop my feet against the railing. "How so?"

"You always look like you're thinking."

"Aren't we *all* always thinking, Einstein?"

He chuckles. "True. But there are *several* ways to help you tame those bad boys.

He reaches down to his side and brings up a black-and-silver glass-blown bong. Producing a lighter faster than I can produce my next breath, he lights the bong and takes a long pull. After a few seconds, he coughs, blowing out the smoke. I watch it curl away like a ghost, its odor colliding with the scent of the harbor and the sweet smell of freshly cut grass.

"One of them being this." He hits the bong again, then he slides it in my direction. "The other's a combination of sweaty body parts, a healthy dose of sheet-clawing stimulation, and me deciding if your lies taste bitter or . . . *sweet*."

"Bitter or sweet?" I stare at the bong, my heart firing off warning shots.

"Yeah. Bitter or sweet." Another smirk kicks up the corner of his mouth. "However, I'd bank my life on the latter."

I wonder if he can see the debate settling over my face. I've never smoked weed. Hell, I barely take anything for a headache. I slowly bring my eyes to his half-mast ones. His gaze is stuck on mine, and it feels like a wrecking ball to my gut. Anxiety piles thick in my throat as I try to level my breathing.

"I've never smoked weed," I blurt, prudence glued to my statement. "I've consumed enough tequila that I was sure my skull was splitting in half the next morning, I've gone skinny-dipping at a house party in front of the entire student body, and I'm almost positive my foster parents' chinchilla tried to rape me one night." I take a shaky breath, my voice a whisper. "But I've never smoked weed."

Tension fills the air as Brock watches me carefully, his smirk sliding away. He stands, rounds the table, and squats before me, capturing both my eyes and waist. Nervousness punches through me, tightening my chest to the point where I feel like I can't breathe.

Brock stares up at me, his brow lifting. "I'm definitely feelin' the skinny-dipping part and look forward to seeing that for myself. But I can't say the same for the chinchilla. It'll now be my life's mission to find the little fucker and beat him to death. Fuck animal cruelty. He fucked with you; I fuck with him right back."

We both smile. His genuine, mine nervous.

"And it looks like I'm on my second apology for the night." He massages my side. "I'm sorry. Like an asshole, I just assumed you'd smoked it before."

I shake my head.

"But I think this will help you to chill." His voice is calm, soothing my nerves in a way I can't explain. "Just a little. That's all you'll need to temporarily forget the shit that's happened to you. It'll wipe it from your head for a few hours. You'll be okay because you're doing it with me. I promised I wouldn't let anything happen to you, Amber."

A silent minute goes by.

Two.

Three.

Four.

I nod, and though I'm somewhat settled by his reassurance, perspiration surfaces on my forehead. I want to say no, that I can't. That I'm more than aware this could lead me to darker places. I want to tell him I watched my parents wither away under their own drug addiction, but the words get stuck in my throat, verbal gridlock holding them captive.

Brock reaches for the bong and lights it up. He sucks a hit into his lungs, keeps it in a few seconds, and brings his hand to the nape of my neck. Gently pulling me down to his face, he stares at me a moment, searching my eyes for a signal to stop.

Though it's only weed—and more than half my generation gets blazed on this shit—I know I'm staring at the birth of what could be my demise. I was born to become an addict, my past sprinkled with needles, paving a path in its dark direction. Still, something tells me to go for it. To finally let go and live. Let go of my parents and the love they held from me. Let go of the day that forever changed the colors of my world. Let go of my fear of loving anything or anyone.

I just want to feel.

Feel life.

Feel this moment.

Feel . . . human.

I nod again, and Brock crashes his lips to mine, coaxing them open with a slow sweep of his tongue. My arteries—just a few seconds before filled with fear and hesitation—are thick with adrenaline and sexual desire as Brock simultaneously licks into my mouth and pushes the smoke into my body. I'm not sure which to concentrate on: the sting in my lungs as I inhale what I hope will erase my past or the feel of Brock's lips on mine.

I do neither. A cough bursts from me, my hand flying over my mouth.

"Are you okay?" Brock asks.

"I think so." I nod, trying to catch a decent breath. "Should I be feeling something?"

His eyes widen. "You *don't* feel turned on?"

"You know what I mean," I half cough with a smile.

"I guess I have to try harder," he says with a grin, repeating the process of taking another hit from the bong as he stands me up with him. After setting it on the table, Brock's hands slide to my hips, dominance wild in their grip, as he layers his mouth over mine. I close my eyes, surrendering to his warmth as I clutch his shoulders and inhale another pull. It doesn't burn as much, and my body welcomes it like an old friend. Brock tastes different from the first time we kissed, but still amazing, an exotic mixture of mouthwash and weed. I barely register my arms becoming lethargic as Brock's hands move up my rib cage, his thumbs grazing my nipples.

"Christ, I could kiss you for fucking days," he growls, sucking my bottom lip between his teeth. He licks into my mouth, his kiss growing relentless with each uneven breath we take. "Please, Ber, I'm begging, baby, let me fuck you like you need to be fucked. Let me give your body what it's craving."

Need, want, and lust lightens my head, his sudden plea spreading over me. Without breaking our kiss, Brock lifts me onto the table, wedging himself between my thighs. A gasp shoots from my parched throat as he draws my legs up around his waist. I rest my palms on the cool marble, my gaze submerged in the hungry look prowling his face.

"Tell me you're gonna let me fuck you tonight," Brock commands, his stare connected to mine with infallible precision.

"Yes," I breathe without a second thought. "You're fucking me tonight." I need, want, and ache for this.

My stomach plummets to my toes as Brock snakes his hand up my thigh, finding and ripping my lace panties clear off my body. He trips a finger over my clit, sending delicious pinpricks of pleasure across my skin.

Another gasp leaves me as his mouth lands on mine, his voice strangled. "Do you like kissing me while you're high?"

I moan, shudders bombarding every previously relaxed muscle in my body as he barely pushes a finger inside me. My head lolls back, my eyelids heavy, hooded like cement's weighing them down as I clutch the table.

"Yes," I answer, thrusting my hips forward. "I love it."

"Do you want to know what it feels like to be finger-fucked while you're high?"

I nod, heat coiling around me.

"Say it," he slowly whispers, his eyes glued to mine as he cups my ass, pulling me to the edge of the table.

On instinct, I bring my hands to his hair, gripping the soft caramel waves. "Finger-fuck me," I beg, shame having no damn say in this moment.

He pushes a scant inch inside me. "Say it again," he growls.

"Finger-fuck me," I pant, digging my fingers into his skull.

Another inch, another finger. My pussy clenches, throbbing for more.

"Again, Ber. Say it again. Tell me to finger-fuck you harder."

At this point, I don't know who's the one begging. The only thing I know is that in some sick, twisted way, he's playing with me. I know it by the way he's waiting for me to answer, his eyes smug with control but still delicious with promise. I know it by the way he's teasing his lips over mine, just enough to make me bite my own when he pulls back. And I know it by the way he's slowly seducing me into loving everything he's doing.

I'm in uncharted territory, every fiber in my fucked-up being aware it's a fiend for the drug that *is* Brock Cunningham. Everything about him is dangerously beautiful, an untapped high I want to fully experience.

Fully consume.

Fully shoot through the curious blood in my veins.

Still, I'm not about to let him steal away my sexual control. It's the only thing that's kept me sane thus far. I'm going in for my next hit, but this addict's not about to make it easy for the dealer.

At. All.

I grip his hair tighter and pull his face to mine, my eyes fierce as uncut gemstones. "If you don't finger-fuck me harder, I'm getting off this table, calling a taxi, and going back to my dorm. A good porno and a dildo's brought me to the *exact* same place you can without the added bullshit. Take it or leave it."

With a wicked smirk, Brock goes knuckle-deep with three of his talented fingers, their rhythm matching the harsh breaths pushing from our lungs.

"Is that deep enough for you?" He buries his face against my sweaty neck.

With words disappearing from my brain—vanished, poof, gone—I can't answer. I can't focus or think straight. Sweet hell of all fiery hells, I can't breathe past the intoxicating sensations pulsing through my body as I claw at his T-shirt.

"Yeah, that's deep enough. This pussy's as ripe and ready as they come." Brock pulls back, his warm breath flirting over my lips as he stares into my eyes. "You want my cock? Need to feel it inside you?"

"Yes," I hum. "I don't care. Just fuck me right here on the table."

Desire buzzes thick through my veins as he rips open my blouse, the buttons scattering against the floor, along with my sanity. He slips the scalloped edge of my bra down, palms my breast, and flicks his tongue across my nipple. I surge forward, my body's primal need to fuck exploding.

"Mm," he groans, suckling the hardened peak, his fingers relentlessly manipulating my flesh. "But you're begging me for it before I give it to you, baby. I wanna hear you beg for my cock."

I cave, crumbling under the sharp scalpel of desire. "Please. I need your cock inside me. Now."

"Ah. There she is," he croons, his voice a dark ache as he pulls his fingers from me. Hunter eyes locked on mine, Brock touches them to my lips, sliding them into my mouth. I accept them without reserve, sucking my moisture from his fingers.

"Fuck, that's right, Ber. You like the way you taste on me, don't ya?"

On a moan, I nod and suck harder, my trembling hands wrapped around his wrist as I stare into his glazed-over eyes. As though the act shattered *his* sanity, Brock sweeps me off the table and up into his arms. He coats his mouth over mine as he carries me into the apartment.

"It's my turn to taste that pussy," he growls against my lips.

He fists the back of my hair, his shoulders slamming into furniture, walls, and the doorjamb of his bedroom before he sets me down on shaky legs. With dark eyes, Brock stares at me. God, he looks like an angelic demon, beautiful, frightening. My pulse thuds, sending blood screaming through my veins. Though the room's scarcely lit—drabs of the moon's potency filtering in through the wooden blinds—I see the hunger in his gaze, his want for me emanating off him.

I blink, my breathing matching his as I become aware of what's happening to my heated body. I feel different, light, something close to nonexistent. My arms are weighed down like bricks, my scrambled thoughts trying to get past a hazy fog clogging my head. A freaky sensation's coating my lips, but for some odd reason, I think I like it. My tongue feels thick like fur, or maybe heavy like lead. Everything's taken on a new shape, taste, and texture. With all of these foreign sensations, the world feels as if it's spread beneath me, airless, intoxicating.

"You're drummed up," Brock whispers, slowly sliding what remains of my blouse from my shoulders. "It feels good, doesn't it?"

It does. It feels *so* fucking good. For the first time in a long time, I'm weightless, almost as though the sins of my parents aren't holding me in their grip.

"Mm-hmm," I hum, thirsty for more.

He tosses the silken clothing to the floor and unhooks my bra. "And I'm about to make you feel so much better."

My bra joins the discarded blouse, the soft wisp of it hitting the carpet crashing the finality of the moment through the air as I suck in a breath. I'm handing myself over to this man. I shiver and stare into his eyes, my senses drowning in his touch.

"Christ, you're fucking gorgeous." Brock's teeth sink into his bottom lip. "There's not an inch of you I'm not gonna cover tonight."

Left in nothing but my skirt and heels, another tremble rocks through me as Brock circles my body. His movements are calculated, a hunter stalking its prey.

He stops behind me and fastens his lips to my neck, his words a deep growl as he palms my breasts. "You want me to make you feel better, Ber?"

My breathing hitches as he twirls my nipples between his fingers. "Oh God."

"That's the answer I was looking for. I *am* your God for the next few hours." Brock glides a hand down the flat of my stomach. I suck in another dizzying breath as he pushes his knee between my legs, spreading them open. My heart beats in anticipation as he hikes my skirt above my waist, his free hand finding my swollen clit. Rubbing it in slow, tantalizing circles, he groans into my neck, his breathing hot against my flesh. I gasp as he dips two urgent fingers inside my warmth. Greedy, I sheathe his fingers, my body hungry for his invasion.

"You like the way that feels?"

"Yes," I pant, my arms flying up around the back of his head. I bury my hands in his hair, my fingers tugging the dampened strands. "Please, Brock, please keep going."

"Can't do that," he whispers into my ear, abruptly stopping his delicious assault.

I moan in protest, my head dropping back against his chest as he unzips my skirt. It drops to the ground, pooling around my heels.

"I need to taste you. Tell me you want me to lick this pussy dry." His carnal demand breaks down every molecule of my blood as he feathers his lips against my neck. "Say it."

He could order me to commit armed robbery, and I'd do so without a second thought. Still, the push and pull's not something I'm used to.

Mindless in my want, I face him, our gazes meeting with equal need. "I want you to lick my pussy dry. However, you're not to stop until I say when. Not you. Me." I touch my lips to his, sliding my hand down his rigid chest. "I want you to lick it until your tongue can't stand the taste any longer. Bitter or sweet, I want you to lick it until it can't function properly without your cock buried deep inside of it." I smile coyly and nip his lip, not an ounce of me ashamed by my filthy words. "You've talked a lot of game, Cunningham. The stage is yours now. Let's see if you can make me ache to the point where it . . . hurts. Good?"

"Yes. Fucking. Ma'am." A slow grin creeps along his face. With one hand, he reaches behind his shoulder and pulls his T-shirt over his head.

My gaze falls to the hard ripples of his abs—trailing lower still to the perfectly defined V, anchoring everything together in delicious slabs of raw muscle. I bring my eyes back to Brock's and, with steadfast determination, work the button of his jeans, my lips on his as he backs me toward his bed. I feel the king frame hit my thighs, my heart hitting the ground as Brock pulls his mouth from mine.

"Get on the bed and spread your gorgeous legs for me." Though his command is whispered with coolness, the urgency on his face is hot, a branding iron to my flesh. "And, Ber," he adds, his stare intent on mine as he slowly rubs the bulge beneath his jeans, "keep your heels on. I want to feel them cutting into my back while your legs go numb around my head." He unbuckles his belt, the promise in his eyes flaring over my skin. "Also, I never talk game. *Ever.* I'm about to lick that pussy undone."

Burn. I'm literally burning with desire, its glorious tongue spitting flames across my body. I sink onto the mattress, a nervous swallow bobbing my throat as I glide along what feels like cool satin sheets. I watch Brock in utter amazement, my breathing a mess as he undresses.

In nothing but black boxer briefs, he frees his cock and palms it, stroking the divine piece as he eye-fucks me with every pull. My heart kicks, every muscle clenching with longing. I lick my lips, aching to taste it.

On a shaky sigh, my eyes close of their own accord as the bed dips with the weight of Brock's body. Grabbing the backs of my knees, and stare honed in on mine, his breathing is eerily relaxed as he pulls me down the mattress. With my ass cushioned against his muscled thighs, I struggle to swallow as he hovers above me.

"I've been waiting for this," he whispers, his mouth landing on my breast.

He flicks his tongue against my nipple, drawing it to a tight bud. I gasp as he sucks it between his teeth, his hand kneading my other breast with skilled precision. Another gasp catches in my throat as he lifts his head, puffing out a chilled breath over my slickened nipple. I lurch in response, goose bumps dotting my skin.

Chuckling, Brock gazes down at me. "You like that?"

"Yes," I say breathily.

He smirks, and moves down my body, his tongue leaving a trail of moisture along its path. Anywhere he can mark, he does. He sucks the hollow of my neck, ribs, the curve of my waist, stopping to dip his tongue inside my belly button.

Another lurch, another chuckle.

"Ticklish?" he asks, his brow drawn up.

"Yes, very, but please—"

"Don't worry, I'm not down here to make you laugh." His smirk is back. "I'll leave that for the spooning and pillow talk."

A sigh of relief leaves me, but it's quickly replaced by a sharp intake of air as Brock sweeps my legs over his shoulders. Positioned on his elbows—centered between my thighs—he gives me one last hungry look before he teases his tongue against my clit.

I tense, and my hands fly to Brock's head, grasping his hair as he sucks the swollen hood into his mouth with a deep groan. Each controlled flick of his tongue sinks me further into both bliss and confusion. I can't remember ever being touched like this. I've had my share of guys go down on me, but none basked in it the way he does. He's literally tongue-fucking my pussy senseless, cataloging its texture, taste, savoring it as though it's his last meal. In and out, out and in, slow strokes, fast strokes, each delicious movement carried out with his sharp gaze pinned on mine.

"Oh my God," I moan, pinching my nipples. Chest heaving, I stare at him, every sense drowning in the here and now. The glorious stinging build between my legs, combined with the rapture of his fingers, sends me into a storm of sensations, a furious need to be fucked overtaking my thoughts. "God, yes, keep going, Brock. Don't you dare stop."

Brock groans and slides his hands under my ass, pulling me flush against his face. "Your pussy tastes too good to stop." He strokes a finger through my folds, exploring the edges of my nub. "It's all the right flavors. Tart." He lowers his head, tonguing the delicate slice of skin below my warmth. "Tangy." He draws my clit into his mouth before releasing it with a pop. "Sweet." He slides two adept fingers inside me, hooking and circling my G-spot. "Pure, fucking, edible, delicious pussy."

I crash, coming apart like a rickety house in a raging storm. Heels digging into his back, my muscles rock, hot ribbons of orgasm exploding through my body.

Holding me snug to his face, Brock laps at my clit, through my center, and down the crack of my ass, sucking me dry like he promised. "That's right," he snarls, gripping me tighter, "give me everything this pussy's got."

Unable to handle the second orgasm I feel coming on, I throw my shaky legs off his back, and sit up, my breath a choppy disaster. "That's en-enough," I stammer, pressing a trembling hand against the skull tattoo on his shoulder. "Please. I'm good. No—no more."

Brock stays quiet for a long moment before he gets to his knees, his hands finding purchase on my waist as a grin moves across his face. "Did you just beg me to . . . *stop?*"

His mouth claims mine in a slow, passionate kiss, preventing me from answering. God, I'm all over him. My taste, scent, moisture, my very essence combined with his dizzies me, suffocating each rushed breath I take. I go limp, my fingers digging into his scalp as he guides me back against the mountain of pillows. Stuck in a sweet daze, I faintly register the sound of him opening a condom wrapper. Before I know it, he's propped on his elbows, hovering above me, his strong hands cradling my head.

"I've never had a girl ask me to stop," he whispers, a soft smile twisting his mouth. "You're my first." Lowering his lips to my temple, he swipes my right leg to the side with his knee. "They usually insist I keep going." His knee attacks my left leg, repeating the process. "It's all good. I'll get you there."

Spread wide open beneath him, the ache at the center of my thighs intensifies as he skirts his lips down my jaw, the base of my throat, and back up to my mouth.

"Are you ready for me to fuck you, Ber?" He teases the tip of his cock against my pussy, drawing a shudder from my body as he sweeps his tongue through my mouth. "Or are you going to beg me to . . . *stop?*"

Everything fades, even the passage of time. I'm lost. Lost in my surroundings. Lost in him. The low timbre of his voice. The sensual promise in his eyes. The musky smell of myself on his lips.

He pulls back a fraction, his gaze roaming my face. "Because that's what I'm gonna do. I'm gonna fuck you. I'm gonna fuck you in ways you've never been fucked. Ever. I know you *think* you've been taken care of, but you haven't. Not the way I'm about to." He licks his lips, and barely pushes inside me, a low groan rumbling from his throat as a moan leaves mine. "But after I fuck you, you're mine and mine *only*. No one else's." He cocks his head and stares at me, the look in his glazed eyes unreadable. "That means you're no longer allowed to kiss my friends . . . in their cars . . . after they've treated you to lunch unless *I* give either of you *permission* to do so."

My vocal cords freeze up, my heart sinking to my toes as he tilts my head, kissing my cheek, jaw, and neck.

"Are we understood, my beautiful, mysterious little . . . liar?"

I swallow, trying to bring some form of moisture to my parched throat. "How di-did you—"

"I have eyes *all* over campus. Never forget that." He drops a tender kiss on my lips, his fingers playing into my hair. "You two put on quite a display earlier. It was bound to get back to me."

He pushes into me again, this time breaching the barrier of my slickened folds. My pussy clenches, attempting to suck him in, but he pulls out, leaving me gasping for air. A shaky breath hurtles from my chest as I clutch his shoulders, the exotic protest climbing from his throat dousing my ears.

Hands still cradling the back of my head, he gazes down at me with a lazy grin. "I know you and Ryder dig each other. That's a given. Though he knew I was trying for you first, I can't blame him for taking a shot. He'd have to be fucking crazy not to." He glides his lips against mine, his fingers lightly fisting my hair. "I know my friend *very* well, and I can't say I'm shocked or mad at him. Ryder and I are both a little . . . fucked up. When we see what we want, we go after it, no matter who's in our way. Seems odd that we're buds, right?"

I nod, wanting to understand their friendship. I know there's more behind it, or less. I'm not sure. Either way, this conversation has me curious.

Brock grins and claims my neck, his tongue sweeping the spot below my ear. "Well, we are, and nothing will ever change that. But unless I give you two permission otherwise, you're no longer allowed to further . . . indulge. *I'm* the one who's going to fuck you straight. The one whose name you're going to cry out several times a day. I'm the one you're going to fall asleep next to and wake up with. The one who's going to know every secret you're hiding. Good?"

I need, want, and crave this. Crave . . . him. *His* secrets. *His* lies. His dark past and uncertain future. His promises and demands. His touch, body. His . . . everything.

"Good," I whisper, tendrils of pleasure tickling my core.

Brock jerks his hips forward, sliding inside me with brutal urgency. I gasp, his heavily veined cock filling every aching inch. The planes of his sweat-slicked torso rub hard and fast against my stomach as we release a string of rushed breaths. My nails dig into his shoulders in pure ecstasy. I'm no longer high, but I feel alive, my deadened cells awakening from a deep slumber. I incline my head, my back arched as I attempt to pull Brock's lips down to mine. With one hand fisting my hair and the other cupped around my thigh, he stares at me a moment, fierce arousal spinning in his eyes. After a beat, he settles his lips over mine, sweeping his tongue through my mouth.

"I need all of you," he snarls, slamming into me. A gasp kicks from my lungs, my body molding to his as though it were clay. He lifts his head, knots of hair spilling over his eyes as possession contorts his beautiful face. "Every inch. Your heart, soul, your past, present, future. All of it. Say it, Ber, tell me you're mine, baby girl."

I feel his desire, his untapped need to claim me, heating everything around us, but there's no method to the way he takes me. One second, he's fucking into me with such force that I feel as though he's about to deliciously split me in two, the hunger in his movements close to paralyzing. The next, he slows down, his eyes locked on mine as if I'm the only thing he ever wants within his line of vision. As if I'm the only thing that exists in his mind.

I've never been made love to, so I'm not sure how to gauge that against what's happening now, but nothing about this is straight-up fucking. Nothing. It's more, deeper. A connection, a thick current of electricity sparking the air, showing no mercy to the emotions it controls.

"I'm yours," I pant. On the heels of my declaration, awareness that I've never committed to such an intimate promise rushes through my gut, fear and longing spiraling through my soul. Still, the words feel right on my lips, a promise penned on my heart long before I knew Brock existed. A groan slips from Brock's mouth as I move my shaky fingers down his shoulders, along his chest, seeking his ass. I squeeze and hook my legs around his waist, letting go of everything I've ever feared. "Only yours. No one else's."

Brock's mouth comes down over mine, his tongue probing with sharp, dominant efficiency as he dives an arm under my hips. With a growl, he hauls back to a sitting position, bringing me up with him. His lips land on my neck, licking, sucking, and biting the sensitive skin. I purr and reach for his cock, guiding it inside me. The air hisses with our ragged breathing as I fully sink down onto him, my pussy swallowing every glorious inch.

"That's right, bounce on this cock."

He fists my dampened hair and yanks, my spine bowing as I plummet into the storm of sensations soaking my muscles. He sucks my nipple into his mouth, his tongue playing over the hardened bud. I jerk forward, a moan punching from my lungs. He stares at me, his eyes wicked. My ass slaps against his thighs, my addiction for this—for him—exploding. I thrust up and down, down and up, stealing what I need from him, but equally accepting what he's dishing out like a fiend. He grips my waist, driving into my pussy, each stab bringing me closer to the edge. With my arms wrapped around Brock's neck—his face buried against my sweat-slickened chest—I slide down again, finding a slow but steady rhythm. I circle my hips, taking him as deep as my body will allow.

"Ah, Christ," Brock snarls, tightening his grip around my waist. "You feel me, Ber? 'Cause I'm feelin' you, baby. Your pussy was made for me. Your tits, ass, lips, all of it."

"Mm, God, yes," I pant, my body vibrating. "You feel so good."

I drag my nails across the width of his back, falling into everything he is. The way his rough yet soft hands are all over my body. It's as if he can't help but touch me, like he's struggling with which part to explore next. The girth of his rigid cock as it slips in and out of me, pulsing into my core with an urgency I've never experienced. The way his erotic groans pitch and lower against my ear with each response my body exhibits.

I might be riding him, but every ounce of Brock is possessing me, staking his claim by the second.

He cushions two fingers against my clit, applying pressure in quick, luscious strokes. "Let go, baby girl. I know you need to come. I can feel it." He rubs at my swollen flesh again, faster, harder. "I want this pussy sucking my cock so deep that it hurts."

Another thrust onto him, followed by his teeth sinking into my shoulder, and I'm done for, gone. My muscles lock up around him, delicious heat flaring from my head right down to my toes as I convulse in what I'm positive's the most brutal orgasm I've ever had.

Brock seizes my waist—his grip unforgiving—and jerks his hips up, fucking into me with the fluidity of a well-oiled pleasure-inducing machine. I crash again, a second orgasm thrashing through my womb. He flips me onto my back, completely withdraws from me, and slides his hands under my ass, lifting the bottom half of my body off the bed. Before I can take a full breath, his mouth is on my pussy, licking through my center, his tongue spearing in and out.

"Are you *crazy?*" I pant, my legs instinctively finding his shoulders. "I can't come again. I can't."

He grips my bottom tighter, yanks me to his face, and drags his tongue lower, probing the puckered flesh no man's ever explored so intimately. "You can," he growls, sucking my clit into his mouth, "and you will."

"Oh my God." I gasp, my hands seeking something to hold as he moves his tongue up and down, down and up, his thumb poking in and out of my pussy in rhythm with his strokes, flicks, and bites. "Please, no. Brock, I . . . I . . ."

Come so hard on his face, I'm sure I've ruined it.

Victorious smile stretching his lips, Brock lowers my listless body back down onto the bed and kisses me hard and deep, his intoxicating groans filling my ears. My belly dips, knotting both welcomed and unwelcomed emotions around my heart. Continuing to kiss me—fierce passion in each delicious lash of his tongue—Brock cradles the back of my head, spreads open my legs, and pushes inside me. Though it's aching, my pussy flares wide, accepting every inch of him.

"You're more than I deserve," he whispers, pulling back to stare at me. Sincerity floods his eyes, a sheepish smile tugging his mouth as he glides his thumbs along my cheeks. "Guys like me never snatch up girls like you. If they do, it's usually because she's rebounding." He kisses my forehead, his voice remaining soft, sensual. "Thank you for sharing yourself with me, Ber. I've never thanked a girl after sex—which now that I'm thinking about it makes me a certified dick—but everything about you is fucking amazing." He kisses my nose, a light chuckle vibrating his chest. "Your sexual skills included."

"*I'm* amazing?" I question breathlessly, convinced the boy has lost his damn mind. I hook my legs around his waist, enjoying his slower movements. "If I'm amazing, I'm not sure *what* you are."

Brock chuckles as I come to the realization I've officially been fucked straight, licked undone, and rewarded with multiple treats. I'm pretty sure I couldn't endure a pounding if I tried.

Still, I kiss his neck, shoulder, and jaw, my need to thank him intense. "Fuck me, Brock. Go ahead. I'm okay."

He draws up a brow, slightly picking up the pace. "You're just . . . okay?"

"I'm beyond okay, Cunningham," I purr, nipping his lip. "You know what I mean."

"Of course. What was I thinking? You want me to"—he thrusts his hips forward, a smirk on his face as I gasp—"*fuck* you, right?"

"Yes." It comes out as a pant as he thrusts into me again.

He grips the headboard with one hand while the other stays securely buried in my hair. "Like this?" he asks with another thrust, his mouth coming down over mine.

On a long moan, I nod, my nails digging into his shoulders.

"And this?" He plummets deeper, his free hand gliding down my waist as he moves fluidly, his balls slapping against the cushion of my ass.

"God, yes. Like that. Please don't stop," I beg, ignoring the sting of my skull hitting the headboard.

It's not long before his body goes rigid, his muscles tightening with his approaching orgasm. Seizing the opportunity, I slip out from beneath Brock, slide the condom off him, and push him back onto his heels. I lower my lips to his cock, teasing my tongue over its engorged head. Brock sucks in a shocked breath, a delicious groan rumbling from his chest. The erotic sound causes my pussy to weep for its loss as I swirl my tongue in slow circles, taking in more of him. Holding the perfect mixture of salt and tang, sex and sweat, the man tastes amazing. One hundred percent pure, unequivocal bliss.

With the fingers of one eager hand caressing the heavy sac of his balls, I take his beautiful cock all the way to the back of my throat, nearly choking on its sheer size and girth.

"Fuuuuck," Brock hisses, fisting the crown of my head. "You don't play games. You feel incredible."

Not only wanting to taste his release, but needing to see it, I keep my eyes on his as I work him from glorious root to tip. Brock pulls his lip between his teeth, his gaze unwavering from mine as I bob my head up and down, moaning around his cock. Grunting in fast, clipped breaths, he fucks into my mouth like an animal, each measured thrust sinking deep into my throat. Rhythm never letting up, I grip his thighs, giving him free rein to do what he wants with me.

"Ber, I'm gonna come," he warns in a deep rasp. "If you don't want . . . Ah, Christ . . ."

On a fast thrust down, I slide my hands to his ass and squeeze, praying my eyes convey to him what my vocal cords can't.

I want every single bit of him.

Eyes locked on mine and gripping my hair as though his life depends on it, Brock lets go, spurting his hot warmth down the back of my throat.

"Goddamn." He moves his hands to my nape, keeping them there as he continues to pulse into my mouth. "That's right, baby. Take it. Take it all."

Thrust after thrust, I swallow and suck every last drop of him, my fingers tweaking his balls with each convulsing jerk.

Before I can rise from my hands-and-knees position, Brock hauls me up, moves my dampened hair from my face, and layers his lips over mine. Deep, long, and passionate, he kisses me, groaning into my mouth. He falls onto his back, dragging me on top of his sweaty chest.

As our breathing descends into an even rhythm, Brock reaches over to a nightstand, flips on a lamp, and slides open a drawer. I squeeze my eyes closed, trying to adjust to the sudden brightness.

"I usually don't blitz in my condo, but hell if I'm not gonna right now. You brought me there." He pulls out a small metal container, produces a ready-made joint, and sparks it up, sucking the smoke into his lungs. After taking another hit, he holds it to my lips as he rubs his free hand up and down my spine. "Here. God knows you deserve it."

I take a deep drag, coughing with a giggle as he slides his hand to my rib cage. "No, no, no!"

"Mm, but this is the *mandatory* spooning-and-tickling part." He dives his hand between our stomachs, tickling the shit out of me.

"Stop!" I blurt, trying to catch a full breath, my face pinched in mock anger as I grip his chin and give it a stern shake. "Did you *like* having sex with me?"

He quirks a brow. "Is that a serious question?"

I nod, trying to contain a smile. "As serious as they come."

Hunger surfaces in his glassy eyes, a slow smirk splicing his lips. "And *come . . . you . . . did.*" He chuckles, kissing my temple. "To answer your question: I didn't *like* it, I *loved* it. I foresee having *tons* of it in the very near future."

"Uh-uh-uh, not if you keep tickling me," I warn with a coy smile. "You'll never, *ever* tap this again."

Joint hanging from his mouth, Brock flips me onto my back and hovers above me. He takes another pull, stubs it out on the box's top, and shotguns the smoke into my lungs, his tongue languidly caressing mine. "Are you threatening me with . . . *sex?*" He cradles my head. "Is that what you're doing?"

"Indeed I am." I cough, nodding. "And if I were you, I'd heed the warning, buddy."

In true rebel fashion, Brock ignores me. This time going full throttle, he pins my arms above my head and tickles my armpits, all the while dropping kisses onto my cheeks. A string of giggles fall from my mouth as I attempt to not only breathe but squirm out from beneath him. As though sent from the heavens above, an angel rings the doorbell, interrupting Brock from his attack on my body.

He slips off the bed, a smile on his face as he shoves into his jeans. "Do you have *any* idea how lucky you are?"

"Do you have *any* idea what a dick you are?" Matching his smile, I pull the sheets to my chest. "A dick who's not getting any more of this."

Ding-dong . . . Ding-dong . . .

"Mm, we'll see about that." Making his way into the hall, he adds, "I'd bank that you're lying yet again, my Ber."

"I'd bank that you're one hundred percent correct," I mumble, fully aware I have every intention of reenacting this evening's events. As sexually sated as I've ever been and floating as high as a cloud, I steal myself away into the silence.

The temporary bliss doesn't last long before, "Jesus Christ! What the fuck took you so long to answer, bro?" cuts through the air.

I whip my head toward the bedroom door, the movement sending my chocolate curtain of hair swinging over my shoulder. The familiar voice seduces my senses, draping my skin like warm silk as oxygen dissolves from my lungs.

Hazed out or not, I know that voice. I'm pretty sure I'd recognize it in a crowded stadium.

Ryder . . .

CHAPTER 7

Amber

I'M CONVINCED THE powers above get off on shit like this. Sitting on their golden thrones—goblet of aged wine in hand—it's their daily dose of laughter. A proper *fuck you* to humanity. And in this very moment, the bigwigs in the clouds are enjoying my little situation.

I take a deep, steadying breath and climb from the bed, my heart kicking furiously as I slip into my skirt and bra. I snag my blouse from the floor, fully aware I can't sport it in its current state of *shred*. I sigh and glance around the room, my eyes landing on Brock's football jersey draped over a leather ottoman at the foot of the bed.

I shrug. There's no better time than the present.

I slip the Hercules-sized black-and-yellow jersey over my head and glimpse myself in the dresser mirror, blinking in disgust at what's staring back at me. Not only do I look like a just-fucked mess—hair a rat's nest of knots and makeup sledding down my face—I look like a damn bumblebee on crack.

"What's up, dude?" an unidentified voice says from the living room.

Curiosity piqued, I decide I'm completely cool with looking like a crack-smoking, just-fucked bumblebee. I also decide I'm one hundred percent baked. Under normal circumstances, considering what happened between me and Ryder today, and what just occurred between me and Brock, there'd be no way in hell I'd leave the bedroom. I've deemed what I'm about to do "weed muscles."

Along with Brock answering the unidentified voice, I hear the front door snap shut, my attention focused on trying to make it down the hall without losing my nerve. As I round the corner to the living room, it's not my nerve I lose.

No. That'd be too easy, and besides, the bigwigs are seriously out to get me tonight.

Instead, I lose my footing, tripping over a barbell. Right about the same time I register a fiery pain blast through my pinky toe—which I'm sure was just broken—my palms hit the maple floors, closely followed by my knees. I land with a thud—doggie style—in front of Brock, Ryder, and Mystery Man.

"What the fuck?"

Though I'm currently staring at a tiny dust ball, there's no mistaking that was Ryder.

"Ber!" Brock bellows, thumping across the living room. He kneels beside me, throws my arm over his shoulder, his face weary as he helps me to my feet. "Holy shit. Are you all right?"

Holding Brock's shoulder, I hop over to the couch, aiming for crass. "Other than the fact that I'm completely mortified and not sure if my toe's still connected to my foot, yeah, I'm just dandy."

Brock frowns and helps me onto the couch, resting my legs over his thighs as he inspects my foot.

"I'll get our clumsy girl here some ice," Ryder pipes up, mirth clear in his deep chuckle. He turns toward the kitchen, but not before adding, "You sure do *love* tripping and falling over things, Moretti, huh?"

I lift my heavy, embarrassed eyes to Ryder's, my breath catching at the sight of him. Lazy grin properly in place, leaning against the archway of the kitchen, he too has that just-fucked look going on. But, boy, does he wear it better than I do.

His black hair has no organization to it. It's spiked up messily in every direction, as though some chick was gripping it while in the throes of *her* pleasure. I contain the urge to bite my lip, watching the way his muscles flex and flow beneath a snug-fitting plain gray T-shirt as he crosses his tattooed arms. He might be a good twenty feet from me, but I can't help but catch his eyes, their clear—almost translucent—blue gleaming as he pitches me a wink.

Completely enthralled or not, again I aim for crass. "Well, Ryder, I'm sure Brock didn't *purposely* stick the barbell in my path so I'd trip over it. Only assholes who are . . . hmm, what's the word I'm searching for?" Eyes locked on his, I tap my chin. "Oh, that's right. Only assholes who are *insecure* in their delivery would do such a thing. They also usually overcompensate by *claiming* that they own huge . . . buildings." I smirk, sending him a wink right back. "So with that, I'd say I *don't* love tripping and falling over things."

Oh God. Did I just say what I think I just said? Maybe I thought it.

Those gorgeous, translucent baby blues flash in amused surprise, staring at me a second.

Then another.

And still another.

Brock's chuckle breaks the silence. "Hot fucking damn. She just put you in place."

OhmyGod. I did say it. Weed muscles. That's what it was.

"Dude," Mystery Man says as he slips into an armchair, "is *the* Ryder Ashcroft short on words? I think we need to call the media. This shit needs to be broadcast nation-fucking-wide."

I've decided I want to cuddle with Mystery Man.

Ryder looks at Mystery Man then swings his eyes back to me. "Amber, this is Limp-dick Lee Mitchel. Limp-dick Lee, this is the clumsy but oh-so-sexy, can-throw-a-slap-better-than-any-girl-who's-ever-slapped-me Amber Moretti."

I feel my face flush purple. Yes, purple. Not red.

"We've met." Lee nods.

I don't remember meeting him. "I don't remember meeting you."

Is there an echo in here?

"I'm your roommate's boyfriend," Lee points out.

Roommate? I have a roommate? Blank, I smile as if I know what he's talking about.

"Oh, and Lee," Ryder says, cupping his balls beneath a pair of Hugos, "that whole media comment? Yeah, bro, why don't you come over here and suck my nuts."

Lee cringes. "Nah, I'm good, dude."

"I thought so, pansy." Ryder turns to me, a small smile tilting his lips as his eyes slither over every inch of my listless body. "Amber."

"Ryder," I answer, waiting for him to continue.

"Kudos, momma. You just managed to do what *no* girl's ever been able to do to me."

"And that would be?" I question.

"Like Limp-dick Lee said, you rendered me completely speech-less." He slides a hand through his hair, kicking me yet another wink. "So on that note, I'm gonna be a *good* boy and go get that ice for your pretty little toes."

Both Brock and Lee bark out a laugh as Ryder disappears into the kitchen.

Brock rubs his hand over my shin, down the side of my ankle, and rests my heel in his palm. "You *do* have pretty toes," he whispers.

I raise a playful brow. "You don't have some kind of weird foot fetish, do you?"

"Nah, you would've found that out earlier." He brushes his fingers up my thigh, his eyes hungry. "But shit if I won't pick one up if that's what you want. I'm not beyond sucking *any* part of your body."

"What the hell is this?" Lee questions, breaking my heated thoughts away from Brock. He points at the television.

"That would be a seventy-inch plasma, dumbass," Brock answers.

"Dude, I'm talking about the show." Lee adjusts his Dodgers base-ball cap, a crooked smile on his face. "It's a bunch of freaks getting down to music my grandparents fornicated to."

I shake my head and giggle, taking in Mystery Man—now turned Lee Mitchel. With tight curls of honey-butter-golden hair, a hand-ful of freckles lining his nose, light brown eyes hidden behind square black-rimmed lenses, and a tall, lengthy frame, he's cute in a sophisti-cated, nerdy kind of way.

"You've never seen *Happy Days?*" I make sure I sound surprised. "Did you grow up under a rock?"

"Hell no, I've never seen it, and I'm *happy all day* that I haven't." He jumps to his feet, his arms spread out as he swishes his hips from side to side. "And no rock here. This dude grew up in SoCal, surfing some of the wildest waves available to man."

"Yup," Ryder says, strolling back into the room. He tosses a Ziploc bag filled with ice to Brock and deposits himself onto the coffee table. "Pansy boy frolicked along the sunny beach, under a sky of rainbows, hand in hand with his hippie parents, Jack and Jill." He smirks and leans forward, resting his forearms on his knees. "But he constructed sand castles, not . . . *colossal* buildings."

Though I roll my eyes, Ryder's words stir a wild flurry of pleasure through me. Still, I'm feeling all kinds of weird. Considering Brock's next to me—fully aware of our earlier car encounter—I'm floored that Ryder's tossing around our "joke" so freely.

"That's right, Ashcroft." Lee sinks back into his chair, beaming. "Other than my parents' names being Jody and Allen, you're correct. I frolicked *and* surfed my way through a kick-ass childhood. Lepre-chauns, sand castles, the whole nine."

"Leprechauns?" Brock asks, his face washed in amusement. "And you claim you've never done any hard-core drugs. Interesting."

Brock cushions the bag of ice against my toe. I flinch, more from the chill than the pain.

"People *claim* a ton of bullshit," Ryder asserts, his gaze stuck on mine. "Makes you wonder what's going through their heads sometimes."

My throat—which feels like the Sahara Desert on crack—seizes up. I glance at Brock, thankful he's occupied with tending to my foot. I lick my lips in an attempt to get some form of moisture to coat my mouth as I stare at Ryder, wondering what's suddenly crawled up his ass.

"It's the truth. I'm high on life," Lee states with a cheesy smile. "Me, my girl, the sun, and a good wave. It don't get no better than that, dude."

"That's deep, Lee," Brock deadpans, gently shifting my legs off his thighs. He rises and rolls his neck. "I think Blue Mountain Greeting Cards just might be your calling. Fuck pushing coke for me. There's some serious cash to be made in your words."

Ryder whips his head in Brock's direction. "Bro, what the fuck?" He looks at me, then back at Brock. "You *told* her?"

"Yeah," Brock answers, his eyes slightly narrowed. "Why?"

"What do you mean, *why?*" Ryder stands and pushes a hand through his hair. "She shouldn't know about shit."

Lee shrugs and plucks his cell from the front pocket of his plaid button-down, punching out a text. "What's the big deal if she knows, dude? Madeline knows."

"*Hello.*" I wave, catching the trio's attention. "In case you all *didn't* notice, I'm sitting right here. Don't talk about me like I'm not in the damn room."

Silence cloaks the air as everyone stares at each other. I can barely lift my arms—or walk across the room, for that matter—but I'm seriously pissed and have every intention of getting to my feet. I rise, and both Ryder and Brock lunge, hooking their hands under my armpits.

Pissed or not, I giggle.

Ryder furrows his brows in confusion.

"She's ticklish," Brock whispers, a slow, sexy smirk lifting his mouth. "*Very* ticklish. Even without that, she's extremely responsive to any kind of . . . stimulation."

"Ah, I see." Ryder's teeth come down on his bottom lip, an equally sexy smirk jumping across his face as he studies me. "Very nice, and *very* . . . lucky."

Though their eyes are different colors, different spectrums of dark and light, their steady gazes—aimed in my direction—are simmering with the same emotion—one hundred percent pure, unadulterated lust. Overheated and sure my legs have melted into molasses, I pull in a staggering breath. After what seems like an eternity, I regain my bearings, my heartbeat falling to an even plod as I test my toe against the floor, tentatively placing my full weight onto it.

"Ya good?" Ryder asks.

"Yeah," I manage, seriously wishing I had a Twizzler. "I'm cool."

With concern edging two beautiful pairs of eyes, they release me, each appearing well aware of what just happened. Something passed between the three of us, an undeniable current charged with want, need, and confusion.

Touching his knuckles to my cheek, Brock clears his throat. "I have to, uh, go take a piss?" It comes out like a question, almost as if he's asking me if it's okay.

I nod and watch him vanish around the corner, taking a sliver of my sanity with him. Ryder goes to speak, but I move past him and his waves of testosterone, somehow finding my way into the kitchen. The only thing lingering in my mind for more than a minute—other than a sweaty threesome with two of the most mentally intoxicating, soul-dangerous men I've ever come across—is liquid.

I feel like a damn goldfish. Unable to focus on anything for even thirty seconds, I open the fridge, my hand landing on its intended target. A bottle of ice-cold water.

Score . . .

I pull it out, twist off the cap, and take a long sip.

Heaven. I'm in it, and I know it.

As I turn around, I almost plow into Ryder. I gulp and try to swallow the H2O that's now lodged in my throat. I tip my head up—way, way up—to look into his eyes. My breath tells me to crap off and catches in my lungs. My heart follows suit, nearly stopping.

"Why are you here with Brock?" he asks with a smug, self-assured grin. "You like switching gears that fast, huh?"

"We're on a *date*." My tone conveys the "duh" I don't say. "And maybe I *do* like switching gears that fast. Maybe I like it more than the average girl should. But you wanna know what I *don't* like?"

"Mm. I'm not sure." He crosses his arms and rubs at his jaw, his grin broadening as he stares at me for several aching seconds. "You've already pulled one of these 'wanna knows' earlier today, and I can't say I enjoyed the outcome."

"Not my problem," I assert with a scowl. "You're gonna hear it whether or not you like it."

"Well, I guess I have no choice, do I?" He inches closer, his voice dropping a notch as I step back. "But I have to admit, your feistiness is turning me the fuck on, so by all means, please continue."

Heart kicking, I clench the bottle of water tighter. "Looks like you so *conveniently* left out your *main* source of income. I may be high, but my memory's machete-sharp." Well, maybe not machete. Apparently I have a roommate. "You never mentioned that you deal for Brock. I don't like being lied to."

"I had no intention of *ever* mentioning it to you. I'm not proud that I do it, so it's not on the list of things I let people in on. And *you* wanna know what *I* don't like, Amber?"

"I really don't care what you don't like," I say, somewhat afraid of what he's going to hit me with.

"Sucks because you're gonna hear it whether *you* like it or not." He smirks, rebellion oozing from his pores. "*I* don't like being kissed and left hanging, so it looks like we're even, peach."

"God! You have no *clue* how much you piss me off," I whisper, sure I'm about to lose my shit and smack him again.

"Ah, quite the contrary. I'm *very* aware of how much I get under that pretty skin of yours. *You're* the one who has no idea what you do to me." He inches closer still, his brow drawn up as I take another step back. "Or maybe ya do know. Maybe it's *you* who gets off on torturing *me*. Yeah, that's what it is. You enjoy this shit."

"You're seriously out of your mind," I say under my breath, not a speck of me convinced otherwise. "Did you know that someone told Brock what went down today?"

"Of course I do, momma. He called me after you . . . fled." His voice is soft as he brings a callused hand up to cup my cheek. Callused or not, my flesh beneath it melts into liquid satin. "Did *you* know he called me?"

I'm breathing faster. I can sense it. I shake my head because, well, that's the only thing my body feels like doing.

"Are ya having fun on your . . . date?" he asks, removing his hand from my cheek.

I feel annoyingly bereft but still manage to narrow my eyes. "I *was* before you interrupted us."

A shadow passes across his face before a devious smile settles on his full, pouty lips. "Well, then I think my timing was . . . *perfect*."

I'm momentarily stunned right out of my high. I look into his captivating eyes, trying to read him. "You think so?"

"I know so." Arrogance reigns over his features as he steps closer. I all but stumble back, my spine connecting with the cold stainless steel refrigerator. Undeterred, he positions his hands above my head, caging me in like an animal. "I also know that you should be at my place, not here."

I bite my lip and stare at him, my fogged-out brain warped in every sense of the word. "Maybe I'd be at your place if you hadn't decided that kissing me *twice* without my permission was a brilliant idea."

"Ah, how quickly you so *conveniently* forget that *you* kissed *me* the last time our lips touched." A slow smile touches his mouth as he taps his finger against the tip of my nose.

My nostrils flare, his smell of cigarettes and musky cologne nearly stopping my heart.

"But I'm a nice guy, so I'll let you off the hook for that one. But going back to *my* less-than-stellar lack of judgment, maybe I already know the two times I initiated kissing you was a stupid idea. Maybe I've lost sleep over it. Maybe it'll eat at me until the day I . . . die." He dips his head, positioning his face right in front of mine.

I swallow, unable to ignore the feel of his sweet, heated breath tickling every muscle in my weakened body as he rests his lips against my ear and whispers, "But even if I've fucked any chance of being with you, I can't say either kiss is something I'll soon forget. I'd kill to experience them over . . . and over . . . and over again." With his hands still pressed to the refrigerator, he pulls his head back slightly, his eyes moving across my face. He smiles again, and it nearly stops my heart a second time. "Our lips fit perfectly together, and I'm pretty fucking sure you know it. Felt it. Want to feel it again as much as I do. I see it in the way you're looking at me. Those gorgeous eyes hide nothing. Neither does your body. The way your breathing's picking up. The way you're shaking just enough to let me know you want another taste of what I have to . . . offer. But you wanna know something about me, peach?"

Before I can conjure up words that make sense, he runs his tongue across his teeth, winks at me, and dips his mouth to the curve of my jaw.

Lightly pressing his lips to my heated flesh, he continues, his voice a low, sexual taunt. "My timing wasn't perfect. I can tell when a girl's been fucked, and fucked *very* well. Earlier, you weren't what I consider *completely* off-limits. Sure, you were halfway there, but you were still on equal playing ground."

A moan slips from my throat as he drags his hand along my ribs, stopping on my waist, his grip nothing short of dominant.

"The game's changed since I last saw you. You've sealed the deal with my friend. Now I have no choice but to play by the rules. You're legitimately Brock's girl, and because of that, I'm no longer allowed to fuck with ya. And I won't. *Ever*. *Again*. Though it may be impossible to believe, no matter how . . . *hard* it is for me, I do have certain barriers I won't crash through. You're now one of them." Smile replaced with a look akin to loss and hands held up in surrender, Ryder slowly backs out of the kitchen, his stare burning a hollow ache into my chest. "It was fun while it lasted, momma. Make sure you take good care of my friend."

Without another breath, he vanishes into the living room. On shaky legs, I move to the center island and set down the bottle of water, my mind racing in a million different directions as I try to talk myself away from the dangerous cliff Ryder makes me want to jump from.

CHAPTER 8

Brock

STARE LOCKED ON Amber, I watch as she fidgets with the hem of her skirt, her nervous attention honed in on the airport doors as she gnaws on her bottom lip. A grin ticks the corner of my mouth, my finger lazily drawing our names on her thigh as we await the arrival of her foster parents. There's something different about her today, a light effervescence exuding from her pores.

Christ. No doubt I'm in deep, this girl the owner of every filthy, twisted beat of my heart.

I can't remember ever using the word "effervescence" to describe a goddamn thing, but hell if this moment doesn't merit it. This beautiful creature—one who has fallen victim to the darkest cruelties of life—is excited to see the only two people who've ever shown her a speck of humanity, a slice of what it feels like to be loved.

Body heating, I take in the undeniable beauty encompassing Amber. The girl who bolted into my life like lightning and has, over the last several weeks, infiltrated every devious desire and jacked-up breath I've breathed. Sitting in my Hummer, her inky black hair's trailing over her shoulders, her fingers clenched in anticipation as she continues to focus on the arrival terminal at BWI. This woman, this mysterious soul, has managed to do what no other has before her.

She's penetrated my hardened shell, wrangled me to her will, and stripped my mind of all control.

When Amber told me Mark and Cathy were coming to see her, I suggested we take them to dinner. I've never met a girlfriend's parents before. Never felt the need to. None of them mattered enough. Not in the pure way Amber does to me, at least. But with Amber I want more, crave more. Meeting her folks seemed like the next step in our relationship. And to be honest, I want to crawl into every crevice of this girl's life, burrow myself so deeply beneath her skin, she can't ever let me go. I've grown to need her in the same way my "clientele" chases after the coke I supply them.

Amber Moretti is my blow, my need for her the best and worst kind of addiction.

When I brought up doing the dinner thing with her parents, Amber immediately asked if we could include mine.

My first thought: Hell fucking no. Not happening. Ever.

I can't stomach the thought of her being in the same room as them. I tried to sweet-talk my way out of it, insisting they would never show. That they had prior commitments scheduled weeks in advance. I fed her every line of bullshit my pathetic mind could conjure up in an effort to delay her coming in contact with the people who created my worthless being. The truth is: my parents hate me, loathe the fact that they mated and bore what they—and most of their elite circle of friends—consider the devil's spawn. Why would they want to have dinner with a son who destroyed their family and a girlfriend they would never approve of? In their eyes, I don't deserve happiness, don't deserve to be loved.

Fuck, to them and their minions, I don't deserve my next breath. It's a gift, something that should've been stripped from me the day Brandon, possibly, took his last.

But Amber . . . Christ, Amber's stubborn, relentless when she wants something done her way. She didn't want to hear a word of what I had to say. The girl flat out doesn't subscribe to the Brock Cunningham world of bullshit. Call me crazy, but in a realm of its own, it's one of the many reasons I've fallen on my pussy-whipped ass at her feet. She gets me. But even when she gets me, every so often, she gives me more crap than I can handle.

Yet all it takes is the disgusting memory of the look of abandonment in her eyes the night I admitted to lying about who I really was—what I really did to maintain the lifestyle I hold—to snap me right back into my undeserving-dick mode. The dick who needs to be who he is in an effort of feeling faultless, his pores wiped clean of the guilt riddling his past, a terminal cancer hell-bent on murdering his future.

The second I fessed up to dealing, I cracked Amber's already-splintered spirit, deepening the bloodied scars of untrusting cells marring her skin. It was in that moment I knew I had to make up for the harm I'd caused her in whatever way I could, in whatever way possible to keep her by my side.

Still, no matter what, I'll never be worthy of the girl who flew into my life like an avenging angel, consuming me hard, stealing my heart faster. At first sight my feelings for Amber were nothing but lust, a carnal desire to control her, to sexually conquer her inner demons. But over time they've grown into absolute need, something I'm sure I can't live without. But knowing me, I'll lose her to my main weakness. Though she's aware I'm a package of fucked-up goods, and I swore I'd never hide anything from her again, Amber doesn't know all my truths, my deepest inconsistency. Telling her I sold drugs was hard enough. Introducing her to the real me—the serpent harboring some of the deepest, darkest secrets imaginable—can sink us. One lie left untold, one obsessive desire that's been awakened, is a truth I'm unsure I'll ever be able to reveal to her.

Nonetheless, after her relentlessly pressing the parents-meeting-parents issue, and batting those damn puppy dog eyes at me, I caved.

Just like that, she chipped away my resolve, crumbling me in her hands like a weakened rock. When it comes down to it, all I wanna do is please her, rip away the pain that haunts her days and terrorizes her nights. That pain, the one that burns like acid behind her eyes, kills me. I need to make this jewel happy, even if it comes at the expense of me being miserable.

Still, I know the second she meets my parents it'll screw with her. And, damn, I can't stand the thought of tainting her with any more of my darkness. I don't want her to experience the painful backlash from the people who despise me. I don't want her to taste the fiery pain that'll rip open every remaining scar I bear, every organ holding a ton's worth of guilt inside its lining when she witnesses the way we handle each other while in the same breathing space. There's a fuckload of crazy shit I don't want Amber doing, meeting my family number one on the long list. It will only blacken her to my world more than I'm positive it already is.

With all of this, I *still* couldn't bring myself to deny her request. I'm a grade-A fucking son-of-a-bitch, but bitch or not, putting a smile on her face compelled me, urged me to set my family issues aside.

I move my hand to her knee, lightly squeezing her warm flesh. "You seem excited."

"I am." She turns those whiskey eyes on mine.

I melt.

"It's been a while since I've seen them." A hesitant pause, a smile flirting with her lips as she wraps her hand around mine. "Are you nervous at all?"

"Who, *me?*" A smirk whips across my face. "Have you ever known me to be nervous?"

"I think you're a little off your game today, so yeah."

"You think so?" I trail my hand up her plum skirt, tickling my fingers along the seam of her silk panties. "Maybe I need to show ya how *on* my game I am."

"Brock." My name rolls off her tongue in a husky warning. "We can't."

"Mm. All I just heard was a challenge."

She laughs, a purr slipping from her mouth. "You're nervous. Just admit it, tough guy."

"Nope." My gaze travels over the flush whispering across her cheeks. *So beautiful.* "Not a chance."

"At some point I'll get you to confess the truth." She sighs, a reluctant pout weighing down her face. "But right now I need you to remove your hand from in between my legs. It's . . . distracting."

I guess trying to finger-fuck my girl right before meeting her foster parents isn't the greatest way to make an impression. I never, nor will I ever, claim to be perfect. That shit'll never happen. It can't. I'm too warped, the person I've morphed into blocking any chance of that being possible.

I wet my lips, my smirk, along with my cock, growing as I obey her request. "But it's distracting in a good way, right? A way you'll never get enough of?"

"Always," she whispers through a little moan. A moan that has me wanting to cancel this whole dinner thing so I can give her what we both really need right now.

The best kind of therapy available to the human race: mental cleansing through angry, physical release . . .

When Amber and I fuck, we go at it like we're running away from something, like our sanity depends on it. While she tries to flee from the ghosts continuing to pull at the last remaining threads of her miscolored past, I resurrect mine, taking out every tormented second of it on her body every time we come within an inch of each other. Tortured, we're both irrevocably broken, a pair of souls attempting to heal the other through sex. The day I was born, whoever's running shit up there knew they were going to put us together, make sure our filthy paths crossed somewhere along the way.

But no matter who's the dick controlling the show, that's how rela-
tionships work. You fight to make up. Initiate war to make love. Fall to
rise. Wound to heal. Create to destroy. Casting a never-ending land-
slide of dirty emotions poisoned by life and the cruel games it plays
with our psyches in our paths, I just hope Amber and I can beat the
maker at his match. Show the motherfucker who's really in charge of
their destiny.

Still, I can't deny one thing. Amber's right. I'm bent about the entire
evening, sweat drenching my palms as Amber's eyes flash wide open.

"They're here!" she blurts, hastily fixing her skirt.

She jumps from the Hummer, her long locks swinging in tandem
with her excited trot toward her foster parents as I smooth a jittery
hand through my hair.

I step out of the Hummer and follow behind her, readying myself
to meet the couple who've cared for the only woman who's ever held
a part of my heart. I take in Cathy, whose arms are wrapped tightly
around Amber in a loving embrace as they geek out about reuniting.
Her vibrant red hair stands out starkly against crisp green eyes and
olive skin. There's a gentleness to her as she murmurs something in
Amber's ear. Amber gives me a sweet smile and moves to hug the
guy to Cathy's left. Mark looks to be in his early fifties with salt-and-
pepper-dappled hair, his tall stature causing Amber to perch up on
her tiptoes to hug him. Warmth floods my chest as I stand back and
allow them all a minute, loving every second of finally seeing Amber
truly happy.

As I watch Amber, I notice a different side to her, one that intrigues the hell out of me. My girl's a fighter. She's had to be in order
to survive. At times, it's felt as though I've had to smash through her
cement walls just to get a glimpse of what's churning inside her head.
However, right here, right now, there's a tenderness to her, something
she's kept hidden from the world in an effort to protect herself from
its ugliness.

Amber rears back and glances between me and her foster parents, an unusual shyness sprinkling the arches of her cheeks. "Guys, this is my boyfriend, Brock."

Cathy and Mark offer me a gracious smile as I step forward, shaking their hands. "It's great to finally meet you both. How was the flight?"

"You as well, Brock," Cathy says, her easy voice filtering through the air as I pluck her bag from her hand. "Thank you. And it went well. Quicker than I thought it was going to be."

"That's great." Amber moves toward the Hummer. "Any screaming kids this time?"

I open the trunk and set Cathy's luggage inside as Mark does the same with his. "No, we lucked out." He chuckles, turning toward Cathy. "It was actually relaxing, wasn't it?"

"It was. I even caught a nap." Cathy winks, a small grin tipping her lips.

Once in the car, I head to the hotel so they can drop off their stuff and check in. After putting on her seat belt, Amber twists her body toward her foster parents, who are sitting in the back. "Are you guys hungry? Brock made reservations at a killer restaurant down in the harbor."

"I am," Mark declares. "We haven't eaten since this morning."

Cathy nods in agreement.

As Amber and her foster parents go over this week's plans, my gut begins to churn. It suddenly feels as though everything is spinning, what little sanity I do possess flying right out the window. I'm gonna see my mother, the queen of making anyone who comes in contact with her uncomfortable, myself included. When that happens, my girlfriend and the people she cares for are gonna endure the same torture. The whole night is a storm brewing, a hurricane waiting to step foot on land. I can't control what my mother says or does, can't control the way my parents treat Amber and her family. I can't control the viciousness that—as sure as my next fucking breath—will spew from their mouths.

As we pull into the hotel valet, I realize I haven't uttered a word since leaving the airport. Guilt hits, pummeling me to the ground. I don't want to be the reason this evening goes to shit. I want everyone to enjoy themselves. However, I'm pretty damn sure that's not gonna happen.

While Mark and Cathy greet the bellboy, Amber turns to me, concern marring her brows. "Are you sure you're okay?"

I feign a reassuring smile. "Yeah, why wouldn't I be?"

"Don't hide from me, Brock. I know you better than that." There's a twinge of hurt in her tone that stings like a rubber band snapping at my chest.

Such a dick . . .

"Hey," I whisper, capturing her face between my palms. I don't want my issues to pelt her with the same anxiety I feel. "I'm fine. I'm just nervous, that's all."

The corner of her luscious mouth twitches in victory. "I knew it! You can never lie to me, Cunningham." Understanding flits over her face, a twinkle of optimism dancing in her eyes. "You know what I think?"

"What do ya think, baby girl?" I ask, pressing my nose to hers.

"I think tonight might surprise you."

Positive Amber . . . now, *that's* different.

A chuckle dips from my throat as I graze my mouth over hers. "Let's get a drink inside."

"Okay, but before we go in, I want you to know something." I nod as she gently nips my bottom lip. Heat floods my veins, my cock responding to her touch like the addict it is. "No matter what happens tonight, I'll take care of you. Make it all better when we get back to your place."

"Damn." My pulse jumps, firing from her promise. "And I'm supposed to get out after you said *that*? I'm about to take you in the backseat. Give ya a little . . . appetizer before the main meal."

"Tuck it in your pants, big boy." Gaze hooded, her voice drops a few octaves. "But in the meantime, instead of mulling over the 'what ifs', the things you can't control regarding me meeting your family, think of how good it'll feel being buried deep"— she licks my nose, those green eyes sparkling with mirth as she gives my cock a squeeze—"so, so deep inside my pussy later tonight."

Sweet Jesus . . .

A groan rips from my throat and she hops from the vehicle, a triumphant, naughty laugh trailing through the wind behind her as she enters the lobby.

I adjust my now-throbbing dick and move inside the hotel, everything in me knowing what I said to Amber when we first met is correct: this girl is sure to be the ride of my life.

With Amber by their side, Mark and Cathy are in the midst of checking in. I head to the bar, deciding a drink will serve me right as I wait for Amber to join me.

Gaze scouring the low-lit hotel, I find a seat and place an order for a shot of scotch. A football game, consisting of the Ravens killing the Steelers, catches my attention on a corner screen, temporarily distracting me from the army of nerves attacking my blood.

Two shots in, and with a third on its way, warm hands sweep around my abs, cashmere-soft lips teasing my ear as Amber's raspberry scent crashes through my senses. I shift and snake my arms around her waist, pulling her down onto my lap. A soft hum escapes her, the sweet sound igniting my desire for her. I've been with a lot of girls, too many to count, but with Amber it's different. She somehow fills the crater inside my heart, giving me a reason to wake up every morning, a reason to push on.

"They're getting cleaned up and changed for dinner," Amber says, her eyes a caress as she loops her arms around my neck. "It shouldn't be too long."

I nod and lean in, sweeping my tongue across the seam of her lips. I don't wanna talk—I can't. I need to feel a part of her inside me. Something to dull the numbness taking up residence in the center of my chest. Amber's sugary-sweet tongue delves over mine, a light moan escaping her as she tightens her grip around my neck. I deepen the kiss, my hands slipping up the graceful slope of her back. My pulse accelerates, my need to fuck her senseless increasing as I glide my fingers across her delicate shoulders.

With palpable reluctance, Amber breaks the kiss, the concern in her eyes ripping through me as she brings her hands to my cheeks. "Talk to me, Brock. Tell me what you're thinking." It's not a request, but a gentle demand.

I swallow the tightness creeping up my throat. "There's a possibility my family won't show."

"Big deal," she whispers. "We don't need them to. We'll still have fun."

"And if they *do*," I bite out, "it'll turn into a shit show and fucking embarrass you. Embarrass all of us."

She sighs, her gaze stroking the planes of my face. "Stop it. Even if it does turn into a shit show, it'll be fine. You're acting like I'm some kind of delicate petal that can't take it. I've been there. Seen worse than anything your parents can dish out."

"True, but you don't know them," I press.

"No, I don't," she answers, her stare resolute, breathtaking. "But I know you, and that's *all* that matters."

I'm about to respond when a peppy voice zips through the air, interrupting our conversation. "Someone *needs* to get a room."

My attention darts from Amber's to the source. A petite pixie blonde with glittering blue eyes and cherry-red lips. My sister, Brittany. I can't help but smile. After Brandon was taken, and I became the target of my mother's hourly hostility and my father's daily put-downs, Brittany kept me hanging on, kept me from murdering someone until I got my own place.

"You gonna buy me a drink or what?" Brittany asks, sauntering in our direction.

My sister defines "spitfire." She makes up for her small frame with a ton of personality and quick wit. A chuckle flips from my mouth as Amber moves off my lap, slipping into the seat next to mine. I watch as Amber studies Brittany, who happens to be dressed as if she owned the hotel. My sister's what most girls would call a fashionista. She wears nothing but designer threads and rarely, if ever, leaves the house without being done up. The total opposite of my Amber, my angel. My vanity-unconcerned gift.

No doubt they'll hit it off.

"Get over here and buy your own drink." I shake my head, my smile widening as I motion her our way. "And while you're at it, buy *me* a goddamn drink."

Brit bumps my shoulder, playfulness glinting behind her eyes. "Still not a gentleman, I see."

I laugh and grasp Amber's hand. "Brit, this is my girlfriend, Amber. Amber, this is my mouthy, pain-in-the-ass, always-has-to-be-right, can't-take-no-for-an-answer sister, Brittany."

Amber smiles, extending her free hand. "It's good to meet you."

Instead of taking Amber's hand, Brit leans in and gives her a hug. "So you're the girl who's finally brought a smile to my broody brother's face."

"*Broody?*" Amber asks incredulously. "I haven't heard that one yet."

"Let's not go there," I mutter, knowing anything, shit included, could fly outta my sister's mouth. I toss back the rest of my drink and order another, including a round for the two gems in my life. Dealing with some of the finest scum on earth has its advantages, getting a fake ID made up for Amber being one of them. "Are they here?" I ask pensively, praying something came up. "Or did we get lucky and they ditched?"

A sigh beats past Brit's lips. "No such luck. Mom had to run to the bathroom, and Dad's waiting in the lobby."

Body stiffening, I inhale a deep breath, trying to quell the stabbing sensation tearing through my gut. It doesn't work.

Brittany looks at me, pathetic sympathy hopping across her features. "Don't stress, bro. Mom wasn't *that* bad when I picked her up. Both seemed to be in a . . . decent mood."

For a million reasons, that doesn't lend me a shred of comfort. When it comes to Debby and John Cunningham, guarantees don't exist. One minute things are cool and the next it's fucking raining fire in the form of word bullets. Silence mantles the air as we all sip our drinks, prepping ourselves for a long night.

"Thanks for coming, Brittany," Amber pipes up, breaking the tension.

"Yeah, of course." She nudges my shoulder, a smirk painting her face. "I couldn't leave this one on his own, *especially* with our parents. He'd shit his pants."

I chuckle, thankful I have Brit. We don't see each other often, but when we do it's always easy. We share a connection, a true understanding. She gets the guilt I carry over our brother's disappearance. She doesn't agree with it, but she doesn't fight me on it either. She knows it's something I have to make peace with on my own. If ever.

"We should probably go," Amber says, pointing to the time on the big screen. "They'll all be waiting in the lobby by now."

Defenses flaring, I stand and slam the rest of my drink back, hating my parents for actually showing up as I chuck a few Benjamins on the bar.

Amber throws her arm around my shoulder, her boner-inducing whisper filled with challenge as she leans into my ear. "Quit being a pussy. Let's get this over with so you can fuck my brains out when we get back to your place. Sound good?"

Gotta love a bad girl.

I weave my fingers through her hair, shifting her face to mine. "Be careful, Ber, you're testing my restraint." I smirk and watch a swallow work the slender column of her throat, her breath catching as I press my lips to her ear, making sure Brit can't hear. "You keep that up, and I'll be doing a lot more than fucking that sweet pussy. I'll light up that pretty ass."

Her eyes flare with arousal, a flush coloring her cheeks as she pushes me away. A laugh rolls from my chest as I slap the sexy ass I just threatened. The sexy ass I *will* teach a lesson to later.

Brit shakes her head, and we move into the lobby, my gaze connecting with Cathy and Mark, who are seated on a sofa, waiting. I tense in anticipation. I'm almost afraid to look for my parents, but after a quick scan of the area I find them standing on the opposite side of the room, their arms crossed in aggravated impatience.

Brit turns to us. "I'm gonna go grab the nutters."

I nod and we make our way over to Amber's foster parents. Cathy spots us and jolts up, a smile beaming on her face.

"You guys ready to go?" Amber asks, glancing across the room at my family.

"Yes, I'm starving," Cathy chirps, grabbing her purse off the floor.

Blood rushing to my head, my muscles tighten. My mother's attention is aimed in my direction. However, I can't tell if she's staring at me, at Amber, or off into fucking space. Black Jackie Kennedy–style sunglasses frame her face, obstructing me from being able to decipher who she's looking at. My defenses surge, my heart rocking my limbs as my fists involuntarily clench at my sides. The sunglasses are a bad omen. End of story: she's halfway to lit up, a few more sips of alcohol sending her into the beyond-tanked zone.

My father and mother make for us, my sister following a step behind as they approach. I square my shoulders, a strained smile slipping across my face. "Hey, Dad. Thanks for coming."

My father grips my hand in a firm shake, his expression stoic as always. "Good to see you, son."

I glance at my mother, forcing my words. "Mom, you look ... well."

She tips her head in acknowledgment, not a single response directed at me.

Releasing a taut breath, I shift my attention to Amber and her family. "Cathy, Mark, and Amber, these are my parents, John and Debby."

After formal bullshit's exchanged, Amber's eyes dance over mine, a small smile tumbling across her expression as she clasps my hand in hers. That tiny gesture alone is all the comfort I need to keep a calm façade. I pull her closer and press a kiss to the crown of her head, breathing her scent deep into my lungs. God, she centers me, brings me down a notch. This girl keeps my world in check and she doesn't even know it.

"You need another drink, Mr. Tough Jock-head?" Amber asks, her voice pitched low.

Her sass has me grinning, but I quickly sober up, making sure she knows what she's causing for herself. "Keep going," I whisper, catching her lobe between my teeth. "You better be ready for later. Payback, baby doll. That's all this jock's sayin'."

Giggling, she winks and turns to my sister. "You know you have to spill some of Brock's dirty secrets. I need something to hold over his arrogant head."

"That can be arranged." Brit laughs, amusement spiking her brows. "I have loads of dirt on this pretty boy."

I shake my head, a feeling I can't describe pouncing in my chest as I watch my girl chatting with Brit. My world tilts, rights itself. God, Amber fucking Moretti is officially filtering herself into the chaotic strands of my life. I've never allowed a woman to get this close to me. Not because I haven't had the opportunity, because I have. But more so because I've never found the *right* girl, the one who'll accept me as I am. With Amber it's been a burst of light from the moment I saw her.

I shift my gaze to my mother and release another nervous breath, taking a step toward her. My father's chatting with Cathy and Mark, and Amber with Brittany, so this is a good time to, hopefully, start the evening off right.

"How've ya been, Ma?" I ask, once at her side.

Face devoid of emotion, she glances at me, then back to her iPhone. "I'm good. You?"

"Doing great," I murmur. "School's going good; football too."

Jesus, she reduces me to a babbling five-year-old. I loathe the need that saturates me to make her happy. Why I continue to try I'll never know. It's an illusion that'll never fucking happen. I'll never meet her expectations.

"That's great, Brock. I'm glad your life is going so well. *Someone's* in this family should." Her voice is tinged with pain. The burning kind that never dissipates. The kind she douses in buckets of liquor to numb herself with.

"I'd love to see you more," I say, discomfort knotting my throat. "Maybe I can take you out for breakfast this week?"

Fuck me. I'm losing it. I gun a shaky hand through my hair, chastising myself for being such a pussy. I'm a grown man who doesn't need his mother's approval. Reining in my features to appear carefree, I smile nonchalantly.

She looks at me, her mouth thinning in thought. Her bitter presence penetrates the air, yanking the oxygen from my lungs. Christ, I wish I could rip those sunglasses off her face and see what's really hiding beneath her stare. Is it thick resentment, festering like a rancid sore? Or just pure hatred? This is what eats at me, the unknown of just how much she detests the man I've become. The man who, in her eyes, will always be the culprit behind Brandon's kidnapping.

"I need to check my schedule," she responds after a short pause.

"Right," I murmur, knowing she's blowing me off. Whatever. Fuck her and the blame she'll forever tag me with, the blame I placed on myself long before she did.

"You booked the reservation for seven, correct, Brock?" My

father's voice breaks me from my and my helpless mother's unrepairable relationship.

I glance at my watch. "Yeah."

"Let's head out, then," he says. "I reserved a limo for the adults. It should be outside by now." He swings his attention to Amber's foster parents. "Cathy and Mark, you can ride with us. Brock, you can drive with Brittany and Amber."

Typical John Cunningham—take charge and direct, a man who doesn't allow others to make their own decisions. A cheating prick who always has to have a say in everything, even if it's a limo ride reserved for adults.

"I'm taking my own car," Brit says, her voice strong, unmoving. "I have work to do after this."

My father nods, his eyes flashing with disapproval. He doesn't like that she's overstepping his order, but he'd never argue in front of people. Unlike my mother, my father's aware of society's perceptions of what the perfect family should look like, how it should smell, talk, and sound. "All right. Brock and Amber can meet us there. Brittany, you follow behind. Let's go. There's nothing worse than being late."

Amber's brows raise, an *are we not considered adults?* confused look pestering her face. I can tell she wants to speak up, her brain working the situation as her grip on my hand turns fierce, protective. Though I'm sure she's mulling over saying something nasty yet flavored with the right amount of politeness to my father, she stays quiet, her jaw tightening as she aims a pretty smile in his direction.

Cathy does one of those girly *eep* things, completely oblivious to the turmoil churning in the air. "This should be fun. I've never been in a limo before."

"*Come again?*" my mother asks, shock rocking her tone.

"A limo, we've never been in one." Cathy's voice is warm, her eyes alight with excitement as she tilts her head toward Mark. "Not even on our wedding day. The funds just weren't there."

My mother's mouth drops agape, but my father shoots her a warning stare, silencing whatever judgmental sludge is about to drip from it. She huffs, going back to whatever the fuck it is she's doing on her phone.

Amber clears her throat. "All right, so we'll see you there, then?"

"Sounds good, sweetie." Cathy grins. "This'll be a treat for us."

My chest burns at the way she converses with Amber. It's clear to see how much she loves my girl. Loves her like she's her own flesh and blood. She looks at her with such a tender expression, my stomach flips, doing somersaults. This evening's already throwing me off my game, and it's just begun. Something's telling me it's gonna take one of Amber's expert blow jobs and at least a pound's worth of green to recover from this shit.

"Awesome," Ambers says, her voice a thin, uneasy stroke as she hugs Cathy and Mark good-bye.

As Brit and both sets of parents make their way out of the lobby, I tangle my fingers through Amber's, squeezing her hand in a display of gratitude, a silent thank-you for putting up with the freak sideshow that is my life. I'm as hesitant of this situation as she's become, my hackles raising with every beat of my heart. But I know I need to man up and give her some form of reassurance. She lets out a breath, stress flaking the whites of her eyes. I take the opportunity to pull her close and wrap my arms around her waist, trying with everything in me to kill the anxiety spitting through her veins. After a few quiet seconds, I release her from my hold and we move outside to wait on my Hummer, my nerves unleashing their torrent on my muscles—tightening each one like a virgin's pussy—as the valet pulls up.

I tip the kid and hop inside my Hummer, the majority of the ride spent silent as the lights heading north on 695 taunt my vision with every wordless breath Amber and I consume.

"Your parents seem ... nice," Amber finally says, her lips two taut, downward frowns as she spreads a thin layer of glittery pink gloss along the heavenly gifts. "Good people."

"I'm glad you think so." I chuckle, entertained by how she so easily tells a lie. If I didn't know better, I would've thought we were siblings—our father's acts of promiscuity the result of us sharing the same fucked-up genetic makeup. We're both liars, two twisted souls cheating our way through the death maze of truth. Amber mentioned having a half brother she's never met. Shit, for all I know I'm him, our chance meeting the dude upstairs' way of saying, *No, motherfucker. I am the one who holds the bolts in the train wreck of your future, the almighty pimp of your destiny. Never forget that, dickwad.*

I flick my attention back to Amber, my eyes drowning in her self-conscious beauty as she drops her gloss into her clutch. "You might be good at stealing my heart, but ya need to work on thieving my intellect. You're full of shit, Ber. I know it, you know it—my parents are assholes. End of story."

"Okay. You caught me. They're as close to douche as you can get." She grins, playfully swatting my arm. "But I've never met a boy's parents before, so this is *still* big for me."

"A *boy?*" I grunt, knowing she's purposely trying to flip the sour mood in her sexual favor. "I thought I'd shown you, on more than one occasion, I'm all man, baby girl."

She laughs, mischief shimmying across her face as her fingers skirt around the shell of my ear. "Am I bruising your ego?"

I smirk, loving how she knows me so well. "I think you need a good spanking."

"I'm not opposed to that very thing," she fires back, branding my cheek with one of her kisses before leaning back in her seat.

I laugh, then sober for a minute. "Thanks for being here with me."

"You're the one that let this happen," she says softly, sincerity streaming from her words.

Something takes over—a tug in my gut, screaming out that I have to make this girl understand how much I need her with me. "I want you in every part of my life, Amber."

She angles her body toward mine. "I want to be there too, Brock. I need to know this side of you."

"Even if it's ugly?" I whisper.

"*Especially* if it's ugly," she says, her gaze tender. "You know my ugly parts, yet here you are."

Jesus. I'm falling for her so fast—almost too fast, and there's no stopping the forward momentum. "Nothing you could ever do or say would scare me away."

"I've never felt happy before," she whispers, her honesty bridging the space between us. "But with you, I think I can be."

My heart stills, my eyes drifting over the vulnerability lining her face. She's giving me a glimpse inside her soul, exposing a piece of herself she rarely does. I tell, if it takes bringing her to meet my insane parents to admit that I could make her as happy as she does me, I'll do it a million times over.

"Why are you looking at me like that?" she asks, a blush burning her skin.

"You kind of . . . complete me," I answer, honestly feeling it.

Without a word, she wraps her hand in mine and we ride the rest of the way in comfortable silence, enjoying the growing closeness between us.

Once at the restaurant—a popular Italian joint overlooking the harbor—the hostess leads us to a private room, where everyone is already seated. The second we walk in, I immediately notice that my father has ordered several bottles of wine. My mother's sipping away at the expensive merlot, her face an impassive mask as she starts to loosen up. She's removed her sunglasses, her arm lazily draped over the back of Brit's chair as I examine the deep lines scratching her forehead, the heavy black bags beneath her eyes. My chest tightens, my body aching as the tortured appearance of the woman who gave me life pummels me down to my core. Another sip, the stem of the wineglass dangling between her fragile fingers as my pulse rises. Instincts alight, the thought of tonight's imminent embarrassment kills me as I unbutton my suit jacket, pulling out a seat for Amber.

Releasing a breath, I take the chair next to Amber's and glance around the table. Everyone else seems to be in good spirits, the chatter flowing freely.

I use the opportunity to speak. "I want to thank everyone for coming tonight." The pitch of my tone wavers as my attention connects to my mother. I search her expression for a hint of life. It's not there, nothing but a desert filled with the skeletal remains of who she was when I was a kid. "It's not often we get together, but it's nice when we do." Most of what I just uttered is a lie—it's usually intense, painful bullshit brought up from the past when we see each other—but I want my mom to know that even though she doesn't want me in her life, no longer loves me because of Brandon going missing, I continue to love and need her in my own way.

"Thank you for inviting us," Mark says with a warm smile, drawing my gaze to his. "This place is really nice, Brock."

I choke back the emotions threatening to destroy me and return his smile. "They make killer food. This Italian princess over here loves it."

Amber taps me in my ribs with her elbow, an embarrassed shake of her head following suit. The waiter comes over and we all order some appetizers.

After he's departed my father strikes up the first conversation of the evening. "So, Amber, what are you studying?"

"I'm majoring in psychology," she replies.

"Why *that* field?" My mother inhales a hearty sip of wine, her venomous glare pounding into my girlfriend as she places her glass on the table.

"I grew up under really bad circumstances, and now that I've *somewhat* found a way out, I want to help others like me."

My mother's brows raise. "And what difference do *you* think you can make to people who've experienced *real* tragedy? Sometimes you can't help those who've lost everything."

"That's not necessarily true," Amber states, her voice thoughtful though her eyes are anything but. They're narrowed, a snake ready to attack. "You have to want help in order for it to work. I'm sure there are plenty of people who want their lives to be different." She pauses, her attention unwavering from my mother's. "Coming from someone who's seen, felt, and tasted *real* tragedy, I know I want my life to change for the better. Sometimes it's just hard to accept help from those who've never been through anything themselves. Hence my wanting to guide others like me toward a mentally healthy existence."

My mother lets out an exhausted sigh, her eyes rolling as she finishes off the wine lingering at the bottom of her glass.

"I think that's great, Amber," Brittany chirps, breaking the tension starting to thicken the air. "Helping people in need is a noteworthy job."

"Agreed," my dad concurs. "And what else do you do besides school? Are you working?"

Amber sits back, ease covering her posture. "Yes. I pull a few waitressing shifts a week at a seafood restaurant down in Riva."

"And she makes good grades too." Cathy's warm voice reaches across the table. "You're working, going to school, doing all the right things for your future. Mark and I are *so* proud of you."

Amber smiles, her face flushing from the compliment.

Intent on adding to her noticeable embarrassment, I feather a finger over the arch of her cheek. "Yeah, she's a great girl. I'm one lucky man." Amber turns toward me, her eyes heating by the second. "Not only is she smart and responsible as all hell, she's also *ridiculously* cute."

A full flush runs the path of her skin, her lips twitching in a soft smile as she clears her throat. "You've raised a *very* smooth talker, Mr. Cunningham. He's never short on strategically timed endearments."

My father nods at Amber, seemingly amused by her statement. "Oh, he's a very smooth talker. There's *little* doubt about that." His eyes flash to mine, clearly insinuating just how smooth I must be to have snowed these people into thinking I was a decent human being.

I look down at my drink, effectively put in place by the self-righteous asshole. Lucky for me, Cathy and Mark don't pick up on his little dig and continue to chatter away with Amber and Brit about the local touristy shit they want to check out.

I just wanna check the fuck outta here.

We're interrupted when a waiter enters the room with appetizers in hand. Drinks are refilled, dinner orders taken. It's in this moment I realize that Amber's a natural around undercover lunatics, her face glowing with a comfortable easiness I have yet to see—one I can't wait to be a part of. In the midst of watching my girl in action, I catch Mark striking up a conversation with my dad regarding what he does for a living. My father's more than happy to tell him how fucking awesome he is, going on and on about the several back-pat-worthy achievements the self-appointed imperial asshole's tackled throughout his lifetime.

Sickened by how high he is on himself, I finish off my whiskey in one large swallow, hoping to catch a decent buzz. A buzz strong enough to help get me through the rest of this night. Inwardly cringing, I yank my attention away from the blue-suited dick, only to have it land on his "better half." Another cringe as I lace my fingers through Amber's, trying to ignore my mother's hateful stare pinning me to my seat. As long as she keeps her mouth shut, I couldn't give a fuck how she looks at me. Still, I fidget in my chair under her silent scrutiny, unable to keep my mind from drifting off to the decent days we spent together before our lives fell apart, before my careless act changed what the future of my family was supposed to become.

Nervous movements catching his attention, Mark turns to me with a wide smile. "Amber tells us you're quite the football star. How's that working out for you?"

My stomach clenches at the topic as my eyes shift to my father. His face is sealed to mine, the dip in his brows showing he's eagerly awaiting my response. I release Amber's hand and tighten a fist under the table, knowing I haven't been that dedicated to the sport the last couple of weeks.

"I don't know about all that," I answer with a chuckle, trying to keep my tone light. "It's been a good season, though. We've had a couple scouts come by the field to watch us play. So who knows, right?"

My father's expression betrays the calm soothing his voice. "I'm glad to hear that," he says, pretending to not even register Mark's start of a reply. "However, a business associate, whose son also plays for Hadley, informed me that you've missed several practices the last couple of weeks. I hope you have a decent excuse for that."

"Of course he does." My mother snorts, tipping her glass to her lips. "This is Brock we're talking about, John."

Amber butts in by clearing her throat, her words spoken sharp. "He was sick with the flu, Mr. Cunningham. That's why he's missed a few practices." The lie drips easily from her mouth, the situation starting to make my pulse pound as I look at her. I wasn't sick and Amber knows it. Truth is, I had something come up and, in my line of work, that happens more often than not. Being that my coaches rarely give me shit about it—the two former potheads letting my and Ryder's dirty piss tests slide by—I don't know why my father feels the need to bring it up.

I shake my head at myself. Who am I trying to kid? I know why he fucking brings it up.

My father acts like my judge and jury. He hovers, trying to control my existence as though it were his own. If it involves my life, and it's something he knows about, then he's all over it like flies on shit. Not because he wants me to make good decisions or avoid getting hemmed up in trouble—that would be one thing. But it's all about not blemishing his name, the façade he's built in the community surrounding his Cunningham clan. It drives me fucking nuts. Even though I've died trying, there's no pleasing these people.

"*Sick?*" my father says. "Unless you're in the hospital tied to an IV pole, you can't miss practices, Brock. You're on scholarship and your future is on the line. It looks bad if you aren't giving a hundred and twenty percent. You know that." His eyes are icy, his struggle to maintain his composure something you couldn't miss a mile away if you tried.

"I got it. It won't happen again," I mutter, the bullshit flowing out of my mouth as easily as it did Amber's. This isn't the place nor the time to discuss my nonexistent football career.

Amber's hand grazes my thigh, causing my attention to shift to her. She smiles at me before turning to her foster parents. "You guys will have to come to one of Brock's games. He's amazing on the field."

"Oh, I bet," Cathy says, her gaze set on Amber. "I still can't believe you watch football. He would have to be something special for you to go to a game."

My mother cackles, her *I'm two sheets to the wind* pitch making me cringe. I wish I could yank the fucking alcohol off the table. Better yet, I wish I could yank *her* from the table. But I can't. I'm as unable to dictate this situation as I am every other time I'm around her or my dad.

Amber's grip on my thigh tightens as she glares at my mother. "I'm surprised too. God knows I couldn't stand the sport *before* Brock."

"Don't worry, Amber." Brit takes a sip of water. "You're not the only one who despises it. I'd rather clean my house than watch a bunch of sweaty dudes throw a ball around. And me saying I'd rather clean is saying *a lot*." She nudges my arm, a smirk twisting her lips. "No offense, bro. Though I love you to death, I'd take a month spent with the vacuum over watching you play any day."

A laugh moves across the table, the easy banter continuing as I fix my attention on my mother, who's refilling her glass with a near-empty bottle of wine. I watch, sickened, as she barely takes a breath in between gulps, her entire body trained on the plum-colored mixture as though it's her lifeline. After inhaling the entire glass in under a second, her gaze catches mine. She raises a perfectly arched brow, my pulse jumping at the darkness dashing over her features.

Shit's about to go south. I know it, can feel it. I've seen this more times than I can count. I grab the sides of my chair and brace myself for whatever poison is about to fly through the room.

After a second, then a third heavy sip of the merlot, her sharp voice hits me in the center of my chest. "How's *Ryder* doing, Brock?"

I meet her stare head-on, wondering how quickly the situation is gonna deteriorate. I know my mother, can see her demons slowly dragging her back to her inner hell. The bomb's about to go off: that I can't prevent. All I can hope for is a mild explosion.

"He's good," I answer, my voice remaining calm. "Working, school, football—the same old stuff."

"Mm-hmm," she hums, tapping her nail on the rim of her glass. "I bet *he* hasn't missed any practices."

Silence simmers midair, a thick tension compounding as I say, "I don't know, Ma. You'd have to ask *him* that. I don't usually keep a tally on what he does or doesn't do when it comes to practice."

A mirthless smile lifts her lips as she once again refills her glass. "I don't *need* to ask him anything," she hisses. "Ryder would *never* throw his future away."

"Neither would I." My words come out tame, despite my wanting to scream them. "I'm thinking about a business law class next semester. Will that work for ya? Make ya proud of me?"

"Not sure *anything* will work or make me proud when it comes to you, Brock," my mother points out through a sardonic laugh. "You look at life like tomorrow's guaranteed. Who knows what will happen? Bad decisions and hedonistic attitudes take away people's will to live." She openly glares at me, then Amber, her hatred palpable as she dangles her glass in the air. "*Especially* when they're running around with white trash."

Angers surges hot and fast, but before I can react, Brittany lets out a quiet moan. "*Put* the wine *down*, Mother."

Cathy and Mark look at each other wide-eyed, not as familiar, obviously, with my mother's lack of couth. Normal people, which the Cunninghams aren't, don't expect someone to be so vicious about another human being, least of all one sitting at the table with her parents.

Though I'm seeing red, I glance at Amber, my eyes flashing an apology as I wrap my hand around hers. She tosses me a tight smile, which only further ignites my anger.

I turn to my mother, making a point to look at her wineglass before speaking, my tone a harsh slap. "We all have different definitions of *who's* considered white trash. In my book, a lush, such as yourself, is right up there in my top three."

"I can smell a tramp a mile away," my mother huffs, glaring pointedly at Amber. "Lush or not, *that* takes the cake in *my* book."

"Excuse *me?*" Cathy's jaw nearly drops into her plate of shrimp scampi. "Who the *hell* do you think you are calling my daughter a tramp?"

Brittany pushes back in her seat, a mix of anger and embarrassment thick on her tongue as she rises. "That was uncalled for. I don't care *how* much you've drunk, this is *completely* out of line. I'm taking you home before you make a fool of yourself."

"She's already *made* a fool of herself," I bite out, tossing my linen napkin into the middle of the table.

"Don't, Brock," Amber whispers, gripping my hand tighter. I know she's trying to protect me, trying to downplay what happened to save me from saying some shit I can't take back. I shake my head at her, silently telling her it's too late. I can't back down, can't let this slide. I refuse.

With an aggravated sigh, my father intervenes. "All your mother's trying to say is that you need to make *all* your practices. There's no reason to miss any."

"Your wife just called my daughter a *tramp*, and you're still talking about *football?*" Mark stands, his eyes fierce as he jabs a finger into my father's chest. "I'm not about to sit here and listen to you put down my child *or* yours! I don't know who you people think you're messing with, but this shit's about to get *real* ugly if you say another word about my kid!"

"That's not what she's trying to say," I tell my father, barely picking up on Mark's comment. I shove to my feet, my fists clenched at my sides, itching to blast something before I blast someone. "We all know what's *really* going on. She's a goddamn alcoholic, but that's still no excuse for her fucking mouth."

"Watch your language," my father says, his tone a resounding warning. "She's still your mother."

"Right," I spit, losing every shred of sanity I own. "I'll watch my fucking mouth when you get your wife under control!"

Everyone in the room stills as our heated stares stay deadlocked. I've had enough of this bullshit. I knew nothing with them would ever be easy after Brandon was taken, but the last couple of years it's been nothing but a clusterfuck of vile comments that have compiled into a storm of hurt and anger. Before Amber, I was able to bury my feelings in selling blow, my choice of employment providing me with a sense of purpose. I couldn't do that in my personal life. There's nothing my parents want from me other than a son who plays football and provides them with some form of status in their elite circle. It ends tonight. They've crossed a line, a major fucking line. There's one thing I won't condone and that's hurtful comments aimed at my girl. You wanna rip me apart, fine, go ahead. But Amber? I'll fucking hunt you down, dismantle you limb to limb, not giving a shit *who* you are to me while I watch you suffer.

"Take her home," I continue, rage blistering my lungs. "Get her out of my fucking sight. She needs help, but you've turned a blind eye to her problem because you get away with more shit while she's lit up. I'm done with it. She can't keep going on like this. It's gonna kill her."

My father stands, his shoulders straightening to full height as fury whips across his face. "Your mother's fine, Brock. The *only* problem in this family is *you*."

"That's not true," Brittany states, her voice forceful. "She has to stop blaming Brock for what happened to Brandon. It's unfair to not only him, but *me* as well. He's my remaining brother and it *kills* me to see the way the *both* of you treat him."

My stare switches from Brit to my mother, who's swaying back and forth, tears dribbling down her cheeks as she lifts her green eyes to mine.

"You're the reason he was stolen from me," she whispers, slashing the knife of guilt—already buried deep within my gut—deeper. "Because of you, I don't have Brandon anymore. I think it's sick that I have to suffer while you get to go on with your life as if nothing's . . . happened."

I hear Cathy and Amber gasp, my breath fucking off at the trail of sheer agony streaming across my mother's face. The agony *I* caused her.

"You think I *don't* think about him?" I snarl, pounding my fists against my chest. "That he's just some memory that occasionally pops into my *mind?*" I drop my head, my fists deciding to connect with the table this time around. "If so, then you're wrong. There's not a *minute* that goes by that I *don't* think about that kid. He was my baby brother, for fuck's sake! I might be the reason he's gone, but you're *not* the only one who *loved* him! Not the only one *suffering* over his loss!"

"I'm not so sure about that," she continues, sniffling as though I didn't just bleed my heart out in front of an entire restaurant filled with mortified onlookers. "The only thing I know for sure, Brock, is you're a filthy reminder of what I'll never have *ever* again. One I can't stand to look at." The last part's whispered as she picks up the bottle of wine, tossing back what remains of it.

Broken to pieces, I watch as she gets up, throws on her sunglasses, and stumbles out of the room.

Bile churns in my stomach as the pain of what our lives have turned into crushes me. I want to run after her, get as far away from the questioning looks I know are being aimed at me from Amber's parents—from the hate getting tossed my way from my own father.

I look at Amber, my only safe place, her expression mirroring my torment as she laces her fingers through mine. I know she gets the level of dysfunction ripping through my world, tearing it to shreds. Maybe that's the reason I've felt this burning connection to her, this insatiable need to have her in my life.

We're two different people who share one common link—our blood families are fucking nightmares.

"Don't listen to her, Brock," Brittany says, anger assaulting her features. "The *only* thing this is about is her being a drunk. You can't blame yourself for something you had no part in."

I can't talk, the pain pulsing through my core so strong, it feels like it's choking the life right outta me.

"I don't know what the hell all of that was about," Mark says, his words strong, unwavering, as he watches, from the corner of his eye, my father toss a couple hundred-dollar bills onto the table. "But your sister's right, Brock. What just happened appears to have *very* little to do with you."

My father tucks his wallet back into his dress pants, shaking his head at Mark's comment but saying nothing as he looks up at the rest of us.

He's not about to make this worse than it already is. God forbid someone he associates with is watching and the word gets out to his circle of friends.

"It was nice meeting you all," he finally says, his face hard as stone, his tone formal, presentable. "I apologize for the way the evening turned out." Without a single look in my direction, he pivots and breezes out of the room.

I scrub an exhausted hand over my jaw, a breath locked in my windpipe as my sister walks over to me.

Sadness digs into the planes of her face as she cups my cheeks, whispering, "I love you. Don't let *their* issues turn *your* life upside down." She pauses, concern, along with tears, edging her eyes. "I want you to remember something. Mom and Dad are *not* a reflection of you. What they think isn't who *you* are as a person. I know who you *really* are, and you're a smart, good young man who I'm *proud* to call my brother."

She stares at me a moment before turning to Amber and her family. I see the Cunningham come out in her, the survival skill she mastered a long time ago—the ability to smooth out a situation, manipulating it to not seem as bad as it was. "I'm sorry tonight didn't go as planned. But it was so very good to meet you all."

"Likewise," Cathy says, her hand on her throat, tears welling up in her eyes. It's easy to see she's never witnessed anything like what just went down.

Amber, on the other hand, has seen much worse than this unfold in front of her.

"Thank you for coming, Brittany," Amber says, a sad, haunting smile touching her lips. "It was nice to meet you."

Brit nods, her gaze remaining apologetic. "I'm sorry for what my mother said, Amber. It's hard to control crazy. Please don't let her comments offend you. It was the wine talking." A shake of her head as she grimaces. "Not that that made it okay for her to say or act how she did, but it's all I have to go on." She casts me a look that speaks a thousand words, none of them audible, before looking back up to the group. "I'm going to head out now. Please have a safe trip home."

Brittany grabs her purse and disappears around a corner. Once she's out of view, I find it hard to look into anyone's eyes, Amber's included. I feel like a dick, shame cloaking me in a heavy, suffocating blanket.

Nobody knows what to do or say, so I suggest getting the bill. Everyone agrees, eager to break free from the filth of the last hour. Over Mark's objection, I hand my credit card to the waiter. I know there's money on the table—my father's way of trying to look cool—but I'll be damned if I'm gonna let the asshole pay for jack shit.

Amber grabs my hand, squeezing it tightly, as I lead us out to my Hummer. Everyone seems preoccupied, still trying to wrap their heads around what just transpired as we all get in. It's just as well. I can't think of anything fucking coherent to say anyway. I'm so goddamn pissed off at my parents, so fucking hurt, but the more I think about it, I'm just as angry with myself. I knew it would come to this. I bite back a laugh as I ease onto the busy highway, realizing I'm the one who caused this shit. I should've stuck to what my gut was saying, insisting to Amber that it just wasn't a good idea.

In the midst of trying to get my head outta my personal problems, I pick up on Mark telling a story about how he got Amber into fishing, and something about her being afraid of the dark—which I didn't know. I knew my girl was scared of very few things, but the dark? She'd kick the dark's ass.

After a few much-needed laughs, we drop Cathy and Mark off at the hotel, promising to pick them up after class tomorrow to go take them out for some crabs. Excited, they walk away, both waving as they enter the lobby.

I pull out of the parking lot and head toward my condo, my mind a Molotov cocktail of emotions as I weave in and out of traffic. Amber stays quiet, rubbing her thumb along my knuckles, letting me have my space but, at the same time, letting me know she's here for me. If nothing else comes of this night, at least my girl sees the evil that's created the monster I've turned into.

Once parked in front of my place, I cut the engine, pluck a joint from the glove compartment, and light it up, taking a long pull as I turn to the angel at my side.

She gives me a wide smile, swiping the mood enhancer from my fingers after I've hit it a few times. "God, I've been waiting for this." She hits it once, twice, her body noticeably relaxing as she blows out a ring of smoke, handing it back to me. "No kidding. Tonight was—"

"As crazy as I told you it'd get," I interrupt, pulling one last, long hit into my lungs.

Amber nods, her smile disappearing as I stub out the joint, slipping what remains of it into my wallet.

I lean over the center console, cupping her cheeks. "I'm not a good man, Ber," I whisper, searching her face. "I have my share of inconsistencies, but I own them, wake up to them every morning, go to sleep fighting them every night." I touch my lips to hers, praying nothing she witnessed will have her running from the twistedness that is my life. "But even though I'm not good through and through, I'll *always* give you everything I am. Take care of you to the best of my ability." I kiss her slowly, ingraining this moment into my memory, hoping this isn't the last time I'll get to. "So please, just chill with me a while, okay?"

Another nod, this one as she places her hands over mine. "I'm not going anywhere," she says, sincerity clinging to each word. "I promise, so stop worrying." It's her turn to kiss me, her cherry-flavored gloss, and little moans causing my heart to beat faster than a drum.

Kiss slowing, we get out of my ride and step into the elevator. As the doors part, I pull Amber into my embrace, praying that any kind of feelings this girl's developing for me, if any at all, will keep her hanging on to her promise.

Keep her hanging on to what could very well cause her some of the most confusing hurt she's ever been through.

Me . . .

CHAPTER 9

Amber

"THAT'LL BE FOUR dollars and fifty cents," the barista announces.
Standing in a Starbucks just off campus, I dig through my purse
for my wallet. No luck. "You've got to be kidding," I mumble. "I don't
have any cash or cards with me." Exhausted, I bring my eyes to hers,
an embarrassed smile on my face. "Can you put it to the side while
I go . . ." I trail off, realizing the barista is my mute roommate, Madeline.

Considering our boyfriends are in *business* together, we've been
forced to hang out here and there, but other than that, we haven't
spoken to each other since the night she told me about Brock.

It's safe to say that the last two months have been nothing short
of awkward.

"There are people who have *jobs* to get to," some douche barks
from the line behind me. I glance at him from over my shoulder and
watch him stretch out an annoyed arm, impatiently checking his
watch. "Can we get moving here?"

I take a deep breath, my muscles trembling from lack of sleep as
I focus on trying not to lose my shit. I decide against telling him to

fuck off, rolling my eyes at him instead. Before I can note his reaction, I bring my attention back to Madeline and she's . . . smiling.

Not a *you're screwed* smile, but a genuine, understanding, sneaky half smile.

"It's on the house," Madeline whispers. "Don't worry about it."

"Aww. She doesn't have any money," a familiar feminine Southern drawl says, its overly sweet tone hitting my ears like acid rain.

I straighten and turn around, locking eyes on Hailey Jacobs. She casts me a snake's smile. I don't return it. Just seeing her after her most recent attempt to drive me insane makes my blood boil. Why bother pretending?

"Now, now, Madeline," Hailey continues, the canny thrust in her words holding the proper amount of malicious amusement. With her hand buried in a Gucci purse—which I'm sure cost more than my car—she steps from the line, produces a leather wallet, and plucks out a ten-dollar bill. "You wouldn't want to lose your job by *lying* for Amber, would you?"

Her statement comes out loud enough, making Madeline's manager whip around, his brows furrowed in concern. Madeline's face freezes, Hailey smirks, and I have a sudden overwhelming need to smack the bitch. With her fiery eyes promising retaliation, Madeline snatches the bill from Hailey and rings up my order.

"No!" I croak over the grumbling sighs in the background. "I don't want her paying for me."

"Just let her," Madeline implores. "My boss is watching, and there's a shitload of people waiting."

Is this what I've been reduced to? Hailey Jacobs—an overprivileged snarky bitch who's been stalking me since I started dating Brock—paying for my four-fifty Frappuccino?

I look at Madeline's worried face and determine that, yes, I have been reduced to this. I grit my teeth, my scowl aimed in Hailey's direction.

Hesitation burns my hand as I take the Frappuccino from Madeline and mouth, *I'm sorry.*

Madeline mouths back, *No problem.*

The reassuring look in her eyes tells me I haven't done too much harm. Still, it doesn't stop me from feeling bad. I turn, pathetically ducking past the line of aggravated, caffeine-crazed patrons. I'm sure the mob is about to pounce on me.

I feel Hailey's wicked presence on my heels as I locate an empty table in the back corner. I take a seat, pull out an essay for biology class, and begrudgingly take a sip of my Hailey-Jacobs-bought Frappuccino.

It tastes sour.

As I scan the drivel I've composed, I can sense the snake-with-tits' eyes on me. It's making me uncomfortable. I can't help but wonder why I'm not used to it by now. In the several schools I attended, I stumbled across her type more times than I care to remember.

Hailey's the girl who'll pledge you her undying friendship, then fuck your boyfriend behind your back. The kind of girl who'll use your weaknesses to her advantage, making you feel beneath her when she's truly the pathetic one. The kind of girl who'll smile pretty in your face, but the second you turn around shove an axe into your spine, slowly exposing every secret you've trusted her with. Rotten to their decaying cores and traveling in hungry packs, girls such as Hailey Jacobs are scattered throughout every school across the globe . . . axes tight in their grips.

A split second before I decide to go somewhere else, Hailey approaches the table and slides into a chair across from me. My chest tightens.

"Amber," she says, twisting her lips into a pout, "why can't we just be friends?"

"This is a joke, right?" I swivel my head, looking for hidden cameras.

She gives a casual shrug. "Why would it be a joke?"

"Let's see," I say, trying to sound unaffected by this bitch's vile attempt to gain anything from me. I cross my arms, my head dizzy from the list of reasons she's not to be trusted. "Where should I begin? Let's start with I know it's you whose been slipping those *love* notes under my dorm door. What was it you called me? Hadley's queen whore?"

"I heard about those." She snorts, her smile smug. "I also heard the student board doesn't know *who* it is because your perpetrator's been dressed from head to toe in black every time one was left. Whoever's been doing it is pretty smart too, since they're using a stamp and not actually writing anything. Seems they have a few ups on everyone." Her periwinkle eyes narrow as her smile widens. "I have *beautiful* penmanship, which I love to show off, and not even for you would I be caught *dead* in black. It's not my color."

"You think I've never been called a whore?" I lean forward, my eyes hardening. "Try being original, bitch. Think of something new the next time you give me one."

"Oh, I'm more than *positive* you've been called it several times, and if we're being honest, there's no way to be original when it comes to whores like you. You're all the same." She mimics my pose and leans across the table, obviously amused. "Anything else you feel like blaming on me?"

"Yeah, there is," I grit out, trying to maintain my composure. "You running me off the road."

"I did *no* such thing," she huffs, her perfectly waxed eyebrows rising. "I'm offended you would think I've done *any* of these hideous things to you."

"You're full of shit," I hiss, my tone doubled up in anger.

Being that she's the only student at Hadley sporting a custom cherry-colored Range Rover, there's no mistaking it was her. Not to mention I caught a glimpse of her golden locks as my car all but careened into a ditch on the side of I-95 the night it happened. I wanted to bang my head against the steering wheel when I failed to catch her license plate.

"Well," she says, screwing her mouth into a sneer as she stares at her bloodred nails, "without proper proof, I'd say all of your accusations are worth not an ounce of anyone's time."

Though I'm shaking with adrenaline, I close my eyes, forcing myself to think of unicorns, puppies, and happy shit like that. Not the best coping mechanism, but if I don't do it, I'll be spending the night curled up on a wooden bench in the local precinct for attempted murder.

I open my eyes and take a deep breath, determined not to let her get to me any further. "What do you want from me, Hailey?"

She rests her elbows on the table, her voice sugary sweet. "So how are things going with you and Brock?"

"That's none of your business," I point out, convinced the girl is bipolar.

"Why not?"

"Do I really need to explain that?"

"I'm just trying to make friendly conversation." She twirls her hair between her fingers as she leans back. "Considering it's almost October, and he's never been known to stay with a piece of ass past a couple of dates, one must assume things are going well. Still, a girl as naïve as yourself may find his . . . *employment* somewhat difficult to handle. I just want to make sure you're happy."

"You want to make sure I'm happy?" I laugh, so over her act. "Enough with the bullshit. I have a paper to finish. What the fuck do you really want from me?"

"I want to get to know you, Amber. *Really* know you." She glances at her nails a second time, her voice sliding into huntress mode. "You come from a *very* tragic past, and I can't help but find myself curious about a girl who's seen such terrible, horrifying things."

My every muscle goes taut, all concerns about spending the night in the slammer vanishing from my brain. "How do you know *anything* about me?"

"I have my *close* . . . sources."

On a shaky breath, I spin over who could've said anything to her. Only Brock, Ryder, Lee, and Madeline know about my warped history. Brock may have told Ryder, but they're best friends, and I know with everything in me that Brock would never say a word to this nut about my life. Never. I'm the guilty one who told Madeline and Lee. In a drunken stupor, I dished out my shit one night when I stumbled into our dorm room. Still, I can't see either of them saying anything. They'd gain nothing from it.

However, Ryder would. Not once in the past month has he made a move on me, looked at me in a suggestive way, or spoken his usual smack. If anything, he's been a total douche, ignoring my presence every time we've been around each other. Still, I thought I'd seen struggle in his eyes, felt it when we got too close. I couldn't have been more wrong.

This must be his twisted way at getting back at me.

Hailey continues her mental fuck as she leans across the table, her tone dropping to a whisper. "So what was it like? Was there tons of blood everywhere? What was running through your mind when they closed their eyes for eternity? I'm thinking about doing a case study on sick psychos and their grieving little spawn. I figured you and your father would fit the bill *perfectly*."

I swallow the hot bile bubbling in my throat, my body rattling uncontrollably with each breath I attempt to take. The ghosts from that evil day trample through my skull, but before I can react, I feel a soft hand on my shoulder.

"Leave her alone, you freak!" Madeline bellows, her brown eyes as wide as Hailey's.

"How dare you talk to me like that!" Hailey jumps to her feet, her pissed-off lips curled over her fangs. "Who the fuck do you think you are?"

Frozen, I watch Madeline take a ground-eating step toward Hailey, their noses nearly smashed together. "I'm the bitch who's about to beat you into the next millennium if you don't get the fuck out of here right now."

"I'm telling your boss!" Hailey spews in true kindergartener fashion. She shoves Gucci's newest bag onto her arm and turns, running smack into the man I'm sure is about to fire Madeline. "Just the person I was looking for. Your employee's threatening me!"

"And *you're* harassing a patron of mine." Though the steel set of his shoulders says he wants to take a good crack at her, Mr. Boss Man's expression is eerily calm. "If you don't remove yourself from my establishment within thirty seconds, I'll be on the phone with the cops."

Not only does Hailey's mouth drop open, but so does mine.

"*Excuse* me?" Hailey's eyes look like hula hoops.

"Do you need a hearing aid?" Boss Man crosses his arms, a cunning smile resting on his lips. "I thought I made myself pretty clear. Get out or go to jail. In my opinion, it's not at all a hard decision."

Hailey casts me one last glare, lets out a huff, and pivots, her body trembling as she pushes through the crowd.

"I apologize about that," Mr. Boss Man says, extending his hand after the nutter exits the building.

I take it, completely confused. I thought for sure Madeline would be first in line at the unemployment office tomorrow morning.

"Once the rush let up, Madeline explained you've been having problems with that girl," he adds.

"I have. Thanks for getting rid of it—I mean, her." I give him a weak smile, my nerves starting to come down. "I appreciate it."

"Not a problem."

"Thanks, Dad," Madeline says, pulling out a chair across from me before readjusting her ponytail.

"*Dad?*" I'm more confused than I was before.

"Yup," Dad answers with a proud smile, smoothing a hand through his salt-and-pepper hair. "She's been calling me that for the last twenty-one years."

Madeline grins. "I'm gonna take a quick fifteen, okay?"

He lays a quick kiss on the crown of Madeline's head. "Take thirty. Maggie just clocked in, and I overscheduled Tim this morning." He swings his attention back to me. "Nice meeting you, Amber."

"You too." As he walks away, I wonder if I'd have any kind of relationship with my parents if they were still alive. "I'm lost. I thought you and Lee are from California."

"We are," she says with a nod.

"But your parents moved here and own a Starbucks?" I crack a smile. "Was your mom *that* afraid of you leaving the nest?"

Madeline shakes her head and laughs. "No. My parents are divorced. My mother's still back in Borrego Springs, and my father's here in Davidsonville with his new wife. When Lee and I came to visit last summer, we decided to give the East Coast a try and settled on Hadley."

"I see," I draw out. "But why aren't you living with him instead? Davidsonville's pretty close, and room and board isn't cheap."

A wicked smile lights her face. "Daddy-o *owns* five of these here Starbucks, so he's got a little cash to burn on the full college experience I so desperately requested. You know: drinking, partying, and tons of sex with Lee without having to answer to Pops."

"Makes sense." I grin, wondering why I didn't catch that to begin with. "Your dad seems pretty cool."

"He is," Madeline says warily. "Caught you off guard with that. I'm sorry."

"Why are you sorry?"

She shrugs, her eyes conveying what she doesn't want to say.

You poor, poor thing . . .

I sigh and take a sip of my Frappuccino, wishing I wasn't a big fat magnet for remorse. "Thanks for what you did. You pretty much saved me from a felony record."

"Don't mention it." She blows out a breath, unties her apron, and tosses it onto the table, disgust marring her features. "I've never liked that bitch. But since Lee lives with Ryder, and Ryder used to mess around with the skank, I had to deal with her. I'm happy that's no more."

"*Used* to?" I ask, her words confusing me all over again. "I thought they were still messing around."

"Nope. Lee said that after she pulled that last stunt with you and your car, Ryder cut her off."

I raise a skeptical brow, not sure what to make of anything. Just five minutes ago, I was sure he'd said something to Hailey. Now I don't know what to think. The only thing I do know is that Ryder's receiving an unexpected knock on his door when I leave here.

"So, listen," Madeline continues, shifting in her chair, "I've been meaning to apologize to you. I was seriously a bitch the day I told you about Brock and the guys. I came off like a judgmental hypocrite, and that's not me at all." She shrugs, hesitation swirling in her eyes. "My feelings toward Brock are . . . complicated."

"You two don't have some kind of history together, do you?" I ask, praying to God they don't.

She giggles. "No, not at all."

I puff out a sigh of relief. I couldn't handle another blow today.

"I don't know . . . Brock's not *totally* a bad guy, and he's been through his share of shit, but I hate what he did to Lee."

"What did he do to Lee?" I ask, completely lost.

"He recruited him into this lifestyle," she says as though the answer should be obvious. "Brock has a keen sense of knowing who he can and can't manipulate."

I scoff. "Manipulated into it by Brock or not, Lee made his *own* choice. We all have to make choices. Sometimes those choices take us down the right road, and it's sunny and bright and filled with sparkles and crap. Other times, our choices sink us down a hole filled with nothing but shit, pain, and regret. Either way, choices are one of the many ways reality pukes its insanity in our faces."

I sigh, hoping the girl understands what I'm getting at. I've made choices I wish I could take back. We all have. But time is humanity's greatest threat, our maturing minds unable to grasp that she's the bitch calling the shots. "You seem pretty cool," I continue, my tone less harsh, my features softening, "but if you want to get along with me at all, you can't blame the universe—or Brock—for things Lee chose to participate in on his own. It's called free will. I don't like people who seek pity for bad decisions they've made on their own. It's also called life. Please deal with both if you want to be friends with me."

"Wow, Amber," she says after a moment, her eyes saucers. "That was . . . I don't know. Kind of inspirational, depressing, conceited, and a little . . . scary."

"*Scary?*" I laugh.

She smiles. "Not really scary, but definitely the other three."

"What can I say? I'm . . . multidimensional, one of my many split personalities jumping into every conversation I partake in." I take a sip of my now lukewarm Frappuccino. I'm in desperate need of a friend—God knows I am—but I'm not about to give up everything I believe in. I've done that more times than I can count. "I'm being honest with you, Madeline. I might seem a little cuckoo—hell, I kind of am—but what you're staring at is what you'll always get from me. That's nothing but the truth."

She folds her hands beneath her chin and studies me. "I'm not sure what to say."

"Say you'll be a friend who can deal with my forwardness and who doesn't think her boyfriend's better than mine just because he's not running the show." I shrug, a grin rounding my face. "Both of our boys are equally as bad because they sell it."

"So you agree that what they're doing *isn't* cool?"

"Of *course* I do. There's not a day that passes when Brock goes to pick up that I don't worry about him."

I've lost sleep fearing that something fucked up is gonna happen to him. That one night, he's just not going to come back. I've never experienced this over a man. My entire existence has revolved around keeping myself guarded.

Regardless of me trying to push love as far away as possible from the cage surrounding my heart, these untapped emotions, whether it's the beginning of falling in love or not, aren't going away. They're changing the color of my blood, adding texture to the palette of my world. Relentlessly destroying everything I've ever known myself to be—to everything I've ever thought I was capable of being to someone else—they're both scaring and making me giddy all at once.

"But it is what it is," I continue, attempting to crush down my fears. "I'm not trying to make light of it, but there are worse things they could be doing." My statement jars me. Am I trying to make Brock seem better for not being a murderer, rapist, or human trafficker? I set my coffee down, attempting to pick her brain. "Either way, they all have their reasons for doing it. What's Lee's reason?"

She stares at me a second. "We started dating our junior year of high school and have always talked about moving to Europe after graduation. We've priced the whole trip, and that shit's not cheap." She shakes her head, a wistful smile pulling at her lips. "I don't know. I mean, I do okay working here for my dad, and if I asked him for it, he'd definitely help me out, but I want that move to be something me and Lee take care of. Lee makes decent money bartending at Ram's Head, but it'll take ten times longer if he doesn't supplement it with something else." She whips her head toward her father, her voice lowering to a whisper. "But what's really a *legitimate* reason to sell drugs?"

"None of their reasons are legit—no matter how either of us chooses to sugarcoat it—but like I said, it is what it is." I stand and shove my belongings into my satchel. "So what's the deal? Are we cool?"

Madeline rises with a smile. "Yeah. We're good, Amber. I *think* I get you."

"Nice. Not many people do," I say, fully aware that a small hole inside has been filled . . . even if it's just a little. "Thanks again for what you did. I owe you. I'll figure out some twisted, fun way to pay you back. Maybe Hailey's head on a platter?" I tap my chin, seriously pondering the idea. "You can showcase it next to the apple fritters."

She giggles, her brow drawn up. "You're scaring me again. You're good at this."

"I am." I laugh, turning toward the exit. "But you have nothing to fear. Just get the bakery section prepped."

I push open the door and hear her drop another giggle, this one holding a hint of genuine nervousness. I can't help but wonder if she thinks I'm serious. As I get into my car—destination: Ryder's place, buried deep in the 'hood—I can't help but wonder the same thing.

*   *   *

I'm pretty sure the crazed southwest Baltimore neighborhood of Edmondson Village can hear the loud pounding of my heart, which is currently trying to leap out of my chest. As I wait for Ryder to open his door, I've decided I'm being paranoid. I killed a blunt on the way over, so one must assume Mary Jane's driving some of my thoughts.

Before I can swallow the pasty saliva coating my dry mouth, the door swings open, revealing my darkest nightmare and wettest dream. As my breathing hitches, the normal sledge-like paradox I've become accustomed to hits me. My toes curl with want for Ryder that I know I shouldn't have. But I do. I do so much, it makes me feel dirty.

Hatred—rooted somewhere between wanting him and despising the fact that I do—simmers in my stomach. Its scorching flames lick across every organ in my body as I allow my gaze to drift over his shirtless chest. Starting at the right side of his neck, my eyes follow a devil's horns and body along the muscled curve of his shoulder, its spiked tail fading into Ryder's name, etched in intricate black tribal ink above his heart.

With the corner of his mouth curled up in that cocky *I'm an asshole* smirk he's known for, he scratches at his balls—which are hidden beneath a pair of navy blue basketball shorts—and rolls his head from side to side. "I'm a little busy right now, peach. I figured you might get bored with Brock, but the chick on my couch may not be down with me inviting you in." He kicks me a wink, his voice dropping to a whisper. "But I'll shoot you a text after I bring her home. We'll get our sex on then."

"You're a dick." My hand darts up to smack his cheek.

He catches my wrist before it can connect. My other hand automatically shoots up and experiences the same treatment from his free hand.

"Let go of me, Ryder!"

"Now *why* the fuck would I do that?" He pulls his bottom lip between his teeth, his smirk widening as his blue eyes flitter across my face. "Besides the fact that you're trying to smack me *again*, I'm kind of digging this. I bet you're a feisty little one in bed." He tugs on my wrists, my chest pressed to his as I attempt to breathe. "Mm. Yeah, I have no doubt you are. I'd gladly welcome *whatever* torture you see fit. But this smacking shit's getting played out, momma. At least while lube, lingerie, and sweat aren't involved. Let's switch it up a bit. Sound good?"

I push up on my tiptoes, my lips grazing his ear. "I thought you were never going to fuck with me again? There goes that willpower."

"A man has his limits," he whispers, his grip on my wrists tightening. "Apparently you *love* testing mine."

"I can't say that I don't. But I *can* say that if you don't let go of me, your balls are my next target." A smirk dusts my lips as his vanishes. "How's that for a switch up and a test?"

"Please don't hurt my brother," a meek voice says from behind Ryder.

Spine tightening, I step back, my nervous gaze landing on the crystal blue eyes of what I'm sure is an angel. Hairless head wrapped in a hot pink bandana, porcelain skin famished of color, and tiny lips quivering, she clutches a teddy bear as she offers me a dollar bill.

"Here." She stares up at me, her eyes glassed over. "Mommy paid me my allowance. I can give you this if you promise not to hurt him."

"I, uh," I stammer, my attention floating between her and Ryder.

Appearing marginally entertained, he crosses his arms and leans against the doorjamb, watching me sweat my way through this beyond-mortifying experience.

Sure I've slammed a dent into her childhood, I kneel in front of her, hoping to undo the damage. "I don't want your money, sweetie."

"Then you're going to *hurt* him?" A tear slips from her eye. "I lied. I have two dollars. I can give you those."

It's official. I'm the devil.

"I have candy too," she continues, her voice shaky. "Do you like candy? I can give you a Hershey bar *and* two dollars."

"I love Hershey bars." I shake my head, a slow smile lifting my mouth. "And I was *never* going to hurt your brother."

"But you said you were going to hurt his balls."

Yep. The devil. Open up the ground and toss me in with the fucker.

"Casey." Ryder rests his hand on her frail shoulder, sending her a quick look of reprimand. "Remember your words."

"But she *did*, Ryder. She talked about your balls."

"She was talking about my football," he corrects smoothly, a grin sliding across his lips as he kneels beside her. Eyes soft, he swipes a tear from her cheek and gives her nose a little pinch.

She giggles and pinches his nose right back.

"This is my friend Amber," he continues, "and though she hasn't played with it *yet*, she loves my football more than she's willing to admit." He looks at me, amusement dancing over his face. "Isn't that right?"

"*Yes, Ryder,*" I grit out with what I know he's aware is the fakest smile I can muster.

"You wanna know *why* Amber's here, Casey?" He looks at me, his amusement exploding by the second.

I narrow my eyes, convinced he's about to sink me.

He turns his attention back to his sister. "I think you'll really like it."

"Yes!" Casey squeaks. "Tell me!"

"Amber stopped by because she's having lunch with us, *and* she's hanging out with you, me, and SpongeBob *all . . . day . . . long.*"

Bouncing up and down, Casey claps. "She *is?*"

"I *am?*" I get to my feet, my need to put my fist through his balls growing. "I don't recall making these plans."

Ryder rises and pinches my nose. "Aww, peach, ya don't remember? Let me refresh that memory of yours. You called me last night and talked for *hours* about how excited you were to chill with me and Case here."

I look at Casey, and the genuine excitement in her eyes causes my heart to stir. I tentatively touch my knuckles to her cheek, and she smiles. Everything inside me screams that there's no way I can let this child down.

"Right." Smiling, I nod. "Now I remember."

"Yay!" Casey snatches my hand, her words racing from her mouth as she leads me into the apartment. "Do you like peanut butter and Fluff? Are you my brother's new girlfriend? Can you paint my nails?"

"Case, you're gonna scare the girl away." Ryder closes the door, a victorious smirk on his face. "Amber tends to . . . *flee* when put under pressure."

I shake my head, wondering how sick he really is. "You're out there," I whisper. "Like, mental hospital out there."

"Mm, see what you do to me?" He pinches my nose again, giving it a light shake. "You have me sinking to the lowest depths of morality."

"At least you're *aware* you're not beyond using an innocent child to get what you want."

"Only for you," he points out, wiggling his brows. "Consider yourself special."

I scoff, convinced he's delusional.

"How can I scare her?" Casey asks with a pout. "They're just questions, Ry. Mrs. Langley says to ask lots of them."

"Yeah, *Ry*." I make a mental note of her nickname for him, knowing I'll use it in the near future. "Just ignore your brother, Casey. He's not right in his head."

Casey giggles and drags me across the living room. My eyes skirt over a multistained Berber carpet hidden beneath an array of roughed-up garage-sale-find-looking furniture. A beat-up plaid couch sits against the far wall. Flanking it, a makeshift end table—made from a blue milk crate and round piece of glass—adds a hint of modern flair to the space.

Riiiggghhhttt . . . That took a ton of imagination.

I sink onto the throwback 1970s couch and take in several posters, every single one highlighting a barely clothed model on a Harley or classic car. I know it's a bachelor pad, but considering both Lee and Ryder make decent money pushing for Brock, I'm shocked they're living so far below their means.

"There's no way you're related to Martha Stewart," I quip, unable to keep the comment to myself. "Not even close."

"Who's Martha Stewart?" Casey asks, sidling up next to me.

"Someone your brother's in desperate need of."

Ryder chuckles and moves into his kitchen that, on its best day, could hold three people crammed shoulder to shoulder. He snags an apple from the counter and makes his way back over to us. After handing it to Casey, Ryder turns his blue eyes on me, a crooked grin breaking out across his face. "Nope. No relation. Now, are you ready for our date with SpongeBob?"

"As I'll ever be," I answer, matching his idiotic grin.

He plops down next to me and flips the television to what I assume is the appropriate station. A whacked-out sailor pelts out a tune, and Casey squeaks in excitement, my presence old news as she hones in on a sponge with eyes and his sidekick starfish.

Ryder nudges my arm.

My breath catches the second my gaze connects with his.

"So, ya plan on telling me why you felt the need to slap me again?" A curious smile crosses his lips, his voice a whisper. "Or are you gonna make me hold you down in a compromising position to get the info from you?"

I stare into his eyes, hating the way my body responds to his slightest touch. Especially when I'm supposed to be mad. It's the universe's way of laughing at me. "You like talking shit to Hailey about my life, *Ry*?"

His brows pull together. "What do you mean?"

"I ran into her today, and she knows everything about what happened to me. Very few people know the full story, and now Hailey's one of them." I pause, trying to gauge his reaction. His face is peppered in confusion. "Was I a topic of conversation after you finished bagging her? Huh, Ry? Did it piss you off that much that I picked Brock instead of you?"

He stays quiet for a moment, confirming what I already knew. The dick told her. I rise—ready to bounce the hell out of here—but he catches my elbow and pulls me down onto his lap.

Casey jerks her head in our direction, nervousness all over her face.

"We're just playing, Casey." Ryder winds his arms around my waist. "Right, Amber?"

"Yep." I give her a reassuring smile. "We're about to deflate your brother's football. He'll *never* be able to use it again."

Tough guy clamps his knees together, and Casey shrugs, the

sponge once again snagging her attention as I try to jack my arms out of the bear hug Ryder has them in.

"Let me up," I whisper heatedly. With my back pressed to his bare chest, I can't see his face, but I hear him chuckle. "You're an asshole. Seriously. I know you know this too."

He touches his lips to my ear, his voice a low sexual taunt. "Come on, momma. Do you honestly think I said something to Hailey? You know me better than that."

"*Do I?*" I attempt to wiggle from his hold. I'd have better luck trying to pry myself away from a hungry anaconda. "I'm not so sure anymore. You're the only one . . . *playing* with her—"

"*Was* playing with her," he corrects, all but tossing me back onto the couch.

My eyes go wide, Madeline's claim officially confirmed as my mouth falls open.

"If you try to get up again, you'll leave me no choice *but* to hold you down in a compromising position." He leans in, his nose inches from mine. "But I won't bring you any form of pleasure when I do. No. Instead, I'll tickle the *fuck* out of you," he whispers, grinning. "I have a killer memory. You're *going* to hear me out. Understood?"

I take a second to regain my bearings. Once fully composed, I lift my hand and smash my palm against his forehead, moving him to a safe "unheated" distance.

It's *his* eyes that are wide now.

"You have two minutes to talk your way out of this. You've already killed what little high I had left, and you seriously don't want to see me pissed off."

He lifts an incredulous brow. "I *haven't* witnessed this yet? Impossible."

"Not even close."

"Mm. Interesting and quite . . . tempting." A lazy grin hits his face as he cups his chin, wicked thoughts swirling behind those baby blues.

I glance at the digital clock on the DVD player. "You now have a minute and forty-five seconds, Ashcroft. I'd use the time wisely if I were you." I cock my head to the side. "I'm happy my situation with Hailey's brought you your daily dose of entertainment. It's good to know my past can amuse *someone*."

He stares at me and rests his elbow on the arm of the couch, his expression melting into regret. "I didn't tell Hailey anything, Amber. She overheard me and Brock talking about it."

"*What?*" My heart thumps with anger. I'm about to swing solo, getting rid of Brock faster than an unwelcome Jehovah's Witness. "You guys talked about me *in front* of her?"

"You're not listening. She *overheard* us."

With my patience wearing thin—but aware there's a child in the room—I dig my nails into my palms, trying to keep my cool. "You have one minute to elaborate before I *seriously* lose it. If you don't, I *will* crush your football."

Ryder blinks, the look on his face showing that he knows I'm not kidding. "He stopped by a few weeks ago and told me your foster parents are coming to visit you again in a few months. Since shit went south the last time they came in, he wants to do something special for you and them when they're here. Something special without involving his parents. One thing led to another, and yeah, we got into the shit that's happened with you." He drags a hand through his hair. "I thought Hailey was asleep, but she wasn't. We both warned her not to say anything, but apparently she did."

I shake my head, wishing Brock would've at least told me the skank found out. Not that that could've prepared me—I'm not sure anything could aid in that department—but it wouldn't have felt like such a crippling invasion.

Ryder slips a finger under my chin, bringing my eyes to his. "You okay?"

I jerk my head away. "Yeah. I'm fine."

"You're not bulletproof, peach. Stop trying to act like you are."

"I'm not *trying* to act like anything," I scoff, uncomfortable with the direction he's taking the conversation. I want to unzip my skin and peel it from my body.

He studies me for a moment, his gaze sweeping over my face. "Pain—in the form of grieving—is healthy, Amber."

"Oh my God, are you *seriously* going there? You're cute and all, but even a dude like you can lose his swoon factor. Fast."

"I possess swoon factor?" A small grin graces his lips as he leans closer. "Is that a girl term?"

I swallow, my head fuzzy from his close proximity, the dizzying smell of his musky cologne and the gray specks in his eyes unfurling my sanity as I back away. "Yeah. It's a girl thing, and again, if you go there, it can lose its potency."

He flicks his attention to my lips, a soft chuckle tumbling from his mouth. "Mm. Well, you, Amber Moretti, make me wanna risk losing my swoon factor." He sobers, his eyes finding mine. "And if you remember *anything* I ever tell you—no matter what—make sure it's what I'm about to say. A kick-ass old man let me in on it before he died." He pauses and taps my nose, his breath soft against my cheeks as he inches closer. "Our past is what shapes us, the scars it leaves behind mold us, and what we do with the shit that's left over is what defines us. Don't let your parents' conflicts define who you are, peach. You're better than that. You deserve more than you're willing to let yourself experience. More than what you think you're . . . worth."

His words, the sincerity behind them, and the way he said them— like he couldn't grab his next breath if he didn't—rain over me, a mist of warmth flooding my heart. Shock stills my tongue, tiny fragments of how to respond jumbled in my head as I stare into his eyes.

As though he knows he's left me speechless, Ryder rises and looks down at me, understanding coloring his features before he strolls into the kitchen. "You girls ready for the world's greatest peanut butter and

Fluff sandwiches?" he calls from over his shoulder. "They'll only cost you a game of Hedbanz."

"I am!" Casey hops to her feet. "Amber, do you like Hedbanz?"

"I do." I smile and traipse into the kitchen, curiosity thick with every step. I sidle up next to Ryder, jerking my hip against his. "But how come I have a feeling they're not the kind I think they are?"

"*Duh*"—Ryder pulls a jar of Fluff from the cabinet—"of course they're not. I'm a shit-ton cooler than that." Like a true connoisseur, he whips together several peanut butter and Fluff sandwiches, piles them on a plate, and plucks a gallon of milk from the refrigerator. Grinning, he juts his chin toward the living room floor. "Go sit, and prepare to get that pretty little ass thoroughly kicked. I'm king at this game."

I snort. "I learn fast, and I'm *extremely* competitive. I have no doubt I'm about to embarrass you in front of your sister."

"You think?" He swipes a stack of paper cups from the counter and hands them to me, his *I'm an asshole* smirk encompassing his face. "Those are some serious fightin' words. You sure you wanna go there?"

"I'm already there," I clip, making my way back into the living room.

"Oh, it's on."

As I get comfortable on the carpet, Casey goes into a detailed explanation about how Hedbanz is played. Considering it includes actual headbands—with little picture cards attached to them that only the other players can see—I can't help but laugh. I figured it would take several shots of tequila and some homegrown vipe to get Ryder to sport anything so girly. Clearly his love for his little sister has no limits. He may not know it, but that alone catapults his swoon factor off the charts.

Splayed out on his stomach, headband with a picture of a bicycle clipped to it in its proper place, Ryder asks, "Can you . . . *ride* any part of me?"

"Yes," Casey and I answer in unison.

The nympho side of my brain cartwheels over thoughts they shouldn't touch in the midst of a child's game. Ryder sends me a wink, and I'm sure I know where he's going to take every single question.

"Do I make noises?" Casey inquires, her expression bright with curiosity.

Ryder tickles her ribs. "Yup. You snore like a man."

She giggles and looks at me.

"Oh, yes." I take in the colorful parrot on her head. "You're definitely something that makes noise." She nods, and I glance at Ryder, ready to twirl his head like a baton. "Am I something you would enjoy . . . *licking?*"

Ryder clears his throat, nearly choking on a sip of milk. I lean back and rest my palms on the carpet, laughing as I watch his pupils turn the size of teacups.

"No," Casey answers with a frown.

"I'd beg to differ," Ryder retorts, a smirk curling his mouth. "I would lick that *all . . . day . . . long.*"

My crossed legs clench of their own accord, my ears humming from the predatory tone in his voice as he continues to stare at me. At this point, I'm not sure whose head I've twirled more.

Casey nudges him, her nose pinched in disgust. "Eeewww, Ryder. That would taste nasty."

He smacks his lips together, his gaze undressing me. "*Nothing* about that would taste nasty, Case. To tell ya the truth, kid, I'd lick every bit—"

"We're getting off track here!" I blurt, my voice cracking like an angry bolt of lightning. Heated, I swipe my hands through my hair, fully aware I've one hundred percent screwed myself. "It's your turn, Ryder. Play. Nice."

Grinning, Ryder crams a piece of his sandwich into his mouth. "Mm. Play nice . . . play nice. Let's see." The look in his eyes tells me he's about to play anything *but* nice. "So I'm something you can *ride*, correct?"

"Yes," Casey answers with a nod, finishing up the last bite of her sandwich.

With his attention locked on my face, dragging his teeth across his bottom lip, Ryder rolls onto his side. "Am I something you'd ride *hard*, fast, and reckless, then easily walk away from the next morning? Or would you experience . . . *sickening* . . . *mind-numbing* . . . *unable*-to-stop-yourself-from-coming-back-for-more insanity by riding me soft and slow, relishing my building for *everything* it's worth on a daily basis?"

"Huh?" Casey asks, appearing completely confused.

I swallow, the effort close to impossible as I come to the realization that both Ryder and I have two very twisted character traits in common.

The first: We're grown adults who are *most* likely messing with the psyche of an eight-year-old child—I'm sure a professional could back up that observation. I'm also pretty sure they'd find that here and now, neither of us would be disturbed by this assessment.

The second: I know that, if given the opportunity, we'd rip our clothes off and fuck until there was no more sexual hostility left in either of us.

"You're a bicycle!" I exclaim breathlessly, ripping off my headband. I get to my feet, aware I've officially lost my goddamn mind, my head cracking like an egg against a sizzling frying pan. "You can be ridden hard, fast, soft, or slow. Either way, no matter how one would *choose* to ride you, I'm sure your building would bring them copious amounts of mind-numbing pleasure. Happy?"

Ryder lifts a single dark brow. "In more ways than you could *ever* imagine, especially since you can dish it but can't handle when it's tossed back at ya." He rises, a triumphant smile cushioning his lips as he yanks off his headband. "And you were a snail, by the way."

I blink, wondering how the hell I went from wanting to kill him, to playing a board game with him, right down to mind-raping him in the span of thirty minutes.

"Cheaters!" Casey jumps up, beaming. "I win! What's my prize, Ryder?"

"You, my beautiful sister, win a visit to Toys-R-Us."

Casey squeals in delight and runs across the room to grab her sneaks.

Ryder plucks a T-shirt from the top of a subwoofer, a smirk reaching his eyes. "You ready, peach?"

"I can't." I feel disturbingly bereft as he tosses the T-shirt over his head and shoves on a pair of Vans. "I have to study."

"*Surely* you're not gonna miss out on her going toy shopping, are you?"

"Uh-uh, Ashcroft, you're not using her again to make me feel guilty," I whisper, firm on not letting him win. "I'm sorry, guys, but I have some things I have to finish."

"*Please*, Amber?" Casey begs, her face turning all kinds of desperate. "You can help me pick out a new Barbie."

"Looks like I don't have to make ya feel guilty." Ryder ducks his head to conceal his smirk-gone-wild as he undoubtedly notices my willpower blow to shit.

"I do love me some Barbie," I concede with a smile, knowing that's a complete lie. Since I never owned one—well, one that wasn't a disheveled hand-me-down that closely resembled our neighborhood hooker—I grew to hate the very fact that the bitch was ever invented. Hate or not, the joy in Casey's eyes has me temporarily abandoning both studying and my childhood issues. "Let's go make your brother spend insane amounts of money on some Barbies."

Casey wraps her arms around my waist, buries her cheek against my stomach, and gives me a hug, a small sigh of contentment pushing from her mouth as she squeezes me tighter. I freeze, my mind locking up against her affection. Against what's supposed to come naturally to a child. Love, trust, and security are pure emotions, a child's God-given right before adulthood swallows them up into a stomach churning with nothing but evil shit. Once we get to a certain age, the devil is around every corner we turn, silently waiting to make us a part of his exclusive club.

For me—at Casey's age—he was hiding under my bed, stripping me bare of feeling any of the emotions I was entitled to.

I catch Ryder watching us, his expression a mixture of pain and understanding. On a shaky breath, I rest my palms on either side of Casey's head, tilting her tiny face up to mine. She smiles, and so do I, my heart falling in what I'm sure is the closest thing to love.

"Casey," Ryder says, struggle thickening his voice. "You have to take your medicine before we leave, kiddo."

Still staring into my eyes, Casey nods and crooks her finger at me.

I hunch over, my face inches from hers as she cups my jaw and whispers, "I like you, and I think my brother does too," she singsongs, but sobers quickly, fear dotting her innocent features. "Do you ever have to take medicine?"

"Sometimes," I answer, feigning a calming tone. Unease coats my stomach as I touch her cheek, hoping to settle her some. "Your brother told me you're the best medicine-taker in the whole wide world."

"He *did?*" she questions, her smile resurfacing.

"Yes, he did. Are you gonna show me how good you take it?"

She nods and reaches for my hand, leading me toward the kitchen. My own fear blisters along my skin as she hops up onto the kitchen table and snaps open the top two buttons of her blouse, exposing a small portion of her chest just below her collarbone.

Casey points at a paper-thin scar on her chest, the delicate skin slightly raised as though a small stack of quarters is beneath it. "This is called a port. There's tubes under here that helps the medicine go into my body. The doctor said this was the best thing so I don't always have to get stuck with needles in my arms."

I drop into a chair next to her, completely disturbed that she knows any of this. My pulse ping-pongs as Ryder pulls a medical kit from the cabinet, sets it on the table, and opens it, a calming smile on his face with each movement he makes.

"That's a tropical antisep—" Casey's nose scrunches in confusion. "How do I say that, Ry?"

Ryder grins, popping a soft kiss onto her forehead. "Topical anesthetic."

Casey tries the word again, failing to pronounce it correctly. She giggles. "Whatever that is, it helps numb my skin so when Ryder puts the needle in my chest, it doesn't hurt as much."

As much . . .

My breath snags. Her statement—the bravery in her tone—seeps dawning through my gut.

Though death stared me in the face when I was Casey's age, it wasn't aimed at me. I spent my days alone while my parents slept, and my nights as equally alone and scared while they ran around town doing whatever they had to do to get their next fix. Concerned neighbors eventually called the authorities. I think the day they died was the morning they were supposed to go to court to prove they were fit enough to take care of me, because it was the first time I'd seen my father in a suit and tie.

I remember staring at him, not sure who he was. His hair wasn't a mess, and his eyes didn't look tired. I remember smiling at him. He smiled back and walked into his bedroom. For a minute I felt calm, like maybe things were about to change for the better. That *they* were about to change. I swallow, knowing I couldn't have been more wrong. He came out of the bedroom, his eyes soulless, empty, and cold. He shook when he told me he loved me. It was then I felt confused. He'd never once said those words to me. Come to think about it, neither did my mother.

Ever.

Numbness rolls through me as I think of our final moments together. The exact moment my father told my mother he was sorry for fucking all of us up. The exact moment he cried, telling her he'd love her forever. The exact second the first bullet rang through the air, followed by the bloodcurdling sound of my mother gasping for a full breath as she looked at me one last time. I saw the demented hollowness in my father's eyes before he shoved the gun into his mouth, blowing his brain straight out the back of his head. In the middle of our living room, where I used to watch cartoons before school, my father's six-foot-two, husky frame landed on top of my mother's tiny body, crushing it.

A thud . . .

My screams

And then nothing . . . nothing but deafening silence.

The memory splinters my soul, but before I know it, it's gone. The splash of running water snaps me back into the present, my past evaporating into the casket of my heart.

"What are you, Casey?" Ryder asks over his shoulder as he scrubs his hands with antibacterial soap.

"Your little cancer warrior," she answers with a small smile.

"That's right." He dries his hands and turns, a proud grin cracking his mouth. "The bravest one ever."

I grab Casey's hand and hold it tight, knowing nothing I've ever seen, heard, or felt compares to what she's facing. This child's living with a fear I can't comprehend. One that'd slay all of my fears put together.

"Ready?" Ryder asks, his tone soft and caring, everything it should be.

Casey nods, clenching my hand. My heart swells, anxiety building thick in my throat as Ryder slips on a pair of medical gloves and cleans the area around her port with Betadine swabs.

Casey looks at me, the cool blue of her eyes misting over. "Are you scared of needles?"

"No," I say, running my free hand along the back of her neck. "Are you?"

"I used to be." She sighs, a single tear slipping down her face. "But not so much anymore."

It takes everything in me not to drag her little body off the table and run out of the apartment with her. I wipe the tear from her cheek, my need to hide her away, sheltering her from the sinister storm she's in the middle of, growing with each unsteady breath.

"A little cold," Ryder warns before spraying the anesthetic on her skin.

"Hurry, Ry," Casey pleads, her voice weak yet panicked. "It doesn't last that long."

"I have to make sure you're numb, Case." Ryder ducks his head and stares into her eyes, trying to keep her focused on the silly faces he's making. His tactic works.

Casey's tiny giggles bounce around the kitchen, their musical notes blocking out the sound of Ryder popping the cap off a weird-looking needle. With a small, clear tube like a tail—and plastic wings stretched out on either side—it reminds me of a dragonfly. Ryder presses his gloved finger against Casey's port a few times, his attention honed in on her face as he says, "Knock, knock."

"Who's there?" Casey smiles at me, completely unaware that Ryder's pricked her skin with the needle.

"Aardvark." Ryder pushes the medicine through the syringe, his attention cutting between Casey's face and the needle.

"Aardvark who?" she manages, a thin sheen of sweat dotting her upper lip.

"Aardvark a hundred miles for one of your pretty smiles." Ryder pulls the needle from her chest, and before she can blink, he rests his lips against her forehead, kissing away her remaining fear.

Close to immobile, my heart tugs, the magnitude of what this man means to this little girl—what they mean to *each other*—scraping tears up my dry throat. I swallow the sound before it can leave me, warmth pinching my stomach into a beautiful knot as I observe them.

"It's over?" Casey asks, uncertainty flashing in her eyes.

"Yeah, kiddo. It's over," Ryder answers, his voice heavy with relief as he applies a small piece of gauze over her port. "You're all set, warrior. Go get cleaned up, and we'll get ready to leave."

With Ryder's aid, Casey slides off the table and heads for the bathroom, the bounce in her step less tangible as she slips around the corner. Quiet reigns, the events from the last few minutes whispering across my mind as Ryder looks at me with exhausted eyes. Stress lines cut across his forehead, wariness drowning his beautiful features. Overcome, I watch him swipe a tired hand over his face and turn, resting his palms against the counter. As though having no control over my body—a magnet pulling in my gut—I stand and move toward him, each tentative step I take carried out with shallow, quick breaths. I come up behind him, lift a shaky hand and tap his shoulder, my pulse lurching as he turns and meets my gaze. Our connection strikes, a bolt of emotions paralyzing us as we stare at each other.

I touch my fingers to his stubbled cheek, my conscience crying out that my actions are wrong, so very wrong, but my heart mutes the warning as I move my palm to the back of his neck.

His muscles go taut, restraint lighting the fiery blue of his eyes. "Amber, don't." The words come out not as a rough warning but a soft plea. "Don't do this."

"I have to," I whisper, trembling. "You're ... amazing, Ryder. What you did for her, everything you *do* for her ... I just ..." I drop my eyes to his chest, my heart galloping as I register his hands gripping my waist. Their heat sears through me, a thrill jumping from cell to cell. "You're tender, cocky, gentle, and an asshole all at the same time. You're kind, giving, nurturing. You're ... everything."

My lips find his, testing, teasing, barely touching. Our breathing comes faster, harder as I pull him down, our foreheads pressed together as we stare into each other's eyes. "Please . . . I just . . . Just once more. That's all I need."

I think . . . hope.

With hunger demolishing all traces of restraint from his gaze, Ryder buries his hands in my wavy curls and looks at me a beat before capturing my lips in a slow, passionate kiss. I sigh into his mouth, my senses drowning in his familiar flavor as I fall in step with his calculated strokes. On a deep groan, he draws me closer, his tongue dipping in and out, out and in. Still, nothing about his touch is rough, yet everything in it screams that he needs me in this moment.

In this wicked space and time of his life.

Every lick and nip is a soft caress, like he's trying to burn the sensation of my lips into his memory. My pulse hammers in staccato mode as I melt the full weight of my body into his. With my blood swimming through my veins, and sinking further into everything that *is* Ryder, I feel the emptiness of his soul slice through me. A dull ache pinches my heart, spreading its misery through my muscles as he cups my cheeks and deepens the kiss with a gentleness I never knew he possessed. My breath catches, wiped from my lungs as he glides his lips along my jaw, down the base of my throat. The cadence of his exotic growl slips through my ears, dizzying my head in the sweetest way.

"Christ, I fucking want you so bad," Ryder whispers hoarsely. He drags his lips back to mine, his kiss urgent, greedy. However, he brings it down a notch, his movements revisiting slow, sensual, worshipping this moment for everything it is. Worshipping *me* for all I am. "So badly, peach. More than I've ever wanted anything or anyone. You drive me crazy. Your smell, skin, eyes." He sucks my lip between his teeth, a groan punching from his chest as he runs his fingertips along my bare arms.

Goose bumps pop, deliciously pricking my skin as I tighten my grip in his hair.

"Your little giggles, pouts, personality. Every single fucked-up scar you own in and out. All of it. All of *you*." He licks into my mouth, his tongue exploring mine with precision as his hands find my nape, their hold possessive. "Fuck. It should've been me. Not him. Me."

And just like that, our moral compasses spring due north, Brock the center of its attention—*our* attention. We slowly break the kiss, our breathing choppy from the loss.

Gaze locked on Ryder's, I shake my head as I fight back tears. "I'm . . . I'm so sorry. I shouldn't have done that," I whisper nervously, shame, remorse, regret, and embarrassment sinking their razor-sharp fangs into my heart. I step back, but Ryder snags my elbow, gently pulling me into his chest. "No, Ryder."

"Don't 'no' me, Amber," he says, his soft voice bordering disciplinary as he sweeps a wayward piece of hair away from my cheek.

I stare into his eyes, their light blue intensity shocking my system, disrupting every mortified thought.

"No one's guiltier than the other here. We got caught up in everything. That's it. Don't get all fucked up on me." A lazy grin surfaces on his lips as he moves another piece of hair off my shoulder. "You're already fucked up enough. I know my kiss has those panties needing a thorough washin', but I don't need your last bit of sanity hanging on my conscience. It was the moment—that's all. You hear me?"

"Ryder," Casey croaks from behind us.

We both spin, the hairs on my neck awakening with fear that she might've witnessed what happened between us.

Ryder's face sparks with anxiety, but he masks it with a cool smile. "You ready, kiddo?" He crouches down next to her, touching his knuckles to her temple. "I just need to grab my keys, okay?"

She shakes her head, a frown dragging across her lips. "No. I don't feel good anymore. My tummy hurts, and I'm getting tired." She tangles her arms around his neck, resting her pale cheek against his shoulder. "I threw up in the bathroom. Can we just go tomorrow, please?"

I push my hands through my hair, my stomach bottoming out. While I was seducing her brother into kissing me, she was in the bathroom, puking. On nervous legs I move across the kitchen and kneel next to her, seconds away from losing my own lunch. Inwardly praying for her forgiveness, I place my hand on her back. She gives me a weak smile, her dusty blue eyes glassing over with unchecked tears.

"Yeah. Of course we can, Case," Ryder says, his voice grave as he lifts her into his arms. She wraps her tiny legs around his waist, her cheek still cushioned against his shoulder as he carries her down the hallway and into a bedroom. Deafening silence swirls around me as I slump onto the couch and squeeze my eyes shut, every ounce of my being convinced I'm the devil's spawn.

Seconds?

Minutes?

Hours?

Feeling detached from my body, I'm not sure how much time passes before Ryder emerges from the bedroom, quietly latching the door.

I stumble to my feet, guilt taking root in my stomach. "Is she okay?"

He nods, his face stressed all over again. "Yeah. She's all right. I should've known better than to expect her to go anywhere after her treatment."

"It's all my fault," I blurt, moving toward the front door. "If I didn't come by—"

"My sister would've never gotten to meet you." He pulls my hand off the knob.

I shake my head, sure I'm the last person she needed to be introduced to. "She wouldn't have thrown up."

"She still needed to take her meds," he counters softly. "Has nothing to do with you."

"You would've been in the bathroom when she got sick, Ryder."

"Not necessarily."

My brows knit together. "How so?"

"She gets embarrassed by it, and doesn't usually call for help. Most days none of us even knows she got sick. Again, nothing to do with you." He rests his forearm on the doorjamb, and with his mouth pulled into a grin, his gaze dares me to continue. "She seriously likes you, Amber. She talked about you until she fell asleep. Believe it or not, she's not a very trusting child, so that says a lot."

"Really?" A small smile forms across my lips.

"Yeah, really. She's digging you." He looks at me through his thick, dark lashes, his expression turning soft. "Nothing that's happened here today's your fault. None. Of. It."

I manage to pry my eyes from his. "You're just trying to make me feel better."

"That's quite possible," he says slowly. "But only because you're making me feel guilty would I attempt this."

Bringing my gaze back to his, I fall silent.

He chuckles, the full hearty sound resonating through the room. "You know I'm only kidding, peach. If you didn't drop by, we *still* would've played Hedbanz, and she would've beaten me like she always does. After she kicked my ass, I *still* would've played the coolest-brother-in-the-universe part and taken her to Toys-R-Us." His attention moves between my lips and eyes.

My body responds the only way it knows how, the only way it has from the second we met. A shudder rolls through me, my skin and thoughts instantly heated.

He clears his throat, his voice a whisper. "I can't say I would've wound up enjoying a kiss from a certain beautiful someone if she *didn't* stop by, though. It added . . . flavor to my day. But I've already explained to that beautiful someone that the both of us took part in that kiss, so we're equally guilty. All we can do from this point on is make sure it doesn't happen again."

I say nothing as I open the door, and step out into the afternoon sun. The late September heat slides down my skin and attaches to my every pore, disintegrating my breath as I turn, meeting Ryder's eyes. For a brief moment, I feel what he said can be achieved. As long as we don't put each other at risk for a slipup, there's no reason we can't remain what we are.

Whatever that is, I'm not sure.

However, as I get into my car—heart thundering in my ears and Ryder's predatory gaze locked on mine—I can't help but wonder if we're both delusional. Have we already fallen, toppled over like two defeated chess pieces, into a pit of emotions neither of us can drag ourselves out of?

I drive away not knowing the answer.

CHAPTER 10

Amber

"THE SOUND OF your clock's annoying," I say to my therapist. "*Really* annoying."

Martin swings his attention to the clock on his desk and jots down the time on his nifty yellow notepad, keeping track of how many dull minutes he has left with me. Each and every "brain picker"—including this one—couldn't give a shit about my problems. But as long as they're getting paid, they'll act like they care for a whopping hour.

Hence the reason I'm in school for psychology. Besides being able to help my screwed-up patients, I swear there won't be a single fucking clock in my office.

"You're trying to change the subject, Amber." Martin's chocolate-brown eyes assess me. "Are you going to make this a habit every time you come to see me?"

With a jittery knee, I stare over his shoulder at the flower-patterned wallpaper. "Depends on what kind of mood I'm in."

"Well, in that case, I take that as a yes. That's what you do every time you're here."

I flick my eyes in his direction, hoping the way I've narrowed them tells him I'm not impressed. Not even close.

"I spoke with Cathy this morning," he continues. "She's really hoping to see some progress with you."

"Ah, the guilt card. Nice touch, Marty."

"Amber . . ." He sighs heavily. "This is our ninth session. You've barely spoken about what happened. I need you to elaborate a little more. Your foster parents want me to help you. I can't do that without your participation."

I drop my gaze and stare at my chipped blue nail polish. I try to think about Cathy's heartfelt talks about how therapy's the key to me releasing the demons possessing my life. Her pleading face flashes in my head, causing my stomach to curl over in guilt. I don't want to let Cathy down. She and Mark have been so good to me, trying everything in their power to help me get better. Still, in an instant, everything goes to shit in my brain, anger playing a wicked game of Russian roulette with the ghosts of my past.

I pull in a deep breath and drag my gaze back to him. "Can I talk about something else instead?"

He nods and rests his ankle over the knee of his navy dress pants. "We can discuss whatever's on your mind."

"I cheated on my boyfriend," I admit, waiting for the judgmental *of course you did, you're a whore* look. He stays neutral. I continue. "It happened over a month ago, but it's been bothering me ever since."

"Why does it bother you?" he asks, scribbling some shit onto his notepad.

"Not sure, Marty. Maybe it's because I have a *conscience?*" I roll my eyes. "Maybe it's because my father used to bang his groupies? Maybe it's because it's a Tuesday? Whatever the case, cheating's not cool. I rank it right up there with attempted murder."

"Attempted *murder?*" His dark brows slash hell-bound. "That's a heavy comparison, wouldn't you agree?"

I shrug. "Not really."

"And why is that?"

"Because you're playing with someone's mental state. Your actions can ruin their life, murdering their trust in anything real. Your indiscretions might as well be a hand wrapped around their throats, squeezing the air from their lungs. You can kill someone's faith in what love is supposed to be." I shrug again, feeling no different from Charles Manson for what I did to Brock. "Murder. Just a tamer definition of the word."

He looks me over, drumming his fingers against his notepad. "You mentioned your father participating in extramarital activities. Do you think your take on cheating has something to do with that?"

I retreat into my past, trying to figure out the answer to his question. Against both of their parents' wishes, my parents eloped when they found out my mother was pregnant with me. She'd just turned seventeen. I think my dad was twenty-one. Both sides of my family wrote them off after that. I've never met any of them, only heard stories about how cruel and distant they were after my parents left Arizona. My father landed a gig as a lead guitarist and followed the band out to Washington State, where they played at local bars. From what I remember, things were good for a while.

A bittersweet day spent in the park dots my memory as Marty waits for me to answer.

A picnic under a tree.

Smiles.

The bright sun and our laughter.

Youth and naïveté at its finest.

Such is life. It slowly sneaks up, fucking you from behind when you least expect it.

Add in a hungry kid who needed clothing, a broken-down car, not-so-steady work, and a wife struggling with depression—voilà, my father started getting high. He also began sleeping with any groupie who paid him a rat's worth of attention since my mother wasn't. Or couldn't. Either way, after Mom found out he'd knocked up one of the chicks, she started jabbing needles of heroin into her arm right alongside the love of her life.

I sigh, wondering where my half brother is at this very moment. If we look alike. If his life is as messed up as mine.

"It's possible," I answer, trying to unfuse my past from my head. "She got tripped up after he did that to her. I hated seeing her sad. It made me sad and apparently it's stuck somewhere in my brain. But it was her fault. She was young and trusted him too much. She should've known better. Supposedly my father was a player from the start. But she had her ways of getting back at him. He just didn't know about them."

Marty taps his pen against his cheek. "Do you think your father's infidelity has anything to do with why *you* don't trust?"

"I don't *trust* because they were in love and he wound up *killing* her." The words are uttered slow and harsh. He knows the answer to his ridiculous question. "*That's* why I don't trust."

Can't trust.

Refuse to trust.

If falling in love can turn into a bullet in your skull, what's the point of giving your heart away? Yet how do you stop your heart from reacting to what it needs?

You can't.

The organ has a mind of its own, disregarding what might be unhealthy for you. Once it's been jolted by that spark, awakened by that all-consuming flame, it plays the dirtiest game of all. With each curious beat of wanting to touch, taste, and feel love, the heart routes all logical thoughts from your brain, siphoning them out of that sucker like a thief, spitting them back out onto a highway piled high with nothing but bloody wreckage.

Causing mass destruction to our mental well-being since the beginning of time, our hearts are public enemy numero uno.

"I think you need to tap deeper into the morning he killed her, Amber." Marty ducks his head, his cantaloupe-sized bald spot aimed in my direction as he flips through some pages of his notepad. He lifts his eyes, the look in them cynical. "The writing therapy is good, but you need to elaborate so we can come up with a solid plan for your recovery."

"What's there to elaborate on? My parents were drug addicts, and my father was a psycho who decided to check himself and my mother out right in front of me. Do I want your help? Possibly. But nothing you can say or do can truly help me. Only *I* can help myself. You overanalyzing my feelings and slight bipolar tendencies can't change anything. My parents will remain dead, and I'll continue to suffer from PTSD. I've found ways to cope with it. I'm simply coming here because I actually like Cathy and Mark, and it makes them feel better knowing I'm keeping up with my therapy visits." I lift my shoulder in an unaffected shrug, though I'm anything but. "I'm not ready to talk about that day with anyone yet. I'm not sure if I'll ever be. Just write my script for my feel-better pills, and for now, let me continue to write in my journal."

I watch my hired mental help shake his head in what appears to be defeat as his timer goes off, relieving me from having to *elaborate*.

Score.

I hop to my feet, sling my black leather satchel over my shoulder, and head for the door.

"Amber," he calls as my hand connects with the knob, "we're eventually going to make progress."

I release a puff of air. "See ya next week, Marty."

I exit his stuffy office, my attention landing on the most yet least complicated part of my life. A part I'm falling for, but sure I'm going to hurt. A part I'm trying to understand, but fear I never will. Lips parted in a sexy smile, and deep green eyes pinned on mine, the reason I'm starting to wake up in the morning, starting to breathe with relief, rises from a chair in the waiting room.

I instantly feel calm, the tension in my shoulders deflating like a balloon.

"So?" Brock grabs my hand, swallowing it in his own. "How'd it go?"

"How do you think it went?" We step out into the crisp air that only October on the East Coast can bring. The smell of fall entices my nose, a network of bright yellow, deep red, and fiery orange leaves fascinating my vision as I climb into Brock's Hummer. "How did your wait go?"

Brock lets free a heavy sigh. "Amber."

"*Brock.*" A smart-ass smirk lifts the corner of my mouth. A tug on the door, a shake of his head, and a dimpled smile later and he's seated next to me. That smile does me in, my heart thump-thump-thumping the way it did the first time I saw him. A second after that, my lips are pressed against his cheek, my hands buried in his wavy, dirty-blond hair as he backs out of the parking lot.

"Get your seat belt on." The smooth, deep timbre in his voice causes my thighs to tighten. Despite my best flirty pout, he narrows his eyes as he attempts to navigate the cobblestoned streets of downtown Annapolis. Despite *his* best efforts, I can tell I've turned him on.

"You're hard as a rock," I tease, settling back into my seat. "Admit it. I get you every time."

He tosses me a shit-eating grin. "The only thing I'll admit is that I'm gonna enjoy sexually torturing you once I get you back to my place if you *don't* get your belt on."

"Demanding," I purr, pulling the stupid belt over my waist. "And kinky. I like."

"Safe," he counters, "*and* kinky. You can't deny I satisfy your wild side. It's a given."

A snort escapes my throat. "Wow. *And* as overconfident as ever."

His mouth lifts into a cocky smile, but it vanishes. "You didn't *talk* to the therapist, did you?"

I bite my lip, knowing where he's headed. "I talked, just not about what he wanted me to." I look down at my pink hoodie, toying with the hem. "I'm not ready to yet."

"You need to talk to him, Amber."

"Please don't start with me." I lean my head against the window. "You're talking in that 'fatherly' tone, and it makes me feel like you're putting me under a microscope."

He rests his hand on the back of my neck, caressing my hair. "I'm not trying to start with you, Ber. I love that you write in a journal. I find it beyond sexy, and have many times told you that you can write your thoughts out across my naked body if it helps you, but you need to open up to him. It'll only help you that much more. I wanna see you happy."

I bring my eyes back to his, a coy smile on my face. "I may just take you up on that offer one day, but seriously, I'm happy, Brock."

"You're *surface* happy." He glances at me, his voice soft. "Don't think I can't see through you. I love you, and I want every bit of you happy. Not just the outside."

My heart twists, stutters, then stops.

Twists.

Stutters.

Stops.

Palms sweaty, I register our vehicle coming to a standstill at a red light. I stare at Brock, and he searches my face, his eyes glazed over in a look I've never seen. I've seen them high, seen them filled with longing. I've even seen anger ignite them, but I've never witnessed them in their current state. They're different, deep, a pool of emotions collecting beneath their surface.

"What did you just say?" My voice comes out weak, thin.

"I love you, Ber," he whispers, his eyes still on mine.

He leans over the center console and cups my cheeks, his touch immediately sending fire crawling through my body. I suck in a deep breath, watching his gaze flitter across my face. It amazes me how something so simple can create a buzzing overload of sensation that wraps me tight, holding me prisoner in its warmth.

"I don't know how you did it, but you did," he says into my ear, his voice soft, sincere. "I know telling you this in the middle of rush hour traffic isn't cool or romantic, but I love you. I love you something fierce, and it scares the fuck out of me, but I couldn't keep it in any longer. I don't expect you to say it back, or even feel the same way about me, but I wasn't about to let another day go by without letting you know that I love you, Amber Moretti."

He presses his lips to mine, causing my stomach to sink and desire to pool between my legs. His words fade into the air, drop back down, and scatter along my skin, sinking into my once-empty heart. The kiss is as intense and mind-blowing as ever, his need for me evident in each slow, deliciously persistent lick. A car horn fires off, and Brock gives the aggravated driver the finger, but he doesn't stop kissing me. No. Instead he kisses me harder, deeper, pouring everything he's got into this one kiss.

Into this moment.

My body responds, wanting nothing more than to climb into his lap and take him right here. Mind in overdrive and confusion knotting my gut, I slowly pull back. Breathing as heavily as Brock, the absence of his lips leaves my core aching with need. His stare ushers a trail of chills over my flesh as I try to wrap my head around his declaration.

Do I tell him that I *think* I'm falling in love with him but am trying my hardest not to? That the mere thought of it makes me ill, wanting to possibly break things off with him, my fear of everything that love represents deadening my cells? Do I explain that at nineteen I'm not even sure if what I'm experiencing *is* love? Close to paralyzed, I go with what I think I need to say before revealing any of this.

The lie I need to wash myself clean of.

I hold my breath and release it, praying I don't destroy the heart of the only man who's ever felt a shred of anything for me.

"A few weeks ago—" I start, immediately second-guessing myself, my motives.

Who gains a thing by me confessing what happened between me and Ryder? More important, who loses something? I can kill a relationship that's barely had time to flourish into something solid, something good. I can abolish a friendship that's lasted years, bulldozing it into something resembling war.

Brock stares at me, his eyes patient. "A few weeks ago, what?"

My pulse thunders, creating a terrifying rhythm of its own, one I've never felt. Another car horn sounds, causing me to jump. My breath snags in my throat as I look over my shoulder at the pissed-off commuter. Shaking, I bring my gaze back to Brock's.

But this time when my eyes catch his, the endless sincerity in them tells me I'm fooling myself. This man stole a piece of my heart the day we met, and though I have no way to gauge the emotions spurring through me, the overpowering feeling that I can't imagine taking another breath without him in my life *must* be love.

The part that terrifies me the most, making me freeze over, is that my feelings for Ryder border on identical.

Who's toxic to whom now?

Worse . . . how's that even possible?

Though the forbidden thought has snuck into my diseased skull, I haven't had sex with Ryder. Surely I can't *love* him. Love's born of sharing your body with someone, the outer shell harboring the demons hidden beneath your hideous surface.

Right?

But if that theory were true, I'd have fallen in love more times than the average first grader can count. Numb, hollow, and broken, I've slipped from both seedy and rich beds smelling of meaningless sex without feeling like I was in love. Leaving every emotion tangled in those soiled sheets, I never looked back.

Is love built from human sentiment alone, the deadly feeling entrapping you in a series of shared moments between two vulnerable souls? Do slices of deep conversations, unspoken words, and stolen glances count? Do those small acts, tiny specks of laughter, unshed tears, and belly-dips grow the foreign feeling, morphing it into what can drive a person insane?

Not knowing if I'll ever understand the difference, I take a deep breath, my pulse thudding as I decide that what I feel for Brock merits attention. "I think I love you too, Brock," I finally whisper, sickened that I'm flying into this relationship on the evil wings of untruth. I'm dirty, the reality of what I am—what I stand for—unsettling me with each passing second.

Though he remains silent, Brock's expression is strewn with devastation. I'm clearly nothing but poison to him and Ryder.

I shake my head, feeling like I'm about to lose my lunch. "I've never been in love," I explain, my voice riddled with confusion. "I . . . I don't know what it's supposed to feel like. All I know is that my stomach twists, in a good way, when I think of you, of us. It also twists in a bad way when I think of never being near you again."

I place my hand on his jaw, hoping I can get him to understand the inner workings of my mind. He tenses, and I lean over to kiss his cheek, leaving my lips there as I continue.

"When we have sex, it's not just sex for me," I say. "I feel you everywhere. In my thoughts, my heart. I've never had that before. You might be fucking me, but you take your time with my body. That makes whatever I'm feeling for you that much stronger." I slowly pull back, watching the late afternoon sun slant through the window against his face. "I don't know what these feelings are, but I know they scare me too."

Brock pulls to the side of the street, his voice gentle as he slips his fingers through mine. "You wanna know something, baby girl?"

I nod, my breath hijacked by his mouth on mine.

"The things you just described *are* pieces of falling in love." He glides his tongue across the seam of my lips, coaxing them open.

Heat paints my cheeks, spreads through my muscles, and colors my heart as he kisses me deep, hard, making sure he steals what little breath I have left along the way.

"And as tiny as those pieces are, I'll take whatever I can. Just knowing you feel a fraction of what you said will keep me fighting for you. Fighting for every one of your thoughts." He kisses my forehead, his touch gentle as he drags his fingertips through my hair. "I want every single memory you own from today on to include me, and nothing will stop me from making sure they do."

Without words, I beg him to devour me in every way he knows how, in every way he ever has. He sees the unspoken urgency in my gaze and, remaining silent, he merges into traffic and drives toward his place. The promise of what I want, what I need, hangs on every breath he takes as the realization that I'm in love, that I'll never look at life the same way again, strips away the last bit of steel encasing my heart.

CHAPTER 11

Ryder

B<small>LITZED.</small>

That's my goal tonight.

Sitting at the bar in Ram's Head Tavern—a local joint in the heart of Annapolis—I throw back a shot of tequila, chasing after a hard buzz before Amber and Brock show up.

It's been a little over a month since I've tasted Amber's sweet lips, felt her soft body in my arms, and heard her lusty little whimper. But Christ if it hasn't felt like a fucking lifetime's passed.

"You ready for another?" Lee shouts from behind the bar, his voice pitching over the live band cranking out psychedelic soul music. "It looks like you can use a few more."

"Just put the whole bottle aside for me." I twirl an unlit cigarette in my hand, wanting to beat the fucking piss out of the dickheads who banned smoking in public places.

"Done." Lee reaches for a Sharpie and an unopened bottle of Patrón and scribbles my name on it. Shaking his head, he sets the bottle and another shot in front of me. "It's all yours, man. But seriously, you need to get the hell out of whatever funk you're in. Where's the Ryder I know?"

I glare at Lee, wishing he would shut the fuck up. If he doesn't, he's joining the infamous ram's head mounted above the fireplace.

"Come on, dude." Lee rests his elbows on the bar, letting loose a sigh as he pushes his glasses up the bridge of his nose. "I know you're balls deep in this shit with Amber, but it is what it is. Move on to the next, Ashcroft. There's nothing you can do about it."

The truth in his words rip through my gut. He *is* right. There's not a goddamn thing I can do about it. Still, as I kill my fifth shot—the burn sizzling my throat—I know the second that girl walks in the bar, any resolve I have about letting it all go is gonna vaporize. If I'd thought I felt an ounce of anything for her before watching her with Casey—the caring way she handled her—I was wrong. After that, I was done for. I wanted to hold her hostage, never letting her leave my apartment, let alone my life.

I gotta get the girl out of my head, but how the fuck do I let go of someone who I feel was made for me? All these months later, no matter how I've tried to fill the void—be it banging chicks I couldn't give a fuck about or drinking and getting high till I can't see straight—I'm still trying to figure that one out. Is someone who'll never be mine worth fighting for? I know what my head tells me:

Fuck. No.

It's the other part of my body—one that hasn't been alive in years—that tells me yes.

Yes, she is. Despite my friendship with Brock, Amber's worth a few rounds in the moral boxing ring.

Before I can think too much about holding her captive in my bed, possibly cuffed to the headboard, I glance toward the entrance. My shoulders tense when I see Amber, Brock, and Madeline waiting to get in.

Close to shitfaced, my body reacts, becoming alert as they navigate through the crush of patrons, heading right for me. My gaze locks on Amber's, and the fiery halo of yellow painting her eyes is almost too much for me to bear. Those angelic irises send me into my own personal purgatory, their heat breathing something words can't explain into the darkest parts of my fucked-up head.

It's showtime.

On cue, Lee drops another shot in front of me, and I chug it back, plastering a smile on my face as the trio approaches.

"You look like you're feeling pretty good." Brock claps his hand over my shoulder and pulls out a bar stool for Amber.

Clad in a black miniskirt, tight pink sweater, and black knee-high leather boots, she's the epitome of every man's dirtiest fantasy. Like candy to a starved tongue or a centerfold to eyes once blind, she throws most of the male population off their game, me included.

Amber sinks onto the stool next to me, a coy smile spreading her lips as she tips her chin up to Lee. "He *sure* does." She swings her eyes my way, her brow drawn up in challenge. "I'll take a double of what he's having. I feel like making Ashcroft look like a fool tonight."

Sweet Jesus. Grinning, I look at Brock. "Is she serious, or is she smoked out?"

Brock tosses his arm over Amber's shoulder. "She's smoked out a little something, but bro, the girl can drink. That's all I'm saying."

I chuckle, snatch up the bottle of Patrón, and throw another shot of the liquid down my throat as I attempt to kill visuals of her gorgeous legs wrapped around my head.

"You sure about that, Amber?" Lee hops onto the bar and lays a kiss on Madeline's lips. "Ashcroft's drinking tequila. Think you can handle it?"

Brock and Madeline bark out a laugh, looking at Lee as if he's lost his fucking mind. Amber remains quiet, a knowing smile on her lips.

"Baby?" Madeline curls her fingers around the collar of his work polo, pulling him in for another kiss. "Brock's not kidding. Didn't you know Amber's a fish out of water, existing only to inhale tequila?"

"Why, no. No, I didn't, babe." Lee slides off the bar and reaches for my bottle of Patrón, holding it up as though asking if it's okay.

I nod, looking forward to the outcome. I've witnessed Amber high, but I've yet to experience her drunk. After setting a Heineken in front of Brock and preparing Madeline her usual Cosmopolitan, Lee pours Amber two shots. A second passes, and she downs them both sailor-style. With an *I dare you to underestimate me* look in her eyes, she wipes her mouth with the back of her hand, not a shred of distaste hampering her features.

"*Damn.*" Lee laughs. "Maybe we *do* have some competition here tonight. This should be interesting."

Madeline knots her arms around Amber's stomach from behind. "Told ya. My girl's got this."

"You bet your ass I do." Amber beams, motioning to Lee for another. "Just give up now, buddy. I may be smaller than you, but you don't stand a chance."

"You *really* think you can outdrink me, peach?" I ask with an amused grin. "Before you answer, I want you to think about what you're saying. I'm a pro at many, many things, but I take drinking seriously. It's an art form. Kind of like huge buildings, it takes time to master the level I'm at."

"You and your building. Blah, blah, blah. I have no doubt in my ability to crush you," Amber replies, her face all kinds of cute with confidence.

"Ah, well, I must warn you, Moretti, my boys can attest to how intimate me and Lady Tequila can get. I make *love* to the bitch. That says something, since that's a rarity for me."

"Very true." Brock nods with a smirk. "Still, I've got a Ben Franklin on my girl taking you down."

Amber pecks Brock's cheek, and I instantly feel tension spark the length of my spine. Yup. I'm gonna need the whole fucking bottle to get through tonight.

"Again, *Ry*, prepare yourself for total annihilation." Amber nudges my ribs. "I'm about to embarrass your manhood right out of this bar. Wa-wa-wa."

"Those are some badass fighting words," Mike Reynolds— a seedy motherfucker Brock and I do business with—snickers from behind us.

Mike sidles up next to Amber, extending his hand. Amber takes it, and I clench my jaw, wanting to break the fucking bottle over his skull.

"Who's the sweet piece of ass challenging you, Ashcroft?" Mike licks his lips, his gaze sweeping up and down Amber's body. "I gotta know."

My jaw clenches again, this time coming close to cracking my teeth.

"*Excuse* me?" Amber drops Mike's hand. "Who the hell do you think you are, calling me a piece of ass when you don't even know me?"

"The sweet piece of ass is *my* girl." Brock stares Mike down, his eyes lit up like coals. "Amber, this is Mike, and you, *my* sweet piece of ass, aren't allowed to look in his direction when he's anywhere in the vicinity."

"Amen to that," Madeline huffs in disgust.

Mike shoots Madeline a look, a sneer working across his deep wrinkles as she gives him the finger. I'm positive Brock's keeping his composure for Amber's sake, but he won't take long to lose his cool with the dick if Mike gets out of line. High school dropout, divorced three times before the age of forty, and spawn spread out from one end of the country to the next, Mike's a walking septic tank. Human shit at its finest. Between slipping Ecstasy into chicks' drinks to get them into bed, to cutting clients' bags of coke with baby powder— which makes Brock look bad since he's the douche's supplier—to smacking around his most recent old lady, he's straight-up poison to the air.

Mike smirks, his yellow train-wreck teeth on display. "Come on, Cunningham. That was a little harsh, don't ya think, kid?"

Amber snorts and downs her third shot.

"I thought I was being pretty fucking nice," Brock deadpans, his voice eerily monotone.

Though Mike's oblivious to it, cocaine hindering any common sense the mutant has left, Brock's composure is wavering. Fast.

Brock takes a pull from his beer and jerks his head toward the back entrance. "Let's go take a walk, Mike. I wanna discuss a couple of things with you."

Mike glares at Brock then swings his attention back to Amber, the corner of his mouth pulled up. "Well, it was nice meeting you—Amber, was it?"

"Lee, can I get another?" Amber asks, ignoring Mike. "This sweet piece of *ass* isn't nearly as tanked as she needs to be."

"I see." Mike drags his thumb across his chin, his words a slow taunt. "I guess I'll catch ya some other time." Mike goes to turn around but halts, his neck craned in Amber's direction. "If Cunningham ever stops doing it for you, hit me up. I'm easy to find. A babe such as yourself needs a man, not a little boy."

I lunge at the asshole, but Brock beats me to it.

Right hand wrapped around Mike's throat, Brock throws a fast left elbow, the powerful blow connecting with Mike's jaw, shattering it to pieces. Mike's shit-brown eyes go wide, his whimpered groan an orgasm to my ears. Dazed, the dick blinks once, twice, then slithers to the wooden floors with a glorious thud, down for the motherfucking count.

"Brock!" Amber wails, shooting to her feet. She curls frantic fingers around his shoulders, her face arranged into a mess of panic and fear.

Brock knots the pussy's greasy hair in his fingers, dragging his body off the floor.

"Brock, don't!" Amber begs, her fingers white-knuckling his biceps. "You already knocked him out. That's enough, baby, please."

Ignoring Amber, Brock stares into Mike's semiconscious eyes. "You think you're a tough guy, you fucking waste of life? Huh, cocksucker? You like talking smack to my girl?"

Mike manages a grin and clams at Brock, the bloody string of saliva slipping down Brock's chin. "Fuck off, asshole." The words tumble out garbled, the strained effort comical considering his jaw's hanging off his face. "You're lucky I didn't *rape* her dirty cunt on the bar in front of you."

Seething, my fists clench and unclench at my sides as the need for his blood hurdles through my chest. But Brock and I never roll like that. Pussies take down assholes like Mike by teaming up. Not us. Unless one of us is in bad shape, really bad shape, it's an unwritten rule that neither of us steals the show from the other. The most amusing part about this whole thing is that the scumbag had a decent chance of walking out of here somewhat coherent. "Had" being the operative word.

My pal's about to fuck him up the ass.

Hands still gripped in Mike's hair, Brock casts a glance Amber's way, seemingly asking permission to continue. Such a gentleman.

Whiskey-colored eyes narrowed into slits—all traces of pity gone—Amber snatches Madeline's Cosmopolitan and pours it over Mike's head. Laughter explodes from a group of onlookers, most of them familiar with who Brock is. A buddy of ours, Kevin, who happens to be the lead bouncer, watches from afar. All six foot nine of him nods, telling me everything's cool.

Let the evening's entertainment commence, folks. Enjoy the motherfucking ride.

A smile splits Amber's glossy lips as the hot-pink liquid slides down Mike's face, onto his brown leather jacket, and soaks through his jeans. She takes a calculated step forward, looks him in the eyes, and spits onto his cheek. "Beat his ass to the ground, Cunningham."

Permission granted, Brock unleashes a string of blows against Mike's head and ribs, each one fucking up the cocksucker worse than its predecessor. Roars and drunken howls ignite the stagnant air, their amped-up pitches drowning out the band jamming away in the back corner.

I grab Amber's waist, pulling her a safe distance away from the growing frenzy. She doesn't resist but instead presses her back to my chest as I relax against the bar. She's tense—I feel it running through her muscles—but with Brock in our view, she plays the good-girlfriend role, allowing him to do his thing.

Though my attention should be on Brock and the plague-ridden asshole infecting the human race, it's not. Fuck, I can't help it. As lethal as I am to her, Amber's no less poisonous to me. She knots me up, twisting my emotions sideways. She drums up every inch of my head, testing my sanity and making me question everything I believe. Her soft, curvy frame, cushioned against mine, hijacks each of my senses.

My hands go to her hips, my fingers gripping her. I feel her jolt, but after a second, she relaxes back into me, a silent whisper from her body giving me permission. I touch my nose to her hair, the act so subtle she doesn't even realize I'm doing it, and inhale the sweet raspberry scent tangled in her long, ebony waves.

Silk. Goddamn fucking silk.

I envision her golden, catlike eyes staring up at me and those silken strands of heaven tickling my abs as her tongue maps its way farther south. My heart kicks against my ribs, speeding blood straight to my cock. I contain a groan, and my eyes flip into the back of my skull as I bite my lip, wishing I was biting hers. I clear my throat, pretty fucking sure *I'm* the plague-ridden asshole infecting the human race, not the douche taking the beating from Brock. I drag my attention back to my friend, knowing I'm right.

A second before Kevin and his sidekick break up the fight—if that's what I can call it—dickwad's barely holding on, so this is more like observing a hungry bear mauling a helpless kitten—Mike gets lucky and somehow connects a lame fist with Brock's mouth. Lame or not, it splits Brock's bottom lip, blood dribbling from it as Kevin grabs Brock by his shoulders and hauls him away from the piece of trash who's now a puddle of bloodied flesh. Moaning, groaning, and most likely regretting stepping foot into the bar, Mike attempts to move from his fetal position, but fails miserably as his body gives out.

Ah, an asshole with a big mouth and the captain of the football team fighting for his girl always makes for a memorable Friday night.

I need another drink ... *now.*

CHAPTER 12

Amber

W*HAT AM I doing!*

I push off Ryder as Brock approaches, everything inside me mourning the absence of Ryder's warmth. Blood dotting his bottom lip, and breathing heavily, Brock wraps a strong arm around my waist, pulling me into him. I nuzzle against his chest, a tangle of emotions twisting through my skull as I war with the filth I've become.

The filth I'll continue to decay into if I don't check myself.

The minute I became aware of my feelings for Ryder should've been the minute I stopped having them. From that second forward, I was conscious they were wrong, unhealthy. I'm not sure how many seconds have passed since that realization hit me. I just know there've been too many to count.

The man I've confessed my love to—the one who's shown me nothing but kindness—wasn't the only man invading my heart as he defended my filthy honor. Right down to my hollow bones, the diseased marrow in between, I disgust myself. Cheating, especially the mental kind—because when we desire something we shouldn't, the ravenous hunger for it consumes each fantasy playing through our immoral brains—can rot a relationship, sending its skeleton to the graveyard of "what should have been."

While Brock dug into the prick who'd disgraced me with his merciless tongue, my eyes might've been trained on my boyfriend, but my mind and all its sickening thoughts couldn't unfasten itself from his friend. Body betraying each unsteady breath I took, I watched Brock, yet my soul ached for Ryder.

As those panicky minutes unfurled, I felt safe in Ryder's arms, his presence soothing the nervousness cording my muscles. Like the whore I was bred to become—the whore I *am*—I let him touch me. Sure, some might consider the act innocent, juvenile at best. Hands on hips will *never* go down in history as being taboo. Well, not in my book.

But the unspoken emotion behind the caress was present, heavy, suffocating.

The deliverer and recipient just didn't . . . care.

I've come to one terrifying conclusion: I'm no better than my father was. I'm dark, weak, broken, and bruised. The only difference is I'm the rightful owner of a pussy, and I'm not aiming a gun at someone I love.

At least not yet.

The band's sharp drums reverberate through my ears as my attention crashes back to the commotion around us. I suck in a shaky breath, watching a bouncer drag my offender to his sloppy feet. A raw groan spills from the asshole's mangled mouth as he attempts to stand, his hand darting to his ribs. Another groan greases the air, this one feral as he cranks his free hand through his dark, unkempt shoulder-length hair.

His face is a fractured mess of swollenness, blood-tinged saliva swinging from his bottom lip before he sloshes it to the floor in a pissed-off hurl. Before I can blink, his demeanor changes. As though unaffected by the damage, he buffers out a malevolent laugh, something akin to hysteria sparking in his eyes as he catches me staring. Glare darkening with revenge, he sends me a smirk, his teeth curling over his cracked lip before he spits in my direction.

My stomach knots, needles pricking their lethal sting along my suddenly frigid skin.

The bouncer—who'd have most NFL linebackers huddled in fear—swings a beefy arm over the man's shoulder and, with waning patience, escorts him out of the bar. I sigh in relief, my nerves settling some. The crowd thins and scatters, leaving me an open view of Ryder, who's perched on a stool. Though he's talking to Lee and Madeline, his blue eyes are zeroed in on mine, their lost, lonely gaze causing my heart to pang in response as I try to take a breath.

No, no, no, I furiously chant to myself. I tilt my head back and look into Brock's eyes, guilt sinking its fangs into my gut. "I shouldn't have said anything."

"What are you talking about?" He lifts his hand to wipe the blood off his lip.

I grab his wrist, halting the motion. He stares at me, confusion thick in his mossy irises. I press onto my tiptoes and brush my lips against his, my tongue collecting his blood in a deep kiss. Salty copper—like a penny rescued from the warm waters of the ocean, the viscous taste lingers in my mouth, further fueling my guilt. I kiss him harder, feeling nauseated for what I did, for what I caused, for what . . . I'm doing.

Brock takes my face between his hands, his eyes searching mine. "What's bothering that head of yours?"

"You fought him for me. You're hurt because I *told* you to do it." I touch my lips to his, every cell aware that I'm unworthy of his love, his trust. "If I would've just kept my mouth shut, this wouldn't have happened."

He pulls me closer, the fusion of his sweat and aftershave rushing up my nostrils. "You honestly think I *wasn't* gonna take him out if you didn't say something?" I attempt to respond, but his finger covers my lips, silencing me. "Wrong, baby girl. He was already on his way down, but after he said that shit to you, he wasn't walking out of this motherfucking place without experiencing what six days a week of hard-core training could do to his face."

He kisses me, and I close my eyes, wrapping my arms around his neck. I feel a smirk curl his lips as he slides them to my ear and whispers, "You made me hard when you poured that drink over his head. You're aware of this, right?"

A soft laugh tumbles from my mouth as I kiss his nose. "No. But I can't say I'm shocked."

"Well, you did, and I'm fucking positive I have blue balls because of it." He grabs his crotch, his smirk stretching into a wide smile. "Yup. Blue as berries."

"Such a naughty, naughty boy." I slip my fingers through his sweaty hair. "Very naughty."

He nips my lip. "Well, since you're feeling shitty about what happened, this naughty boy's willing to accept your apology in the form of you fixing my . . . *problem* in whatever way you deem necessary. Fair?"

"Fair," I purr. Brock's well aware of my sexual dependency issue, and he uses it to both of our advantages, fucking the numbness right out of my mind as he fucks his own social-pressured thoughts and family bullshit right out of his body.

"You two gonna do the dirty right here?" Madeline dangles a shot of tequila in my face. She digs a palm into her waist, her fiery red strands of hair falling over her shoulder as she tilts her head. "Or can you wait until *after* we're finished partying?"

"That's a tough one." Brock swipes the shot from her and tosses it down his throat. "Actually, it's worse than tough. It's like asking a kid not to peek at his Christmas presents."

"That shot was for *Amber*." Madeline frowns, snatching the glass from him. "You best plan on refilling her, Cunningham."

"Yeah." I lift my chin in playful defiance. "You better *refill* me."

Brock's hand swallows mine, and he leads me toward the bar. "Ah, you have no idea how many times I'm filling you after we bounce outta here."

"Sounds hostile," Ryder deadpans, twirling an empty bottle of Sam Adams on the bar. He cranks back a shot of whatever's in front of him, the dimple on his cheek deepening as he studies me. "Just make sure you don't hurt her while you're at it. That is, unless she's into pain. Then, by all means, light it the fuck up."

I narrow my eyes at Ryder, and mirth flashes in his as he twirls his stupid bottle. He loves dissecting the mechanics of my brain.

Ugh! I'm about to take that bottle and show him the copious number of ways I'd use it to inflict pain. On his ass in particular.

"Still," Ryder continues, swinging his attention to Brock, "you might piss off Amy. You know how she gets, bro. That's one jealous gal. The worst you've ever dealt with, and you've dealt with your share of them. She wants *all* of you to herself. Definitely not the *sharing* type."

I glance at Brock, my heart pulling. "Who's *Amy?*"

"She's . . ." Hesitation smothers his face. "Well, she's kind of . . ."

My heart pulls again, the viciousness in it making it difficult to breathe.

"He's never told you about Amy?" Shock tinges Lee's voice. "Wow. Not cool, dude."

"No." My response comes out weak, anxiety clumping thick in my throat. "He's never told me about her. Who *is* she?"

I'm sure I've lost it. Who the hell am I to question anyone or anything Brock may or may not be doing behind my back? Not only did I kiss Ryder after being warned not to do it again, but I've mentally banged Ryder right in front of him.

"No way. I don't believe that shit." Lee lines up five shot glasses and pours a red concoction into each, topping them off with a squirt of whipped cream. He slides me one, amusement creasing his forehead. "Brock's never let you in on his number one *fan?*"

Madeline giggles, Brock chuckles, and Ryder quirks a wiseass brow. I sigh in frustration, the need to slap an answer out of someone coating my stomach. I flip my attention between each of them.

Nothing. They're mute.

No longer giving a shit if I should question who or what Brock's doing behind my back, I throw my shot down my throat, wipe a frustrated hand across my mouth, and slam the glass on the bar. "No! He's never told me about her. But somebody here better. Who. The. *Fuck.* Is. She?"

The air rockets with their amusement, their laughter drilling through my ears. Pissed, I rise, seriously ready to get the hell out of here.

"She's a ghost who haunts this here tavern, peach." Ryder grabs my wrist, preventing me from leaving. "Now sit back down and ch-ch-chill."

"*What?*" I drag my gaze to Brock. "She's a . . . ghost? You pricks put me through that for a ghost?"

Shrugging, a guilty grin tramples Brock's face. "She indeed is, and we indeed did." He slugs back his shot, his grin melting into a pout. "But, babe, pity me. She's a psycho."

Madeline tips her glass in Brock's direction. "She only gets that way with you. Sure, her obsession's become a little off the charts, but her intentions are good, mainly fueled by her desire to get it on with you. But at least she actually *likes* you, Cunningham. That's more than Ryder can say. She all-out hates him."

"She doesn't *hate* me. She just can't handle the . . . *swoon* factor I possess." He kicks me a wink. "Yes. That's what it is. My swoonworthiness intimidates her. She couldn't handle me if she tried. Ghost or not, my shit would bang her up. Bad."

I sigh, regretting that I ever gassed up his head with that bit of information. "So let me get this straight." I reclaim my seat, trying to understand this comical yet somewhat disturbing story. "Amy's a psycho ghost who haunts the bar and wants Brock?"

Lee uncaps a few bottles of beer for a crowd of customers whose drunken attentions are hanging all over our conversation. "She doesn't just *want* him. She wants to give birth to his ghost kiddies."

Laughter erupts from all directions. I can't help but smile as I watch Brock shake his head in embarrassment.

"From grabbing his junk when he's taking a piss to making her frustration well known when he leaves by smashing everything from pictures to glasses, she wants the dude more than a pie-eating prick-goblin wants a kinky slut-waffle," Lee adds.

Hoots of laughter gurgle the air, oiling every surface.

Embarrassment long gone, Brock bows his head, superiority taking over his expression as he nods at me. God, my man's so damn cute, each inch of him a morsel of deliciousness. Square jaw, edible full lips, and eyes that can cut through steel. It's no wonder Amy—in all her deadness—wants him.

"It's rumored the place was a brothel in the late seventeen hundreds," Lee goes on, a smile stretching the freckles sprinkling his nose. "Our fine young Amy entertained the Johns. But sadly, she was murdered in this very building while in the midst of . . . performing. A new owner took over in the fifties, and during a renovation, they found her skeleton mangled between those walls." Lee throws a thumb over his shoulder at the bricks surrounding an ancient fireplace. "Brock's not the only customer she bothers, but he's *definitely* her favorite."

"And Amy hates Ryder?" I ask, eerily enthralled. "I mean, how do you know she hates him? Does she . . . abuse him?"

"She doesn't *hate* me," Ryder reiterates, stabbing a finger in my direction. "She does, however, *abuse* me. Mm. Hell yeah, she does. But I'm cool with her pulling my hair. I dig the kink."

"She pulls your hair?" I giggle, motioning to Lee for another shot. "Oh, then it's definitely hate."

"It's not hate, peach." Ryder's gaze stays heavy on mine as he rests his forearms on the glossy mahogany bar. "I told ya, it's my swoon factor."

I roll my eyes, positive I've inflated his head to the point of explosion.

Madeline scoffs. "How do you know it's your swoon factor? She just really might *hate* you."

A lazy grin curls his mouth. I hold my breath, knowing he's about to further mutilate the mechanics of my brain.

"Some pretty little thing *told* me it's my swoon factor. I didn't believe her at first, but after I really thought about it, I couldn't help but agree. My informer's extremely intuitive when it comes to the male anatomy." Ryder flicks his eyes to my lips as he swipes his tongue along his. "Especially their . . . *mouths.*"

Mechanics screwed beyond repair, my heart catapults from my chest, taking with it what little oxygen my lungs are harboring. I try to force myself to swallow. It doesn't work. Ryder lets loose a light chuckle, pleased with my reaction.

"Here ya go," Lee says, producing my much-needed shot.

I nearly yank it from him, and before I can say thanks, I empty it, my throat welcoming the sizzling sensation.

"I give up," Brock booms over the music. "I know I'm a business major, but what the fuck is swoon factor?"

My buzz is thicker than molasses, but I'm aware it's not the alcohol dizzying me. Between Brock and Ryder's testosterone lighting up my girly parts, I'm sure there's not a command I wouldn't obey, a wish I wouldn't grant, or an immoral act I wouldn't participate in with either of them.

Madeline kills her shot, her pebble of a nose scrunching up. "It means he's hot, spicy, *muy caliente.* Like Jagger, he's got swagger. Makes the ladies drool. Sets panties aflame. Gets them tingling in all the right places. That kind of crap."

Ding . . . ding . . . ding . . . We have a winner!

Yeppers. I'm officially toasted.

She blows Lee a kiss. "But it's nothing like the swoonworthiness my man's got. He beats them all."

"That's my girl." Smiling, Lee throws a dish towel over his shoulder. "She knows where the *real* sweetness is."

Brock snorts. "If Ashcroft *or* Lee's got an ounce of swagger, then I'm drowning in it."

Ryder flips Brock the finger, a wicked smirk shuffling across his face. "Bro, you're the cat who's got a ghost wanting to multiply with you. At least my following has—I don't know—a *pulse.*"

Brock rises, and with a smirk rivaling Ryder's, he tangles his hand in mine, gently dragging me to my feet. "This fine specimen owns a pulse," he points out, his tone thick with reverence as he pulls me into his muscled chest. Laying his fingers against the curve of my neck, he nibbles and sucks my lips, his tongue swiping their seam in soft, slow strokes. "And right now, her beautiful pulse is quickening."

I part my lips and fall in step with his rhythm, my body aching for his touch, his drugging warmth. He licks into my mouth, his familiar taste a reprieve to my system, his increased breathing nourishment to my soul. Whistling catcalls and hoots of encouragement reach my ears, but the blood roaring through my veins buries the sound, cocooning me in a tomb of desire. My heart clatters—its strength shaking my rib cage—and the world around me vanishes as my fingers sneak into the silky caramel strands of his hair. He bites my lip, his free hand gripping my waist with complete ownership.

"And still faster," he whispers roughly, cushioning my back against the bar as his erection prickles the flat of my midriff. "And . . . still . . . fucking . . . faster." He trails his lips down my jaw, resting them on the hollow of my neck. "To be honest, it's beating so fucking fast it's scaring me."

"Then maybe you should stop." Ryder's voice electrocutes the air, a conduit of hostility stabbing my ears. "I mean, if you're afraid for her health, why fucking continue?"

Brock slowly pulls back, an entertained yet lethal sneer etching his mouth. "Yeah, bro. Maybe I should stop."

Boos, heavy sighs, and laughter from the crowd ignite the bar as Ryder and Brock stare each other down, their eyes alight with venom, possession hardening their jaws.

Adrenaline girds my spine as Ryder's gaze slithers over me. Though he attempts to mask his pain with a chuckle, the hurt on his beautiful face is palpable, his jealousy stripping the air from my lungs. Guilt crashes an angry wave of nausea through my gut. I take an unsteady breath, confusion tripping over the mess of emotions piled high in the dark corners of my mind.

"Lee?" Ryder calls. His gaze holds mine, the steadiness in it wrapping phantom fingers around my throat.

"What's up, buddy?"

"I need another shot. *Now.*"

"I think you need a few." Brock steps toward Ryder.

My heart stills, the organ stuttering to a deadly plod. But when Brock claps a hand over Ryder's shoulder, a breath of relief rushes from my lips.

A genuine smile dusts Brock's mouth. "I think we all could use a few. Wouldn't you agree?"

Ryder rolls his neck and pulls his gaze from mine. "Sure. Why the fuck not?"

"Come do a couple of shots with us, Ber," Brock says, jerking his head toward me.

Both men sink onto bar stools next to each other, their demeanors eerily calm as Lee lines up six shot glasses. Hesitation flitters through me, and I gnaw on my thumbnail, my breathing increasing as debate hinders my muscles from reacting to Brock's demand. A stone's throw from the two men who've had my heart and mind warring since the day we met, I'm frozen, Super-Glued to my spot.

Urgency widens Madeline's eyes, snapping me from my internal battle. My steps are tentative, cement weighing each one down as I bridge the distance, approaching them. A nervous smile teeters on

Madeline's lips, and she rests a calming hand on my back. But my heart pounds anew as Brock slides his arm around my waist, positioning me between him and Ryder.

On shaky legs, my gaze shoots between what I'm positive are heaven's visual gift to humanity. Chiseled, masculine pieces of art for all to indulge in, they're gods in their own right, making it impossible for both sexes not to wish they could snag a taste. One minute my senses are drowning in the cool, icy blue gleam shadowing Ryder's eyes, the next they're hijacked by the sincere love squatting heavy across Brock's face.

Little does the world know that each of these men—each of these simple yet complicated gifts—harbor so much more than their looks.

They're soft, yet hard.

Sweet, yet bitter.

Perfect, yet perfectly imperfect.

Each is an inescapable mixture of everything that's captured fragments of my dreams, nightmares, thoughts, and soul. They've become my reason for going on.

"Hey, sweets," Brock croons, dragging his fingers up my spine.

Goose bumps flare my skin, the deliciousness of his touch curling through my weakened muscles. "Hey." I sound breathless, a whisper of uncertainty stealing my voice. *What the hell is wrong with me?*

I've never been meek with a guy. In love or not, confused or not, I care for both of these men. Their well-being is the first thing that springs into my head the second I crack open my eyes. I know I have to tread with caution—shit's already ugly—but I'm not about to let their alpha tension bruise the rest of our night, let alone their friendship.

I've had many guilts in my life. I refuse to add the demise of a long-term friendship to my list.

Deciding to take control—and knowing I'm the only one who can fix this mess—I swing my hip against each of them, hoping to lighten the mood. "Lee, these boys are lightweights at best. Double me up to four shots. It's time to school them on how drinking's *really* supposed to go down."

Steadfast, Lee obeys my request, plopping two additional shot glasses in front of me.

"Mm, you love pushing it, don't ya?" Ryder chuckles, a grin softening his face.

"Ah, she knows nothing else," Brock agrees.

"What's wrong, fellas?" I fling my arms around their necks and yank, cushioning their jaws against my ample C cups. "Are ya feeling . . . threatened?" I tease, a wiseass smirk plastered across my lips. "'Cause I'm smelling fear, and it reeks like shit."

A giggle bursts from Madeline as Lee pours liquid bliss into each glass. "She's about to take you both down. Saddle up, my brothers, and watch how it's done."

Before either can respond, I untangle my arms from their necks and down my quartet of shots. The leftover sting in my throat, spliced with waves of nausea, convinces me I've gone too far.

Yep. I'm gonna hurl.

Still, the fluidity in which I conquered the task garners me not only a round of applause from the patrons, but impressed smiles from my sexy opponents.

Following my lead, they toss back their double shots and slam their glasses onto the bar, Ryder beating Brock by a split second.

"Not bad," Madeline appraises, clapping. "But Amber *still* outdid you guys."

"I did. And for this, they owe me for the victory." I smile, my brain in overdrive as I think of a proper "trophy."

Brock rests his hands on my hips, his eyes narrowed. "I know that look, and it's not good."

"Be a good boy," I say, tapping his nose. "You'll both be fine."

Ryder lifts an incredulous brow. "Which translates into: we're royally fucked."

"Maddie," I call, jutting my chin toward Ryder. "You get him, and I'll get Brock. I need to work off some of this alcohol."

"Oh, *hell* no." Ryder shakes his head. "I don't—"

"Dance," Madeline finishes, yanking him by the collar of his T-shirt. "We know. We know. Stop being a baby, Ashcroft. You lost. You dance."

I laugh and thread my fingers through Brock's, leading us through the horde of sweaty bodies and out onto the dance floor. With the band on break and a DJ taking over, I twine my hands around Brock's neck and pull his ear down to my lips, licking along the shell as we sink into the rhythm of Usher's "Scream."

"Is this my punishment for losing?" Brock squeezes my ass and jacks me against his chest, his mouth finding the contour of my jaw. "If it is, I have absolutely no problem losing every time we battle it out."

"Again," I say, a purr biting my tone, "such a naughty boy."

"You bring out the bad in this good boy."

I scoff. "Yeah. Like you weren't bad before me."

"You got me there." He smirks, tipping his head toward Madeline and Ryder. "Look at those two."

I glance over my shoulder, amused at what I'm witnessing. With his collar acting like a leash, Ryder begrudgingly makes his way through the throng, a pout on his face as he and Madeline step onto the dance floor. However, his pout disappears when Madeline bends over, curls her fingers around a pole, and shakes her ass against his crotch. Seemingly more than okay with what she's doing, a smile pops across Ryder's face.

"*Now* you're good?" Brock asks.

"How can I *not* be?" Ryder grips her shoulders, grinding his hips against her. "I *do* have a dick, and she just kind of woke him up."

"Ryder!" Lee bellows from the bar, "I'm off in ten minutes, and I'm beating your ass if you fuck with my girl."

"Bro, I'm innocent," Ryder throws back, a shit-eating grin curling his mouth as he fists her hair. Grinding harder against her ass, he gives it a whack and chuckles as Madeline squeals in delight. "See? It's all her. I ain't doing nothing she doesn't want."

Narrowed eyes locked on Ryder, Lee dashes into the kitchen, a cart of dirty glasses in tow.

Continuing her tease, Madeline giggles and flips up her head. "You're asking for it, Ryder."

"No, Madeline, *you're* asking for it." Ryder plucks a bottle of beer off a passing waitress's tray. With a wink, he fishes out a couple of twenties from his jeans, handing the hearty tip to the chick. "Don't ya think she is, beauty?"

Saucy smile in place, the redhead nods and slowly shoves a ready-made card between his lips. "If she doesn't want it, I'll *gladly* take it. I get off at two. Call me if things don't work out."

I roll my eyes as Red shimmies through the crowd, flipping Ryder one last seductive glance before she disappears around a corner.

"The nerve!" Madeline huffs with a pseudo-pout as she faces Ryder. "You're dancing with me, but you take a number from some random chick?"

Ryder pulls the card from his mouth and tucks it into his pocket. "Sorry, Mad. A man's gotta do what he's gotta do."

"I concur," Brock says, discreetly gliding his hand below the waistband of my skirt. Heart rate spiking, my breath slips as he moves his free hand to the small of my back, tugging me closer. "Ah, no panties. I like."

Predatory stare locked on mine, he pushes a finger inside me, hooking my G-spot. An uncontained moan leaves my throat as my pussy spasms, stretching around his fingers.

"What are you doing?" I breathe, my head falling back as he slides in a second, then third finger.

"Why, I do believe I'm . . . finger-fucking you." It comes out as a low growl. He catches my mouth in a hard kiss, our bodies moving against the unsuspecting crowd.

In and out, out and in, he finger-fucks me ripe, the pulsing beat of the music adding to the exoticness of his onslaught. My eyes flutter closed, my instinct to fuck kicking in like a starved animal.

"Dude, your time's up." Lee's voice cracks through the air, causing me to jump.

Brock chuckles, and I hold my breath, letting it go as he slowly drags his fingers out, making sure he brushes my clit before completely pulling them from my skirt. Hungry eyes locked on mine and still smiling, he lifts his fingers to his mouth and sucks my moisture from them. Legs quivering and breathing a stuttered mess, I'm ready to take him right here.

A groan crawls from his chest as he stares at me. "Do you have any idea the damage I'm gonna do to that pussy when we get back to my place?"

I nod, trying to get my body under control. "I think I have an idea."

"Nah, baby girl. I really don't think you do. I'm gonna wreck it the way you like it, and *then* some."

"You're gonna wreck what?" Madeline slurs, wiping her sweaty forehead. "Her sanity?"

"I plan on coming close to doing just that." Brock nods with a smirk.

"If you *haven't* already wrecked it." Lee snakes his arms around Madeline's waist and drags her backward into a dark corner next to the bar, straddling her over his lap as he falls into a chair.

Brock turns to Ryder, his brow drawn up. "I gotta take a piss. Can I trust that you won't maul my girl to death while I'm gone?"

"Are you *high?*" Ryder smacks his lips together. "She's done for if you leave her with me, and I'm not responsible when she doesn't come back to ya."

"She'll come back," Brock calls from over his shoulder. "Just be nice."

"Oh, I'll be *very* . . . *very* nice." Ryder finishes his beer, bows his head and reaches for my hand, his eyes glimmering with mischief as he sets the empty bottle on a table. "Madam, may I have this dance?"

My pulse lurches at the thought of physical contact with Ryder. Smiling, I lay my hand in his, aware that he's about to make the next five minutes . . . interesting. "I thought you didn't like dancing?"

"Well, two things have changed since then." He laces his fingers through mine, pulls me into his chest, and wraps his free arm around my waist. My heart sinks as he dips his mouth to my ear and whispers, "First, I like *slow* dancing, and in case you didn't notice, the band's playing 'Sail' by Awolnation."

Drummed up from too many shots and mind askew from Brock's recent attack, I smile like an idiot, just now realizing the band's back.

Lips continuing to tantalize the shell of my ear, his voice tangles with the sultry beat. "Second, the girl in my arms is a better match for me. It makes the act more . . . bearable, if you will."

"Is she?" The question scratches up my throat, a sheen of desire further dampening my skin.

He drops his hand from mine and reunites it with his other around my waist. "She is." Another whisper, this one breathed soft against my cheek. He pulls me closer, his erection stroking my stomach as we sway to the music. "She can throw a man off balance, leaving him with nothing but tiny fragments of what used to be a pretty sane mind." He runs his fingers up the dip of my waist, along the curve of my breasts, and curls them around my elbows, dragging my arms around his neck. A grin tugs at his lips as I knot my fingers in his hair. "And you wanna know something, peach?"

I nod. My vision blurs, a million sensations tumbling over my skin as he sinks his forehead to mine, keeping it there.

"I think she knows what she does to a man." His hands find my hips, slowly clenching and unclenching. "How she completely takes over every goddamn thought he owns. Whether he's awake or not, she's there in his head, jacking up his universe. But hell if he wants her to stop. He's addicted to her eyes, the way her sweet taste lingers on his tongue, and the way she moves when she's near him." He takes a deep breath, his barbell peeking out as he licks his lips. "So fucking in tune with her, he hears the silent call from her body when she craves his touch."

Blood overheated, I stare at his lips, my own quivering as he moves his along my temple, down the side of my cheek, resting them against my jaw. "Yes. I think she knows *exactly* what she does to a man."

I shiver, my words strangled. "I think you're wrong."

"I think he's right," Brock whispers into my ear, gripping my waist from behind.

I jump, my heart speeding toward implosion. I go to turn, but Brock holds me in place, his nose buried in the sweaty waves of my hair as he pushes his pelvis against my ass.

"Without a doubt, he's correct."

"There's no question I am." Ryder's voice comes out a hungry rasp as he steps back. "I'll meet ya at the bar."

"Don't leave, bro." Brock moves my hair from my neck, his mouth landing there, teasing, taunting. "Amber won't mind if we both dance with her, will you?"

"No," I breathe, immediately shocked at my answer as I sink into the soft touch of Brock's fingers kneading my hips. I hesitate a second, embarrassment seizing my thoughts. "Do . . . *you* mind?"

"Not at all. That's why I'm offering, baby." Brock lightly bites my shoulder, his breathing heavy as he hooks his thumbs in the waistband of my skirt. "The thought of you sandwiched between us turns me the fuck on."

Convinced the alcohol's talking for Brock, a nervous giggle erupts from my throat. I stare at Ryder, waiting for him to make a move. Frozen, Ryder offers a guarded smile, surprise evident in his loss for words.

"Stop being a pussy, Ashcroft," Brock says, "and put your hands on my girl."

Ryder blinks. "Well, since you put it that way, how can I resist?"

He steps toward me, takes my face in his hands, his eyes searching, gauging my reaction. Chest pressed to mine, he whispers into my ear, "Are you sure you're cool with this?"

I nod, my heart galloping as our bodies sway in unison to the slow, sultry beat. Ryder grins, his fingers tiptoeing down my cheeks, along my collarbone, their journey ending on my waist, where he grips them.

"She feels nice, doesn't she?" Brock lifts my arms, swathing them around his neck as he feathers his mouth against my ear.

A soft moan escapes me as I hold Ryder's gaze, his heady cologne swamping my senses. He bites his lip, raw hunger surfacing over his face as he moves his hands to my rib cage, his thumbs drawing small, tantalizing circles just below my breasts. My pulse rocks, the perils of their seduction wrenching the oxygen from my laboring lungs.

"Like fucking heaven." With his eyes locked on mine, Ryder's thumbs continue their gentle persuasion along my ribs, each pass testing new limits, nearly brushing my nipples. They bud, hardening like gemstones. Flames of sin ignite me, chills skidding across my skin as he pushes a knee between my legs. My lips part on a second moan, and Ryder smirks, my heart bouncing out of control as he grinds his hips against mine. "She's a beautiful gift. One neither of us deserves."

My muscles go limp, my need for him—for *them*—mounting by the second. I dig my nails into Brock's scalp as he tips my head back and slides his tongue against my neck, licking the sweat from my flesh.

"She *is* a gift. But I'm not sure she realizes this," Brock points out. "I wonder if there's anything we could, I don't know, *do* to make her aware of just how fucking sweet she is."

"That might be difficult," Ryder says, a delicious grin spreading over his mouth as he coils a piece of my hair around his finger. "But I'm sure we could come up with something that would . . . satisfy her."

"Oh, you two are good." I smile, their dual stimulation sucking the last vestiges of morality from my brain. "Did either of you go to school for this?"

"No. They're just players." A hiccupped giggle freezes the air. "They're about to do you real good, but *real* dirty."

I twist my head, my gaze landing on an inebriated Hailey Jacobs. Blonde hair hanging messily over her shoulders, red lips puckered into a sneer, and an arm wrapped around her friend's waist, the chick can barely stand.

"Christ," Ryder mumbles. He drops his hands to my hips, a scowl anchoring his face as he stares at Hailey.

"What's the matter, Ryder? Afraid you and your buddy's secret's gonna come out?" She turns her wicked blue eyes on mine. "I thought I was the only one they liked double-teaming. Apparently I was wrong."

My breathing screeches to a stop. I jerk back, neither man's possessive hold able to keep me in place. "What the hell did you just say?"

She stumbles into my chest, and beer from her bottle splashes onto my sweater. "I'll make it quick, bitch. Don't feel special that they're all over you at the same time. You're nothing but—"

"Shut the fuck up, Hailey," Brock growls. He grips the back of her neck, tugging her away from me. "You're drunk, and you're about to catch a fucking beating if you say another word."

She drags a finger down Brock's cheek, a purr seducing her tone. "Since I know you'd never rough up a woman, I find your threat entertaining but sexy. If *anyone* knows that I like it rough, it'd be you and Ryder, wouldn't it?"

Blood.

Hers.

I want it.

But the poison in Brock's eyes stills my rapid heart. What the skank said is true—Brock would never lay a hand on a woman. But she can only taunt a hungry lion for so long, and I know that look. I've lived in homes where it was the last warning before a man lost it.

"No, Brock!" I yank his hand off Hailey's neck, my pulse hammering as I glance between him and Ryder.

Remaining silent, Ryder shakes his head.

Rage coils through my muscles as I bring my confused gaze back to Brock's. "What are you hiding from me?"

"I'm not hiding anything, Ber. Let's go." He levels Hailey with a glare and wraps his fingers around my waist, attempting to herd me out of the bar.

"Are you kidding me?" I spit, my tone clotted with venom. Forget not taunting the lion. I shove against his chest, hardly moving him. "Are you fucking that skank behind my back with Ryder? Is that what's going on?"

"No!" Brock argues, his voice barely controlled as he reaches for my hand. I wrench it back, my lips parted in silent shock. "Calm down."

"Calm *down*?" I feel heat explode, blotching across my face. "You didn't answer the question. What the hell is she talking about?"

"What a mess I've caused," Hailey interrupts through a slur. She tilts her head, the movement unsteadying her. She falls against my shoulder, her listless weight knocking me back a few inches.

Ryder catches her by the elbow, hauling her away from me. "What the fuck are you doing, Hailey? Huh? You getting off on this shit?"

"I'm *totally* getting off on it." She pulls her arm from Ryder's hold. "And I'm telling the truth. I'm done with you and Brock warning me to stay away from her and not open my mouth about what happened."

"What the heck's going on?" Madeline asks, confusion pinching her forehead as she and Lee approach. "I go to the restroom, and all hell . . ." Her words die in her throat, her eyes narrowing on Hailey. "What's *she* doing here?"

"The last time I checked, I was allowed in *any* bar in Maryland." Hailey turns to me, one side of her mouth curled up. "But *she's* not. Maybe I should let the owner know her ID's fake?"

"Goddamnit! Just shut the fuck up already!" Ryder booms, a muscle ticking in his jaw. He looks at Hailey's friend. "You sober?"

The petite brunette nods, something akin to fear breaking out across her face.

"Good. Get her the fuck outta here before she makes me do something I can't take back."

The girl swiftly obeys and snags Hailey's hand, but as though unaffected by Ryder's threat, Hailey yanks it away and resumes tripping up my brain. "Let me guess, your lover boys here had the ID made for you? No surprise. They conjured up one for me too, while they were *fucking* me, *together*, at the *exact . . . same . . . time*. Again, you're nothing special, bitch."

Confusion dips its poisonous rods into my alcohol-soaked brain as voices fade into nothing but sinister notes of chaos. I take a deep breath, my hearing sparking back to life when Hailey speaks again.

"The only thing that actually has me surprised is that they're willing to share a bitch whose father wasted a bullet on her mother instead of her."

The hairs on my neck jump, prickling at her words. Every wicked thing the skank's ever done to me has nothing on this very moment. All coherent, rational thoughts peel from my head, tearing the sanity right out of my skull.

I lunge, my hand gripping her neck faster than any of us can comprehend. Before I can process what's happening, I have her on the ground, my legs straddling her Coke-bottle waist, as my fist connects with her dainty nose. Twice. With blood streaming down her rosy cheeks, she no longer looks like a porcelain doll. I barely have time to relish the destruction I've caused to her overpriced nose job before I'm hauled off her by Brock, his hands under my armpits as he drags me into the amped-up crowd.

"Ber, look at me." Brock's voice is panicked, his hands all over me.

Face, shoulders, arms, neck, he inspects every inch of my body. "Look at me, baby."

I catch his eyes, the sincere worry in them sinking me. But it only lasts a second. Resting against a metal pole, I turn my head and bask in the sight of Hailey crying as she scrambles to her feet. Blood's spilling from her nose, seeping between the grains of the wooden floorboards as her friend and a bouncer help her toward the exit. Eyes flaming hot as coals, I lunge again, attempting to nip one last piece of her before she leaves.

Brock stops me, caging me in. "Ber, no! She's not worth it, baby."

"She's not," Madeline says, approaching us with Lee. She swipes my hair away from my face, a sad smile on her lips. "Are you okay?"

"Not worth it?" I scoff, ignoring Madeline's question. "Not worth it, Brock? Apparently she was worth it to you at some point. My God, how could you *lie* to me about her?"

He drops his forehead to mine, anguish thrumming through his whisper. "I didn't lie to you."

"*What?*" I take an exasperated breath. "Yes, you did! I asked you about her."

"And I told you the truth. That she meant nothing to me. Every time we hooked up, I was drunk, she was drunk. That's all it was."

"But you so conveniently left out the part where you double-teamed her with *Ryder?*"

"Yeah, I did. Why the hell would I tell you that?"

My eyes bug from their sockets. "Why the hell *wouldn't* you?"

"That's not something I'd tell Madeline," Lee interrupts, curling his arms around Madeline's waist from behind. "Definitely not."

Madeline swivels her head. "Oh, *really?*"

"Don't get upset, pussycat." He burrows his face into her neck. "It's just not something a dude's gonna tell his girl. Amber knew he messed around with her. She didn't need to know the specifics."

"Mm-hmm," Madeline hums as I debate whether or not to release the rest of my anger on Lee. "Did you know that Ryder and Brock . . . did the little whore?"

"Of course I did," he admits as Ryder approaches. "It was impossible to fall asleep while these two fuckers were banging the shit outta her in the next room." Lee grinds his pelvis against Madeline's ass, his tone a high-pitched, mocking squeak. "Ryder, please don't stop. Brock, yes. Oh God, Brock, right there."

Ryder smacks him upside his head, his eyes drilling into Lee's. "You're an asshole."

Lee shrugs. "Bro, Amber knows what happened. What's the big deal?"

"Go take a walk before I make it a huge deal," Brock grits out. "Now.

Madeline drags him toward the exit. "You knew about what they did with her and didn't say anything to me?"

Lee's response is indistinguishable as they push through the crowd and out the doors.

I look at Brock. "You two really did share her."

"*Did.*" Brock's stare is pinned on mine as he brushes his knuckles along my jaw. "I haven't messed around with her since the first time I talked to you, Ber."

A tear slips down my cheek. "You expect me to *believe* that?"

"I swear to fucking God I haven't," he implores, sinking a nervous hand through his hair.

"He's not lying." Ryder's words come out soft, his face tormented. "He cut shit off with her the second he saw you."

Confusion and betrayal eat at the lining of my stomach, rotting away my trust. But more than anything, one emotion swells through my gut. One emotion I never thought I'd feel toward Hailey: jealousy. My heart its smorgasbord, it's feasting on the muscle like a famished king as thoughts of that bitch enjoying their talents attack my head. She's had what I haven't. What I've craved. Visions of Brock kissing her, taking her, while Ryder indulges in some other part of her body freezes my blood.

I sniffle, trying to find my words. "Have you two done this with any other girls, and how many times did you both bang her together?"

"No, just her," Brock whispers. "And I'm not sure how many times. Maybe a few over the summer."

I hug my stomach, my watery gaze landing on Ryder.

Ryder lifts a tentative hand to my cheek, his finger soaking up a tear. "She was the only one," he admits, his voice soft. "Are you all right?"

I step back, embarrassed that I'm crying. "Yeah. I'm fine. I just wanna get out of here."

"Brock," a deep voice calls.

A glance over my shoulder reveals the bouncer approaching.

"What's up?" Brock hesitantly pulls his eyes from mine.

"My boss is vexed." King Kong's twin rubs a hand over his buzzed head, shaking it as he sighs. "It was bad enough I let you pummel Mike, but what just happened with your girl *will* get me fired if I don't toss ya outta here. I'm sorry, man, but I got bills to pay."

"Nah, I hear ya, bro." Brock nods. "We were just getting ready to jet."

"Cool." King Kong slaps a hand over Ryder's shoulder, mischief tap-dancing across his face. "I gotta make this look good, okay?"

Ryder spikes a brow. "Kevin, I don't give a fuck how big you are. You touch me, I'm dropping your ass right here."

"Come on, Ashcroft. You're gonna deny me playing this the way I should?"

"You bet I am."

"All good. I'll make up for it at Saturday's game." Kevin turns on his heel, a chuckle rumbling from his chest. "Your quarterback ass is mine for the sacking. Now get outta here before you guys get me canned."

A second of awkward silence stretches between the three of us before I head for the exit, my pulse rocketing with every step I take out into the parking lot. I pull in a deep breath, the chilled October air not much of a reprieve to my nerves as I lean against Brock's Hummer. Emotions straddling the sharp edge of insanity, I peer up into the cloudless sky, the night washing over me like an angry wave as Brock and Ryder approach.

"Amber," Ryder whispers, his throat tight, rough, "I'm sorry. I'm sorry for the way you found out about Hailey. Sorry for taking advantage of you." He shoves a hand through his hair. "I'm just fucking sorry about everything, peach."

The sincere remorse and vulnerability on his face drops me, confirming what I already knew. I'm nothing but poison to these men, a dangerous vine of fucked-upness spearing its ugly thorns through their flesh.

"God, Ryder, you didn't take advantage of me. Please don't apologize. You have no reason to be sorry." I wipe my eyes with the back of my hand, sure I'm close to a mental breakdown. "I'll talk to you later, okay?"

Ryder palms the back of his neck and stares at me for a few seconds, sending me an understanding look before nodding and walking away. Heart in my throat, I round the vehicle and open the door, exhaustion taking over as Brock gets in. Silence shrouds the air before Brock's soft sigh laps at my senses. My breathing skids to a stop, goose bumps beating across my skin when he leans over the console, touching his lips to my temple.

He slowly pulls back, his green eyes beckoning my soul. "Hailey meant nothing to me, Amber. Nothing. The second I saw you, I knew you'd be mine. Needed you in my life. Our scars come in different shades, but they bind us together, baby. I know you can feel that. Can sense it when we're together. I'm not trying to hurt you. I'd never intentionally do that. I—"

"But you *have* hurt me." I press my finger to his lips, silencing him. "And I don't mean by you being with Hailey. I can't hold you responsible for something you did before me, and I never would. But you keep giving me half-truths. Not telling me about selling coke. Hiding what happened to your brother. Now this bullshit with you, Ryder, and Hailey. What *else* are you keeping from me?"

"Nothing," he says softly, guilt thick in his tone. "I swear on my fucking life there's nothing else."

I close my eyes, wanting with everything in me to believe him. But who am I not to? Infested with lies, I'm harboring the mothership of untruths. "What was all of that before? You letting Ryder dance with me?" I open my eyes and stare into his, trying not to choke over my words. "Were you . . . for *real* about what you said, or was it just the alcohol?"

"Why?" A slow grin pulls at the edge of his mouth. "Did you . . . *like* what we were doing to you?"

"No." Another lie. Anxiety tenses my muscles. "Why would you even ask?"

"Come on, baby. I know you better than you think I do. You feel something for Ryder, admit it."

"*What?*" My breath disintegrates from my lungs as I stare at him.

"You heard me. There's something between you two. I've known it since the day we met. I feel it every time we're all in the same room. It's undeniable, but it's okay. It's human nature. Just admit it."

"I'm not talking about this." Guilt cloaks me as I look off into the parking lot, my gaze catching Ryder's as he gets into his car. He stares at me for a long moment, my heart shredding before he closes the door and pulls onto the road. "I'm not."

"No. You're not running from this, Ber." Brock's voice is soft as he captures my chin, bringing my eyes to his. "Clean slate, baby girl. No more lies for either of us. We're talking about it, and we're talking about it *now*." A nervous swallow pinches my throat as he kisses my lips. "No one's denying the chemistry you two share anymore, and like I said, it turns me the fuck on."

"It seriously turns you on?" My thighs quiver as he cups my cheeks, dragging his lips to the curve of my jaw. "How's that even *possible?*"

"How can it *not* be?"

"I . . . I don't know. A chick all up on you would do nothing but piss me off."

One truth. The thought alone sickens me.

He chuckles but sobers quickly, lust dominating his features. "I'm aware of the attraction and not at all threatened by it. I'm confident in what you and I have, and I'm cool with you exploring your want for each other while in my presence." Brock's mouth finds mine again, taking what's rightfully his in a deep kiss. "The two of us together would bring you *so* much fucking pleasure, you wouldn't be able to think straight. Let us, baby. Let us give you what you want. What you need."

The whore in me jumps at his proposal, my darkest fantasies screaming to life. Opening every door, Brock's giving me permission to entertain the man whose mere presence has held me captive from the second our eyes met, colliding our worlds together in an explosion. Thoughts of both men taking me, possessing me, ravishing every inch of my body flip through my head, seduction crooking a drugging finger in my direction as Brock kisses me harder.

Still, my heart's saying this isn't right. Love may know few boundaries, but surely this is one of them. If you love someone, have truly handed over your soul to them, this line should never be walked, let alone crossed.

Right?

"Say it, baby," Brock whispers over my mouth, burying his hands in my hair.

I moan, my body lighting up as he kisses me deeper, his tongue seeking mine in ways it never has. There's an urgency to his strokes, a silent plea for me to give in. On a groan, he pulls me over the console, straddling my legs over his waist.

He stares into my eyes. "Tell me you want this. Don't be afraid to say it."

"How can I *not* be afraid?" I question, trying to understand where all of this is coming from.

"Why would you be?" Brushing his thumb over my lips, his brows dip in confusion. "Is it the physical part? If that's what's bothering you, we'd make sure to take our time with you. Neither of us would hurt you. I promise you this. It'd be nothing but pleasure for you."

"No. It's not that. Well, I mean, I've never . . ." I pause, my brain skirting over unwelcomed thoughts of my past sexual encounters. Though I've had what anyone would consider an unhealthy number of partners, I've never engaged more than one man at the same time. "I haven't had—"

"Two guys take you together," Brock finishes, his voice husky as he brings my face to his.

A blush burns my cheeks, my breathing heavy as I nod.

Grinning, he nibbles my lip, his hands gripping my waist as he rocks his hips, making sure I feel how hard he is. "Like I said, we'd take it slow with you, baby. Nothing"—his hand floats under my skirt, his thumb circling my clit—"and I mean *nothing* we'd do to you would hurt." Words a strangled whisper, he stares at me as he dips two fingers inside my warmth. "I know you want this. I can feel it. This pussy's begging for what it needs. Let us give it to you."

The stimulation makes my body jerk, my nipples hardening. Before I know it, I'm riding his fingers like I would his cock, my back chafing against the steering wheel as he watches me, lust dilating his eyes.

Do I care that I'm in a parking lot while my boyfriend's finger-fucking me? In my world, complicated questions have very simple answers. No, I don't care. I wouldn't care if the owner of the bar walked up and banged on the door. At this point, I'd probably ask him to watch, if not join in.

"Come on, baby girl. Say it," Brock demands, his breathing ragged, his strokes becoming faster, harder.

I moan, one hand sinking through his hair, the other resting on his thigh for support as I continue to pound down onto him. Brock growls, his mouth abandoning mine, attacking the sensitive flesh where my shoulder and neck meet. He plunges in a third finger, and my pussy clenches in response, my body melting. I can't breathe, can't think. All I can do is feel. Feel every inch of the numbness I crave seeping from my pores and deadened spirit, awakening something dark, but still awakening . . . life.

Brock breathes heavily against my cheek. "Say it, Amber. Fucking say it."

Pussy drenched and a mere heartbeat away from losing my mind in an orgasm on his fingers, I pull Brock's face to mine and latch my lips to his. I bite down, drawing a small amount of blood into my mouth. The heavenly copper taste washes over my tongue with our frenzied kiss.

Brock hisses but continues his mind-fucking assault. "Jesus, Amber. Say it. That's all I need to hear."

"You already did this with Ryder and Hailey," I pant, tearing my mouth from his. "You said she meant nothing to you. What would make me think I'm not going to turn into the same thing?"

His fingers slow, and before I can blink, he removes them from me. Sighing, he pulls me down to him and rests his forehead against mine. "Because I'd die without you. That's why. She was a mistake, something I can never erase. But you . . . Christ, Amber, you'd never become a mistake to me. It's impossible. Ryder was right; you *are* a gift. One neither of us deserves. But you're one we'd treasure, making sure to take care of your every mental and physical need." He drags his lips to mine, kissing me soft, deep. "I fucking love you, Ber. You're the purest air that I have around me. I need you to breathe, to wake up. To just . . . exist. You're my lifeline. That's what you are and will always be to me. I need you to know that."

"But people don't share someone they love," I whisper, still confused by what he's asking of me and even more confused that I'm so intrigued by his proposal.

Are we both just one clusterfuck of a mess, or in some sick, demented way, did *I* cause this? Ignoring what I knew could harm us all, have my piteous existence and disgusting thoughts for Ryder become the culprit in Brock fearing he'll lose me unless he shares me?

"Am I right?" I cup his cheeks, tears stinging my eyes. "If you love someone, you don't share them. You wouldn't want to. I mean, you're the first man I've ever felt anything for, so I have nothing to go on, but isn't it bad that we're even entertaining this thought at all?"

"Do you think I *don't* love you?" His voice breaks, his gaze drilling into mine as he clenches my hips. "Because I do, Amber. Fuck, I love you with everything in me."

I shake my head and press my lips to his. "I know you love me, I do, but I'm trying to understand the suddenness of this. You never told me this is what you wanted. I'm just . . . confused, Brock. Confused about how I feel. Confused for you, for us. That's all."

He stares at me, his thumbs kneading slow circles on my hips as I wait for him to say something. Seconds, minutes, hours crawl by. I don't know how long, but the silence is killing me.

"I kissed Ryder again," I whisper, my spine stiffening the second the confession falls from my mouth.

Face a brick of placidness, Brock swallows, his eyes never leaving mine.

"You said no more lies. A clean slate for us. I . . . I don't want to lie to you anymore, Brock. I can't." I pull in a ragged breath and climb off him, praying my cleansing doesn't bathe him in hatred for me. Hands shaking, I twine our fingers together. "I went to his apartment back in September. It was the day I thought he'd said something to Hailey about my parents. His sister was there, and he was helping her. I got tangled up in the emotions of everything. He tried to stop it, he honestly did, but I wouldn't let him. It just . . . happened."

Remaining silent, Brock fires up the engine and pulls out of the parking lot. With not a single word spoken between us, by the time we get to my dorm, I feel as though the only good thing ever to happen to me is about to vanish in the disarray of my life. I want to stop thinking, stop the loud clatter clogging my head. No matter how sweet they start off, lies will forever wind up bitter in the end.

As I grip Brock's hand tighter, I can't help but acknowledge that this may be *our* end.

CHAPTER 13

Brock

I KNEW SHE'D KISSED him.

Felt it in my fucking bones, in the center of my chest.

Parked in front of Amber's dorm, I glance at her, my heart dropping into my balls as I stare into her beautiful, confused eyes. Those eyes caught me off guard the second I saw them. They blinded me, their sorrow calling out to me like a fucking banshee. It was then I knew that no matter the cost—no matter who or what I had to give up—I had to make her mine.

She's holding my hand like her life depends on it, guilt for giving in to what she craved shadowing her face.

Christ. What the fuck have I done to this girl? Like a dick, I've corroded her mind, tossing out some pretty heavy shit. I can't deny a part of me is pissed that she kissed Ryder again. Hell, I'd let her kiss whoever she wanted to if it made her happy, but I told her she wasn't allowed to further indulge in him without my permission.

I jerk my head, summoning her. "Come here, baby girl."

She blinks, a tear dripping from her eye. *Fuck.* My heart crashes again. She pulls in a staggered breath and crawls onto my lap, her body shaking.

I lift my hands to her face, cupping her cheeks. "I threw a lot at you tonight, didn't I?"

She nods, trepidation marring her features. "Yeah. But I guess we both did." She ducks her head. With her lips inches from mine, she seems afraid to kiss me.

I sigh, feeling like the king of assholes. The last thing I want is for her to fear me. I'd rather die. I breathe for this girl. No questions asked, I'd kill for her.

"Kiss me, Ber." I gather the silky waves of her hair in my hands, my body aching to feel any part of her. "I need you to kiss me, baby."

"Are you mad at me for what I did?" she whispers, hesitation flashing in those gorgeous yellow orbs. "I'm sorry, Brock. I'm so—"

I don't let her continue. I can't bear to hear her apologize for something I wouldn't crucify her for to begin with. I pull her to my lips, melting them over hers. Goose bumps pop across her milky skin, her little moan increasing the speed of my blood, the thudding of my heart as I slowly lick into her mouth.

The keeper of all things pure, sweet, and whole in my life, the girl's unaware that she owns my fucking soul. She has from the second she and her love for Twizzlers stumbled into the chaos of my world.

I slide my hands down the curve of her spine and under the swell of her ass, hauling her chest to mine. I deepen the kiss, my greed for her mounting with every unsteady breath she takes. Before I know it, she's unbuckling my belt and tugging my cock from my jeans. I grin and drag her sweater up over her head, her ebony hair spilling onto her shoulders.

"Wait," I whisper, the effort nearly killing me.

She stills, uncertainty hopping across her beautiful face.

"I need to look at you."

And I do.

Most guys would jump right into the fucking. Not me. Not with Amber. The hungry gaze in her unsated eyes, the soft sway of her clipped breathing, and the small tremors of need rolling through her unhinge me, driving me animalistic. The fucking is a blessing I'll never be worthy of, but it's the sight of her that does me in, releasing me from reality.

I unclasp her bra, her gorgeous tits falling free with a light bounce. Christ, she's fucking perfect, and she's mine. How I got so lucky, I'll never know. Mouth watering, I take one breast in my hand and draw her nipple between my teeth, lightly biting. Her back bows, her lusty moan filling my ears, causing my cock to pulse, the throb close to painful as I suck harder.

"You wanna fuck me, Ber?" My free hand travels up her back, fisting her hair. I stare at her, my tongue making a second, then third pass over her nipple. "Is that what you want?"

She answers the only way she knows how. On a moan, she sinks down onto my cock, her pussy clenching around me as she bounces up and down like it's the last time she'll ever get to. I suck in a quick breath, my balls tightening as she feathers her nails against them. Sweet Jesus. She feels so goddamn good. When we fuck, Amber becomes an extension of me, her essence the missing link to the chains encasing my heart.

I dig my fingers into her luscious hips, attempting to slow her movements. "You keep going like that, this isn't gonna last too long."

Ignoring my warning, she slams down harder, her sweet pants music to my ears. "I don't care. I want to make you feel good, Brock. I need to."

Hooded eyes glued to mine and licking her lips, she paws at the back of my neck. A gasp falls from her mouth as I jerk my hips up, hitting her deep within her slickened cunt.

Another jerk, another gasp.

Over and over, I fuck into her, our bodies shredding to pieces within seconds. Nothing compares to the way Amber looks when she's letting go. I've known that since the first time I took her. My name the only thing in her mouth, my body the only thing possessing hers, and my eyes the only thing in her line of sight, she's ravenous, her need to fuck unlike anything I've experienced.

I guide her face to mine, sweeping my lips over hers. "Thank you," I whisper, kissing her soft, slow. "And no, I'm not mad at you, Ber."

"You're *not?*" Shock swamps her tone as she cushions her cheek against my chest.

I bury my nose in her hair, my senses hijacked by the smell of raw sex and her raspberry shampoo. "Well, I was pissed for a hot second, but I'm cool now. We'll talk more about it when we get up to your room."

Amber nods, the tension in her muscles dissipating some as I help her get dressed. Once she's fully clothed, I spark up a joint, take a long hit, and pass it to Amber, who does the same. She smiles, her body fully relaxing. She leans over, hands the joint back to me, and coats my lips in a luscious kiss. For a beat, I stare into her glassy eyes, my gaze roaming her beautiful face. My cock twitches, telling me it wants another go. However, Amber straightens, reaches for her purse, and casts me one last glance before swinging open the door.

By the time we get up to her room, not only am I happy that Madeline crashed at Lee's place, but my dick is hard as a mother-fucker. Still, I know there's too much shit I have to explain to Amber. Shit I pray I can get her to understand, but I'm not sure it's gonna happen.

I kick off my shoes, tug my T-shirt over my head, and dump my jeans onto the floor. Falling onto the twin mattress, I crook a finger in Amber's direction. "Come lie down with me."

"I'll be right back," she says, digging through her makeup bag. She lifts her head, a smile sliding across her swollen lips. "I have to take my pill. No little mutant Brocks and Ambers for us."

"Mm." I nod, grinning. "Can't say I disagree. Go do your thing. I ain't going nowhere."

She swipes a pair of shorts and a tank top off her dresser and makes her way out into the hall, latching the door behind her. Crossing my arms behind my head, I fix my gaze on a poster of Jared Leto, whose eyes are staring back at mine, on the ceiling. I chuckle, wondering what the fuss over the dude's about. Before I can dwell too much on why chicks find the pansy-looking motherfucker appetizing, Amber comes back and sinks onto the bed.

I envelop her in my arms, tugging her onto my chest as I jut my chin in Jared's direction. "You think he's sexy? He looks like he bats for the other team."

She slaps my shoulder. "He does *not*." She twists her head around, looks at him, then back at me. "You should talk, buddy. Don't you go both ways?"

"*What?*" My balls hit my stomach. "Where the fuck did you get that from?"

She lays her cheek on my chest, tracing the tattoo on my bicep as she shrugs. "I don't know. I just figured because you and Ryder were with Hailey, that maybe you two were . . . also together."

God help me. My girl thinks I dig guys. She might as well tell me she's faked every orgasm I've given her. I slip a finger under her chin, bringing her eyes to mine.

"Ber."

"Brock," she replies with a shit-eating grin.

"Your assumption couldn't be further from the truth. That was some of the finest homegrown vipe we just smoked, so I'm gonna go with you being fucking blitzed. I swing one way, and that's in the direction of pussy. Nowhere else."

She pops a brow. "Who are you, Tarzan?"

"Hell yeah, I am. And you're my Jane, not my Jay. Got it?"

"Oh my God." She giggles and sits up, straddling my waist. "Do you know how cheesy and clichéd that sounds?"

"You think I give a fuck?" I slide my hands up her silky thighs, sneaking my fingers beneath her shorts. Gotta love a girl who hates wearing panties. I graze her clit. "Ah, there it is. *This* . . . this right here is the *only* thing your man touches, plays with, or wants. Understood?"

"Mm-hmm," she hums as I push a finger inside her, breaching the barrier of her sweet pussy.

There was doubt in that little hum, and I'm not about to ignore it. "You don't believe me?" I slide in a second finger, my thumb circling her clit. "Huh? You think I secretly want dick?"

"I never said that." She closes her eyes, a soft moan falling from her parted lips as my third finger makes its way inside her.

"You don't sound too convincing, Moretti." I pull my fingers out and lift them to her mouth, watching in amazement as she sucks them clean.

"Do I sense . . . insecurity from *the* Brock Cunningham?" Coy smile lighting up her face, she sits up on her knees and shimmies off her cotton shorts. Her tank top follows them to the floor as she glides my boxer briefs down my legs.

Sweet Christ. I lick my lips, ready to fuck her raw. "No insecurity, baby girl. I'm all man. So is Ryder. We set a firm no-contact-what-so-fucking-ever rule before anything happened."

"Mm-hmm." She nods, staring at me as she tugs on her nipples.

Grinning, my cock stands at attention. "Ber, if you 'mm-hmm' again, I'm gonna make sure you can't walk for a week. That's a threat you know I'll keep."

"Well," she purrs, "you *did* tell me earlier that you were going to . . . *damage* my pussy." Legs flared over my waist, she dips her head, dragging her tongue across my chest. My muscles tighten. "But before you do, I want the deets."

"Of what?" I groan as her hand slips down my abs, her fingers skimming the head of my cock.

"Of how it all came about with you, Ryder, and Hailey." Going in for the kill, she licks my neck and cups my balls.

Another groan, my breath halting.

Seduction 101. My girl should teach the goddamn course.

"Also," she adds, "I wanna know everything you did to her."

Convinced the weed was too strong for her, I sit up, my eyes pinned on hers as I carefully position her over my thighs. "You want me to tell you *everything?*"

"Yes." She leans in and sucks my bottom lip between her teeth. "I do."

"Why?"

"Because I deserve to know," she whispers, the look in her eyes gutting me. She shrugs, dousing my jaw with kisses. "Like I said, I wanna know how it first happened. I also want to know why you wanna share me with other guys."

"*Not* other guys, Amber. Only Ryder." Tucking her hair behind her ears, I kiss her lips, lingering there. "And I told you how it happened. We were all drummed up, and it just . . . happened. That's it."

"Right, but you said you weren't sure how many times you two banged her. Were you drunk every time you all hung out?"

"Yeah. Either that, smoked out, or both."

A hazy memory of Hailey straddling my waist, taking a pounding from me beneath her while Ryder fucked her fast from behind decays my thoughts. At the time, there was no limit to what a few hits of the good stuff, several shots of tequila, and a willing cheerleader could bring to me on a Friday night after a big win. Before I knew it, it was happening a few times a month.

Now, considering the shit the bitch has done to my girl, it's become the biggest regret of my life. Still, I can't deny that it opened me up to a darker side of myself I never knew existed. One I want to revisit. One I wasn't too sure I'd ever let Amber know about.

Amber slides off me and lays her head on my stomach, propping her feet against the wall. "So get to it. What's the deal? Why do you all of a sudden feel like sharing me?"

I coil a piece of her hair around my finger, trying to find the right words to explain where my sick head's at. "I think after doing that with them, I found that I dug the domination of it all. Not that there's *not* domination in doing it without a sidekick, but when another

dude's involved, it's a total breakdown for the girl. A complete surrender of her body. I liked it. Liked it enough to wanna do it again." I
pause, knowing I sound like a freak, but I need to experience that feeling with Amber. "I'm layered, Ber. I want to give you every goddamn
thing I can. Open you up. Help take away the pain you carry around."

Peering at me through hooded lids, hunger drenches Amber's face
as she touches her neck. "You don't think you already do that for me?"

"I'm not sure," I say in all honesty.

I know we fuck like animals, not a single sexual act gone undone.
We put the entire porn industry to shame. But my girl's different from
all the rest. An uncut diamond. Amber's need for release during sex—
to let go of everything tainting her memories—runs deeper than anything I think I can conquer on my own.

"Well, you do."

"Yeah?" I ask, hoping she's not just trying to gas up my head.

"Yeah, baby, you do." She gathers her tits in her hands, squeezing them as she drops her feet from the wall. Spreading her legs, she
swipes her tongue across her glossy lips. "You always have."

Fuck.

Soft as silk and glistening, her pussy's screaming for a pounding. I
swallow, rushing a hand through my hair. "Finger yourself for me, Ber.
Show me how badly that pretty cunt wants my cock."

Before I can inhale, she's knuckle deep, two fingers sliding in and
out of her pussy. A groan sneaks up my parched throat, the high that
is Amber intensifying mine. I take my dick in my hand, stroking it as
I watch her go at it.

"Tell me more," she pants, getting to her knees. Free hand swathed
over her tits, she continues to pleasure herself as she stares at me. "Tell
me what you two did to her. What you'd do to me."

I hesitate, but only for a second. Her little mewls and the insatiable look in her eyes nearly make me come. I lie back, my mouth
begging to taste her. "Sit on my face."

She obeys, and a moan filters from her lips as I grip her ass, holding her just enough above me to give me some maneuvering room. I spread her open and slide my tongue through her soft folds, lapping up every bit of her juices.

"Mm. Fuck yeah. No other pussy tastes as good as yours, baby girl. None." And that's not a lie. The perfect mixture of what a ripe pussy is supposed to taste, smell, and feel like, if I could, morning, noon, and night, Amber's pussy would be the only thing I'd consume.

Balls aching, I look up and catch her gaze.

She digs her fingers into my hair, tugging hard. "Please tell me," she begs over a long moan. "Tell me what you two did to her."

I shake my head and suck on her swollen clit, my teeth holding it prisoner before letting it go with a pop. "Don't worry about what we did to her. I just want you to think about what we'd do to *you*."

She nods, her hands flying to the wall as she starts riding my face like a jockey.

I continue to dig in, feasting on the real deal. Amber makes a man want to tongue-fuck her pussy. Some chicks turn into corpses, making not a goddamn noise while getting licked. Not my queen. She lives for this shit, her hips swaying in unison with my strokes, her moans painfully hardening my cock.

"You like when I fuck into that little ass of yours, don't you? The burn. The pain. The way my cock fills you."

"Yes," she hisses, her nails clawing at the wall. "Mm. God, yes, I love when you fuck me in my ass."

"That's right, you do." And she does. I've never encountered a girl who can take it the way she can. I drag two fingers through her silk, slowly circling the puckered rim of her ass. "Now picture having a cock inside of that pretty pussy of yours at the same time," I growl, licking through her as I burrow my fingers into her ass as deep as they can go. "Picture it, baby. Feel it."

She rides me faster and drops her hands to her tits, tweaking her

nipples as she looks down at me. "OhmyGod, Brock. Fuck. I'm . . . I'm
. . ." A shuddered breath, two, three, four, and she comes apart, a string
of spasms rocking her body.

I lift her off my face, flip her onto her back, and haul her legs over
my shoulders, fucking into her like a machine. Her body goes taut,
my name flying from her mouth as she breaks again, a second orgasm
slicing through her muscles. Christ, I live for the look in her beautiful,
sated eyes. It's pure heaven to the hell that was my life. The hell it'd still
be if I didn't have her.

I grab the back of her neck, pull her lips to mine, and kiss her long,
hard, and deep, our flavors mingling as she claws my biceps. "I love
you, Ber," I groan, seconds from erupting. "So fucking much."

Though Amber's not big on making love, I slow my pace. What
I'm asking her to do merits every bit of love I have for the girl. Every
ounce of repayment for what she's already brought to my world.

"I love you too, Brock." Amber looks into my eyes, confusion cascading across hers as I stop moving. She pulls her legs from my shoulders and cups my cheeks, worry crashing over her face. "What's wrong?"

I cradle her head, praying to God my twisted desire doesn't cause
me to lose her. "I just want to give you everything you want. I know
this whole thing's fucked up, believe me, I do, but I trust Ryder with
my life, and I'm okay with you wanting him. I can tell you're uncomfortable that I know how you feel about him, but I don't want you
feeling that way. You have enough shit plaguing your thoughts. I don't
need guilt fucking with you."

I kiss her lips, unsure if anything I've said has eased some of her
guilt, her confusion. "Everything about doing this with him would
fulfill *both* our needs. Your pleasure would become mine in ways you
can't imagine, baby. Hopefully mine would do the same for you. Just
think about the two of us taking you, worshipping you like the princess you are."

She stares at me, her heart thumping wildly against mine. I swallow, everything in me screaming that I've gone too far this time. Master of douchery, I've ruined the only good thing I have. The one person who makes me feel alive after years of feeling dead.

Amber drapes her arms around my neck, guiding my face within inches of hers. Her sweet breath brushes my cheeks. I inhale, burning her scent into my skull, scared to fucking death that this is the last time I'll hold her. I close my eyes, shivering like a full-blown pussy. Pussy or not, I deserve whatever's coming.

"Do you *really* love me, Brock?" she whispers shakily.

My heart skips a goddamn beat as my eyes burst open. "Christ, baby, more than you'll ever know." I slide my thumbs over the seam of her lips, sure the devil himself is gonna walk me through the gates of hell. "I love you more than anything. Need you more than the air in my lungs."

I kiss her forehead, ashamed that I've allowed my temptation to override what she truly needs. A real man. A man who would never toss this shit at his lady. A man who, no matter how much he desired something, would never put his wants before the goddess in his life.

"You're everything that completes me," I say. "Everything that was missing from my fucked-up universe. I'd lose it if you ever left me. Done deal. I wouldn't make it one day without you in my life."

"Then fuck me, Brock." She wraps her legs around my waist, her fingers sinking into my hair as she touches her lips to mine. "Make me forget who I am. What I've been through. That's all I want. I don't want to think about anything else. Not my parents, not Ryder, not tomorrow, not next year. I just want to think about you and me." She sweeps her tongue over mine, urgency thickening her tone. "I can't make a decision about anything right now. I can't. I just . . . need you to heal me, okay, baby? Just heal me right now. Please."

Soul hers until the day I die, I do as she asks, layering my mouth over hers as I try to take away her pain.

I only hope to God I didn't add to it.

CHAPTER 14

Ryder

I'S A LITTLE past two in the afternoon when I pull up to my mom's house nestled in the less-than-thrilling neighborhood of Glen Burnie. Supposedly it used to be a great area before it went to shit in the late eighties. Either way, my mother refuses to move because it's the home she grew up in. She, along with half the world, hates change. I'm sure she gets that from my grandmother, who also lives here.

I have just enough time to catch my mom before her five o'clock bartending shift, where she'll work until the early morning. It makes me sick. Did I mention she does this after she's cleaned a few rich bastards' homes along the bay?

Yeah. It sickens me.

"Hey, baby!" my mother squeaks. She tightens her brown hair into a ponytail, a smile beaming on her tired face as she strolls across the lawn. "Long time no see."

I kill the engine, flip open the glove compartment, and pluck out a small bottle of Visine, squeezing a few drops into my eyes before she approaches. I get out and give her a smile, hoping she can't tell I'm baked. "Yeah. Been working a lot." I pull her into a hug, realizing how much I've missed her. "Sorry, Denise."

Bad habit. I started calling her by her first name when I was fifteen. It began as a joke. My mother—when pissed off—refers to herself in the third person. She really didn't care too much for my ribbing on her, but she eventually softened up to it. Now it's the norm.

She pulls back and swipes a motherly hand through my hair, her smile melting into a frown. "Mac's working you boys to the bone, huh?"

"Yeah, but it's been a pretty busy season, so I'm stoked." I try to sound genuinely happy I'm getting work.

Though my boss is a cool cat, I use his construction company as a front. At the ripe, young age of twenty-four, I'm killing close to a hundred and fifty thousand a year between hanging drywall for Mac part-time, running grades for moronic students, and pushing coke for Brock. But unlike Brock and his bling-dripping apartment, clothes, and vehicles, I cover my tracks by making it look like I'm poor as snot.

I'm far from it. Retirement—somewhere along the Caribbean—is looking pretty fucking sweet.

"True," my mother points out. "A lot of people are out of work right now, so it's good you have something coming in."

I nod. "Wait. I thought your shift doesn't start until five." I look at my watch. "It's not even four."

She frowns again. "Pete called me in early."

Pete Flannigan, owner of—you guessed it—Flannigan's Irish Pub in Brooklyn Park, is a man who so badly needs to suffer a slow, blood-curdling, screaming death that I'd willingly hand over my left nut on a platter to watch it happen. Cheap with salaries, well practiced in fighting off sexual harassment lawsuits, and brutal with his employees' hours, Pete's the epitome of every douche-cock employer who's ever run a business.

Here's where that whole "change" thing—which gives my mother issues—poses a problem. She's worked for the prick for close to ten years. God help her, I'm not sure why the woman stays. I've talked to her about quitting until I was blue in the face. Needless to say, I constantly lose the battle.

"Denise, I can take care of you, Casey, and Gram." I rest my hands on her shoulders. They feel frail, overworked, and my chest tightens with something I can't describe. Guilt, possibly. "Let me pull the weight. Casey's hospital bills are too much."

She shakes her head and looks into my eyes, a retort perched on the tip of her tongue.

"Stop being stubborn and listen to me," I continue before she can say a word. "Switch jobs. Go work in a Laundromat to keep yourself busy if you have to. But let me take care of the bills."

"That's not your job, Ryder." She sighs, the lines cracking her face showing her exhaustion. "I'd never allow you to pay for anything in my home. You don't even live here anymore."

"And your point would be what?" I question, honestly trying to understand her madness. "I'm the only man left in this family. I not only feel that it's my duty to help out, but I *want* to help you, Mom." Using the name I should be calling the woman who gave birth to me usually works in my favor. "You've taken care of me my whole life. Let me do something for you in return."

Another shake of her head, her tone resolute. "No. Again, Ryder, it's not your job; it's his. He might be backed up seven years, but your dad's finally sending something every month. It's a decent amount, and we're doing okay for right now."

Though the asshole left her when I was fourteen, my father recently started paying child support for my sister.

At least that's what my mom *thinks*.

Last summer, after saving a fuckload of cash, I took a trip to California and used a cousin's address to open an out-of-state checking account.

Since I've been graced with the prick's first, middle, and last name, sending monthly payments as Ryder Jacob Ashcroft Senior is relatively easy. It's all good. I'm a firm believer of *what you don't know won't hurt you*, and in this case, Denise having no clue it's really *me* sending the cash, and *not* the sperm donor who helped create Casey and me, is something she'll never lose sleep over. Still, I make a mental note to send more.

"You're a tough one." I pull a cigarette from my pack. Before I can put it in my mouth, my mother swats it out of my hand.

Her nose scrunches up. "Disgusting! I can't believe girls kiss you smelling like that."

I lift a brow, a smirk twisting my lips. "*Many* girls kiss me smelling like this. The way I kiss them is how I make their noses forget how to function."

"My baby boy." She places a warm hand on my chilled cheek. "You need to take care of yourself. Kisses from the ladies won't get you longevity. Clean lungs will."

"I disagree." Shoving the pack back into the pocket of my sweatshirt, I kiss her forehead. "I'm pretty sure *both* will help prolong my life."

A smile lifts her green eyes but vanishes the second she looks at her watch. "Dammit. I have to get going." She pushes up on her tiptoes and plants a quick kiss on my cheek. Digging her keys from her purse, she starts for her beat-up Corolla. "Call me, okay? I'm getting tired of you being a stranger. We've missed you the past couple of weeks."

I nod and clasp my hands behind my neck, watching her back out of the driveway. My attention stays on her car until it makes a left out of the neighborhood. With a sigh, I bolt up the stairs onto the front porch, sliding my key into the lock. The second I step into the modest rancher, I hear Old Blue Eyes crooning "The Way You Look Tonight" from my grandmother's vintage record player. I can't help but smile when I see the black-and-white photos of my grandparents scattered from one end of the living room to the next.

I round the corner to the kitchen and catch a glimpse of Casey and my grandmother dancing to Frankie's smooth voice. My smile widens, and my grandmother dipping Casey elicits an uncontained chuckle from my chest. Stopping dead in their tracks and beaming in my direction, two of the three women who'll forever own my heart bum-rush me.

"Ryder!" Casey squeals, jumping up and throwing her arms around my neck.

I stumble back, laughing. God, she's growing so fast. It feels like it was just yesterday my mother brought her home for the first time. She was the sweetest goddamn thing to ever cross my vision, her existence making me understand what it is to truly love someone. The asshole who legally claims the title of her dad has no idea what he's missed. With a single look, the kid can fucking blind you, bringing the brightest ray of light to anyone's dark day.

Having taken well to her last chemo treatment, she's put on some much-needed weight. "Where've you been?" Casey tightens her hold around my neck. "You didn't stop by last week. Is Amber with you?" She cranes her head to the side, looking over my shoulder. "You better not have a new girlfriend. I like her, Ry."

My heart sinks to the ground. I've texted Amber a few times this week. Though she responded, her messages were clipped, using work, exhaustion, and something as fucking lame as laundry as excuses to jet. I even ran into her on campus, but her usual wiseassery and quips were missing. She felt distant, almost embarrassed to be in my presence. I can't blame her for hating me. Disgusted with myself, I've come to realize that her finding out what Brock and I did with Hailey was too much for her to swallow.

Apparently, the second Amber started dating Brock, Hailey's had it out for her. From snide little remarks in front of an entire frat party to leaving threatening letters under Amber's door, Hailey's mentally steamrolled over the girl. Other than her attempting to run Amber off the road—because that's when Amber finally said something to Brock—I didn't find out any of the shit the nut was doing to Amber until last weekend. Had I known a morsel of what was going on, I would've been done with the psycho long before.

Picture now clear, it's pretty simple: Hailey's jealous of Amber. Like a fiend, she couldn't get enough of Brock and me fucking her. Other than mastering a deep-throat blow job, begging for double penetration became her expertise.

But once Amber stumbled into the picture, Brock cut off Hailey from not only the free coke he was supplying her but also his dick. Once I got rid of her too, her hatred for Amber intensified, morphing out of control.

Hailey catching a beating from Amber last weekend was long overdue.

"Oh!" Casey hops out of my hold, breaking me from my thoughts. She snatches my hand and drags me down the hall to her bedroom. "I have something to show you!"

Jesus. They've painted again. It looks like a bottle of Pepto-Bismol threw up all over her walls.

"Come see the new clothes Mom bought for me," she squeaks, pulling me toward her closet. "You know I'm in third grade this year, right? In a few years, I'll be a preteen. Then a few years after that, I get to date boys like you!"

That freezes my feet.

I kneel and reach for her shoulders, steadying her excitement. "Case."

She nods, her blue eyes twinkling with innocence.

"One: I've been working. That's why I didn't come over last week. I'm gonna be busy for the next few months, so it might be hard for me to stop by every day, all right?"

She frowns as she nods again.

"Two: Amber's not my girlfriend. She's just . . . a buddy. I don't

have a girlfriend. Never count on any nieces or nephews from me."
I chuckle, taking in her cute little pout. I need to fix this. "Three: I'm
excited to see your new clothes. I bet you look like a princess in them."

That statement erases the pout, a megawatt smile replacing it.

"Four: You're not now, nor will you *ever* be, a preteen. I've created
a potion that's going to keep you eight years old *forever*. All of the boys
you're *not* going to date will also never, *ever* reach puberty."

Shit, the frown's back. I suck ass.

A laugh wrinkles my grandmother's nose, her caramel eyes dancing with joy as she enters the bedroom. "Pay him no mind, Case. Your
brother's just being overprotective. Right, Ry?"

I stand, caging my grandmother in a bear hug. "Umm, that would
be a big, fat, sloppy no. Her chastity belt's in the back of my car." I flash
my pearly whites. "It's called a bat to the head, courtesy of her older
brother."

"You bought me a belt?" Casey's excitement colors her voice. "I
like belts!"

I swish my hand over her peach fuzz. "Sorry, kiddo. No belt."

She lets out a huff, climbs up onto her bunk bed, and crosses her
arms. "No fun, Ryder."

I swipe a teddy bear from her dresser and toss it onto her lap.
"Next time I come over, I'll bring you one, deal?"

She chucks said teddy bear at my head. "Promise?"

At least she didn't smack my dimpled cheek.

"Cross it." I draw an X over my heart.

Amusement sparkles in my grandmother's eyes as she laces her
soft hand in mine. "Come on, overprotective brother. Let me feed you
while Casey gets dolled up in one of her outfits."

I leave my sister to get prettied up and follow my grandmother
into the kitchen, my stomach growling as I drop into a chair at the
island. It doesn't take long before I have her infamous chicken cutlet
parmesan plated up before me.

It also doesn't take long before my burner cell goes off, flashing Brock's number. I send it to voice mail and tuck it into my pocket. My grandmother's smile—as she waits for me to take my first bite—takes precedence over whatever shit he wants.

The fucker can wait.

"So, how's school going?" she asks as I sink my teeth into generation upon generation of practiced perfection. "Only one year left."

I nod, thinking about her statement. I've focused and sacrificed for the last five years, working toward my MBA in banking and financing. There's no doubt I'm ready to finish school. Amped, I'm more than eager to join the rest of the scum-sucking investors in corporate America. The industry's hostile, fierce, and competitive. It's a perfect storm that'll suit my fast-paced lifestyle, intense love of money, and quick-talking personality.

"I'm hanging in there," I answer, chewing. Before I can take my next bite, my burner goes off again. I pull it from my pocket and scan a text from Brock.

Monthly pickup. Meet me at my place by 3. Don't be late.

Mentally disconnecting from the temporary joy I've found, I delete the text and pocket the fucking thing. After I bid farewell to my girls, I'm out the door to go earn a living until corporate America welcomes me into its fucked-up, twisted game. As twisted and fucked up as it is, it's somewhat more legal than the shit I'm hustling now. The shit I plan on getting away from forever.

Eventually . . .

CHAPTER 15

Brock

"Maybe I'll go get laid or something." Attempting to piss me off, Amber stares dispassionately at her nails, her foot tapping against the pavement. "Some guy slipped me his number at the restaurant last week during my shift, and he was definitely fuckable."

I exhale a deep breath, trying to keep my cool.

"Goddamn." Ryder chuckles. "Talk about retaliation."

I shoot him a scathing glare, about ready to knock him the fuck out.

Amber lifts her eyes to mine, a pseudo-dreamy sigh rolling from her lips. "Yep. I'm calling him. I'm sure he'll find multiple ways to . . . *occupy* me while you're gone. Between your monthly pickups and away games, I'm constantly being left alone. He'll keep me busy."

Head officially fucked sideways, I hop into the rental van and slam the door closed. "Ber, every time I leave to make a pickup, you pull the same shit. How many times do we have to go through this?"

Pouting like a child, she crosses her arms. "As many times as I feel like it, bastard. That's how many."

I let loose an aggravated sigh, knowing she's as feisty as they come.

Still, that feistiness was the first thing that had me falling for the girl, my existence wrapped around her finger the second she smacked Ryder. But whipped or not, Amber knows this subject's nonnegotiable. No matter how much seeing her upset twists my head, I'll never drag her out to West Virginia with me. Besides putting her at risk for getting pinned for something she's not involved in, exposing her to the demented fuck I score my shit from is never happening.

Done deal. She's wasting oxygen.

Ryder flips a cigarette into his mouth, lighting it up as he sinks into the passenger side. "At least you're a bastard today, bro. No doubt that's a step up from the last time you didn't take her along for the ride." He turns his eyes on Amber. "What was it you called him, peach? A twat-waffle?" He taps his chin, his brows dipped in mock thought. "You know my IQ's close to genius, but I can't say I've ever come across that term. Good one. But what exactly *is* a twat-waffle? This boy's a *very, very* good student, so I promise to pay close attention while you school me."

Amber blows him a kiss and gives him the finger. "Do me a favor and use that huge brain of yours to figure out how to go to hell, Ryder. Sound good?"

Puffing out a ring of smoke, he gives her a slow smirk. "Mm. You're beyond goddamn sexy when you're pissed. This student gives the teacher an A for that alone." He reclines his seat back, tossing his feet onto the dash as he looks at me. "How do you *not* fuck her into submission when she disobeys you like this?"

Amber pokes her head through the window, her eyes narrowed. "Because he loves me, *twat-waffle*." Smiling, she blows him another kiss. "Make sure to add that to your dictionary, Mr. Genius."

Chuckling, Ryder shakes his head, defeat slumping his shoulders as Amber pats herself on the back.

I let out a laugh. "Ashcroft: zero. Moretti: one."

"Seriously, Brock," Amber continues, her pout resurfacing, "there's no reason why you can't take me with you. I know *why* you're going down there. I know what you sell, Mr. Big, bad coke man. You act like I'm an undercover or something." She slides into vixen mode, her eyes dripping with seduction as she gives me a once-over. "It's not fair. I wanna come with you."

"You *came* with me this morning." I take her face between my hands, pulling her sweet mouth to mine for a soft kiss. "Did you not?"

"Very funny, wiseass," she mumbles against my lips. "I'm being serious."

"So am I." I grin, slipping my fingers through her hair. "If I'm not mistaken, you came *twice*."

"But, Brock—"

"But nothing." I kiss her again and start the engine. Killing what's about to become a fight, I back out of the parking space. "Just go upstairs. It's too cold out here for you. I'll call you from my burner to let you know if we'll be back tonight or tomorrow morning."

She stares daggers at me, her middle finger making me its second target of the day. "I'm getting sick of this crap!"

"Come on now, why you gotta get all kinds of crazy?"

"Because you suck!" She spins and stomps toward the elevators.

Her ass—hidden beneath a pair of tightly fitted pink sweatpants—instantly hardens my cock. "Love you too. And you better answer when I call, Ber. I have no problem spending the rest of my life in prison if I have to come back and put a bullet in Mr. Fuckable's dick."

"Yeah, we'll see about that." Another finger before she disappears around the corner.

Christ. She owns my heart, but my girl knows how to fuck with it when she doesn't get her way. Guilt coats my stomach as I make a left out of my complex.

Ryder flicks his cigarette out the window, an entertained smile on his face as he slides a joint from behind his ear. "She's no joke, huh?"

I sigh, shaking my head. "You know how she gets."

"I guess I do." He sparks the joint, passing it to me after killing a few hits. "Still, she throws me off a little something every now and again."

"You and me both." I swipe the joint from him and take a long pull. Potent as hell, it instantly works its magic, wiping away every speck of guilt over leaving Amber behind.

"So what's been up with her this week?" Ryder drops his feet from the dash, curiosity moving over his face. "Other than just now, she's been . . . off. I know last weekend fucked with her, but there's more. Are you two all right?"

Sinking into the mother of all highs, I glance at Ryder, debating whether or not to tell him what I asked Amber to do with us. I haven't yet explained to him how far shit went that night.

How far *I* went that night.

After fucking around, we talked more about my request, how it'd benefit us all in a multitude of ways. With some heavy coaxing on my part, she eventually admitted to having fantasized about being with me and Ryder, but she ultimately decided it's something she's not ready for yet.

Figuring I'd give her time to sit on it, I haven't tapped the subject since last weekend. Born with the gift of persuasion, I know if I wanted to, I could easily get her to give in now. As tempted as I am to do just that, it wouldn't be right. Pressuring her into making a decision that's not truly her own isn't something I can bring myself to do. I love the girl too much to put her in that predicament.

Besides, I've already done enough harm.

Still, her curiosity's piqued. Sexual wheels spinning, Amber's brought it up several times, asking questions about how we'd all get through something so intimate without someone getting hurt. It's obvious she's worried about not only her heart, but also mine and Ryder's.

I've tried my best to assure her we'd all ease into it, taking our time to adjust to whatever bullshit might come along with the scenario. As twisted as I am, I know I'll be able to decompartmentalize. It sounds sick, but that's just the way my brain works. Knowing she uses sex as an escape from reality, I'm more than positive Amber will be able to separate the two, tossing aside any feelings she may cross. That's just the way *her* brain works.

"You two good or what?" Ryder's question snaps me from my thoughts.

I kick him another glance, wondering how the fuck I should go about telling him.

"This is some of the finest Gold Culiacan available, and you haven't answered me yet. You're not starting to bug out, are ya?"

"Nah. I'm cool." Deciding I'm gonna need more to get through this conversation, I take another few pulls from the joint and hand it back to him. "I gotta talk to you about something serious."

If I thought he looked curious before, I was wrong. Jesus, now he looks all-out disturbed. Ryder nods, his face peeled over in anxiety as he waits for me to continue.

I take a deep breath, knowing I just have to come out and fucking say it. "I told Amber I wanted to . . . share her with you."

The confusion in his eyes tells me this is gonna be an interesting ride at best.

CHAPTER 16

Ryder

I STILL, SHOCK FREEZING my muscles. "You're . . . fucking with me, right?"

"No, man, I'm not," Brock admits, his tone devoid of humor. "I know you two've got something going on. You have for a while, and I'm cool with it. No shit, I really am." He looks at the road then back at me. "I want to show her the highest level of pleasure possible. That's where you come in. We'd know how to work her, how to give her what she needs. Only the two of us can do that. She's undecided right now, but I know she wants it. Wants . . . us."

Tripped the fuck up, images rush through my mind of me exploring every inch of Amber's body the way I've repeatedly imagined I would if given the chance. My pulse speeds, thwacking like a drum as I try to digest his words. I take one last hit from the joint as I look out the window. Just thinking about Amber makes me hard, makes my balls throb. Still, my feelings for her go far beyond physical. Something close to a compulsion, my need for her has deepened.

When she talks, I want nothing more than to cover her lips with mine.

When she's upset, the ache to hold and comfort her is close to unbearable.

When I make her smile—Christ—I feel like a man, my heart bursting at the seams.

Though she's Brock's, the girl's supposed to be mine. From the second I saw her, something in my gut, a premonition of some sort, told me that. Fuck. I don't know what the hell it was—what the hell it is—but it happened and it hasn't let up, its claws digging into the hollow of my chest more with each passing day. Yeah. Way past physical.

Convinced Brock's playing a sick joke on me, I kill all thoughts of Amber, demolishing them as fast as possible. I know the asshole's trying to trap me by getting me to admit how much I crave his girl.

How much I need to make her a part of my life in whatever way I can.

Stubbing out the joint on the bottom of my boot, I swing my attention back to Brock. Blood drains from my face, pooling a clump of nervousness in my throat as I realize this isn't a joke. The skeptical look in his eyes, rigid set in his shoulders, and uncertainty dousing his face say it all.

He's dead . . . fucking . . . serious.

Brock shifts in his seat, casting me a sidelong glance. "Did you hear what I said? She's not sure what she wants right now, but if she decides she's cool with it—and I'm pretty positive she will—I want to share Amber with you."

The English language disintegrates from my fucking skull.

He sighs. "Come on, man. Say something."

"*Say* something?" The words snag in my throat, causing my voice to crack like a pubescent teenager's. Jesus. *I* must be the one who's bugging from the weed. "You want me to *say* something?"

He chuckles, the sick fuck, enjoying my reaction. "Yeah. That would be the point of me asking."

"How's about 'have you lost your goddamn mind?' Does that work?"

His eyes narrow, their light green turning sinister. "What the fuck is that supposed to mean?"

"Exactly what it's intended to mean. Have you lost your goddamn mind, Brock?" I pull out a cigarette, light it up, and take a drag, my nerves bouncing around as I stare at him. "Because I'm starting to think you have."

Confusion mars his forehead. "Why do you think I've lost my mind?"

"Jesus Christ. Do you *love* the girl or not?"

"Yeah, I fucking love her," he growls, gunning the gas. "That's why I want to do this for her. I liked doing it with Hailey, so I know I'll like it a fuckload more with Amber. I'll get off on watching her with you. She'll get off on being with you. For fuck's sake, you'll get off on finally being able to have her. If I don't have a problem with it, why the hell do you?"

"The problem is Amber's, *not* Hailey's." Aggravation grips me tight. Hailey couldn't hold a candle to Amber if she tried, and the fact that he's comparing the two has my nuts twisted. Since all truths are out, and I'm beyond caring if I piss him off, I'm not about to hold back. "I'm trying to understand why you'd ever want to share a jewel like Amber. If Amber were mine, end of fucking story—the thought would never cross my mind to share her with anyone. You included."

Brock shakes his head, frustration hardening his jaw. "You're not getting it."

"No, I guess I'm not. Enlighten me, bro, because I'm lost."

Legit, I am. Never in a million years would I think I'd pass up an opportunity to be with Amber. She's different, untouchable. A woman trapped in a past that killed who she was meant to be, her hardened outer shell hides nothing but pure, undeniable beauty. But, sweet Jesus, when the girl lets you in, you're done for. Other than beating for her, your heart is rendered useless, everything you knew yourself to be vanishing like the last breaths from a dying body.

With all of this, I'm hemmed the fuck up, anger at Brock for not seeing what he has with Amber controlling every tormented emotion kicking me in the balls.

"I love Amber in ways you'll never grasp," Brock says, his shoulders tightening as he merges onto an exit ramp. "You have no goddamn idea what she means to me. How much I need her. What she's brought to my empty existence after everything that happened with Brandon."

My stomach drops, distant memories of his brother plaguing my mind. The man lost himself the day that kid went missing. Unable to release himself from the guilt—no matter what he did to cover up the pain—Brock's been forever changed. His soul disappeared in an instant, never to be found again.

Considering his logic—if any—I stare at him long and hard. Blank, I got nothing. Kid brother gone, pressure from his parents, none of it makes sense or has anything to do with wanting to share Amber.

"Give me more," I demand. "Help me understand what the fuck's going on in your head. I get that you liked doing that shit with Hailey—so did I—but the playing field's different with Amber. There are raw emotions involved. None of that existed with Hailey."

And it didn't.

It was nothing but mindless fucking while I was banging Hailey with Brock. Even after he dropped out of the picture, my feelings for Hailey didn't change. They couldn't. She'd never grabbed me that way. We'd fuck, then fight, then fuck and fight some more. That's what we were good at.

Do I feel like an asshole for using her? Sure. The most important people in my world are women. Despite the nut she turned into, Hailey's someone's daughter. I'd kill any man who ever tried to pull that shit with the women in my life. Done deal: I'm the man I am because of my mother, grandmother, and Casey.

After my dick of a father bounced, it didn't take me long to realize there's beauty in all women. Even the ones who don't strike an emotional chord with me. Fragile as flowers, yet as hard as a mindfucking jigsaw puzzle, every woman warrants respect from a man. The very foundation of humanity, they deserve to be worshipped, their minds, bodies, and souls a gift from the heavens above.

Still, Hailey was aware of what we were. She went into the arrangement knowing neither I nor Brock had any intention of making her something serious.

But this? This would be a whole new level for all of us.

Brock flicks his eyes to mine, scrubbing a palm over his face. "I don't think I can get you to truly understand. I'm not sure *I* even understand it. I just . . . I need to give her everything she wants. You're part of that equation. You may not realize it, but you are." He inhales a long breath and lets it out, hesitation slowing his words. "She . . . Christ, she dreams about you."

I blink once, twice, blood roaring through my eardrums. "What do you mean she . . . dreams about me?"

He takes another breath, his tone dropping a notch. "Man, I've heard her say your name—more than once—while she's sleeping."

I palm the back of my neck, my nerves wired beyond repair. Hell, what the fuck do I say to that?

A part of me wants to bolt from the van, hitch a ride back to Brock's, and pull Amber into my arms, telling her she knows she belongs with me. Like she does mine, I'm invading her dreams, undeniable thoughts of me taking up residence in every crevice of her skull. Yet the other part of me has my stomach tumbling with nausea, my conscience aware that none of this is cool. My feelings for Amber, her feelings for me, Brock wanting to share her: it's all a dangerous shit storm of emotions brewing, waiting to demolish us all.

Still, how do any of us control how we feel? It's not as simple as erasing something. If it were, my need for Amber would be written on my heart with a fucking Sharpie—impossible to remove. The heart fires off warning flares when something's not right—and hell if they aren't exploding in mine right now—but how the fuck do I stop wanting someone I know was made for me?

The answer's a clear-cut, jagged piece of glass. One I'm sure is gonna bleed me the fuck out at the end . . .

I can't.

I haul in a breath, my lungs begging for air as I try to wrap my head around everything Brock's dumped in my lap. "I don't know what to say."

He swings his attention to me, his expression a lethal blend of determination, pain, and confusion. "I'm not losing it, bro. I just love the girl, and want to fulfill every fantasy she has. I know you think my reasons are self-serving, but they aren't. This is about the pleasure *we'd* give *her*. We could help get rid of everything weighing her down." He pauses a second, a smirk twitching his mouth. "You have no idea what she's like in bed. The filthy things she says. The way she moves. It's like she was a dude in a former life. She kills it, knowing exactly what to do. No joke, my girl was created to fuck a man into oblivion."

I gnaw on my lip, sure I've drawn blood. His statement ignites a series of explicit images that trample my mind, my cock awakening as jealousy simmers deep within my gut.

"I'm not saying that to sway you," he continues. "You don't need swaying, Ashcroft. I see the way you stare into her eyes. You think you look controlled around her. You might fool Amber, but I've known you a long time. I'm quite aware you're a fucking mess when she's within a mile of you." He chuckles lightly, shaking his head as he drags his attention back to the road. "To be honest, it . . . fascinates me. You've only been broken once, and after Stephanie pounced all over your heart, fucking that dirty old man, you shut down, never allowing another bitch to get into your head. Amber's got ya hooked, and you have yet to fully experience her."

Wondering how I've maintained a friendship with the prick for as long as I have, I grit my teeth, positive I'm about to beat him to the fucking ground. "You're a douche, you know this, right?"

"Ah, but I'm a giving, sharing douche, my friend." He grins. I shake my head, still trying to understand the dark depths of his brain. "I even know you two kissed ... again, while she was at your apartment."

Christ. This keeps getting better. I rush a hand through my un- kempt hair, wishing she would've given me a heads-up that she'd told him. "You know about that, huh?"

"Yeah. She said you tried to stop it, so I have to give you props for that, right?"

A medal's more like it.

He's lucky I didn't bang the shit outta Amber right there in my kitchen. Had Casey not been in the next room, it would've happened.

I sigh, knowing I'm fooling myself. I wouldn't have taken her like that. I crave Amber, God knows I do—but unbeknownst to her, I was seconds from stopping before she pulled away. I knew she de- served better than a quick fuck on my counter. I've lost control around her multiple times, screwing Brock over to no end. Since the day he started dating the girl, I've relentlessly pursued her, willing to throw away our friendship for a taste of what's rightfully his. And *I'm* the one questioning *his* darkness?

"Why?"

He glances at me, his brows dipped in confusion. "Why what?"

"Why, after knowing what I've done behind your back—even if it was just kissing—would you ever consider sharing her with me?" I take a breath, feeling like the asshole I've become. "I don't get it."

He stays quiet a minute, thoughts moving behind his eyes before saying, "Because you *didn't* fuck her when I know you could've. Call me nuts, but instead of making me not trust you, that made me trust you more."

Trust. Something I've tarnished, tainted beyond recognition, but am being rewarded with.

"So now what?" I ask, unsure what to do, what to say. Hell, I feel psychotic, my head a tangled mess.

Brock grips the wheel as he stares straight ahead. "Tell me if she's down with it, then so are you." He turns to me, his eyes imploring. "Help me give her what she needs. What she . . . wants."

A fiend at his worst, this junkie's eager to get his fix no matter what he has to do. Amber's my obsession, the sweetest addiction a man like me can have. And right now—even if it goes against what I would or wouldn't do if she were mine—I nod, praying the deal I've struck with the devil doesn't sink us all.

. . .

By the time we pull up to Dom's farmhouse in Harpers Ferry—a lifeless town in no-man's-land West Virginia—my mind's spun in every fucking direction. It's close to six in the evening, the sun long past its descent, as Brock parks the rental van around the back.

Though I've been through this routine more times than I can count, I can't help the unease churning my stomach. In this business, it's impossible not to run across a few freaks here and there. But Dom Lawrence steals the goddamn show. From offing fuckers who've stopped buying from him to the whacko's racist, redneck, neo-Nazi lifestyle, the dude's head is jacked up, no doubt.

What the sick fuck doesn't know is that when pushed, this cat's head can twist the same way. If not worse.

I open the glove compartment and grab my trusty thirty-eight Smith & Wesson, checking to make sure every chamber's loaded. Brock does the same with his nine-millimeter Sig, chuckling as I hop out of the van.

I shove the gun down the waistband of my jeans. "Why the fuck are you laughing?"

"It never fails. Every time we come here, you look like you're walking into your own funeral." A smirk slides across his face as he plucks a bank bag that's holding triple what a middle-income family earns in a year from the center console. "I swear to God, you turn into a certified pussy the second we step foot onto this property."

"I'm no pussy." I shoot him a glare, gravel crunching beneath my boots as I round the van. I spark a cigarette, blowing the smoke into the late October air. "Furthest thing from it. Never mind that I actually *like* my life—and want to live it as long as possible—I just realize how warped Dom is. For whatever reasons, ones I'm positive I'll never understand, you don't."

"You think I *don't* know how crazy the asshole is?" Brock jumps out of the van, his smirk disappearing. "Come on, man. I may not be able to claim the 'genius' title like you, but I'm not clueless. I'm plenty aware he's missing a few nuts and bolts."

I shrug, sliding the hood of my sweatshirt over my head. "I have no fucking clue. All I know is he's not the only supplier on the East Coast."

"Ah, but he's the only one selling me a load for ten grand less than all the rest of the pricks out there." He slaps my shoulder, his smirk making a comeback. "Cash, my brother. Not that we don't have enough, but by the time we're thirty, we'll be balls deep in it. We take a lot of risks pushing this shit. Might as well make it count."

Profit—that's what it's all about for Brock. Fuck our lives. As long as he's getting a deal, everything else—including the oxygen we breathe—is a nuisance to him. But I can't deny my buddy understands numbers.

This far north, a kilo will bang your pocket a cool thirty-five thousand. Most of the time, the shit's recompressed with every kind of cutting agent imaginable, making your loyal fan base unhappy when their high's not tight. Besides producing pure, uncut coke, Dom sells a kilo to Brock for twenty-five thousand. On the norm, Brock yanks up two a month.

Never messing with shit amounts like eight balls, Brock goes hard, dumping nothing less than ounces out to his buyers. Knowing he has the best blow available, Brock gets rid of those ounces for a few hundred more than what they'd go for on average.

Clientele a mixed bag of small street dealers, the highest-paid lawyers money can secure, CEOs of corrupt corporations, and scum-sucking politicians, Brock's got half the DC/Bay Area sniffing their stress away out of the palm of his equally dirty hand, their need to stay on top running his profit margin close to one hundred and fifty percent.

America: home of the free, land of the finest waste available on the fucking planet.

"Now grab your balls and stop being a pussy." Brock checks his gun again before shoving it and the bag of cash into his jacket. "If you have to, think about your mother, Casey, and your grandmother. All the ways you've financially helped them. You're their goddamn savior."

I blow a ring of smoke into Brock's face, guilt for lying to my mother stabbing my heart. Guilt or not, he's right. Their well-being's the only thing that's fueled me this far. A few more years of this shit, and I'm out, never to compromise my morals for this filthy lifestyle again.

With that in mind, we make for the warehouse, my hand on my gun as we reach the back door. Entering, the domed metal bay lights nearly blind me before I see Dom.

Sitting at his desk—in the middle of enjoying a blow job from some blonde knelt before him—Dom jerks his buzzed head up. An aggravated frown hits his face as Blondie whips her attention to me and Brock, putting the brakes on her pleasure-inducing skills.

I inwardly smile, getting off on fucking up the asshole's night.

"I'll call you later," the blonde says through an embarrassed whisper.

"Get your lips back on my cock," Dom growls, shoving the barrel of his pistol against her temple as she attempts to scramble to her feet.

I'm about to fucking lose it. I take a ground-eating step forward, but Brock seizes my arm, hauling me back.

"I never told you to stop." Fury ignites Dom's words. "Who the fuck told you to stop? Are you hearing voices, whore? Is that what this is?"

"No . . . bu-but two guys came in," Blondie stammers, clearly freaked out. "I thought—"

Dom's free hand crashes down on her shoulder, holding her in place as he cocks the gun. "Don't make me repeat myself," he half snarls, half chuckles. He lifts his dark eyes to me and Brock. "I'm sure these men don't feel like seeing your pretty little brains splattered across this warehouse. That would make for such a mess, wouldn't it?"

She nods, a whimper caught in her throat as he fists the back of her skull.

Continuing to hold the gun to her temple, Dom pets her golden locks, a jeering smile splitting his mouth as he commands, "Finish me off or wind up buried somewhere beneath the horse shit stinking up my property. The world couldn't give a fuck less about finding girls like you."

Heeding his warning, Blondie's head disappears under the desk.

"How long ya been doin' business with me, Brock?" Dom's hollow stare stays on ours as the slurping sound of Blondie sucking him off sneaks into my ears. "Huh? How long?"

"Sorry, man, I—"

"Don't *ever* come in here without knocking." Aiming his gun in the air, Dom pops off a shot into the ceiling, tiny fragments of mortar, Sheetrock, and metal falling to the ground as Blondie stifles a petrified cry. Still, the girl keeps at it, her head furiously bobbing up and down. "That is, unless ya feel like a bullet from this here Desert Eagle tearing through your skull will add some excitement to your day. You know the fucking rules. *Abide. By. Them.*"

"Go fuck your cousin, you hillbilly, wheat-smoking asshole," Brock hisses, vengeance lighting his eyes. "Don't threaten me, dick. I don't give a fuck *who* you are. I'd gladly take one of your bullets before *ever* giving you the satisfaction of letting you think you intimidate me."

I rest my hand on my gun, ready, waiting, and itching to show this prick what's up. Glaring at Brock, Dom slowly rises and yanks up Blondie by her hair, shoving her to the ground as he pulls on his camos. Her knees scrape the cement, her naked body trembling as she scurries into a corner like a scared, helpless animal. My stomach twists at the sickening sight.

Dom scratches his head, his combat boots echoing through the chilled warehouse as he approaches us. An unnerving laugh rips from his chest as he lifts his gun to the center of Brock's forehead. Unblinking, Brock smirks, his teeth curling over his lips as I pull out my Smith & Wesson and pin it to Dom's cheek. Finger steady, I cock it and suck in a slow breath, preparing myself for what's to come.

My first kill.

Before I can swallow the last remnants of morality I have left, I feel the icy barrel of a shotgun against the back of my skull. The chilling sound of it being cocked causes goose bumps to jump across my skin, sweat instantly forming on the back of my neck. Heart pounding, I slide my gun to Dom's temple, visions of my grieving mother, sister, and grandmother jamming my thoughts as I accept my fate.

"Well, looky what we got here," Dom says. "Looks like the only fucker *not* dying tonight is Bobby."

"Ain't that the truth." Bobby jabs the shotgun harder against my head.

Dom flicks his lifeless gaze over my shoulder, a small grin glued to his face. "It's a shame too, because I was excited about sawing through Cindy's cunt before the wife and kids got back from my in-laws'. No comparison, she fucks better than my old lady ever has."

The blonde—who now has a name and remains curled up into a tight ball—whimpers again, tears plopping down her cheeks as she stares at us from the corner.

Brock brings his gun to his temple and cocks it. "I'd rather put a bullet in my *own* head than let you get off on killing me. Go ahead. I dare you to test just how warped this college boy really is." Eyes locked on Dom's, Brock juts his chin in my direction. "But keep in mind my dick will be as hard as they come knowing my buddy here blew your head to fucking pieces. Just a little something for you to ponder while you're trying to make a decision. In the meantime, I guess I'll be seeing ya in hell."

Time's suspended above me, fragments of memories popping in and out of my mind as I wait for the dick to say something.

My father's last drunken words before walking out of our lives. The confusion of what we'd done to make him leave taking over . . .

The day my mother placed Casey's tiny body in my arms. The fear running through me when we found out she had cancer . . .

The cherry scent of my grandfather's cigars as he spoke of his many years in the Marines. The proud look in his eyes when I became the man my father never could . . .

My grandmother's petrified face when her lover of fifty years took his last breath. Her beautiful smiles when I helped my mother and Casey get through the emotional shit girls endure . . .

The second mine and Amber's eyes met, down to this very moment of knowing I'll never be anything more to her . . .

I swallow. I'm not ready to leave behind the women who make up every good and bad memory I have. Staring into the cold, calculating eyes of the Grim Reaper himself, I'm not sure how many minutes creep by before Dom clears his throat, breaking the silence.

But as sure as I'm holding a gun to the head of an evil asshole, I'm positive about one thing . . . This memory isn't mine to make.

The decision to kill a man lies solely in a loaded gun in the hand of a man I'm certain has Satan's blood coursing through his veins.

"I always knew I liked you, Cunningham." Dom taps the barrel of his gun against Brock's cheek. "So because of that, I'm willing to let ya walk out of here with your head intact. But this here deal hinges on two things: Ryder lowers his weapon, *and* you buy the load you came here for."

"Fuck you, cocksucker," I spit, my free hand joining the other as I grip the pistol tighter. "You can bet your mother's saggy tits we're yanking up the blow we came here to get, but you're crazier than I'd ever thought if ya think for one fucking second *I'm* dropping my gun first." My eyes shift between Brock and Dom.

Brock nods, telling me all I need to know. Unless the sick fuck listens to what I say, I get to paint the goddamn walls with his blood.

"If *you* wanna walk outta here with *your* head intact," I continue, "you and your pussy friend are gonna play by my rules."

Dom tilts his head. "So now we're playing a game?"

"Yeah, motherfucker," I snarl, inching closer. Bobby moves with me, making sure his shotgun doesn't lose contact with my skull. "We're playing a game that, I assure you, I'll win. I haven't got a thing to live for, so the idea of dying tonight has me lit the fuck up. This shit's the most exciting thing to happen to me since I found out how to rub one off."

"Don't ya go listening to him, Dom," Bobby urges. "They disrespected ya. Ya can't let them get away with that. If ya do, it'll show you have vul-vulner-vulnerabilities."

"Go back to school, you fucking re-re-retard," I quip, wondering how the imbecile knows how to handle a gun. "You mean it'll show he's vulnerable, numb-nuts."

"Fuck you, Ryder," Bobby all but cries, sliding the barrel of the shotgun to the center of my spine. "The second one of these here slugs slices through yer' bones, you'll never walk again. I'm about to turn ya into a pa-par-paramedic. How ya like them there apples?"

"Jesus Christ, it's a paraplegic!" I'm positive I'm already in hell. I narrow my eyes at Dom, pissed that he's going to allow the stupidest man on the face of the planet to take my life. If I'm dying tonight, it needs to happen right the fuck now. This is an embarrassment to my ego. "I'm getting annoyed, and when I get annoyed, bad shit happens. When bad shit happens, no one's happy. When no one's happy . . . well, that's not good. Actually, it's pretty fucking bad." I smirk. This shit's comical. Yup, I've lost my goddamn mind. "If you don't tell your boy to drop his gun, everyone—*including* the naked whore—is getting their beauty sleep in the morgue tonight." I swing my eyes to Blondie and kick her a wink. "You ready to die, sweetcheeks?"

Full neon pink lips trembling, she lets out a cry, her body convulsing with a severe case of the shakes as I bring my attention back to Dom. "Despite what they say, brunettes have more fun, and they fuck a whole lot better. Besides, I've always wanted to add a bitch to my list of kills."

Dom stares at me for several agonizing seconds, his mouth pressed into a hard line. "What are your terms?"

"Ah, they're quite simple," I answer. "First, Einstein's gonna remove the barrel of his shotgun from my spine. The pressure it's putting on my back isn't good for a young buck like me. What can I say? I'm conscious of scoliosis and shit like that." I hear Brock chuckle. Like mine, the bastard's mental state's in the middle of snapping. "Then"—I crane my head toward a row of monstrous shelving units—"Einstein's gonna kick his shotgun over to those metal racks. After that, the rest is technicalities. You're gonna follow your buddy's lead and make sure your nifty little Desert Eagle also reaches those metal racks."

Dom looks at Brock then back at me, skepticism brimming in his eyes. "Ya think I'm an asshole? How do I know you're not just gonna kill us both?"

"Why, I give you my scout's honor, of *course*." I shrug, a lopsided grin tugging my mouth. "And—*only* because you asked—I do happen to think you're an asshole. You've ruined a perfectly good Friday night for me and my friend. I'm feeling a tad bit . . . hostile because of this." I sigh, feigning disinterest in life or death. "I'm getting bored, and my arm's startin' to hurt from holding it in this position. You have ten seconds or . . . well, need I further explain?"

Other than Blondie's soft cries, silence cloaks the warehouse, suffocating my thoughts. Once again, time stops, holding me prisoner in its wicked grip. Dangling my future in front of me, Mother Time is in control. She's the relentless cunt making the ultimate decision.

Vision tunneled on Dom's expressionless face and sweat sluicing from my pores like filthy buckets of water, I take what could be my last breath.

Dom jerks his head toward Bobby. "Do what the kid said."

"Are ya shittin' me?" The words tumble from Bobby in an exasperated rush. "Ya gotta think about—"

"Don't question me!" Dom's eyes narrow into slits, fury reddening his usually pale complexion. "Just do it!"

Relief spirals through me, my pulse pounding out of control as Bobby drops the shotgun. Christ. The sound of it hitting the cement hardens my cock. A second ticks by and he kicks it, the sight of it sliding under the rack a goddamn visual orgasm.

Gun remaining pinned to Dom's head, I nod my approval. "Well done, gentleman. If my hands weren't occupied, I'd give ya's a fucking round of applause. Considering Zipperhead thought the correct term for a paraplegic was 'paramedic,' I wasn't sure he'd understand the logistics of kicking something." I smirk, needing to make the dick pay a little more. "Now tell him to go stand in the corner—his back facing us—until I'm ready for him to load up our van."

Jaw clenched, Dom stares long and hard at me before jutting his chin toward a corner. "You heard him."

"This is insane, Dom!" Bobby stomps toward some random corner. "Complete bullshit!"

My smirk explodes as the fucktard does as told. "Looks like it's your turn, Dom," I point out with a casual shrug, well aware—but not giving a single fuck—that I pushed my luck past its limit several minutes ago. "Let's see if you're as responsive as your buddy is. Drop your shit or end up the reason we'll all get to experience rigor mortis tonight."

"I've got cameras all over this bitch, Ashcroft," Dom warns, his voice disturbingly calm. He lowers his gun from Brock's forehead and tosses it to the ground. He kicks it, the weapon joining Bobby's across the warehouse. Staring into my eyes—the evilness pouring from him fisting my balls—he grins and points at the four corners of the ceiling. "Say hello, prick. You're on television."

I don't lift my gaze from his. I don't have to. I know he's telling the truth. The asshole's as paranoid as a prison escapee. From motion detectors to an arsenal of weapons stockpiled in his stables, the dick has every acre he owns covered.

"You pull anything shady," Dom continues, "it won't take long for Derick to figure out it was you and Brock. You'll be begging for the cops to come get ya's after he finishes what ya's started here. Bet on that."

Older than Dom by five years, Derick Lawrence—if at all possible—makes Dom look like an altar boy. After their mother died from an overdose when they were in high school, and their father took his last breaths in prison for murdering an innocent family during a home invasion, Derick raised Dom. Having no other living relatives, and knowing nothing but violence, Derick dragged Dom into the lifestyle he currently leads.

It's safe to say Dom's threat's not a threat but indeed a fact.

Dom swings his attention to Brock, a sardonic smile resting on his lips. "But I can do better than that. I know where ya live, Cunningham. Never forget this, motherfucker. It was just the other day me and Derick took a trip out to Annapolis for a little get-together. I might've had a few too many beers in me when we passed your complex, but I could've *sworn* I saw a tight piece of ass getting out of your ride. Dark, wavy, long hair. Tits you could suck on for days." He licks his lips, his smile vanishing. "It'd be a shame to hurt such a cute little thing. But no worries, my friend. I'd make sure to fuck her pussy *real* good before I made her pay for your disrespect."

I automatically react, my fist connecting with Dom's rib cage.

Hunched over like a cripple, Dom curls his arms around his stomach, a wheeze of pain slipping from his mouth. "Guess I hit a soft spot." He lets out a scornful laugh and straightens. "I'll keep that in mind when I'm scrubbing her bloodstains off my clothing."

Bobby lunges for his gun, but I lift mine, halting his forward motion.

"Too slow." I aim it at his head. "You tryin' to piss me off, dick?"

His hands shoot heaven-bound in surrender as I approach him. "Fine! I ain't doin' nothing, man! Just calm down, okay?"

I scratch my jaw, wondering if I should kill him or scar his mental state a little more than it already is. Not about to take any risks, my fist graces the side of his skull, knocking him clear the fuck out.

After watching all two hundred and fifty–plus pounds of his fat ass slither to the ground, I walk back over to Brock and rest my hand on his shoulder. "Wanna add a few colorful bruises to Dom's face before we get back to business?"

"Yeah," Brock answers, his voice eerily cold. A chill of unease shoots down my spine as he steps into Dom's face, revenge lighting his eyes. "As a matter of fact, I do."

It takes me a second to realize what's about to happen, but by the time I've gathered my thoughts, Brock has his gun shoved in Dom's mouth, his free hand gripping the psycho's collar as he whispers, "You threatened my girl's life. Say good night, motherfucker."

Adrenaline expands my veins as Brock pulls the trigger, blowing Dom's brains straight out the back of his head.

Blondie screams, her deafening cries slicing through my ears as I try to process what's happened. Fuck. Frozen, I can't breathe, can't think. The only thing I'm capable of doing is watching a tidal wave demolish my dreams, wiping out my future as Dom drops to the ground. Lifeless body twitching, blood pools around what's left of Dom's head, his eyes wide open as his last garbled breath evaporates into the air.

I blink, oxygen rushing into my depleted lungs as Bobby comes to and reaches for his gun. "No!" I yell, snagging Brock's attention. He swings around and pops off a shot, the bullet hitting Bobby in the center of his chest. The impact knocks him back, his body coiled into a ball.

Brock crosses the warehouse and stands over him, the tip of his boot pressed to his throat. "What's the code to the room holding the blow?"

"Fuck you!" Bobby wails in pain. "You ki-killed Dom." Another hiss of pain follows a measured smile stretching his lips. "Derick's gonna ea-eat you alive."

Brock digs his boot harder against Bobby's esophagus. "Answer me now, motherfucker, and I won't kill you. What's. The. Code. To. The. Room?"

A glimmer of hope sparks in Bobby's eyes as blood bubbles up from his mouth, oozing down the side of his cheekbone. He coughs, gurgling out, "The code spells 'die pig.' 343744."

Brock tilts his head, not a hint of remorse on his face. "Thanks for the information, but I changed my mind, asshole." Before I can take a breath, Brock sends a second bullet into Bobby's chest, this one tearing through his heart.

God help us . . .

Hysteria riffles through me as I sink my fingers into my hair, gripping the sweaty strands. Brock's lost it and I'm right behind him, my sanity splintering by the second. Muscles strung taut with anxiety, I hunch over, my stomach threatening to hurl. The whore's hiccupped cries knife at my ears, her howls drowning out the sound of my dry heaves as Brock steps over Bobby's body and stomps across the warehouse, his piece aimed at the girl's head.

Raw fear dilates her pupils, her lips quivering as Brock kneels beside her.

"No, Brock! Listen to me!" My voice cracks midsentence as I come up behind him, resting my hand on the back of his neck. "Don't do this, bro. She didn't do anything."

"She has to die," Brock says flatly, his tone hollow as he shoves the gun under her chin. "She saw everything. Knows what we look like, our names. We gotta get rid of her." He tucks his hand under her armpit, dragging her up off the floor. "Wrong place, wrong time. That's all."

A cry drops from her mouth, tears swallowing her pale face. "God, please don't. I—I won't say a word." Rivulets of mascara darken her cheeks, her frail, naked body shaking as her stare bounces between me and Brock. "Please. I'll leave here, and you'll never hear from me again. I . . . I've seen men kill other men. Seen Dom do it a coup-couple of times, and I never said a word. I swear on my *son* I won't tell anyone."

Christ. The whore's a mother. I can't let this happen. Though she's a risk, I'd never be able to live with myself.

I hit the place I know will hurt Brock the most. The only place that might stop him from taking her out. "Think of Brandon, bro. If you do this, you won't be around when they find the kid." I cringe, knowing I'm spewing false hope—but fuck—it's all I got. Hope that my words will penetrate somewhere inside him in a way that not even the mention of Amber can. "He's gonna need his older brother to teach him shit about life. Shit he's not gonna wanna learn from behind a partition when you're serving a life sentence for killing anyone else."

The second I see a flash of sanity in his eyes, I lay my hand on his, guiding the gun away from the girl's face.

She grabs her stomach and pukes, her dinner splattering the cement.

"We don't have to kill her," I continue, cautiously taking the gun from him. "There's other ways of doing this." For the sake of the whore's kid, I'm about to do something that'd never normally cross my mind. But in this very moment, I'm not who I used to be. My mind, along with my morals, fucked off the second Brock killed Dom.

I fist the back of her greasy hair, my voice a fiery whisper as I pin the gun to her cheek. "You have a purse here with you?"

She nods, a sob on the heels of the shaky movement. "It's under Dom's de-desk."

"Grab her purse, Brock." I pull her into my chest, the stench of her vomit-tinged breath curdling my stomach. "We're about to play another game."

Brock cuts his eyes to mine and—with little hesitation—fetches her purse.

"Find her license and read out her name and address." Gaze stuck on hers, I hear Brock shuffling through her belongings, my heart surging at the lines I'm about to cross. To keep Brock from killing her, I need to turn into an animal, erasing everything I was taught never to do to a woman.

"Cindy Lewis," Brock announces. "Four eighty-three Culvert Road, apartment B, Matoaka, West Virginia, two four seven three six."

"Repeat what he said." I clench her hair tighter. "*Now.*"

"Cin-Cindy Lewis," she cries, her lips trembling, "Fo . . . four eighty-three Culvert Road, apartment B, Matoaka, West Virginia, two four seven three six."

"Very good, Cindy. You wanna live?" I question, sick at what I'm doing. "Wanna wake up to your kid tomorrow? See him grow up?"

Another nod, snot dripping from her nose.

"Answer me!" I untangle my fingers from her hair, the back of my hand singeing her cheek in a ruthless smack. She loses her footing, but I catch her by the nape, dragging her flush to my chest. "Don't just fucking nod! This is serious! *Do. You. Want. To. Live?*"

"Yes!" she sobs, her naked body falling limp against mine. "I want to live!"

"'That's what I thought." Though I'm anything but, my words come out calmly. I grip her chin, digging my fingers into her flesh.

"I want you to listen *very* carefully, Cindy Lewis from Matoaka, West Virginia. You ready?"

"Ye-yes."

"I'm gonna let you walk outta here alive so you can see that kid of yours grow up. But I'm keeping your license—as insurance, if you will. Understand?"

Relief loosens her muscles as she sniffles. "Mm-hmm. I—I do."

"Again, very good, Cindy. Now, do you have a vehicle here or did Dom pick you up?"

"I drove here in mine," she whispers, her sobs quieting. "Dom wanted to pick me up, but I ju-just got it for my sixteenth birthday, so I wa-wanted to drive it."

Jesus. She's only a kid. Nausea rolls through me as I glance at Brock. After looking at her license he nods, confirming her age. The pig wasn't just fucking around behind his wife's back, but he was banging a minor. Another piece of my morals disintegrates, flames igniting any guilt I had over Brock killing Dom into ashes. If I could, I'd resurrect the asshole, take a dump in his mouth, and stick a bullet in his crusty thirty-five-year-old balls.

"Perfect," I say, sliding back into character. "You're gonna get in your car, drive home to that kid who needs you, and forget what my and my buddy's faces look like. You're *especially* gonna forget what happened here tonight." I suck in an uneven breath, feeling like scum. I've never hit, threatened, or fucked with a girl like this, but I push through, knowing my hideous acts are saving her from Brock making her his next target.

I bring the gun to her head. "If you *don't* do what I said—and decide to call the cops—once I get out of prison, I *will* hunt your coke-sniffing ass down, and knife your body open from your dirty cunt all the way up to your chapped lips. Ya hearing me?"

Whimpering, she nods. "I—I am. God, I am."

"Good." I stare into her dark, chocolate eyes, hoping she can see

I'm not the monster she thinks I am. I release her chin and, with the gun still pinned to her head, I glance at my watch. "You have one minute to get dressed and disappear. Your time begins . . . now."

She snatches her purse from Brock, gathers her clothing, and—without getting dressed—scurries out of the warehouse, her sobs piercing my ears as the door slams closed behind her.

"Fuuuuck," Brock groans, swinging his fist through the air. "I should've had you test the code before I killed Bobby. Come on." He starts for the room harboring the coke. "We have to yank up the shit and get the hell outta here."

Numb, I stare at him, unsure of what either of us has morphed into. Willing my body to move, to react, to do something, I follow Brock, my heart thumping at dangerous levels as he punches the code into a security panel flanking a metal door.

A long beep, a red light turns green, and *bam*: I'm staring at enough pearl to keep the entire Eastern Seaboard geeked up for months, if not years.

On top of accessory to murder and threatening the shit out of a minor, I'm about to add theft to my growing list of immoral acts. No amount of visits to the confessional booth is gonna get me outta this one . . .

I enter, my eyes landing on endless stacks of kilo bricks lining a room the size of a small office. If I had to estimate the street value on the shit, it'd be somewhere around fifteen to twenty million.

"Grab that." Brock points to a black duffel bag cushioned against a filing cabinet as he starts swiping the coke from the shelves.

I walk over to the bag and lift it, my bicep getting a workout from its weight. Other than a small body, there's only one thing that can be inside it. I set it on top of a wooden table and unzip it, my intuition proving right as a slew of AK-47s, a shiny twelve-gauge shotgun, and at least twenty pistols hit my line of sight.

I dump everything onto the table and lean against the wall, my arms crossed as I watch Brock fill the bag. Nerves mounting, my head begins to fully digest what's gone down. What started as a normal pickup ended in complete chaos, two assholes losing their pathetic lives because of us. I didn't pull the trigger, but Bobby and Dom's blood is on my hands as much as Brock's.

Movements carried out with quick precision, and stare narrowed on mine, Brock continues to stack out the bag. "We should've gotten rid of her."

"I wasn't gonna let you kill an innocent kid," I mutter under my breath. "I get that you snapped when Dom threatened Amber—so did I—but that's where it needed to end."

Having nothing more to say, I turn and walk out. Barely stepping foot into the open warehouse, a pang of nausea razors through me as my gaze lands on Bobby and Dom's bodies. I clamp my eyes shut, nightmares of what I've turned into—what I have yet to become—seeping into my thoughts.

I snag a breath, aware with everything in me that I'm never gonna be able to look at my mother or grandmother without fearing they'll smell the stench of my lies, see the demon hiding beneath my flesh.

My heart trips, knowing I'll never hold Casey the way I used to without feeling diseased, the warmth my arms once brought to her turning into icicles.

I exhale, my conscience screaming out that if I ever touch, taste, or take Amber, I'd spread nothing but poison over her beautiful body, not an ounce of me capable of giving her what she needs, what she deserves.

Taken by the evilness ravishing the air around me, the last remnants of who I was finally disappears, leaving me tainted, broken beyond repair.

I open my eyes, blinking my vision into focus. Another pang rips through me—this one rocking my skull—as the realization hits me that there are cameras all over us. Close to cracking, I head for the main office and locate the surveillance equipment. After ripping the cables from the control module, recovering the disks, and snatching up the monitor, I haul ass back into the warehouse, everything tight in my grip.

"Christ. I forgot about that shit." Brock slings the duffel bag over his shoulder, his attention frozen on the cameras watching us from above. "I'm not worried about our prints because neither of us has a record. And, besides taking Dom and Bobby's guns, mounds of other fuckers' prints are all over this place. But the cops *gotta* have some kind of technology that can hone in on our profiles, right?" His eyes shoot to mine, concern lining his face. "Don't you have to destroy the cameras or at least bring them with us? We can't just *leave* them here."

"They don't need to be destroyed." I brush past him, making for the back door. "And yes, we *can* leave them here. The video feed's stored on the computer's hard drive, not the cameras."

"Are you *positive?*" he asks, his tone itching with doubt. "I know you're a computer whiz, but you gotta be sure. This is our fucking *lives*, bro."

I spin, fury hardening my jaw. "Yeah. I know this is our lives. *I* remembered that minor detail the second we stepped foot into this motherfucker. *You're* the asshole who let that slip your mind. Not me." A showdown of glares ensues between us before I start for the door again. "Let's go. We've wasted too much time. There's no reason to clean up anything because—as you pointed out—the cops couldn't trace shit back to us if they tried. We've got everything we need, so now the only thing we have left to do is get the fuck outta here. Fast."

I don't wait for him to respond. No. Instead, I step out into the chilled night air, my nerves rocked as I open the van, tossing everything inside it. Mentally wasted, I turn and Brock's standing behind me, his expression depleted of emotion as he pitches the duffel bag into the back of the van and closes the doors.

"I'm gonna be honest with you, bro, and you might not like it."

Brock wets his lips, any compassion he owned before tonight vaporizing as he shakes his head. "They were dying the second Dom pulled his gun on me." Demeanor unnervingly calm, he slips around the vehicle and into the driver's seat. "And for *no one* will I *ever* apologize for that. Not a goddamn fucking soul."

Frozen, I stare at him, my brain knocking around his admission.

Dead the second Dom pulled his gun on me . . .

Dead the second . . .

Dead . . .

Christ. No matter what I did or said to get us the hell outta there without anyone getting hurt—the two assholes included—was all in vain. Brock knew he was taking the fuckers out the minute this nightmare began. I suck in a disturbed breath, aware this night will haunt me down to my bones, every sick detail played out in slow motion, terrorizing the rest of my life.

Brock fires the engine, his eyes vacant of the nervousness, fear, and regret feasting on each cell in my body. "Get in, Ryder."

Jaw clenched and head fucked sideways, I hop in, my spirit beaten to shreds as I spark up a cigarette.

Brock kicks the van into drive, gunning it down the dark, graveled driveway. He cuts a hard right out of the property, a blaze of dust surrounding the vehicle as guilt returns, wrapping its lethal fingers around my neck.

Brock glances at me, his tone remaining calm. "I had to drop them. There was no way in hell—"

"Fuck!" I punch the dashboard, my knuckles splitting on impact. Sanity officially cracked wide open, I punch the dash again, blood seeping down my wrist as I try to catch a full breath. "Are you fucking nuts? We *killed* two people!"

"Am *I* nuts?" he growls, navigating the back roads of bumble-fuck nowhere. "No, my brother. *You're* nuts. You need to wake up. If you thought for one goddamn second Dom was letting us walk outta there *alive*, then I don't give a *shit* if you're a genius on paper. You're a moron if you thought he *wasn't* killing us first."

"You don't know if—"

"If *what?*" He slams on the brakes, the van screeching to a stop. "If Dom was gonna spare our *lives?* Gonna invite us over for a *bar-b-que* next weekend? You know what? Maybe it *is* me who's nuts. Maybe I confused him shoving his gun in my face with him wanting to ask me to be the godfather of his newborn."

Silence reigns, nothing but our heavy breathing shrouding the space as Brock sinks a nervous hand through his hair. "Goddamnit, Ryder, think about what you're saying," he whispers, the first sign of morality swamping his eyes. "For fuck's sake, think about how it went *down*. You *know* we weren't getting outta there without him putting a bullet in our skulls. If *I* hadn't done it, done deal—right about now— *he'd* be dumping our bodies into a shallow grave somewhere on his property. It'd be *our* families grieving, not his. It'd be *my* girlfriend, not his wife, losing her goddamn mind when we never came back. Fuck no. Amber's been through too much shit. And did you *honestly* think I was gonna let him threaten her *life* the way he did? You think I'd be able to sleep, knowing the psycho knew what she looked like? I didn't wanna kill him. Jesus Christ, I wasn't born a murderer, bro, but I *had* to fucking do it. I had to because if I didn't—whether you wanna admit it or not—Dom knew he was taking us out the second I opened my mouth to him."

He hauls in a slow breath and punches the gas, the van speeding down the road as he stares straight ahead. "Again, I'll *never* apologize for what I did. For what I *had* to do to keep you, me, and Amber *alive*. If I had to, I'd do it again." Another breath as he swings his attention to me, a flash of fear jumping across his face. "I just pray my judge and jury remember what happened tonight when my time's up."

The remainder of the ride is spent in silence as I mull over what happened in the warehouse. I take a drag from my cigarette, feeling sick that I actually agree with Brock's actions. He's right. We were never walking outta there alive, and even if by some miracle we had gotten away without killing them, the fucker *did* threaten Amber's life. Does this make me as warped as Brock? As shut down and cold as he's become? I flick my cigarette out the window, unsure of any of the twisted emotions speeding through my head except for one thing . . .

The evilness of the night has forever stained who we are, stripping us bare of anything resembling a normal future.

The worst part?

The petrifying feeling that our time *is* almost up . . .

CHAPTER 17

Amber

"YOU LOOK LIKE a sex kitten," Madeline appraises from the mini-bar as she prepares me a shot of tequila. "Amber Moretti in a black strapless leather dress is one badass vision. You're gonna make every dude *and* dudette in the casino wanna get it on with you." She shimmies her sequined skirt down her thighs, beaming as she ungracefully wobbles into the bathroom. "Guy and girly parts all over the Borgata will be on high alert."

I inwardly giggle at her attempt at walking with poise in six-inch stilettos. "You need practice in those things."

"Ugh! Tell me about it." She hands me the shot and looks down at my four-month anniversary gift from Brock: a pair of *fuck me now* seven-inch animal-print Louboutins.

"You make walking in them look like second nature. It's like they're a freaking extension of your body." She frowns as she messes with her fiery red strands of hair. "*Me?* I'd be better off sporting circus stilts."

I smile, chucking my lip gloss into my beaded clutch. "Stop. Like I said, with a little practice, you'll be able to walk in them like a model *with* your pretty brown eyes closed."

"I highly doubt that. But thanks for the encouragement." She grins, bumping her hip against mine. "You look amazing, really, but we gotta jet. Lee texted me *twenty* minutes ago, threatening to auction us off to the highest bidder if we weren't downstairs at the craps table within *ten* minutes. Considering he's down a grand, I'm treating his threat with the utmost seriousness."

I toss the shot down my throat, shoot one last glance at my reflection, and head out of the bathroom, my nerves a mess as I grab my room's key card. Though I'm excited we're in Atlantic City celebrating Brock's twenty-third birthday, and my man spared no expense for the Piatto suite, I can't help but worry what the next forty-eight hours are going to bring.

The last month with both Brock and Ryder has been the closest thing to what I imagine living in a psychiatric ward would be like. Absolute mayhem. Between their sudden bursts of anger, secretiveness, drinking until they pass out, and even going as far as getting lit up last weekend on their own supply of blow, I feel like I'm losing my mind. Add all of that to Brock skipping out on sex with me, and I'm sure it won't be long before one of us ends up in a straitjacket. Brock's denied it, but since their last pickup, they've turned into two completely different men, each one acting out in ways that petrify me.

Though I may be reaching, my best guess is they're vexed I decided against being with them. The night Brock brought it up, my world was rocked, its very foundation sinking into a state of Brock and Ryder euphoria. The mere idea has taken over my life, visions of each man bringing my body to new heights—to its glorious limits—dominating my every breath, dream, and fantasy, reducing me to nothing but a sloppy, masturbating mess.

Masturbating mess or not, after considering the repercussions, my conscience won't allow me to go along with it. I have a feeling the whole thing will backfire on us, leaving me the reason these two men—whom I equally hold close to my soul for different reasons—

will lose a friendship. More than that, I'll wind up being the culprit of two broken, unrepairable hearts. I wouldn't be able to breathe knowing I hurt either man. Although I bounced between what I long for and what I already have, the decision was somewhat simple.

For the first time in my life, I put my sexual addiction to the side, choosing our sanity instead.

Still, though I'm pretty sure their abrupt change in demeanor is because of me, I've been unable to ignore the unwelcomed voice in my head telling me I have *nothing* to do with it at all. It's whispering that something happened while they were in West Virginia. Something dark, a monster born from an evilness I couldn't even begin to understand. It's screaming it's the reason Brock has woken up most nights since they returned in cold sweats, his body riddled with the shakes. Its sinister cries keep telling me it's the motive behind Ryder's decision to quit football, his love of the sport ending overnight.

Either way, no matter how many times I've questioned them, I'm left with the same answer: I'm overreacting to something that doesn't exist.

On a sigh, I follow Madeline to the elevator. Sweat threatens my makeup as the doors part on the casino's main floor. The air—rife with the smell of stale cigarettes and sweet cigars, along with the hum of slot machines—awakens my senses. A thick layer of excitement bubbles in my stomach, my attention sweeping the span of the casino as Madeline hooks her arm in mine and drags me toward the craps tables.

Overwhelmed, my eyes take in a concoction of strategically placed numbers, stacks of colorful chips, and tumbling dice, ultimately landing on Ryder and Brock. I smile, my pulse whipping my blood into overdrive at the dual beautiful sights before me. In a crowded space, filled with the heavy buzz of commotion, they still manage to command a room, the eyes of women spread out all over the casino appraising them with heated interest. Decked out in tailored suits, they motion me over, both chuckling at the confused look on my face as I approach the table.

God, it feels so good to hear them laugh again. Depleted of their usual wittiness and jovial spirits, the past month demolished my existence as a whole, every agonizing second killing off a section of my heart.

Brock curls his arms around my waist and pulls me into his chest. "You know I dig you in leather, right?" He grips me tighter and slides his lips to my neck, his erection tickling my stomach as he nibbles my flesh. "It does things to me no man should have to bear in public."

Madeline smiles, an *I told you so* look aimed at me as Lee gathers her in his arms.

"I hmm." I tug on Brock's tie, my brow playfully drawn up. "Although it's been a while—*ahem*—I do recall you having a healthy fetish for me in this material. Is this going to pose a problem for your gambling prowess, birthday boy?"

"My birthday isn't until tomorrow, wiseass. Don't make me older than I am." He kisses my lips, the tantalizing swirl of his tongue tasting of whiskey. "And no. It won't pose a problem. Once I get you back to the room, I'm *destroying* your dress. I dig you in leather, but I love you out of it. Especially when it's on the floor, next to your naked body, while your legs bug out around my head." He releases me from his hold, his grin turning the best kind of sinister. "But, as usual, I'll require that the heels stay on."

Heat liquefies my muscles at the thought of fucking him. It feels as though an eternity has passed since he last nourished my body with what it requires. For some, a month without sex is a piece of cake. For me, it's akin to drinking rat poison, each deadly swallow bringing me closer to my coffin.

"You sure did paint her a vivid picture, bro," Ryder points out, his gaze passing between mine and Brock's. "She no longer looks like a hot, confused mess. Well done." He tosses back what remains of his shot, sets down his empty glass, and motions over a passing waitress. "*Very* well done."

Bloodred lips spread into an eager smile, and making sure the sway of her hips holds Ryder's attention, the waitress nods and skirts toward us. "Ryder," she drawls, her voice thick with sex as she brushes up against him, shoving her double Ds in his face. Batting what I'm positive are fake lashes, she taps his nose. "What can I do for you, cutie?"

"What *can't* you do for me, Leslie?" He toys with a strand of her dyed blonde hair, his eyes jumping from her rack to her lips. "That's the *real* question."

Her giggle makes me want to hurl. "Well, I *did* give you my number earlier, and you know what time I get off, so I'd say it's up to you to find out *exactly* what I can or can't do for you."

He chuckles and leans into her ear, whispering some shit I can't hear over the din of the casino.

Another giggle, this one on the heels of a playful gasp. I roll my eyes, positive I'm seconds from losing my dinner. She taps his nose again, squeaking out in nauseating delight as Ryder slaps her ass. Relieving me of the vomit-inducing scene, she slips around a corner, craning her neck in his direction until she's completely out of sight.

Ryder unfastens his attention from the waitress, bringing it back to me and Brock. "What was I saying? I got a little . . . sidetracked."

"You gotta be as shit-faced as I am." Brock polishes off his whiskey, then swings his arm over my shoulder. "How the hell that wrinkled piece of leather does a *thing* for you is beyond my understanding."

"Sorry, dude, but I'm with Brock," Lee says, cringing. "She looked old enough to be your mother."

Points scored for Lee and Brock.

"I'm not sure which one of you assholes is more smoked out." Ryder sparks up a cigarette, taking a cool, long pull from it as a lazy smirk strokes his mouth. "I might be hammered a little something, but I know a fine-looking piece of ass when I see it. Besides, she's thirty-four. That's not old. That's *experienced*."

Chuckling, both Lee and Brock shake their heads.

Unaffected by their taunting, Ryder blows a ring of smoke into Brock's face. "Now, again, what was I saying?"

"Brock's picture of Amber in leather," Madeline answers, wiggling her brows.

"Ah, that's right." Grinning, Ryder looks at Brock. "Well done on the picture you painted for our girl here. Amber Moretti in leather. How the fuck could you go wrong?"

"You can't." Brock cups my cheeks, his gaze roving over my face before he kisses me as though it's the last time he'll ever get to. I sink, realizing this is how he's kissed me since he got back from West Virginia. We may not have had sex, but we've kissed—a lot—and when we have, there's been underlying torment attached to each one.

My pulse takes off, shards of unease slicing my heart. As I fall in step with his sensual rhythm, it hits me that the voice inside my head's not a voice, nor me overreacting—but instead—my intuition firing off warning shots.

Something happened to my man while he was down there.

"I love you," Brock whispers, something parallel to paranoia surfacing across his expression. "You'll never understand how much I cherish you, baby girl. I'd do anything for you. *Anything.*"

Soul aching in question, I clutch his lapels, everything in me needing to understand what's happening to him.

"I'll be right back." He tosses a hand through his hair, a smile on his face. "I have to hit the ATM. I got killed on the blackjack tables before you girls came down."

"I'll take a walk with you," I blurt, aware his smile's an act, hiding something I fear he'll never tell me about. "I could use the exercise anyway. Dinner did me in. I'm positive I look like a pregnant elephant. God knows I feel like one."

"You're crazy. But you're a beautiful psycho, so it's all good." Brock drops a kiss onto my forehead and checks his Rolex. "Just hang here. I have a few phone calls to make, so I might be a while. Besides, Ryder's gonna teach ya how to play craps. Isn't that right, Ashcroft?"

Ryder tips his empty glass in my direction. "Yup. I'm about to turn her pro."

Brock shoves a wad of cash in my cleavage, and stares at me a beat, desolation returning to his eyes before he turns and walks away. I pull the cash from my cleavage and watch him bleed into the throng, my heart sinking as I thumb through the knot of hundred-dollar bills. There's at least two grand in my possession. He might have a few calls to make, but he's not hitting the ATM.

Another lie, this one managing to confuse and worry me further.

The second Brock's out of view, Ryder rests his hand on my nape, guiding my face to within inches of his. The spiced scent of his cologne, combined with the warmth of his touch, curls a live wire of adrenaline around my limbs.

"You're the most goddamn beautiful thing ever created," he croons, his words spoken soft against my cheek. "I might be a little hemmed up, but that doesn't mean I can't see straight. I'm positive I'll never come across anything as breathtaking as you." He wets his lips, the sight of his delicious barbell causing my body's temperature to jump. "Cats like me don't usually use the word 'breathtaking,' but hell if the good Lord above wasn't on his game the day he made you. In leather or not, you, Amber Moretti, are an angel to tainted eyes."

"Thank you," I murmur, sure I've squeezed my clutch into the shape of a pancake. I inhale a shaky breath, trying to replenish the oxygen his declaration yanked from my lungs.

"You're very welcome." He steps back and nails his gaze to mine. "Also, we're here to have a good time. If I have to beat a *real* smile outta ya, I will. I'm not beyond getting . . . physical if the occasion calls for it.

You think you're an expert at hiding your thoughts, but it's not your forte, peach. You suck at it."

"I'm fine." The lie slips from my mouth with excruciating effort. "Besides, shouldn't you be worrying about what your *waitress friend* is or isn't going to do to you after her shift, and not what's bothering me?"

"Asking me not to worry about you is like asking me not to take my next breath, Amber." He tilts his head, genuine concern darkening the turquoise in his eyes. "I'm also starting to think ya get off on making me call you out on your bullshit. You're far from fine. I'm not an asshole, Moretti. You haven't been fine for a few weeks."

"You win, Mr. Genius. I'm not fine. But how am I *supposed* to be when you and Brock aren't? Something happened when you guys went on your last pickup, and no one's saying shit to me about it. I know I'm not supposed to ask questions, yada, yada, yada, but *I'm* not an asshole, Ashcroft." I sigh as I look away, a plethora of nerves attacking my system as I shove the knot of cash into my clutch. "Something's wrong. I can sense it."

Ryder hooks his finger under my chin, dragging my attention back to his. "Would you stop?"

"No. I *won't* stop." Though my words are a whisper, they come out as harsh as I intend them to. "While we're at it, let's talk about you quitting football out of nowhere. Or maybe we should discuss Brock not wanting to have sex with me—no matter how many times I've initiated it." I tap my chin, aggravation bubbling in my chest. "Oh! And let's not forget that you and Brock snorted so much blow last weekend that I was positive you two were overdosing when I found you both—after three straight days of *not* sleeping—passed out on Brock's kitchen floor. Look me in the eye and tell me I'm losing it, Ryder. Tell me—once again—that I'm imagining this . . . this *change* in you and Brock, and I'll forget everything."

"You're losing it," he replies without skipping a beat. "So forget whatever twisted shit that pretty head of yours conjured up."

I may not be in his mind—chained to whatever's holding him hostage to his thoughts—but I can see *his* lie took excruciating effort too. Guilt, fear, and anger. It's all there in his eyes, masking the truth.

"Thanks for being honest, really. You've put every doubt I had to rest." I let out a dry laugh, making sure he knows I'm aware he's talking nothing but smack. "Your integrity's something I—and everyone in your life—can always count on. Again, I appreciate it."

"I'm begging you to chill the fuck out, Amber." Ryder rushes a hand through his hair, his plea lost on me amid the sewage seeping from his mouth. "Come on, momma. We're here to have a good time. Just drop it, and relax, okay?"

"And if I *don't* relax and drop it, it'll be my fault everyone's weekend turned to shit, right?" I snort, digging a hand into my hip. "*I'll* be to blame for ruining what should've been a good time?"

"Amber," Madeline interrupts, touching my shoulder. "Let's go take a walk, all right? We'll hit up a couple of slot machines. Maybe catch a few hotties in the high-roller room."

With anger churning my gut, Madeline's words fly over my head as I narrow my eyes on Ryder. "You guys can talk about *sharing* me, but can't tell me what *really* happened during your last pickup?" I catch him by his silk tie, tugging his face to mine. "Huh, *Ry*? It's easier to shoot the shit about how you two plan on fucking me sideways? How you boys are gonna rock my world as you fuck away my *pain*?" Seething, I yank harder, his nose smashed to mine as a flurry of tears dribbles down my cheeks. "You and Brock are lying con artists, and you know it. All you two have done is hurt me *more*."

"Goddamnit, Amber! Kill your thoughts!" Ryder grits out, his threat raising over the hum of the casino. He cups my nape and presses his forehead to mine, our quickened breaths mingling as he brushes his thumbs along my cheeks, swiping away my tears. "Tuck them back where they belong. Everyone—*you* included—is having a good time this weekend." Shame trots across his face as he steps back, dropping his voice to a torturous whisper. "We all need it. Ya hearing me, peach? *We. Need. It.* And what you're doing is . . . Fuck, Amber, it's making it worse. Please . . . just . . ." He trails off and rests his lips against my temple, his shoulders slumping as he moves his hands to my hips, gripping them. "Just let it go."

Heart fraying, I swallow back the wave of emotions flooding my throat. I'm pissed, confused, and hurt. Still, I know I've pushed him too far, my explosion nearly causing him to lose his cool.

My instinct to jet sinks through me, embarrassment burning my chest as I spin, searching for an exit. Ignoring Madeline's calls to stop, I shove through the crowd, my cries lost amid the frenzied atmosphere. With tears blurring my vision, the blistering breath of late November blown its poisoned chill across my skin as I step outside, into the clusterfuck that is Atlantic City.

Drunken partygoers slam into me as a rainbow of lights pop over a gang of prostitutes gathered around a corner streetlamp. With sheer chaos surrounding me, I'm alone and empty, the core of who I am completely hollowed out. Though two amazing men want me—desiring all of my broken pieces, each tortured imperfection—I feel more alone than the day I watched true evilness seep into my father's pores, blackening his soul before he took his and my mother's lives.

On autopilot, I walk. I walk until my feet ache, until it feels as though my skin has turned into cement, the bitter cold wind beating against my face with every step. My heart a dumping ground for tainted memories, I think. I think until my skull feels like it's about to split in half, my head replaying every torturous minute of my life. I think of each second that's crawled by since my parents died, of the rare amount of good times we shared, the countless bad that gutted us. I think of the damage I've done to myself, using who and what I can to mask my pain, forever hiding in the shadows of my reality.

Body prickled numb, I lean against a brick wall of an abandoned storefront and sink to the ground, losing myself to the vengeance of life's cruelty. Arms curled around my bare shoulders, I rest my head on my knees and—after years of needing to—fall apart, tears dripping from my eyes as I suck in a string of shaky breaths. Praying to a God I'm unsure ever existed in my world, I purge every wicked emotion from my system, releasing my parents to where they've always belonged . . . my past.

Still, I'm bound to my present, a prisoner chained to the hurt diseasing Brock and Ryder. I never thought I'd be capable of letting a single person into my life, yet I've opened myself up to two men, allowing them to see through all of my disturbing layers. Left feeling so helpless to what's going on with them is wearing me down, my spirit eroding by the second. They're embedded in my soul, each man a beautiful thread stitching my once-broken heart back together. Knowing something has them scared not only scares me, it's cutting me to pieces.

Time creeps by—for how long, I'm unsure—before I feel a hand touch the side of my face. I look up, my weary gaze landing on Ryder. I wipe my eyes and manage a weak smile, but it's quickly replaced with more tears as he lifts me from the ground, pulling me into the safety net of his warmth. I throw my arms around his neck, holding on to him with what little strength I have left as I sob into his chest, each tear an exorcism of the demons that have forever controlled me. Resting his lips on my forehead, Ryder wraps his suit jacket around me.

"Christ, I never meant to hurt you," he whispers, his voice cracking as he holds me tighter, not a single inch separating us. "I'd *die* first before ever trying to hurt you, peach. I'm so sorry."

I lift my watery gaze to his, my breath snagging as I bear witness to what I never imagined I would . . . tears building behind Ryder's eyes. Fighting them back, he looks away, his face contorted with the anguish of a man who's done something unperceivably wrong. I touch his jaw, my need to console him overwhelming.

He stares beyond my eyes—straight into the hollow of my soul—

the pain emanating off him shattering my last bit of resistance to him, to the idea of . . . us. Unable to convey with words my heartbreak over his silent torture, I do what feels right, what has felt like second nature from the moment we met.

I kiss him.

I kiss him until I'm warm, the heat from his gentle touch melting the cold from my muscles. I kiss him until the quickened notes of our breath drown out the sound of my crying, his hands gripping my waist as he slowly sweeps his tongue over mine. I kiss him with everything I am, my concern for him imploding as I taste the bitterness in his need to tell me what's kidnapped who he used to be.

"Please," I beg as he deepens the kiss, his strokes becoming possessive, urgent. A soft moan claws up my throat, my body confused by the lethal blend of hunger and hurt. "Please tell me what's wrong. I need to know what happened. I love Brock more than anything, and I . . ." I break the kiss, watching in agony as a lone tear slips down his face.

My breath catches again, my tears falling in a torrent of thick sheets. This beautiful, selfless, caring man's exposing his opened wounds to me, setting his vulnerabilities on the operating table of my heart for me to repair.

"I care more for you than I know I should," I whisper, aware I'm crossing a dangerous line as I press up on my tiptoes, layering my mouth over his. I kiss him soft and slow, my need for the truth growing. "I have from the second you stole that first kiss from me. Your smile, your laugh. The way you love and take care of your family. All of it, Ryder. You're a magnet I know will never stop pulling me to you. Even when you're not near me, I can feel you. Hear your voice. See your face in my dreams." I move my lips to his jaw, my hiccupped cries misting the air around us. "The feelings I have for you scare me. *You* scare me. But even if I wanted to stop them, I couldn't because I don't *want* to. I'm tired of fighting what feels . . . right. You feel right to me, Ryder, and I need you in my life. Couldn't imagine it without you." I pull back and gaze into his eyes, hoping my confession will break down his defenses. "Please let me *help* you. Let me fix what's happened to you and Brock."

"You can't help us," he murmurs, torment capturing his words. "No one can. What happened, what we did . . ." He sucks in a slow breath, his body shaking as he drops his forehead to mine. "We're burning in hell for it."

Fear bolts through me, its menacing strike threatening my sanity. I knew something happened, felt it down to the marrow in my bones, smelled the presence of evil rotting the air. But the sinister whisper tormenting my eardrums is telling me what they did is worse than anything I could imagine. Still, I push through, unwilling to accept that I can't somehow help them get through this—even if it's something that serves as my undoing.

I sniffle, my whisper barely audible. "You can't just keep *lying* to me. You *and* Brock. It's not right."

"Our lies are *protecting* you." His hands fall to my waist, his grip ironclad. "Don't you see that?"

"I do. But I have no idea *what* you're protecting me from," I answer through a cry, his words petrifying me. These men are all I have, two of the very few people who matter a rat's ass to me. As scared as I'm becoming, my safety's an afterthought, their well-being trumping mine. "Please don't close me out. If either of you care for me at all, then you'll tell me what happened." I pause, knowing what I'm about to say is the truth, my heart breaking to pieces at the mere thought. "You might be trying to protect me. I get and adore the both of you for that, but I'd rather be alone—not *ever* knowing what really happened— than be with you or Brock under false pretenses. It'll kill me. It's *already* killing me, Ryder." I tangle my fingers through his dark, wavy hair, unsure if tonight will be the last time I lay eyes on either of their beautiful faces. "Please don't make me walk away from either of you because of this. I don't want to. You have no idea how much I *don't* want to, but I will if it comes down to it."

Forehead still pressed to mine, he stares at me for the longest minute of my life, surrender eventually painting his face as he nods. "No fucking way in hell I'm letting you walk away from me, peach. You can give it a decent go, but I'm telling ya now, it ain't happening. If you know me at all, then you know I'm one big, fat persistent prick." He moves his lips to mine, a spark of possession flashing in his eyes as I tremble under his touch. "I know you're not mine to claim. Hell, you might not ever be. This I know *all* too well. But the little bits of you I've got—the beautiful, painful, amazing, Twizzler-loving, crazy pieces of yourself you've shared with me—mean way too much to my goddamn sanity to give up." He palms my cheeks, apprehension floating across his face for a brief moment before he brushes his lips against my ear. "I need you a hundred times more than I need my next breath, a thousand times more than I need my next heartbeat, and a million times more than I need to wake up to the sun hanging in the sky."

He kisses me soft, slow, his words strumming the hollow ache in my soul as he gathers me in his arms. "I'm sorry I caused you any pain the last few weeks. Again, it was done to protect you. I need you to know this. I speak on behalf of Brock when I say that. But no more lies. No more bullshit. Though I have to be honest, if it didn't mean losing you, I'd never think about telling ya what happened. Ever. It'd never cross my mind. But like I said, I ain't losing you over this. I've already lost too much against what . . ." He pauses, his expression becoming distant as he shakes his head. "What we did has already stolen too much from us. I'll be *damned* if I let it take you away from me."

My tears slow as I rear back, staring into the weary blue sea of his eyes. Pain, fear, and confusion are all present, the deadly trio trying to suck the last vestiges of who Ryder used to be out from beneath him. My heart trips, skids, and crashes into a brick wall spray-painted with his and Brock's anguish, my mental state bruised from the collision.

But worse: my mind's left wondering if any of us will ever be the same after tonight.

It doesn't take long before I need to feel Ryder again, my body aching for his touch. Seeking his warmth, I twine my arms around his neck, holding on to him with everything in me. Pressed to his chest, both calmness and my own fear surround me, the soft beat of his heart a safety harness to mine.

After a second, Ryder releases me from his hold, his hand swallowing mine as he leads me in the direction of the hotel. Pulse thundering, it's only just now I realize I've won the battle. I'm about to become a part of their truth, the rightful owner of a piece of their nightmare. It's also just now I realize I'm walking into what I'm positive is going to be the hardest conversation of my life.

I take a breath, knowing my new normal has already killed off my old.

CHAPTER 18

Amber

"HIS CELL WENT to voice mail," Ryder says as we approach my suite. "Lee and Madeline said they haven't heard from him either, so I'm banking on him being here."

Hands shaking, I slide my key card into the door and step into the dark entryway, my ears clogged with the suffocating sound of a chick's heavy panting. I still, my heart rate going nuts as her husky moans fill the weed-laden air.

The weed-laden air I can't seem to inhale enough of in my current state of *I'm about to kill a bitch.*

Ryder catches my elbow, attempting to lead me out of the suite, but I yank it back, rage fueling me as I follow the sound of snarls and flesh slapping against flesh. Barely able to see in the darkness, and prepared to happily spend the night in jail for de-dicking Brock, I pursue a path of his clothing into the living area, where I find him passed out on the couch, undeniably alone. Sure I've thrown up in my mouth, I suck in what I'm positive is the largest breath of relief possible. He's wearing nothing but boxer briefs, an empty bottle of whiskey at his side, the light hum of his snoring a sure sign he's tanked.

331

Ryder chuckles as he points across the suite to the gigantuous plasma television. I turn around, taking in the offender: a panty-dampening porn showcasing two chicks getting it on with an extremely well-endowed dude. Though my nerves are still revved up, I can't help but laugh, my heart rate settling some as I flip on a lamp.

Eyes flying open, Brock jerks awake, the speed with which he darts up to reach for his gun on the end table killing my "tanked" theory.

"Are you goddamn nuts, Ber?" He shoots to standing, uncocking the weapon. "I could've *killed* you."

I plop onto the couch and, with no sign of stopping, continue to giggle. God, it feels divine. Ryder sinks into an armchair and clicks off the television, laughter bursting from his chest as we release the stress that's built up over the last hour.

Brock sets his gun on the end table, confused. "Is there a reason either of you find this shit *funny?* It wouldn't be so comical if her brains were splattered all over the fucking couch right now, would it? I bet *neither* of you would laugh then."

Ryder and I glance at Brock, then back at each other, our thoughts on the same wavelength. Brock's statement isn't possible, the empty bottle of whiskey proving to be a hindrance to his intelligence.

Silence, then—yet again—Ryder and I bust out laughing, our bodies rocking like two ships caught in the angry undertow of a tidal wave.

Mouth dropped open and hands dug into his hips, Brock stares at us with widened, defeated eyes.

"I have to agree with ya, bro," Ryder admits, his point made with difficulty as he chuckles, if at all possible, even harder. "She wouldn't be laughing at shit if her brains were part of the décor right now. Dying will *usually* do that. You know? Prevent someone's ability to do . . . well, *anything.*" He reaches for a joint perched on a stack of magazines and fishes a lighter from his pants pocket. "And if she *could* do anything, even if it was something as minuscule as licking her pretty lips"—he sparks up said joint, takes a long pull from it, and coughs before passing it to me—"then I can safely say, with all certainty, I'd turn into a pussy *real* fast. Though I'm sure she'd remain sexy as all fuck—scoring the lead role of *The Walking Dead*'s hottest zombie—that shit would be *way* too much to handle—even for someone who's a self-proclaimed crazed, masochistic, kink-loving psycho, such as myself." With a wink aimed in my direction, a smile deepens his dimples, his likeminded playful dementedness strumming my nerves to a complete rest as he mocks a cringe. "No offense, peach, but I think I'd pass on tapping that."

"None taken," I toss back over a giggle, instant gratification swelling through my muscles as I inhale a second, then third hit from the joint. I hand the smoking stick of happiness back to Ryder, a coy smile flirting with my lips. "There's something understandably undesirable about a cold—excuse my French—pussy. I get it, really."

"You're both nuts," Brock says with an aggravated sigh, stomping toward the bathroom.

A slam of a door and the mood in the room shifts, all pretense of joy gone as the reality of what's to come pokes its menacing head into the moment. *It was fun while it lasted . . .*

Attention stuck on me, Ryder's smile vanishes, a thin line taking its place as he pulls in one last hit from the joint before stubbing it out in an empty shot glass. Denial. Realizing we've been in it over the last few minutes, our demeanors deflate, a needle—held in the dirty hand of a bratty child—popping our bullshit-filled balloon of false hope. Nothing, not even jokes about me perfecting the role of one hot apocalyptic zombie, can keep us from facing what's about to go down. Silence shrouds the air, the look in Ryder's eyes mirroring what's eating me from the inside out, trying to kill me.

Fear. It's smothering my breath, its cancerous poison set on making me its next victim.

After what seems like forever, Brock reemerges, instantly picking up on the anxiety wiring the air as he sits next to me. "What's wrong?" Frowning, he kisses my cheek and slides my legs over his lap, his finger toying with a strand of my hair as he stares at me, waiting for a reply. "No more giggles?" He kisses me again, his voice tinged with regret. "I'm sorry, baby girl. I need your giggles more than you'll ever know. I was a dick before. It's just watching you get off on what *legitimately* could've happened messed with my head. I'd never be able to live with myself if some shit like that ever happened."

"That's not what's bothering me." Nervous, I flit my gaze to Ryder.

He hesitates, clears his throat. "We have to tell her, bro," Ryder whispers.

Brock whips his attention to Ryder, fury lighting the green in his eyes. "What the fuck do you mean, *tell* her? There's nothing *to* tell her."

Brock tosses my legs off his lap and rises, but I catch his wrist, preventing him from taking a step. Peering up at him, I silently beg him not to fight. He touches my cheek, a flash of remorse sweeping over his features, but it vanishes, a look of resolve setting in.

"Nothing happened." He hooks a finger under my chin. "We've been over this a million times, Amber. *Nothing. Fucking. Happened.*"

I nod, wanting with everything we are to believe him, my conscience screaming that I'm nothing but a lovesick fool as he glances at his watch. He pulls me up from the couch into his solid, shirtless chest and wraps his arms around me, cocooning me in his hold. For a split second, I honestly believe him, my stubborn soul winning the battle with what I already know. Every excuse he's used has been nothing but an attempt to distract me from the truth, each lie a steel blanket protecting me from the shadows of his reality.

Confused, I don't know if I should kiss or castrate him.

"Now that I'm officially twenty-three," he continues, grinning, "it's time to celebrate until we can't think straight. I just gotta get dressed, and we'll head down to the tables. Cool?"

Another nod, this one filled with hesitation as he presses his lips to my forehead.

"Either you tell her what happened, or I will." Ryder stands and walks toward us. "She deserves to know. I can't—no, I *won't*—lie to her anymore. It's hurting her." He gazes into my eyes, regret swallowing his expression. "I care too much for her. Her life's been filled with assholes who've hurt and used her. I'm not about to become one of them."

Brock twists his head toward Ryder, his glare lethal. "Shut the fuck up. I'm not kidding, man. Go sit back down, smoke some more vipe, and chill while I get ready." Brock flips his attention back to me. "You know what? Fuck this." He grabs my hand, tugging me toward the bathroom. "You're showering with me. I ain't taking any chances that this asshole will say some stupid shit to you."

"Brock!" I wrench my hand back, my mouth dropped open. "Have you lost your *mind?*"

"Maybe I have, but I love you more than I love myself, so I don't give a fuck. But you wanna know what's really messed up? What's hurting *me?* You questioning me trying to protect you from something you have no business knowing about. That's more fucked up than anything I'm doing to save you from more pain you don't need."

Tears needle my eyes as I try to wrap my head around what's happened to him, what's happening to all of us.

"We shot and killed two men," Ryder whispers, his voice cracking through the air like a whip. "Two men who, before threatening your beautiful life, peach, deserved to die."

I nearly trip over my feet as my back hits the wall, my barbed-wire thoughts tangled over his confession.

"Goddamnit, Ryder!" Brock reaches for my arm to steady me, curling his free hand around my nape. "Look at me, Ber." His soft plea is barely distinguishable over the blood roaring through my veins— all sound muted as I lift my watery eyes to his. "You gotta—"

"You . . . *murdered* two men?" I interrupt through a cry, unable to believe the question I'm asking. I can't deny a sliver of me thought that's what happened. Still, hearing myself say it, tasting the poison-riddled word—"murdered"—has me feeling like I'm stuck in a nightmare, screaming for someone to wake me up. "Did you, Brock? Did you *kill* them?"

"You gotta listen to me, baby girl. I didn't mean for it to happen," he chokes out, his eyes misting over as he moves his hands to my waist. "That wasn't my intention. You have to believe me. But after everything went down—as it started falling the fuck apart—I had no other choice *but* to kill them. Christ, I knew it was a bad move getting nasty with Dom, talking shit to him after he'd tried to act tough, but before I knew it, he had his gun to my head. Ryder pulled his gun on Dom. Dom's buddy pulled his piece on Ryder." His face a bed of shame, he sucks in a slow, staggered breath, his fingers nervously clenching my waist. "Everything happened so goddamn fast, Amber, but I swear on my kid brother's *soul*, I had no other choice."

My breath falters at the realization that he acknowledged Brandon in the past tense. I blink, tears dripping down my face, his silent admission that he's aware his brother's gone forever killing off a piece of who I am. A piece of who he is.

"He didn't," Ryder offers from behind me. "Honest to God, he had no other choice." He sweeps my hair off my shoulder, his touch warming me as he, too, rests his hands on my waist. "You might not have been there, peach, but you *were* with us. You were all we could think of while everything fell to shit. All that kept our hearts beating, kept us . . . hanging on. Hell, you're *still* keeping us holding on. Without you, there's no doubt we would've lost our shit by now." He takes a deep breath, his grip on my waist tightening. "You're the reason we're alive. The reason we're still breathing, why we've woken up every day since and pretended to be okay when we're not." He sighs, his head shaking against the back of mine as Brock's finger absorbs a tear from my cheek. "We're not bad men, Amber," Ryder continues. "I know you know this. Can feel it. We just got caught up in some really fucked-up shit, and the only way out of it was to kill the source. But know that without you, Christ, peach, without you, we're . . . nothing. Absolutely nothing. Try to see past what happened, what we had to do to keep ourselves—you included—safe."

Brock lifts his trembling hands to my cheeks. "Everything Ryder said is the truth. I'd go nuts without you, baby. I need you by my side. I'll lose it if you walk away from me now. I will." He pauses, anger cutting across his expression. "The sick fuck threatened to hurt you. He threatened to . . . kill you. To take you away from me. To never allow me to wake up next to you, holding you, ever again. Never kiss your lips or feel your body against mine. To never build a . . . life with you." The fear haunting his eyes bleeds me out, my body aching raw from the wave of emotions pouring off his slumped shoulders. "No damn way was I gonna let him do that. I'd die a million times over if something ever happened to you. *Especially* if it was something I could've stopped."

His words, *their* words, the sincere remorse behind them, and their silent plea for help sinks me, pain fisting my soul as I try to breathe. Brock blinks, the reflection from a tear slipping down his face blinding me. Beautiful in all its purity, everything that tear represents fills my once-empty heart as I watch it follow the square curve of his jaw and drop onto his bare chest. Staring into the eyes of the man who's forever changed my life—having painted a rainbow of light onto the darkened canvas of what was my world—my finger soaks up the warmth from his tear, my body instantly flourishing with his love as he returns my stare.

Trembling, I look out the floor-to-ceiling window, the bright lights of the vibrant city below trying to distract me from the ugly presence in the room, the undeniable camaraderie every single human being shares.

Death . . . It's all around us, its wickedness hovering above our heads.

I try not imagine what they went through, my thoughts running rampant as I turn my attention back to Brock. I touch my lips to his dampened cheek, the overwhelming need to save him and Ryder from the pain they've endured—the pain continuing to feast on their mental stabilities—so powerful and unforgiving, it takes everything in me to hold myself together.

"I can't hear any more of this." The words drop from my mouth with urgency as I move Ryder's hands to my midriff, surrendering to what I've craved for so long. I slide my lips to Brock's, my heart letting my body take over. "I don't want to hear any more. I just . . . I need the both of you right now, and you both need me. We can heal each other from this nightmare. I know we can."

Brock breaks the kiss and stares into my eyes, his shadowed with uncertainty. "Are you . . . *positive*? I didn't say any of that to make you feel like you have to do this, Amber."

"We don't want you to feel forced into anything you're unsure of," Ryder whispers, his lips pressed warm against my ear.

"I don't feel guilty or forced," I say in all honesty, my ache for them growing. "I want this. I've never been more certain about anything in my life." And I haven't.

Every fiber of who I am—who these men are sure to turn me into—knows this moment is right. *They're* right. I capture Brock's mouth in a desperate kiss, my legs quivering for their touch as I guide Ryder's hands up under my dress.

"I want you to use my body," I purr, not an ounce of shame in me. "Use it to escape what happened. Let it be your release from what you had to do to keep us safe. Use it to help you forget everything that happened that night."

An understanding that we're about to become one—united through death and tragedy—shifts the air hot, thickening the space between the three of us. Brock looks at me then Ryder, their eyes communicating in a way I've never witnessed.

Brock studies Ryder for what seems like forever before taking my face between his hands, his touch gentle as he dips his head, teasing his lips against mine. "You want us to fuck you?" he asks in a low rasp, his gaze glistening to the measure of how turned on he is. I nod, and his lips fully connect with mine, his tongue seeking untapped depths as he groans and hitches my leg around his waist. He drops a hand to my pussy and slips two fingers inside me, deepening the kiss as he works my inner flesh. "Is that what you want, baby girl? Want us to make you feel better? Wipe your mind blank?"

"Yes," I moan, a flame of desire licking its delicious tongue over my heated skin. "Please."

Ryder's fingers slide down my stomach, in between my legs, the soft hum of his heavy breathing dissolving my senses as he rolls my clit between them. "Say it," Ryder whispers, his fingers joining Brock's in their delicious onslaught. "Tell us what you want us to do to this sweet pussy."

"I want you to hurt it," I say breathily, my hands curled tight around Brock's shoulders for support. I need them to take their pent-up aggression out on me—every disturbed bit of their torment drenching my mind, battering my body, unleashing their anger and confusion into my soul. Leather dress hiked up over my hips, I dig my nails into Brock's back, grinding down against their hands as they finger-fuck me ripe. "I want to feel your pain, want you to feel mine. The pain I have for what you had to do. The pain I went through before I ever met the two of you. Hurt me, then heal me. Please. I need it." I kiss Brock harder. "Take from me what you need, and let me take from the two of you in the same way."

Lips pressed to the side of my mouth, Brock's breath dances scalding challenges across my cheek, his groan causing my pulse to quicken.

"Turn around and look at Ryder," he demands through a whisper.

They remove their fingers from me, tripping them over my clit before Brock releases my leg from his hold. I turn and face Ryder, searing curiosity reaching up from my stomach as he glides his dampened fingers along my lips. Goose bumps rise, chasing after his touch as I wrap my hands around his wrist and pull his fingers into my mouth. I suck on them, inhaling the infusion that makes up the deadly storm that defines me, Brock, and Ryder.

Hurt.

Pain.

Confusion.

Attraction.

Lust.

All a lethal but beautiful cocktail that's about to combust, exploding each of us into a state of numbness, a state of healing through what we need.

Each other . . .

Almost in awe, Ryder stares at me, his damaging blue eyes piercing through every intention I'd had to keep myself balanced between what's right and wrong and my desire for him. I ache to tear off the clothing covering his sun-kissed body, to feel him inside me.

His disheveled jet-black hair teases me into knotting my fingers through it as he snags my nape, guiding me to his luscious mouth. He groans, stealing a greedy kiss from me, this one taken with my permission as my longing to feel him fucking me raw burns across my skin. I moan, matching his eagerness as he kisses me harder, deeper, his heavy breathing working in tandem with mine as Brock slowly unzips my dress. It hits the ground and pools around my heels, my lace corset following as he unhooks each clasp. Brock latches his mouth onto my neck, his tongue laving the sensitive flesh where my shoulder and neck meet as he palms my tits, his fingers pinching my nipples into hardened buds. I furiously work Ryder's belt and fly, my need to feel his lips tracing the swell of my breasts, the swirl of my stomach, and the devilish pull of my pussy igniting into near pandemonium, my fingers not moving fast enough for my growing ache.

"Want us to taste this beautiful cunt?" Brock's question is spoken hot against my ear as he slips his fingers inside my warmth. Continuing to tweak my nipples with his free hand, he grinds his cock against my ass. "Take turns tongue-fucking it until you can't take anymore?"

"God, yes," I breathe, devouring the familiar yet unfamiliar taste of Ryder. "Yes, baby, please."

The second I've got Ryder down to his boxers, shirt, and tie, he lifts me from the ground, fastens his lips to mine, and carries my naked body to the couch, kissing me one last time before setting me down on shaky legs. Gaze locked on mine, he kicks off his shoes, his socks following in their wake as he looks me up and down with scalding reverence.

"Christ, you're beyond goddamn gorgeous," Ryder says, unexpected nervousness cutting across his features as he slants a trembling hand through his hair. "A fucking angel." The isolated dimple I've claimed as my own appears on his cheek, hidden under the stubble shadowing his face. "You're . . . I don't know." He shakes his head. "You've rendered my mind blank. I haven't got a single fucking thing." Another shake of his head, his voice cracking as he captures my face between his hands, gliding his thumbs along the seam of my lips. "Thank you for everything. For the last couple of months, for tonight, tomorrow, for . . . you, peach. Even if this is the only time we do this— hell, even if we all freeze up and stop halfway through—thank you. This very second alone is something I'll never let go of. Ever."

God. This beautiful creature's nervous—I feel it, sense it through and through. He lays his lips on my forehead, his movements carried out with that of a man who's unsure if the territory he's about to explore should be walked at all as his palms slither up my shoulders, barely smoothing over my skin. Instantly, every objection I had to doing this falls away.

"It's okay, Ryder," I whisper, nervousness grabbing me tight. "I want this. I want . . . you."

Silently, I grab his tie, sliding it from his neck. Somewhere deep in the crevices of my soul—the unseen compartments of my heart that he and Brock have already dissected—I know Ryder never intended to refuse Brock's request for this to happen. I also know I didn't either.

Time—a thief of decisions—kept me from acknowledging that this moment was always meant to be. Despite the mixture of fear and excitement in my chest, as Brock and Ryder stare at me with hungry eyes, every wound I ache to have healed splits open, allowing them to medicate me, their touch a numbing agent to the demons of my past. Everything I want this night to be, no matter how right it feels or how wrong it is in others' opinions, is my way of letting go of my control—the control I'm willing to hand over to them. I want them to own me, both men breaking down my defenses. My body pulls and strains, longing to be filled with everything Ryder and Brock want to give me, with everything I need to give them in return.

Gaze prowling the length of my body, Brock steps behind me, his voice an untamed whisper as he slides Ryder's tie from my hold. "Close your eyes."

My pulse takes off as he slips the silk tie over my eyes, knotting it across the back of my head. With my sight gone, silence sweeps through the room, nothing but their heavy breathing in my ears.

A soft kiss graces my cheek, followed by another along the opposite curve of my shoulder. I stretch my neck, pushing my chin toward the ceiling, my senses rocketing awake as a hand skirts across my breasts, down the dip of my stomach, and settles between my legs. A finger, then a second, breaches the barrier of my warmth, my body bucking of its own accord as they slide in and out, each pass dragging moisture up along my clit.

"Jesus, you're already wet for us." Brock's husky whisper moves across my cheek, my pulse hammering through my chest as my G-spot's found and hooked with skilled precision.

"So goddamn sweet," Ryder says, the heat of his mouth blazing a line of urgency down my spine. My back bows, my pussy clenching around a third finger as it works its way inside me. "Do you know which one of us is finger-fucking you?"

"No," I pant, my head dizzy with curiosity. My hips rock with my pleasure-inducer's steady rhythm as I grind against his talented fingers. "I . . . I don't."

"It's both of us," Brock offers, his voice encased in a delicious, tempered growl. "Now it's time to guess which one of us is about to lick this pussy until it aches to be fucked."

Before I can say a word, they simultaneously withdraw their fingers, the chilled air rolling across my dampened flesh in their wake. Wasting not a single second, a pair of hands shackles my wrists, gently lifting my arms over my head. A surge of adrenaline floods my listless muscles, my heart thrashing as fear, desire, and excitement create a craving so intense—so brutally intoxicating—I feel as if I'm about to explode.

Another pair of hands brushes down my collarbone, along the sides of my breasts, the soft silk of a tongue stopping to lick, suck, and lightly bite my nipples before coming to rest where I need it most. I moan, my fingers gripping a shoulder for support as my leg is guided onto an unknown surface.

Hands still held captive above my head, I shimmy my ass against the hardened cock of whoever's behind me, each of my senses tested as I hear what I assume are knees hitting the ground, followed by a soft, cool breath over my slickened folds. A hand grips the underside of my thigh, lifting my leg higher, as a tongue laps my clit, sucking on the swollen bud with a long, deep, mind-numbing groan.

"Oh my God," I pant, ripping my wrists free from their confines. My fingers seek the hair of the man whose tongue is pleasuring me as I thrust my hips forward, grinding my pussy against his face. "God, yes. Please don't stop."

From behind, a hand comes around the side of my jaw, tugging my head back as soft lips capture mine in a ravenous kiss, a groan on the heels of each greedy swipe of his tongue. Before tonight, if someone had asked me if I could tell the difference between Brock's and another man's touch, I would have said without a doubt I could. But once whoever was just devouring me pulls away, I'm left clueless as to who's where and doing what. All I know is I'm surging with an intense desire to feel these men fill me, take me, use me up until I beg them to stop.

Almost perfectly timed, the mouth buried between my legs halts its delicious intrusion as I'm swept up—bride-style—into strong, thick arms. Another deep kiss, this one just as intense as all the rest, before I'm gently placed on the bed. My back melts against cool silk sheets as anticipation lights me up, yearning dizzying my head with every nervous breath I try for.

"Spread your legs." Brock's voice threads through the air, his heated command spoken from too far away to determine where he is.

I obey, no inhibitions or fear hindering my movements. I'll give them whatever they want, whatever they need, my entire body Brock's and Ryder's to keep.

Large hands wrap around my ankles, spreading my legs wider, opening me up, not an inch of me unexposed to their eyes. I'm pulled to the very edge of the mattress, the reality of what's about to happen yanking me—in the best way possible—clear out of my weed-induced high.

Not expecting to feel anything so soon, my breath escapes me in a harsh rush as Ryder and Brock each take a breast in their hand and sweep their tongues over the hardened peaks of my nipples. I lurch forward, tingles screaming across my skin as my heels hit the wood floor, their echo lost amid the increased pounding of my heart.

They pull away for what feels like an eternity before I feel a touch again on my inner thigh. The bed dips with the weight of a body to my left, a tantalizing groan to my right. A tongue licks a fiery trail up the bend of my calf as fingers trace my swollen lips, the shell of my ear, and the curve of my jaw. A mouth descends upon mine, kissing me soft and slow. Its addictive taste is familiar yet unfamiliar, but delicious all the same as its rhythm picks up, kissing me faster, harder. Another talented set of lips finds the flat of my stomach, moves up the arch of my ribs, the sensitive swell of my breasts, and ultimately lands on my neck, where it sucks with vigor, each teasing bite and masterful flick turning me into a fiend for them, for this, for us.

Drowning in an ocean of bliss, I let out a shaky whimper. My fingers delve into a thick mane of hair as a glorious tongue dances with mine. Another meets my ankle, its warmth traveling to the back of my knee, the curve of my waist, and the dip of my navel before heading back south, lapping at my clit with urgency.

My womb jerks in ecstasy, sweat gathering between my breasts as two fingers effortlessly slide inside me. Letting out a guttural groan, my boy licks me slow—ripening me up—his mouth attacking every inch of my pussy as my muscles buckle under the pressure of my approaching orgasm.

"You taste better than I could've ever imagined." Ryder's snarl travels across the room, his free hand digging into the back of my thigh. "I could suck on this pussy for days."

Curiosity burns across my body, scalding everything in its path, intensifying my need to watch Ryder take me so intimately as I spring up onto my elbows and yank the tie from my eyes. Breathless, the delicious sight of him buried between my legs annihilates the air in my lungs, my already explosive want for him igniting into something dangerous, mentally lethal.

On instinct, I flit a nervous glance at Brock, scared of what his reaction to all of this is, petrified of how I'll receive it.

I gnaw on my lip, guilt edging the deceitful corners of my self-indulgent mind as I touch his jaw. "I love you," I whisper, praying he believes me, hoping I haven't killed off his ability in being able to fully trust me after tonight. "I love you so much. I need you to know this, _feel_ it without a speck of uncertainty."

"I do, baby girl." The drowsy cadence of his voice feels like the finest cashmere, its warmth coating my stomach. "I know it more than you'll ever understand." He tucks a strand of my hair behind my ear and swathes my lips in a kiss, each deep, probing press of his tongue absorbing another piece of my heart into his. In one fluid motion, he drops his mouth to my breast, capturing my nipple between his teeth, gently biting it. A gasp kicks from my throat, my spine arched as the healing caresses of his and Ryder's tongues send a bolt of electricity through my limbs. Brock pulls back, his heated grin detrimental to my sanity as he juts his chin toward Ryder. "Like the way he's taking care of you?"

Slowing his strokes, Ryder pins his eyes to mine, his grip on my waist easing as he swirls his tongue around the rim of my ass, making sure he catches every last drop of my excitement. Taking his time—worshipping me like a peasant would his queen, his mouth making love to my pussy—Ryder kisses my clit as he stretches his hands up my stomach to my breasts. He squeezes them, then groans, the sound so erotic, so insanely intense, I start to fall apart. My muscles lock up as a delicious army of flames spit hot tendrils of pleasure over my sweat-saturated pores, my orgasm milliseconds from exploding into the air.

However, every heavenly sensation comes to a screeching stop as Ryder stills.

I moan in disappointment, my body aching in protest. "What are you doing? I was almost there, Ryder. Why'd you stop? Just keep . . ." I pause, suddenly self-conscious. I reach between my legs, making sure my Brazilian wax is still good to go. All clear. I furrow my brows, praying to God I'm cool everywhere else. "Wait. Is something . . . *wrong?*"

He slithers up my stomach, his rigid body hovering above mine as a lazy grin fills his face. "No. Nothing's wrong, momma." He cushions his mouth to my ear, his words a soft whisper meant only for me to dissolve. "Something as perfect as you are can *never* be wrong. It's fucking impossible."

Soft and slow, he kisses me like he'll never get to experience feeling my lips on his ever again, like someone's about to steal them away from his possession. The infusion of my unique taste on his tongue, coupled with his, fires me up, my fingers white-knuckling his hair as I buck my hips, seeking his cock. He growls and deepens the kiss, both of us unleashing months of pent-up sexual energy with each deep lick and angry stroke.

"Christ. Just kissing you fucks me up," he says with a heavy rasp, sucking on my bottom lip. "I knew you'd become an addiction."

I wrap my legs around his waist, despising that his boxers are still separating me from what I so desperately need. I move my hands to his waistband—insistent on remedying the problem—but Ryder snags my wrist.

"Uh-uh-uh," he chides playfully. "Not yet. Patience, beautiful one."

My pout only fuels the unmistakable amusement swallowing Ryder's expression as Brock joins in on the taunting, nipping my earlobe.

I sigh, feeling ganged up on.

"And you're correct," Ryder continues, a smirk catching the corner of his mouth. "I *knew* you were almost there. That's why I stopped." He lifts my hand to his lips and glides his tongue around my fingers, down the center of my palm, brushing it over my wrist before trailing it to the inside crease of my elbow. "I *believe* we had this conversation before, remember? I get off on the whole prolonging thing. Don't worry, though. I have every intention of bringing you back to where you were, Pip."

"*Pip?*" I drop my eyes from his as he unbuttons his dress shirt, his

rippled muscles—soaked in ink, from his glorious neck to the beautiful V of his waist—flexing as he pitches the material across the room.

"Yeah . . . Pip," he answers in a low growl, all playfulness gone as
he wets his lips. I watch him carefully, a breath fighting up my throat
as he slides down my stomach, shackling my ankles in one hand. He
dips his head and stares at me a moment—raw hunger lighting his
baby blues—before kissing the contour of my calf, the back of my
thigh, and the bend of my hip, each tantalizing movement sucking
me into the vortex of beautiful oblivion that makes Ryder who he is.

On a groan, he spreads me wide, his tongue gracing my inner
thigh as he settles on his elbows, tugging my legs over his shoulders. I
freeze, the *I'm about to tear you up* look bolting through his eyes seizing my heart as he blows a cool breath across the slickened pleats of
my warmth.

"It's short for Pretty"—his finger circles the entrance of my ass,
his tongue prowling the edges of my clit—"Italian"—he captures the
bundle of nerves between his teeth, groaning as he pulls me flush to
his face—"Pussy."

"Oh. My. God," I moan, my body humming hot as he lifts my
bottom from the bed, spearing his tongue past the puckered, sensitive
flesh of my ass. "Mm, yes. Please don't stop this time, Ryder. I need to
come so bad, it hurts."

He and Brock go all out, nothing soft or gentle in the way either
takes me. I rock my hips in tandem with the strokes of Ryder's tongue
fucking into me, my back bowed as Brock's mouth comes down over
my nipples, neck, and lips. Devouring me like a hungry animal would
its prey, but still in tune with what I mentally need, they shower me
with praise, each man telling me how much I mean to them as they
continue to go at it. Their confessions sing to me, their words filling
the gouged-out wounds scarring my heart.

With their soft yet rough hands running over my heated skin—
their touch wiping out every hideous thing that's ever harmed

me—I crumble, my legs convulsing around Ryder's shoulders as I let go.

"I want more than one from you," Ryder snarls, nipping my clit as his free hand teases my nipples. "I need more than one, peach. You taste too fucking good, and I've waited a long time for this. I ain't stopping until you come for me again."

"Oh, she'll deliver." Brock slides across the bed and tosses my leg over his shoulder. A grin kicks up the corner of his mouth as he joins in, working two fingers inside me. "Bet on that."

My pulse jumps, the delicious pressure of their dual stimulation eating me alive as they ravage my flesh. It doesn't take long before I'm dangling over the edge of pleasure's cliff, my heart speeding toward implosion as I hold my breath, feeling another orgasm building.

"I'm . . . Oh God, I'm about to . . ." Unable to finish my sentence, I sink my hand into Ryder's hair and pull him against my warmth, the fingers of my other hand clawing Brock's nape as a second, then a third orgasm rocks through me. "Yes! Oh my God, yes!"

Before I can take a breath, Brock and Ryder crawl up the bed, laying rows of kisses along my hips, waist, and tummy. Anywhere they can kiss, they do. I bite my lip, my head dizzy, my heart warming with each greedy yet gentle touch against my dampened skin. They roll onto their sides, sandwiching me between them, reverence thick in their eyes as they worship every inch of my body, each man making sure they play with a different part from what the other's indulging in. Ryder grins and toys with a strand of my hair, his teeth snagging my earlobe in a gentle bite as Brock sweeps a slow hand over my breast, lightly pinching my nipple.

"Other than coming again," Brock says against my lips, a smirk shadowing his face, "which *will* happen—what do you really want?"

Though I know exactly what I want, a sense of betrayal burns in my chest. I get to my knees, my words a whisper. "I feel . . . weird saying it."

"I could be wrong, but I think weird happened three orgasms

ago," Brock deadpans, his reassuring smile settling me some as he, too, sits up on his knees. He drags his fingers down my stomach, circling my navel before sinking them inside my pussy. I moan, my forehead falling listless against his chest, my nails biting into his shoulder as I grind down on his hand. Knowing my body better than he does his own, Brock finds my G-spot faster than I can blink, his free hand fisting the back of my hair as I start riding his fingers like I would his dick.

Panting, I swing my gaze to Ryder's. My head instantly splits with the need to be fucked as he frees his cock from his boxers, palming the Prince Albert–pierced piece. Shocked, I take in the circular barbell, an excited edge of fear slicing through me as he strokes it, his eyes locked on mine with every teasingly slow, measured pull. Dear Lord, this man's as sinfully bad and deliciously good as they get. The best and worst part? He knows it. Working every blessed inch of his irresistible charm, triple-take good looks, and hard slabs of muscle, Ryder Ashcroft's fully aware he's a king in his own right.

The only piercing that I was remotely aware of is in his tongue. Judging by the grin shifting the corner of his mouth and the overly entertained look on his face, I'm more than certain he's enjoying my embarrassing reaction. Continuing to stroke his cock, Ryder slides his tongue over his lips, the desire in his baby blues scalding my already-heated skin as he watches Brock finger-fuck me. Trying but miserably failing to look away, I drop my eyes from his, moving them down every inch of ink, which tells his story one masterful image at a time, resting them on what I'm positive is going to pleasure me in ways I've never been pleasured.

If there's such a thing as a beautiful cock, Ryder Ashcroft's the proud owner of one. Long and thick, an indescribably perfect engorged pierced head, and veins straining beneath at least nine rock-hard inches of delectable, *give it to me now* male flesh, it's the epitome of what dampens panties around the globe.

My lips part, tingling to taste it.

Brock's groan breaks me from Ryder's hidden gem as he removes his fingers from me and brings them to his mouth. "Can never get enough of this," he whispers, sucking my moisture from them. Eyes glued to mine, Brock dips his head and flicks his tongue over my nipples, giving equal attention to its twin. "Remember, your pleasure's mine and then some. Nothing's off-limits. Just say it, Ber. Tell me what you really want."

I swallow my nervousness, allowing his needs to let mine run free. "I—I want to suck Ryder off while you fuck me," I answer in a timid whisper, still in shock that any of this is happening, that I actually spoke those words to my boyfriend. I pull him to my mouth and kiss him hard, needing to show him how much I love him, how thankful I am that he's letting me explore this side of myself. I dump my past, present, and future into the kiss, adrenaline expanding my veins as I reach behind me, seeking Ryder. The bed dips with the weight of him rising, his chiseled chest pressed to my back as I continue to kiss Brock.

"You wanna taste me, peach?" Ryder asks, his lips ravishing my neck, his hands finding my waist. "Is that what you want?"

"Yes," I moan, one hand buried in Brock's hair, the other drifting over Ryder's balls. "Please. I need to taste it right now."

The sound of their heavy breathing explodes through the room as they circle my body, changing positions. From behind, Brock slides his hand up my stomach, trailing fire over my skin as he pulls me back to rest against his chest. Lips cushioned to my ear, he sucks my lobe into his mouth, his tongue undoing me as he drags it down my spine, along the dip of my neck, and back up to my ear. Stuck in a mindless, lustful haze, all thoughts of right and wrong, of yes and no, disappear as the heat of his cock glides down the seam of my ass, lighting me up with every slow stroke.

"Suck his dick like you do mine." The dominance in Brock's low rasp thrills me as he presses a hand to my shoulder. Sneaking the other around to the flat of my stomach, he bends me onto my hands and knees, then pulls in a ragged breath as he teases his cock against the entrance of my pussy. "Wrap those pretty lips around it and suck it *real* good. *Real* slow, baby girl. Show him how it's supposed to be done. What he's been missing."

I look up, desire spinning a deadly web through my head as I meet Ryder's gaze. The intensity of his stare pierces my skin, its potency demolishing every last ounce of my uncertainty in its destructive path. My hunger for him surges, pitching my thoughts beyond the room filled with the two men I crave more than air, more than life itself. Words vanish, morphing into flashes of mine and Ryder's past, our undeniable ache for each other flipping through my mind as I watch him watching me.

His jaw tightens as he touches hesitant fingers to my cheek, brushing them along my parted lips, lingering there before resting them on my nape. Still, though his eyes are screaming that he can't wait to fuck me raw, for the second time tonight, nervousness washes over him, his hands trembling as he wets his lips.

God, the thought of this beautiful man feeling even the smallest bit of nervousness lifts my heart, my urgency to taste him exploding into pure insanity as I try to breathe. Core throbbing, I wrap my hand around his glorious piece, my tongue soaking up the tiny bead of silk dripping from the head of his cock. Hot ribbons of desire sear my skin, my eyes fluttering closed as I swallow the liquid pearl. Ryder tastes every bit as divine as I imagined he would, if not better. Like Brock, he's the perfect combination of salty and sweet, an addictive blend of smooth and bitter.

Passion intensifying, I run my eager hand along his shaft, each stroke releasing more of what I need. What I'm sure is going to turn me into a junkie, not a single day passing without grabbing a fix.

"Mm," I purr, fastening my gaze to Ryder's as I stroke him from root to tip, repeating the process with every ragged breath he attempts.

"Ah, fuck," Ryder hisses, fisting my hair as I lick the head of his cock, relishing its pierced tip. "Your mouth's so sweet." His eyes fall closed, his hips rocking in tandem with each slow swirl of my tongue. "That's right. Just like that, momma. Keep doing what you're doing."

I push him back onto his heels, sucking a few scant inches of him into my mouth. He groans, his grip on my hair tightening as I slip my nails under the smooth sac of his balls. Another groan as my tongue makes a pass over them.

"Jesus," Brock snarls, his cock plunging deep into me. "You're drenched." Finding a slow, easy pace, Brock seizes my shoulder and teasingly presses the pad of his thumb around the rim of my ass. "You want it? Need it, baby girl?"

He pulls out a fraction before thrusting back into me, causing me to strain into his touch. Feverishly nodding, I moan around Ryder's cock as Brock's thumb barely breaches the sensitive entrance. "Want my fingers inside this pretty ass?"

"Oh God," I pant, my walls clenching his hardened length. "God, yes. Please give it to me." My body vibrates as he glides his thumb inside me, gently parting the tender flesh as he thrusts into me again.

"I don't think one's enough for her," Ryder says through a groan as I draw the head of his cock into my mouth, sucking and flicking my tongue over it. "Want another?"

"Yes," I beg, their dominance caging me in as Brock slips a second, then third finger inside me. "Mm. Ohh, yessss."

Brock pumps into me faster, harder, his angry tempo eliciting a gasp from me as I take every inch of Ryder into my mouth, stretching my lips to accommodate his girth.

"Fuuuuck." Ryder gathers my face in his hands, slowly guiding me back and forth along his rigid length. "You look so fucking hot, so goddamn beautiful sucking me off. It's enough to kill me."

Like a wild animal, I snap, unleashing everything I've got on

Ryder, my moans matching both men's as I find the taut muscles of Ryder's ass, squeezing them. Pleasure ripples through me, each slap of Brock's balls against my sweat-soaked skin nourishing my entire being with what it requires as I hollow my mouth, taking Ryder as deep as I can.

His head falls back, his Adam's apple glistening with sweat as he once again fists my hair, fucking my mouth with brutal yet equally fluid motions. The tip of his cock hits the back of my throat, and my nails dig into his ass as I swallow him deeper, nearly gagging on his size. Still, I don't stop. I can't. My need to watch him cave, to crumble under my power, is something I've fantasized about, this moment beyond surreal as Brock stretches me, filling me to the core.

"I can't wait anymore," Ryder says through a strangled groan.

He cups my cheeks, his cock slipping through my lips as he pulls back, instantly killing my pleasure. Adding to my torture, Brock removes himself from me. Feeling crazed, I watch both men slide from the bed, their gazes latched on mine as Ryder starts for the living room.

"What are you doing?" I get to my knees and slide off the bed.

Ryder turns and looks me up and down. "I have to fuck you, Amber. I have to fuck you right now. Couldn't wait another minute more if I tried."

I look at Brock, silently seeking permission to react. Gleam wicked, he falls into an oversized armchair and palms his cock, stroking it as he nods his approval. On shaky legs, I bridge the space between Ryder and me, my mind reeling as I approach him. Head tilted back to stare at him, I smooth my hand across his tatted pecs, down the planes of his abs, and ultimately curl it around his cock. He sucks in a sharp breath, the length of his towering body tensing under my touch. His subtle nervousness sends a wave of anticipation tumbling across my skin as I press up on my tiptoes.

"Then ... fuck ... me, Ryder," I purr, my lips cushioned against his ear. I stroke him once, twice, each slow pull eliciting a low groan from his chest. "Don't wait another minute longer. Fuck me now, and fuck me. *Hard*."

A slow smirk twists his mouth as he closes his hand over mine, aiding me in pumping his cock. "Oh, I'm gonna fuck you, peach."

His free hand grips the back of my thigh, hitching my leg around his waist.

"I'm gonna fuck you until thinking straight's no longer an option for you. Until you have no goddamn clue who or where you are." He dips his head, biting my shoulder as he teases the tip of his cock between the slickened pleats of my pussy.

I gasp at the double stimulation. Groaning, he runs his lips along my collarbone, the curve of my jaw, eventually resting them over each of my eyelids as he kisses them.

"Do you hear me, beautiful girl?" he whispers gruffly. "I'm gonna fuck you mindless until *all* you can remember is what I feel like buried inside this." He presses the pad of his thumb against my swollen clit, circling it before pushing a finger inside me. "Sweeter than sweet . . . peach."

My walls clench around his finger, a moan shooting past my lips as he removes it from me.

Smirk returning, his voice is soft as silk as he presses his mouth to my ear, licking my lobe. "I'm being the gentleman my mother raised by giving you fair warning that, well, honestly, I'm about to fucking unhinge you from reality. Consider it . . . gone."

He brushes his nose against the hollow of my neck and slowly inhales, his grip around my thigh laced with fervent ardor as he once again thrusts his hips forward, this time completely breaching the barrier of my warmth. Dizzy, my eyes roll back, my hips bucking of their own accord. The pleasure only lasts a second, though, devastation falling from my mouth in the form of a gasp as his rigid length slips from me faster than I can blink.

He kisses my lips, the languid caress of his tongue destroying the last remnants of my control as he releases my leg from his hold. "But before I fuck you into submission"—flecks of promise flash bright in his eyes—"I gotta grab a condom."

Impatience hurdles through me, tightening my chest. "No, Ryder." I swallow, and glance at Brock.

Watching us carefully and continuing to stroke himself, Brock nods, the knowing look in his eyes giving me permission to proceed.

"I don't want anything separating us," I go on, not an ounce of hesitation in my words as I twine my arms around Ryder's neck. "I *want* to feel you. *Need* to feel all of you. I'm on the pill, and Brock and I trust you if you say you're cool. If you've been tested and are clean, there's no reason to use a condom. No reason for us to not fully become . . . one."

He doesn't respond with words. No, he answers with his body, kissing me deeper, harder, each desperate stroke of his tongue etching his untamed passion for me across the sky. Without breaking the kiss, he drops his hands to my ass, hoists me from the ground, and in one swift movement, pulls me down onto his cock. Unable to believe how amazing he feels, I whimper into his mouth, our bodies moving in sync as he bounces me up and down his thick, rigid length. With another whimper, I tighten my legs around his waist, his piercing hitting deep within my core.

Knowing we've broken all the rules, not a single line left to cross, and convinced I'll never get enough of him, my grip around Ryder's neck tightens, my fingers knotted in his hair as I rip my lips from his and pull back, gazing into his hungry eyes. With nothing but the sound of our heavy breathing curling through the room, a mountain of emotions rains down upon us, releasing its energy into the heated air before redepositing its potency through our limbs. Time stops, halting everything outside of this moment. There's nothing left. Only the warmth of his body as he slows his rhythm, the strong security of his arms as he grips my bottom tighter, and the steady pounding of his pulse as he feathers his lips over mine. Staring into my eyes as though I'm the only thing that matters, the absolute center of his existence, Ryder kisses me, each soft, slow sweep of his tongue opening my heart to him even more.

Beautiful and torturous all at once, thoughts resurface, my mind flashing with every memory of him asking me to kiss him, to touch him, every stolen glance and agonizing second we spent aching to taste each other when we knew we shouldn't. In an instant, it all merges, blurring into images I cling to, but equally fear. What was once simply lust for us is now exploding into something deeper, the magnitude of what it was nothing compared to what it's morphing into.

I milk every glorious inch of him as his pace picks up, pounding into me with brutal force.

"Yes," I grit out, needing the pain as a punishment for ever thinking I could do this without developing feelings for him. "Harder, Ryder. Fuck me harder."

Eyes prowling every crevice of my face, Ryder pumps into me once, twice, three times, completely burying himself to the hilt. He stays there a second, his gaze fastened to mine, before lifting me clear up off him only to slam me back down in the same breath. My head jerks back with a cry as he ravishes my neck with an urgency I've never experienced, not even with Brock.

"Christ, you feel fucking incredible," he snarls, sparking nerve endings I never knew existed. "So goddamn perfect, peach. I could fuck you for days without needing anything else but this sweet pussy." His free hand digs into my backside. "And I don't care what Brock thinks. Your pussy was made for me. Not him."

"Told ya she felt exquisite."

A quick glance over my shoulder reveals Brock standing behind me, his light green eyes darkening.

"And don't get too high on yourself, bro," Brock says, mild warning lacing his tone as he runs his tongue along my nape. "My girl knows *exactly* where her pussy belongs. It's all good, though. She seems to be enjoying what you're doing to her. That's all that matters."

"*Seems?*" Ryder circles his hips from side to side, back and forth, and up and down, each glorious movement sinking me further into a state of mind-numbing bliss. I moan, both from his talented hips and my core throbbing to feel Brock. Still, I'm nervous, anticipation rising inside me, hindering me from taking in enough oxygen. I pull in a slow breath, attempting to calm myself.

"Like how he's making that pussy feel?" Brock's voice is a strangled whisper as his hands guide my hips, bouncing me up and down Ryder's punishing length. "Like how he's beating into it?"

With one hand wrapped around the back of Ryder's neck, I bury the other in Brock's hair, my fingers white-knuckling his wavy caramel strands as my head falls back against his shoulder. "Yes," I answer through a pant as Brock grips my waist tighter, again slamming me down onto Ryder. "Oh my God, Brock. I need you now. I can't take it anymore. I need to come, and I won't until you're inside me. Please, baby. Please don't make me wait anymore."

"That's my girl." Brock drags the head of his cock up and down the seam of my ass as my legs involuntarily tighten around Ryder's waist. "I fucking love when you beg. You're so goddamn hot when you do it, so fucking sweet and vulnerable, it drives me crazy." Chest pressed to my back, Brock brings his free hand to the front of my neck and palms it as he continues to tease me. "But sorry, baby, you're not getting anything from me until you tell me how much you love feeling Ryder inside of you. Say it, Ber. Tell me how good his cock feels."

I snag Ryder's hot gaze, hesitation hindering my response. He wets his lips and jerks his hips up, the groan ripping from his chest matching the intensity of mine as his sheer girth stretches me, flaring my pussy wide open. Brock chooses the exact moment to thrust me down onto Ryder again. My head snaps back against Brock's chest, a gasp springing from my throat as they work me to the very edge of insanity's sweet blade.

"Say it," Brock repeats, his voice harsher, hoarser. With the tip of his cock barely penetrating my ass, Brock tightens his fingers around my neck, both men groaning as Brock slams me down onto Ryder once more.

"Give me what I need. I wanna hear you say it," Brock insists.

"I love how good he feels buried inside me." I moan, tugging Brock's hair as I angle my head just enough to capture his mouth in a ravenous kiss. Tongue twined with Brock's, I flick my eyes to Ryder's, our gazes glued to one another's as he pumps his hips, his tempo matching the furious pace of mine and Brock's kiss.

Brock roughs his hands up under the swell of my breasts, his fingers pinching my nipples as the head of his cock pierces my ass. The delicious burn makes me cry out, but still, he continues to tease me, retreating the second he's got me where he wants me.

"Look at his face. Look at what you do to him." Brock slides his hand down the flat of my stomach, his fingers playing with my clit. Lost in their pleasure, the steady pressure nearly splinters me apart. "Keep talking. Keep fucking up his head, baby girl."

Ryder watches me arch against Brock's chest, his grip around my ass ironclad as he pumps into me.

"I love the way he's fucking my pussy raw," I breathe, sweat dewing my skin as I ride him faster, harder, my nails clawing his back.

"Christ," Ryder snarls, his nostrils flaring. Blue eyes hardening, he palms my nape and pulls me to his mouth, his lips taking small, greedy kisses from me as he digs his fingers into my backside. "You're so goddamn tight, so fucking wet, I ain't gonna last too much longer."

"Think she's ready for the both of us?" Brock asks, his question hot against my ear, his fingers tweaking my nipples as he grinds against my ass.

"Yeah, bro. Of course she's fucking ready."

Though Ryder's response is immediate, I see possessiveness flash in his eyes. He's trying hard to conceal it, but it's all over his face. Jealousy. Steadfast, he dips his head to the valley between my breasts, his tongue gathering the beads of sweat dotting my skin as he grips my bottom tighter.

My legs clench around his waist, my hips rocking with his as he draws my nipple into his mouth, tripping his barbell along the aching peak. Suckling it, he pumps into me with urgency, our bodies locked in sync.

Almost as though he knows it'll be the last one we share without Brock being involved, Ryder kisses me hard, his tongue probing the deepest parts of my mouth. "I know I said it earlier, but thank you for tonight." His words are soft against my cheek, their meaning flavored with desperation. "You're a fucking jewel, Amber. The queen he deserves."

Before I can let his pain eat me alive, I tense, my muscles locking up as Brock starts to ease inside me.

"Don't hurt me," I whisper, touching Ryder's face. "Although I've done this before, I—I've never done it with two men at the same time. Please don't hurt me."

Ryder stops moving, and behind me, Brock completely stills.

"You think we'd ever . . . *hurt* you?" Ryder's eyes dilate in surprise, his hand coming up to cup my cheek.

Fear of the unknown spirals through me, my heart thrumming as Brock strokes his fingers down the side of my ribs. I gasp, involuntarily relax.

"There's no pain here, baby girl." Brock lays his mouth on my neck, kissing it. "None at all. We want you lost in the pleasure we're going to bring you, giving in to it until nothing else exists but your hunger for release."

"Keep your eyes on mine." Buried to the hilt, Ryder remains still, his strong hands gripping my underside, holding me in place as Brock slowly works his cock inside my rear. "You hear me, sweets? Don't take those beautiful eyes off me."

"Ryder," I moan, digging my nails into his shoulders. "Oh God."

"Shh. I have you," he whispers, his gaze moving over my face. "I've always had you, Amber. Always." He presses his lips to mine, hungry, fierce, and gentle all the same.

His words calm me some, their sincerity coating my belly with warmth. "If you want us to stop, you only have to say so. Understand?"

I nod nervously as Brock presses into me a little more.

"Just let it feel good," Ryder whispers against my lips, picking up a slow tempo. His hips rock in tandem with his tongue sweeping over mine. "Bare for him, and just . . . feel us, beautiful girl."

Fighting to drag in more air, I obey. I need to be taken, to be loved. I let their pleasure surround me, allowing it to fill the darkest corners of my mind, forcing my muscles to relax as I pull in a calming breath.

"That's right." Brock kisses my neck, his movements measured as he slides in, fully burying himself inside me. "Let us take care of you. Every single inch of you is ours to touch, taste, worship, and pleasure."

Body flared wide open to the max by both men, my head jerks up as sparks of white-hot pleasure ignite in front of my eyes. I writhe between them, feeling myself dissolve into their rock-hard bodies, becoming one with them as they move against me. Taking their time, they slide back and forth, entering and retreating, each slow thrust and careful manipulation of their hips, hands, mouths, and fingers, wiping my mind clear of everything dark, evil, and cruel—at least for the time being.

Nails biting into Ryder's back, I gasp, burying my face in the crook of his neck as I feel my release approach, one I fear will destroy every future contender. At first, it tiptoes across my skin, building in intensity, until it strikes with hot, wicked bolts of passion deep within my womb. My legs lock around Ryder's waist as I tense, attempting to prepare myself for an orgasm I'm positive is about to rock my skull.

A lethal blend of pleasure and searing flames tears through my core as I buck between them, driving myself onto their cocks in synchronous rhythm. I hear their groans and curses as I gasp again, my muscles buzzing under their attack.

"Ah, fuck. She's starting to come." Brock clutches my ass tighter and Ryder pumps into me harder, deeper.

"Let go, peach." Ryder rears back, our gazes colliding before he jerks his hips forward, plunging into the furthest depths of my pussy. My eyes roll back, my heat milking his cock, swallowing every inch of it as a sharp intake of air fills my depleted lungs. "Let it all go for me."

Mindless, my ribs stretch, my shoulder blades pulling together as my back bows under a swirling mass of ecstasy. I try to scream, but can't as I come apart. The most intense, beautiful orgasm I've ever experienced arcs through my core, destroying me from the inside out. Legs convulsing around Ryder, I let out a wail of completion as the torturous need for release in my lower belly explodes, shattering the fragments of the tainted woman I'd once been. Seeking their own releases, Brock and Ryder clench my waist, hips, and ass, their cocks shifting, throbbing inside me as both men control me, owning my soul, my very existence, in ways I never thought possible. So close to breaking down, they groan in unison, the deep, primal sound sweeping through the room.

"Brock!" I cry out, his cock filling my ass, flaring me wider. Still, the physical pain's nonexistent, a whisper of nothing compared to the pleasure surrounding me. The need and agonizing ache for more of him, of them, of this . . . that's the real pain, the near devastating mental addiction. Feeling every pulse of blood speeding through his heavily veined piece, I gasp, reaching behind me, my desperate fingers sinking into his hair as he works me over.

"Christ," Brock snarls, his hips bucking in fast, clipped pumps.

With one last thrust, he catches my jaw, turns my head to the side, and angles his lips over mine, stealing my breath with a kiss that sends me higher, hotter, each languid pass of his tongue bringing me closer to another orgasm as he comes inside me. "Ah, fuuuuck," he groans, his tempo slowing as he runs his mouth along my flushed cheeks.

On a satisfied sigh, he carefully removes himself, my body immediately feeling ten notches past bereft the second he does. Green eyes sated, he lays a row of kisses on my neck, and backs away as he goes to settle on the bed, propping his back against the mountainous pile of pillows. "I'm just gonna hang out and watch the rest of the show." Folding his arms behind his head, he springs a wiseass brow. "Make sure you finish my girl off the right way."

Paying Brock no mind, Ryder snags my lips in a slow kiss, his need for release darkening his gaze as he whispers, "You're the sweetest sin there is, and this here boy's gonna *more* than finish you off the right way."

Though he's kissing me like an animal, like a man on death row devouring his last meal, his desire to prolong this moment is palpable.

"Look down so you can watch my cock slip in and out of you," he commands through a deep growl. "I wanna see the look on your face as you watch me fuck this beautiful pussy."

"Oh God," I whimper, my chest seizing at the sensual sight as I watch every thick, magnificent, rigid inch of it—glistening from root to tip with my juices—slide in and out.

This is intimate—almost too intimate—the simple act alone trumping every sexual act of my past. I'm all too aware that not only are we physically one in this moment, but also mentally and emotionally— our hearts melding together. My legs convulse around his waist as he lifts and slams me back down onto him. "Yes! Oh my God, Ryder, yes!"

"Say it again," he grits out through a strangled whisper. "I need to hear you say my name."

"Ryder." My fingers white-knuckle his hair as he thrusts me back down onto his cock.

"Again," he growls. "Say it again, Amber."

"Ryder," I moan, his ragged breath on my cheek as I circle my hips, my core seeking the head of his cock with each punishing thrust. "Ryder," I pant, licking the masterful streams of art painting his sun kissed skin, my tongue laving a devil's fiery horns splayed across the curve of his neck. Blazing bright red, the demon's wicked eyes stare back at me as my tongue follows the beast's progression, flames, and Chinese writing lining the sinister, black-shaded body, its tail curling under Ryder's right bicep. I moan again, my gaze lost in the beautiful pops of color, my body lost in Ryder's talent.

He presses his forehead to mine and utters words meant only for me. "Sweet Jesus, you're a goddamn dream. I'm afraid that's all this night is—a fucking dream. I'm scared to death I'm gonna wake up and find that none of this really happened."

His confession stills my heart, thieving the breath from my lungs, as my body races toward another climax. He moves across the room and sets me on the minibar. My eyes flash in surprise, the cold granite surface racing a chill up my spine. However, it only lasts a second, flames searing my flesh as he tugs my legs over his shoulders, pulls me to the very edge of the bar, and sinks his cock inside me. Shot glasses and bottles of liquor clink against each other in rhythm with our frenzied coupling, nearly crashing to the floor before Ryder sweeps them out of the way.

Staring into my eyes, Ryder drives deeper inside me, the force of his beautiful intrusion nearly painful as he finds my clit, circling the pad of his thumb over it. I arc against the pressure as my fingers join his.

"That's it," Ryder hisses, grabbing my wrist. "Finger yourself for me, beautiful girl. I wanna feel them on my cock as I fuck you."

Mind bent with ecstasy, I obey, not a single second of hesitation before I plunge them into the deepest depths of my sex. I'm an un-tamed creature of pleasure as I go at it, finger-fucking myself like I never have before. Though my eyes are wide open, I can't see; I'm in a place no man has ever been able to take me, Brock included.

I meet Brock's heated gaze across the room as he slowly strokes his cock, watching us from the bed.

Every glorious sensation, confused emotion, and excited beat of my heart is all too much, the sheer erotic intensity of this moment setting me off.

"Oh God, Ryder," I pant, my hands flying to his forearms, my hips bucking beneath him. "I'm—I'm going to come."

Ryder grips my hips, driving into me with one long, hard thrust. I scream, the final explosion of my orgasm bursting a rainbow of color through my vision as I hear Ryder growl, "Mine."

A single word, barely audible to my ears, let alone Brock's, as he loses himself in his own pleasure, spurting his release deep inside my core, covers me in warmth. Its silky echo slides through my bloodstream, balling into a knot of dirty emotions in my belly, before welding its meaning around my heart.

Mine . . .

His . . .

But all the same, that single word cloaks me in a blanket of paranoid confusion as Ryder's strong, hard body convulses over mine, his fingers fisting the back of my hair with each violent shudder.

A strangled curse, my name falling from his mouth, and one last thrust has him spilling his remaining release inside my womb, his head falling against my chest with a light thud as we start to come down from our high.

Surely it was just the moment. Ryder can't possibly mean what he said.

The heat of our joining, the intensity of the last few hours, and the agonizing wait for each other made him go temporarily insane.

"You're mine, Amber," he whispers raggedly against the shell of my ear, his hands cradling the back of my head.

So much for my temporary-insanity theory.

Opening his baby blues, he gives me a slow, passionate kiss. "You've always been mine, peach. I think you know it too."

My heart swells with equal parts confusion, emotion, and my own temporary insanity, my insides lighting up like lightning as my conscience screams that he's right. Though I've tried to fight it, Lord knows I have, it was a battle fought in vain from the second our worlds collided, our pull too magnetic, strong, and powerful to ignore.

I stare at him for what feels like an eternity before slipping from his hold, my instinct to flee kicking in. As my feet hit the cool marble floor, all the control I thought I'd gained tonight unhinges, unraveling faster than either of us can blink.

CHAPTER 19

Ryder

I CATCH AMBER'S ELBOW, hoping to calm her down. Fuck. I knew I shouldn't have told her she was mine, but sweet mercy if I could help myself. The moment she reached her plateau I knew she belonged to me. Hell, I knew it the second she tripped into my universe. Tonight only magnified my feelings for the girl, doubling them into something I didn't expect.

If I'm being brutally honest, it's scaring the shit outta me, bringing me right back to a place I swore I'd never revisit after Stephanie blew my heart to smithereens.

But, Christ, this angel's worth every ounce of pain and torture that might very well careen me into a ditch of regret if this little setup doesn't work. The way Amber felt wrapped around my cock, her cries for more, the way her eyes glimmered while watching me fuck her, the addictive taste of her excitement on my tongue . . . Yeah. I can't even.

All of it did me the fuck in, adding to the petrifying knowledge that no one's ever felt so good, tasted so sweet, or been so goddamn right for me. The whole thing's something I know is gonna burn me. Something I'm completely cool with getting burned by. Not only did she accomplish what she set out to do—rid my mind of that fucked-up night—but Amber made me forget all the rest who came before her, memories of my time spent with numerous women vanishing with every soft touch she branded across my skin.

Lips hued ruby red from our frenzied kissing, Amber looks up at me from beneath a fan of thick, dark lashes as she nibbles on her thumbnail.

"Did I scare you?" I keep my voice soft and soothing, trying with everything in me to toss it away from the stalkerish level.

Considering her breathing's a mess, and she's staring at me as though I'm a maniac, I'm not quite sure if my attempt to level her out is working. I gather her cheeks between my hands, the silkiness of her flushed skin searing my palms as I study her face. She tenses, another round of panic swelling her beautiful features. My asshole-ometer dings, going off like a siren. Jesus, I can't tell if she's nervous because she wants to get the fuck away from me, or if her trembling is the result of my touch, her usual reaction.

Either way, I'm about to test it out, praying it's the latter.

I drop my hands to her waist, clenching her soft curves, while trying to control my own choppy breathing. This girl has no idea what she does to me. Hell, I don't think she ever will.

I lower my head and stare into her widened eyes for a beat before brushing my lips over hers. The hairs on my nape jump the second we connect. "Because if I did, I apologize. That wasn't my intention, peach."

"No. You didn't scare me, Ryder. It's . . . it's just . . . me," she whispers, her muscles going lax as I part her lips with my tongue.

I still, hold it there a second, trying to gauge her reaction. She gives me what I want, what's all too fast becoming an absolute necessity to my sanity.

She whimpers and clutches my forearms, her eager tongue peeking out to seek mine. Dizzy from her touch, taste, and scent, I reciprocate, kissing her deep, ravishing her slowly, the need to take her again thickening my blood as she twines her fingers through my hair. Her exasperated mewls tease my ears, each one of her needy little pants driving me fucking nuts. A groan hurdles from my throat as she claws at my back, whispers my name, and hooks her leg around my waist, the pain fisting my balls worth the torture. I snag her lip between my teeth, every cell in my body getting off on the warmth of my release— easing from her pussy—swathing my hip, her sweet nectar coating a thin sheen of our juices along my flesh as I drown in everything she is.

Just knowing I'm in her, on her, my stamp surrounding every inch of her beautiful body lights me up. Soaring, completely motherfuck- ing high, I rough my hand down the back of her thigh, gripping it, my cock throbbing against the smooth surface of her belly as I lick through the silk of her mouth. She moans, a glorious sound. Though my confession might've momentarily made her second-guess her de- cision to go through with this, Amber's not running from me. She's running from her feelings, trying to free herself from the confusing emotions tripping up her head. She loves Brock. This I know. Been aware of it for more than four months. However, I know she feels what I feel, knows what I said is the undeniable truth. Done deal: Amber's been, is, and will always be mine, the reality behind that fact scaring the fuck outta her.

Still, as she kisses me, her feverish little tugs on my hair, urgent strokes, and hips bucking against mine like a crazed nympho says all this cat needs to know. All that'll help him sleep like a goddamn baby tonight.

She's cool, we're cool. That's all that fucking matters.

In the same breath, my confession bugged her out a little something and, for this, I can't help but acknowledge my douchebaggery for mak- ing her panic. I'd rather die than fuck up this girl, this unique gem.

No matter how worthy I become of her, I'll never be worthy enough.

I gotta fix the damage I've done, making sure she knows tonight wasn't just sex for me. That no matter how twisted this scenario gets, I'm in it for the long haul, remaining by her side every tormented second of the way.

I sweep Amber up off the ground, her legs dangling over my forearms, her eyes popping with surprise as she tangles her arms around my neck. A smirk cocks my mouth as I kiss her forehead, reveling in the heavy scent of my cologne, saliva, sweat—hell, my entire body—layering her skin. Not an ounce of her vanilla perfume remains, the sweet fragrance buried beneath one hundred percent pure, raw, unabashed sex.

"C'mon." I kiss her nose, knowing if I could worship her twenty-four seven, it'd still never be enough. She's turned me into a fiend, her touch the crack to my goddamn pipe. "I think this gorgeous body needs some *insane* spoiling."

"It sure does," Brock concurs with a grin, slipping from the bed. He saunters across the room and kisses Amber's pretty bow of a mouth, his grin widening as he drags his lips to her nipple, tugging it between his teeth. She gasps, her hand darting out to playfully swat his shoulder. "*Tons* of spoiling."

Sobering, she stares at him a second, a hint of guilt shadowing her features as she cups his cheek. He softens against her touch, the silent exchange between them punching me in the gut as she leans up to kiss him.

With Amber still in my arms, and me feeling out of place—a third wheel observing their undeniable connection from the sidelines—I start for the bathroom, abruptly breaking their nauseating moment of affection. Not giving a single fuck that I have, I gently set Amber down on the edge of the Jacuzzi, trying to kill my jealous thoughts as I swipe a strand of her hair away from her face. I knew what I was getting myself into when I agreed to this setup.

Now I just have to figure out how to cope with sharing what I know the good Lord above created for me, and me only.

I might be determined to make this . . . unique arrangement work, but I'm sure it won't happen without me losing my shit somewhere along the way. It's nearly impossible. If I do reach my goal of keeping the peace in our little trio without killing my best friend, there's no doubt a pair of cuffs, a blindfold, a dark cabin hidden away in the woods, and a warrant for my arrest—regarding Amber's kidnapping—will be involved.

Sure. My IQ borders genius, but I've never once claimed to possess much in the way of sanity. Where Amber's concerned, all bets and every lick of common sense are off.

Amber looks up at me, concern edging her eyes. I swear the girl can read me like a goddamn book, her thoughts in tune with everything—except my plan of possibly holding her captive against her will—flying through my head as she studies me.

I grin, attempting to brush off what I'm aware she can see.

She casts me one last worried glance before she sighs, her pout all kinds of cute as she leans against the marble tile surrounding the Jacuzzi. "Lord help me," she says with an exhausted groan, "you two are predators, sex addicts at their best. Believe me when I say there's not a muscle in me that's *not* sore, weak, and pissed for what I allowed you two to put it through. So, sadly, I must RSVP no to your invitation."

Brock and I shake our heads, chuckling as an impish smile colors her face. "On top of feeling like I can sleep for an entire month, I think I broke a rib during our little sexcapade. I couldn't go another round if I tried." She pauses, her demeanor flipping from depleted to vixen in under a second. "Well, not *yet*, at least."

Clearly intent on driving us nuts, she slides her hands up her thighs, along the flat of her stomach, over the gorgeous swell of her tits, and into her hair, where she knots her fingers through the dark, wavy strands. "Give me a few hours to recover." She spreads her legs, her soft moan causing me to swallow what feels like a lump the size of a golf ball as she lifts her thick, silky mane off her neck, piling it on top of her head. "I beg thee both, *masters*, for mercy."

Sweet fuck.

I might've brought her in here with the intention of spoiling her *without* using my cock, but I'm about to "master" the "master" right outta her if she keeps this shit up, all thoughts of treating her to a simple bubble bath and massage vanishing with every come-hither look she tosses my way.

Struggling to maintain what little composure I have left, I pull my attention from the temple of Amber's body and begrudgingly bring it to the double granite sink, my balls aching as I pluck a small bottle of apple-scented bubble bath from a glass shelf. I pop off the top and, before I can take a whiff of the stuff, catch Amber's reflection. With a coy smile aimed in my direction, she pinches her nipples and spreads her legs wider, the sweet sound of her lusty little whimper adding additional pain to my balls as she kicks me a wink.

I've never found a mirror to be so resourceful yet so goddamn torturous at the same time.

I approach the tub, dumping the entire bottle of bubble bath into the thing. Bubbles. Only bubbles can save Amber now. If she isn't covered from her glorious neck right down to her pretty pink glitter– painted toenails, it's on. I'll have no other choice but to show her what a true "master" is.

"Mm. You're *real* good at this, peach. *Real* goddamn good." I look at Brock. "I should've been warned about her ability to cause such sweet, agonizing torture to a man. It's a talent unlike any I've ever encountered. Not cool, bro."

Appearing to struggle with his own restraint, Brock wraps a towel around his waist, and takes in Amber a long moment, hunger darkening his eyes as he lifts her up, gently setting her inside the Jacuzzi. He reaches over her shoulder and turns on the water, steam thickening the air as he twists it to the hottest setting.

He sinks to his knees, flanking the marble oasis, and leans over, pressing his lips to Amber's ear. "Talented she is," he says with a grin. She gasps, her eyes fluttering closed as his finger draws a slow circle around her nipple, his touch instantly hardening the luscious, pink bud. "And you, my friend, have yet to experience all her *many* delectable talents. *If* she grows to like you enough, maybe she'll show ya everything she's got. If not, it'll blow for you."

The sight of him sucking her lobe between his teeth, noticeable shudders moving through her, and his douchebag statement further ignite my jealousy for what they share, for what I'll most likely never get to experience with Amber. She might mentally belong to me—hell, for all I know, she might not even, the whole damn thing just wishful thinking on my part—but their bond is too strong, an impenetrable connection that—on my best day—I couldn't come close to touching.

Brock pulls his attention from Amber, a smile cracking the asshole's face. "And I wasn't about to warn you about shit. I suffer, *you* suffer right alongside me. If you're gonna hang around, enjoying my girlfriend, you better get used to it."

Ignoring my urge to snap his neck, toss him out the window, and worry about cleaning up the mess after I've enjoyed Amber by myself, I yank a towel off the rack, knot it around my waist, and squat on the edge of the Jacuzzi. Her toe sneaks up from beneath the pool of bubbles, pressing against the chrome knob to shut off the water.

With a sated smile, she rests her arms on either side of the Jacuzzi and cushions her head on a spa pillow, tiny beads of sweat dotting her skin as she looks between Brock and me. "God, I needed this. Tonight was . . . It was amazing. Everything I could've ever imagined it'd be, and *then* some. I've never been one to gas up a dude's ego—whether or not it's merited—but both of you made me . . . forget about my past for a while. Gave pleasure to my body, but more importantly, gave me a sliver of peace." Her voice softens to a whisper. "There's no way to fully explain it. Even if I could, it wouldn't be accurate." Her smile falls as she touches her hand to my knee, then Brock's. "You were right, baby," she says, staring into Brock's eyes. "Being with the two of you took some of my pain away, even if just for a few hours."

My stomach dips, my heart aching for the shit I know will forever plague her thoughts. "*But,*" she continues, seemingly catching herself opening up to us a little more than what's usual for her, "you two did a number on me."

She closes her eyes and runs her fingertips along the hollow of her neck, a sigh leaving her as she sinks below the storm of bubbles. My breath blasts from my chest as she pops up from beneath the water, the sight of her dragging her tongue across her lips, her hands brushing her soaked hair away from her forehead, and the small smile on her face all fucking with my already-fucked mental state.

She opens her beautiful whiskey-hued orbs—their deep exotic shade nearly blinding me—and wags a finger at me and Brock, a healthy dose of warning encasing her expression. "So I wasn't kidding when I said I needed some time to recoup before going at it again. Understand, twentieth-century cavemen?"

I dip my hand into the boiling pot of H_2O, sure Amber's flesh's melting from her bones. "It's *you* who's the twentieth-century cave-*woman.*" I yank my hand out of the water and give her a shit-eating grin. "We're simply innocent bystanders to something you just *assumed* was our intent."

Amber sits up and wraps her arms around her bubble-covered knees. "Are you trying to get one past me by saying you two had *no* intention of having sex with me when you dragged me in here? Hmm, wiseass? Is that what you're *attempting* to do?" Before I can nod in agreement, *I'm* the one who's swathed in bubbles as Amber splashes me. "'Cause if so, *that's* what I think of your failed attempt."

With my free hand being utilized as a towel to dry my face, the other curses me out as I sink it into the awaiting lava, scooping a decent amount into my palm.

I smirk, enjoying the flash of fear in Amber's eyes. "We're going *there,* are we?"

"No!" Amber half squeaks, half giggles, regret painting her expression as she gauges mine. She cautiously reaches for my arm, rests it on the edge of the Jacuzzi, and pets it, seduction showering her tone as she turns on her charm. "I don't know *whatever* could've come over me." She bats her lashes, a coy pout puckering her lips. "I'm sorry, *master*. I *truly* am." Another bat of her lashes, her pout turning into an *I've got you now, prick* smirk as she draws tiny figure eights along the inside crease of my elbow. "Maybe it's sexually induced insanity? I mean, considering all the *delicious* things you boys did to me this evening, it's quite possible I've sustained *some* kind of injury to my brain." She lifts my hand to her lips, kissing my knuckles. "*Puh-lease* forgive me. I couldn't go on without it."

It's enough the girl's a walking eye-boner, but add knowing how to seduce a man—and seduce him very *well*—to her already-long list of appealing physical and mental attributes, and you've got yourself a deadly combination. Cock on heightened alert, unable to resist the cute yet sinful look on her face, and officially welcoming myself into the *Amber's turned me into a pansy* club, I grin, caving like a certified pussy as I let the water slip through my fingers.

"I'll let you off on this one," I say with a mock frown, "but you *severely* missed the mark on your assumption. Having sex with you wasn't in the playbook when we brought ya in here."

"But in our defense," Brock cuts in, twirling a strand of her hair between his fingers, "you make it impossible *not* to turn into a predator. So, in my opinion, *you're* the guilty one, not us."

"I'm not convinced. Not even close. Still, I gotta give you both kudos for attempting to *swoon* me into believing your bullshit story."

"It's not bullshit, Ber." Brock tucks a wayward strand of her hair behind her ear, his voice soft as he leans over, resting his lips on the crown of her head. "Like Ryder said, we didn't bring you in here to sexually attack you."

She pulls her brows together. "Well, why *else* would either of you bring me here, if not for the purpose of having sex with me again?

Makes no sense. I mean, that's what tonight was about. Sex. Nothing more, right? The two of you taking out your anger, frustration, fear, and stress on me, using my body as an outlet to bring you back down to the somewhat stable mental level you were at before . . ." She trails off as she gnaws on her thumbnail. ". . . before what you two were forced into doing to those men that night."

Her eyes glass over as she looks between Brock and me, trembling. "I shouldn't have brought that up. I—I apologize." She takes a breath, her shoulders slumped as she shakes her head. "The point I'm trying to make is that neither of you has to make me *feel* like tonight was anything more than what it really was." A tear rolls down her cheek, and plops into the water. My heart splits open as the raw pain emanating off her causes a swell of torture to rip through my muscles. "To be honest, all this . . . this *act's* doing is making me feel like an idiot. So just cut it out, all right?"

Seemingly aware that she's spilling her vulnerabilities—every one of her disturbed thoughts on display for Brock and I to dissect—a bolt of horror strikes through her eyes. "Look, I'm sorry. I overreacted. But it's okay, really. I'm used to it. Sex has always been that for me. Just . . . sex. A mindless physical act with nothing attached to it." Her hands shoot to her cheeks to swipe away her tears, her meek voice feigning composure as she continues to tremble like a withered leaf caught in a storm. "Before Brock came along, I was never treated special afterward. No flowers, chocolates, or calls the next morning. No spooning, following a long-winded proclamation of how much I'm needed. No . . . nothing." She hugs her knees to her chest, a noncommittal shrug tugging her shoulder. "I guess I became used to it, and prefer it that way. So please, just . . . just keep it at that, okay?"

I glance at Brock, his expression as lost as mine—if not more—as I try to digest every warped word she bled out. Head tripped the fuck up, I find her shoulders and gently turn her to the side, my breath disintegrating as I take in the defeated woman before me. I swallow hard, the final piece of who I was before tonight disappearing, the man who's left becoming an extension of Amber's bruised soul as I watch her rock back and forth.

It's as though she's embarrassed to look at me, her attention focused on the water. I hook my finger under her chin and lift her beautiful face to mine, my heart sinking the second I catch her eyes. There's so much pain and hurt drowning in them—pain I want to erase from her brain forever. I touch my lips to hers, trying to understand why this jewel doesn't see herself worthy of anything more than being used for some asshole's sexual satisfaction.

The afternoon I kidnapped her away to the diner, it was apparent she'd lost herself somewhere between the filthy pages of her life's story, her corroded past enough to fill a novel. How could it not? The last toxic memory her asshole father gave her left the girl a hollowed-out mess, visions of that sick, twisted day something I'm sure is on constant replay in her mind. Still, the exact moment she gave up on her self-worth, the number of dickheads who helped strip it from her, and why she continues to close herself off, never allowing anyone to truly break down the steel cage surrounding her heart, is something I fear she'll never let me in on.

But hell if I won't die trying to crack her open.

"Sorry, but we're *not* keeping it at that," I whisper over her lips, my hand cupping her nape. She attempts to pull back, her battle fought in vain as I tighten my grip, preventing her from moving. "You can spew *your* bullshit lies to me all day long about how you don't wanna be loved, respected, or treated the way you should be because you're not *used* to it, but—as usual—I'm calling you out, Moretti. *I* ain't buying *your* story. Nice try, but it ain't happening. Not with me. Not now, not . . . ever, peach." I press my forehead to hers, our sporadic breaths intertwined as I thumb away her tears. "And based on our earlier conversation, you know I'm one big, fat, persistent prick, so good luck at any wasted effort you dump into trying to change my mind."

She shakes her head, an exhausted sigh falling from her mouth. "Ryder, please. I don't—"

"You don't *what*, Amber?" I hold her gaze, challenging, testing. "Don't want us to show you our thanks for what you gave us? Christ, you *shared* yourself with us. Willingly handed over not only your body but every one of your beautiful, fragile, fucked-up emotions, trusting that we'd do right with all of it, with all of . . . *you*. Do you know what that means to two assholes like us? Can you even begin to understand what that made us *feel* like? And I'm not just talking about the physical part, peach, because this shit goes beyond that. Sorry, you might not want it to, but it does. You were right when you said tonight was about sex. True indeed, a small fraction of it was. But you were *dead* wrong when you skewed it into something that was *only* about sex. Sex is the easy part." I press my nose to hers, doing one of those Eskimo-kiss things girls love. "It doesn't hurt that it's one of the most . . . *interesting* parts of getting to know someone." I move my lips to her jaw. "It was more than . . . *fun* getting to explore you inside out. I could be wrong, and I apologize if so, but I think you feel the same way about your experience getting to know *every . . . single . . . inch* of me."

She gives me a hesitant smile, its glow lifting the boulder weighing down my heart as she nods. "I definitely enjoyed it."

"Mm. That's what I thought." I kiss each of her cheeks, praying I can get this girl to understand what she means to me, how just a single look from her unhinges everything I am. "It's *after* the sex is outta the way that the hard part comes. The mental ride, if you will. The part where you're learning to trust someone with your feelings, secrets, past, present, and future. The part where, right as you start to feel yourself falling for them, you wanna bounce because you're afraid of where your heart's gonna take you, but mostly scared to death of what *they're* gonna do to it. How much they're gonna hurt it, leaving you numb to ever loving again. But something tells you to stick around, that they just may have something to offer you, something to teach you. Something that—if shit doesn't work out—you might be able to use with the next person who stumbles onto your path."

She knows it's she whom I'm referring to, my words telling the story of us. "Still you don't let go. You keep at it, fighting the fucked-up thoughts diseasing your head, all the while trying to hold on to the small bit of hope you have for you and that person. The hope that shit'll work itself out, that the two of you will find your way through to the end. The hope that there'll never *be* another person who stumbles onto your path. That they're it for you, and you for them. That you're each other's . . . forever."

Amber takes me in for several silent seconds before surrender douses her features, one last tear sliding down her face as she pulls in a shuddered breath. She nods, her muscles going lax as I work my fingers into her shoulder blades.

"Let us spoil you," I whisper against her forehead, watching as Brock stands, drops his towel to the ground, and sneaks into the Jacuzzi with Amber, positioning himself behind her. "You gave us a gift most men can only *dream* about, let alone experience. You can deny us anything you want, whenever you want. But hell if we're gonna let you take away our *right* as men to worship you the way you deserve to be worshipped."

"The way every asshole before us should've worshipped you, baby girl," Brock adds as he too starts working away her stress. Caressing her neck, arms, and shoulders, his touch releases the last remnants of tension from her limbs. "The way we'll *always* worship you before, during, and after sharing yourself with us."

Amber rests her arms on Brock's knees, cushioning her back against his chest. "I'm not used to this." She sighs in contentment, a wary smile playing around her lips as Brock strums his knuckles up and down her spine. "To be honest, I'm not sure I'll *ever* get used to it. Again, before Brock, it wasn't my norm."

"Ah, don't worry about that one. We'll make *very, very* sure ya get used to it." Grinning, I reach for a washcloth and squeeze a dot of vanilla-scented girly shit onto it, my hand screaming out in pain from the searing temperature of the water as I dip it below the bubbles. Trying to avoid sounding like a pussy by whimpering, I quickly lather up the cloth and rub it over Amber's shoulders, around the back of her neck, and down by the sides of her breasts, enjoying the sound of her little gasp as I circle it around her belly button. "And what the fuck's up with the entire female population taking baths and showers that make running into a burning building look appealing?"

Amber giggles and reaches for a razor blade, shaking her head as she perches her leg on the side of the Jacuzzi. "It's relaxing." She slides the blade down her thigh, her knee sneaking up from beneath the fading bubbles as she shrugs. "Who wants to sit in a lukewarm bath? The thought gives me the heebie-jeebies."

"I agree," Brock says, taking the razor from Amber. With her back remaining pressed to his chest, he shackles her ankle in his free hand, lifts her leg from the water and touches his lips to her ear, a grin surfacing on his face as he cautiously runs the blade up behind the silken bend of her knee. "Nothing beats a hot bath. *Except*," he adds, his whisper spoken against Amber's neck, "shaving your insanely *hot* girlfriend's legs and other delectable body parts while she's in that hot bath. Not even the finest green can trump that shit."

Grin turning sinister, he lifts Amber's leg higher and trails the razor down the contour of her calf, back up over her thigh, the asshole ultimately sinking the purple, flower-dotted weapon below the water. No longer in my line of sight, its final resting place is a mystery to me. However—and I'm just throwing this out there—judging by the little gasp that shoots past Amber's lips, I can pretty much figure out which "delectable" part of her body he's giving attention to.

"You good, baby girl?" he asks as Amber relaxes back into him.

"Better than good," she purrs, her lack of fear heightening mine as her eyes flitter closed.

I've always known Amber defined crazy, that very characteristic the main reason the girl caught my attention. But this shit's gone too far, her limitless trust in Brock reaching a whole new psychotic level as she continues to allow him to shave what I'm sure she's unaware is the most goddamn beautiful pussy the big man above ever graced a woman with.

On a sated sigh, Amber twines her right arm around Brock's neck, her fingers dipping in and out of his hair as she rests her left elbow on my thigh. Her eyes open, a coy smile flirting with her lips as she strums her nails over my knee. I suck in a breath, the soft, slow manipulation of her fingertips throwing me under the deadly wheels of her trance.

"You're pale, Ryder," she says with a giggle, "like, ghost white. Are you okay?"

"Am I *okay?*" I rush a hand through my hair, cool with sounding like an overpossessive douchebag. "No, I'm not *okay*, peach. Besides not *needing* to be shaved—considering you've got minimal hair down there anyway—is what you're letting him do to you even goddamn *safe?*" Not waiting for her reply, I look at Brock, my jaw hardening as I stab a finger at him. "Bro, no joke, if you hurt her—even just a little— I swear on my kid sister I'll fucking kill ya."

Instead of appearing even marginally defensive, Brock simply smirks, his demeanor as calm as an uninhabited lake as he pulls the razor from the water. "Here," he says, handing it to me. "When I told you I was willing to share my girl that meant being able to partake in *everything* I do to her. You can shave her, if you want. That is, if she's good with it." He lifts Amber's hair and kisses her neck, his voice smooth as aged brandy as he moves his mouth to her ear. "Feel like letting Ryder in on this?"

Amber slowly rises and rests her foot on the edge of the Jacuzzi, her hourglass shape shimmering with a thin layer of bubbles. I blink, my heart lurching as she buries a hand in my hair for support. Bared

wide open—every glorious inch of her exposed to my hungry eyes—
Amber looks down at me, her smile vanishing as she tilts her head.
"Yeah. I think I'd enjoy that," she says, an edge of nervous excitement
cutting through her whisper. She reaches for my hand, my cock awakening as she guides the razor over the barely visible landing strip of
hair positioned above her pussy. "I think I'd enjoy that . . . *a lot*."

Beginning to tremble, I swallow, and fuck if it doesn't feel like
shards of metal are scratching down my throat, my unexpected reaction worse than a teenage boy who's about to get laid for the first time
as I try to think straight. I swing my eyes up to Amber's as she waits
for me to make a move.

No doubt there's a certain amount of seduction involved in what
she wants me to do to her, the lust shadowing her eyes enough to drive
me to my knees alone. Hell, who am I kidding? There's *more* than a certain amount of seduction, her request landing a first-place position on
any straight man's list of things he'd die to be asked to do by a woman,
let alone one of Amber's caliber. I'm one lucky bastard and I know it.
Aside from participating in tonight's pleasurable acts, this is the hottest
fucking thing I've *ever* had a girl ask of me, nothing else coming close.

Still, I can't bring myself to do it, my cock warring with my mind
as I release the breath trapped in my lungs. I yank back my hand,
letting the razor slip through my fingers. It hits the water, sinking to
the bottom of the Jacuzzi alongside my ego as I take in the confusion
in Amber's eyes. Though I've enjoyed a shit-ton of kink in my sexual
lifetime—usually not giving a single fuck as to how I do it, where I
do it, or the number of spectators observing me and my partner while
we're going at it—I've never done something so intimate to a girl,
something I feel I can't do to someone who doesn't *fully* belong to me.

This here, folks, is a prime example of dropping the ball midplay.
I stand and swipe a towel off the rack, wrapping Amber in it. "I want
to, peach. Christ, you have no idea how *much* I want to, but I can't."
Silence reigns, each passing second Amber stares at me with confused

eyes making me feel like a bigger asshole. "But I don't know. It's just not . . . right."

She touches my jaw, worry slashing her brows. "I'm sorry," she whispers, something parallel to shame cracking her voice. "I shouldn't have assumed you'd be okay with—"

"Nah, beautiful girl," I interrupt, placing a kiss on her forehead as I help her out of the Jacuzzi, "don't go apologizing for something I'm struggling with. It's *me*, not *you*. Understand?"

Pensive, she nods, my words barely dousing the uncertainty torching her eyes. Great. I've officially reached the *you're a loser* level in her mind. Mentally slapping myself upside the head, I watch as an equally confused Brock steps out of the Jacuzzi.

He knots a towel around his waist and drapes his arms over Amber's shoulders from behind her, an entertained smirk replacing his confusion as a light chuckle pelts past his lips. "*All righty, then.* I'm curious as all hell, and have no goddamn clue *what* the fuck just happened with that one, but I'm too tired to ask. Tonight's your lucky night, Ashcroft. I'll leave it alone."

"Good," I growl through gritted teeth, my muscles strung taut with the need to bury him in a shallow grave. "It's better if you *don't* ask." I scratch at the stubble coating my jaw, an entertained smirk tweaking *my* lips as Brock drops his arms from Amber's shoulders. "Believe me, in the end, your face *will* thank you for keeping your asshole remarks and questions to yourself."

"What the hell's your problem?" Green eyes lit up, he circles Amber and steps in my face, his chest puffed out like a blowfish as he cocks his head to the side. "Because *you* pussied out on an opportunity any *legit* dude would give his last breath for, we're supposed to suffer through your dramatic bullshit?" He sniffs haughtily, his smirk thinning into a hard line. "Yeah, I don't think so, bro. Save that shit for someone who actually gives a fuck, because this asshole doesn't. Believe me, *your* face will thank *you* for it in the end."

Red.

All I see is red, visions of drowning him flashing through my mind. I suck in a measured breath, attempting to bring myself down a notch. It doesn't work, not even close. If anything, it's cranked me up, his threat spreading its poisonous vines through my mind, each branch further diseasing my thoughts. I clench my fists, my palms itching for his blood as I inch closer, daring him to make a move. I size him up, secure in my capability of destroying him, every lick of me positive I can put him to the ground. He might have me by an inch or so in height, but if it came down to it, the motherfucker wouldn't last more than a couple of seconds with me—and that's being generous.

"Why don't we get ready for bed?" Amber's suggestion zips from her mouth in a nervous rush, fear lacing her voice as she curls her hands around our biceps, clearly set on saving her dicknugget boyfriend from the worst beating of his life. "It's been a crazy few hours, we're all emotionally spent, *and* we have a long drive ahead of us tomorrow morning. Let's just chill and call it quits, okay?"

With neither Brock nor I unfastening our glares from each other, silence—dark and menacing—swoops in, its evil wings bringing with it a tension so thick, so goddamn impenetrable, not even a jackhammer could break through it. However, Amber works her magic, her touch pulling us from our showdown as she moves her hands to our cheeks and gives us a playful look of reprimand. "*Besides* you two being best buds, this whole night was meant to *relieve* me of my insanity, not *add* to it. Don't think I won't kick *both* your asses if you ignore that piece of info and decide to go with the classic caveman pissing contest instead." She presses up on her tiptoes and pops a kiss onto each of our jaws, her smile widening as she wags a disciplinary finger at us. "I might be smaller than you boys, but *never* underestimate my ability to kick some major ass. When I'm hyped up, I can throw a punch faster than a fiddler's elbow."

With twin grins threatening our mouths, Brock and I glance at each other then at Amber, wash, rinse, repeat as we attempt to keep our childlike game of silence going. Try as we might, we crack, our "pissing contest" coming to a relief-filled end as we bust out laughing. Hard.

Amber slips out from in between us and crosses her arms. "What the heck's so funny? You don't believe I can kick some ass, do you?" She blows on her knuckles as she lifts her chin in defiance. "Care to find out for yourself, then, Ashcroft? Size—in *this* case—has nothing to do with *shit*. It's speed that counts, how fast you can knock someone off guard *before* the battle begins. Everyone in the universe knows the first person to throw the punch wins the fight."

I lose it, shaking with laughter as Brock falls apart beside me, chuckling as hard, if not harder.

"You sure do have a cute but odd way of describing shit." Brock pets her hair. "A fiddler's elbow? *Really*, Ber? Again, cute, but still odd as fuck, baby girl."

"*That's* what you two've been laughing at this entire time?"

"Hell yeah." I give her towel-hidden ass a whack. She jumps with a squeal. "That, and you honestly *thinking* you can kick our asses. The delusional faith you have in being able to beat us down, without us *letting* you win, merits—at the very least—a C-plus." I cup her cheeks, my mouth pressed to her forehead as I chuckle at her melodramatic sigh. "And if you run around telling people your punch is faster than a 'fiddler's elbow,' then it's *you* who's gonna get dropped."

She places a lingering kiss on my jaw, her tongue grazing my stubble before she slides it down my neck.

I tense, preparing myself for what, I'm unsure, but fuck if she doesn't look like she's about to rearrange my face, my cock next in queue on her mutilation list as she pulls back, gazing deep into my eyes. I try to play it off, acting as though the girl hasn't burrowed herself beneath my skin. But she has, and she's done so unlike any other before her. When Amber gets like this—pissed, playful, and dirty all at once—it's nearly impossible not to bend her over and show her how I *really* feel, every attempt at playing it cool turning into one huge pile of worthless shit.

"Thanks for the mediocre grade, Mr. Ashcroft," Amber purrs, something akin to revenge cutting through her eyes, "but this here student's *already* kicked *both* her teachers' asses." This time around, Brock's her target, her fingernails running down his chest as she works his neck like she did mine. He tenses worse than I did, the faggot's breathing jumping past his lips as one of Amber's many split personalities continues to keep me on heightened alert. Just to be safe, I cover my balls, my hands serving as a shield to my baby-maker as Amber licks a line up behind his earlobe. "But, sadly, they just don't *know* I kicked their asses."

"How so?" Brock asks, his question spoken through a groan as Amber sucks his lobe between her teeth. "Sorry, but I ain't seeing any kind of ass-kicking going on in these parts of town."

"*No?*" She steps back, her eyes turning sinister as her towel hits the ground, leaving her naked before us as she rests her hands on her hips. "How's *this* for some unseen ass-kicking? Is the vision in focus, or do we need bifocals?"

Like two speechless idiots, Brock and I move our gaze up and down the length of her body, not a single comeback leaving our mouths as Amber lifts a triumphant brow.

"Hark. What's that?" She spins on her heel, a giggle moving through the air as she starts for the bedroom. "Ah, that's right. I believe I just kicked *both* your asses without even having to throw a punch."

With nothing but her apple-shaped ass in my line of sight, I swallow, watching as Amber sways around the corner and into the bedroom.

Brock palms his neck, his voice grainy as he yanks his attention from the empty doorway. "Did she—"

"Just school us? Put us in our pitiful places? Show us the almighty power of pussy has spoken?" I sigh, a grin creeping across my face as I make my way into the bedroom. Amber's already dressed in a pair of Hadley U sweatpants and sweatshirt, her smile lighting up the room as she gets cozy dead center of the California king bed.

"Now, now, boys," she says, patting the mattress, her widened smile creating a new category for wiseassery as she slips beneath the silk sheets. "Don't look so grim. Everyone needs a good ass-kicking every now and again." With a stretch of her arms, she feigns a yawn. "Come on. This gal needs a little spooning right about now. Good?"

Brock dives onto the bed, entombing Amber in his embrace, the grizzly-like attack causing her to hoot out in bubbly laughter. I stroll over to the bed, unsure where I belong in this fucked Rubik's cube of emotions the three of us have manufactured.

I scratch at the hairs lining my stomach, hesitancy softening my words as I pluck my briefs off the chaise lounge. "You two go ahead. I'm just gonna head on back to my suite."

Amber casts me a look that crushes my heart. Steadfast, she untangles herself from Brock's hold and sits up on her knees. "No, Ryder. You're not leaving. You're staying here tonight. In this bed. Next to me. That was the deal."

"There was *never* a deal for what comes after, peach," I point out, an edge of irritation cutting through my tone as I stare into soft, golden eyes. Soft, golden eyes my asshole statement's brought what appears to be tears to. Fuck me. My heart crushes again. Still, my mouth keeps moving, my words meant to push her away, to hurt. "*Deal?*" I ask through a disdainful chuckle. "I think I sealed my end of the deal, no?" Hands gripping my hair, I move across the room, my head ticking back and forth as I throw on my pants and dress shirt. "Did what we all did *not* make you forget about your past? Unload some of that pain you've been carrying around?"

She jumps to her feet, fire in her whiskey irises as she follows me to the front door, stabbing her finger into my shoulder the entire time. "Turn the hell around, Ashcroft," she demands, a hiss biting her breathless tone as my hand makes contact with the doorknob. Playing the dick this situation's turned me into, I freeze, my need to make her sweat it out hardening my cock as I ignore her order. "Now, asshole. I'm not kidding. If you don't turn the fuck around right now, then I'll have no other choice but to show you the damage my punch *will* do to the back of that thick, idiotic, greasy skull of yours."

Is there nothing the girl can say that won't make me fall harder for her? This I highly doubt.

I turn, my gaze meeting hers with the same intensity it always has, the same *I'm about to fuck the fuck right outta ya* look it'll forever possess.

An unsteady breath, followed by an unsteady step forward, and Amber's chest is pressed to mine, our heart's beating in bullet-fast sync as she takes my cheeks prisoner between her shaky hands. I try to look away, but she tightens her hold on my face, her eyes narrowed.

"What the hell's your problem?" she asks through an aggravated huff. "Can't handle the pressure?"

I slide my hands to her hips, gripping them as I try to contain my urge to kiss her until she begs me to stop. "What the fuck's *that* supposed to mean?"

"Now all of a sudden the genius is stupid?" she tosses back, her glare unwavering as she all but smashes her nose to mine. "It means exactly what I said. You're a pussy, Ryder Ashcroft, a softy. The big, bad, tattooed, pierced former quarterback can't handle the pressure of sharing me when he thought he could. You agreed to this setup as much as I did. Now all of a sudden it's too much to take?"

At this point, I have two options, both I'm quite fond of.

One: strip her bare of her Hadley gear, bend her over the entry-way table, and show her how *un*soft I currently am, her anger hardening my cock by the second.

Two: repeat option one until she can't take it anymore, her inability to walk straight, for at least a week, my top priority.

I decide on an unplanned option three, my mouth crashing down over hers with lightning speed. She reciprocates with the same angry passion as I tangle my fingers in her hair.

"I hate you," she hums through a moan, her nails leaving their stamp on the back of my neck as she kisses me deeper, harder. "I swear to *God* I do."

"Right," I growl as I hike her leg up over my waist. "I can tell. I guess our hatred for each other is a mutual feeling, then, peach."

A moan floats past her lips, her breathing choppy as I lift her off the ground, pressing her back to the cold mahogany door. "You're staying here tonight," she says, insistency thick in her rasp as she knots her legs around my waist. "I'm not kidding." She pulls back and stares straight beyond my soul, a glimpse of sorrow drowning her eyes. "I *need* you to stay here. Don't make me feel like you used me, that this was a onetime deal." She pauses and my heart comes to a dead stop, my breath faltering as a tear slips down her flushed cheek. "I don't want that with you. I—I don't know what I want or how either of us is going to deal with any of this, Brock included. All I know, all I feel with everything that makes me, is you and I *can't* be a onetime deal. We weren't placed in each other's lives to become that. God's cruel, but I have to believe he has his moments."

Before he died, my grandfather told me I'd know if I was falling for a woman based on my reaction to her words—that if it wasn't just simply lust, and I was truly in way over my head, the girl would be able to demolish my senses the second not only her flesh connected with mine but the very moment she opened her mouth. As it stands, Amber's already the keeper of each and every single one of my senses, the owner of every breath that moves in and out of my lungs. The potency of her touch, her smile, hell, her goddamn spirit, has blinded me from being able to see anyone else but her, her eyes a constant image playing in my head. She's thieved my ability to hear, the angelic tune of her voice the only sound in my ears. Whether or not she's near me, the scent of her skin lingers in my nose, my body incapable of smelling anything else but her sweet vanilla perfume.

Yeah, I'm in deep, every inch of me past the point of being in way over my head. What started out as lust for Amber is gone, my absolute need to have her by my side replacing it. This girl's a rose amid a garden of weeds, her mind, body, and soul a representation of her beautiful petals. Though I know how to take care and love her in the purest way—which is constantly through the silence of time—I'm aware I have to tread lightly. One ugly tug on those petals, one uncareful touch, and she'll fall apart, withering away, my fingertips bleeding from the painful prick of her thorns.

With that, I nod, however, not without setting boundaries. "All right, peach, you win. But I'm staying on the couch. I don't belong sleeping in the bed with you and Brock. I just don't."

"But if—"

"No," I whisper, setting her down. I cup her dampened cheeks, my thumbs grazing her quivering lips. "The couch. That's my limit. I'll be here when you wake up. I swear I will." I kiss her forehead, my words remaining soft, calming. "Besides, how can I resist seeing what you *truly* look like when you crack open those pretty eyes?"

She gives me a weary smile, surrender painting her features. "Okay, but I'm tucking you in, though. No arguing with me on that, or else, got it?"

"Mm. The 'or else' has me curious." I pull her into my embrace, my heart thrumming at how perfectly she fits in my arms. She presses her cheek to my chest, her silken skin a piece of heaven to my racing thoughts as she releases a small sigh of relief. "I'm sorry," I whisper, realizing how much my douchebag move impacted her. "The last thing I'd ever intentionally do to you is make anything resembling a tear fall from your eyes. I don't know what's wrong with me."

She looks up at me, the devastation coloring her whiskey orbs telling me all I need to know . . . She's just as deep in over her head as

I am, both our hearts struggling with this hazardous situation. "No, Ryder, I'm the one who's sorry," she admits.

"All right. So you're both sorry." Brock steps from the bedroom, scratching a tired hand over his face. "Glad to see the two of you've made up. Ber, tuck the baby here into bed, and I'll warm up the bottle before we turn in, cool?"

"Stop being a dick, Brock," Amber huffs, seizing my hand in hers. She shakes her head and drags me past him, our glares glued to each other as Amber flings open a closet, yanking a spare pillow and blanket down from a shelf. "Seriously. Contrary to what you think, it's not one of your finer attributes."

"Chill, baby girl." He chuckles, making his way over to the couch as Amber sets up my temporary sleeping quarters. "Ashcroft knew this arrangement would come with its share of emotional shit. Now he just has to figure out how to maneuver his way through the mental maze. Isn't that right, bud?"

Keeping Amber's sanity in mind, I grit my teeth, somehow managing to conjure up an unaffected smile. "Yeah, I guess we all do, isn't *that* right, bud?"

His glare intensifies, his eyes narrowed on mine before he turns, heading back into the bedroom. "I'm giving you ten minutes with him, Ber," he calls over his shoulder, clearly aggravated. "After that, I expect you to come to bed."

He slams the door, the power behind it knocking an oil painting clear off the wall. I glance at Amber, the confusion dripping from her face causing my stomach to roil with anger.

"He's just . . ." Amber starts, her words trailing as she stares at me. "I don't know. He's just . . . a mess right now, Ryder. He took a big step allowing us to do this."

I touch her jaw, knowing if she were mine there'd never be any confusion on my part. No questions asked: I'd never share her with another man, the thought sickening me down to my bones. Still, I keep my thoughts to myself, placing a soft kiss on her forehead before slipping onto the couch. She goes to sit next to me, but I gently grab her wrist, preventing her from doing so, my chin jutted toward the bedroom.

"Go inside, peach," I whisper, fighting the animalistic urge to kick open the door, and beat the man I've called a friend for so many years into a coma for putting Amber through this. "He needs you. I'm cool. I promise."

She can tell I'm lying, trying to keep her emotions guarded. I see it in her eyes, the shadow of uncertainty in them. She nods hesitantly, then turns and disappears into the bedroom, the door softly clicking shut behind her as I cross my arms behind my head, wondering if any of us will ever be the same after tonight.

More important, as the minutes creep by, ticking into silent hours, I can't help but feel like we're all standing in the path of a dangerous storm. A storm I'm positive is gonna take one of us out—if not all of us—leaving the bloodied remnants of our hearts spread over a field of nothing but pain, hurt, and regret.

CHAPTER 20

Brock

"Breathe, motherfucker," I murmur to myself, my teeth gritted as I attempt to keep my cool. "You did this, asshole. Not them." Sitting in my Hummer, watching Amber and Ryder say their goodbyes, I inhale a calculated breath, trying to keep myself bolted to my seat as the girl I love—the girl I'd die for—places a soft, lingering kiss on my best friend's lips.

Fuck. What've I done?

The mind can change what the heart *thought* it wanted—both unrelenting in their battle of wills—and right now, my mind's winning the war as visions of making Ryder disappear swallow my thoughts.

Witnessing Amber show anything resembling feelings for another man is killing me, my soul shredding to pieces, as Ryder pulls her into his arms, his mouth devouring hers the same way mine does when I want her, when I crave her the most. I know letting them be together was my doing—my need to give and receive pleasure to and from Amber clogging whatever rational sense I had before last night—but I'm starting to think it was nothing short of the second-worst decision I've ever made, not making it home in time to get Brandon off the bus holding the number one spot on my list of regrets.

Sure, I played it cool while watching them together last night, but hell if I didn't want to stop the whole thing from happening the moment Amber said she needed us.

Bipolar? Maybe.

Psychotic? Killer possibility.

But after having had almost a month to *really* think about sharing her with Ryder before she finally gave in to my request, I'd decided I wouldn't be able to watch any dude—best friend or not—touch my girl. I just never got around to telling Amber I'd changed my mind. Besides my having to lie low after outing Dom, Amber seemed so goddamn steadfast on *not* letting Ryder and I take her together, I figured the subject was dead. Still, the second Ryder opened his fucking mouth about what went down at the warehouse, and Amber's gut-wrenching reaction to it, I felt I had no other choice but to allow that shit to happen. To sum up my birthday weekend: I unwillingly, yet willingly, let my buddy fuck the girl I'd give my last breath for, the girl I've already killed for and would kill a million times for over again.

Happy fucking birthday to me . . .

Either way, this shit's gonna haunt my nightmares for the rest of my life, every ounce of me loathing my on-the-fly decision. Like a delusional, self-centered asshole, my thoughts were skewed when I convinced myself that I wanted to share Amber. More so, screwed when I thought she'd be able to separate the physical act of being with Ryder from the emotional.

As I continue to watch Ryder shove his tongue down her throat, I'm starting to realize my girl isn't separating shit from shit.

Finally, Ryder enters his apartment, the asshole looking back at Amber one last time before closing the door behind him. After he disappears, Amber stills, her attention aimed on where he was standing. I sigh, wondering what the fuck's going through her head. As she slowly turns around, her weary eyes catching mine, I think I know the answer to that question.

My girl's hurting, torn.

Christ.

Since I'm the one who initiated this fucked-up scenario, how do I end it? With my mind and heart continuing to battle it out, that's one question I don't have a single answer for, my hatred for myself growing by the second as Amber slips into the passenger seat.

"You okay?" I ask, knowing she's not.

She nods, a weak smile slanting her lips as she leans her head against the window. "Yeah. I'm cool."

"You're cool?" I parrot, an edge of sarcasm in my tone as I pull onto the road. "You sure as hell don't seem like you're *cool*, baby girl."

She twists her head in my direction. "What do you want me to say, Brock, huh?"

"I don't know," I bite back. "The *truth*, maybe? That you're an emotional mess right now? That you want more of him because he *thinks* you belong to him?"

She opens her mouth, but quickly snaps it shut, her gaze landing everywhere else but on me as I slam on the brakes. My Hummer screeches to a stop, the tires leaving a thick, inky stain on the street as I grip the wheel.

"I heard what he said to you, Ber," I whisper, trying to calm the rage scorching my skin. "That you're his. That you've always been his." Her eyes widen, shock thickening their depths as she lifts them to mine. "I heard *everything* last night." I pause, acid crawling up my throat as I try to get out the question that can forever change our relationship to move past my lips. "Do you, Ber? Do you belong to . . . *him?*"

Nervousness plagues her features as she leans over the center console, brushing her fingers through my hair. Before I know it, she's seated in my lap, her arms knotted around my neck, her cheek pressed to mine as she trembles under my hold. I take an unsettling breath and keep it locked in my lungs for as long as I can, her silence scaring the fuck out of me as I await her response. This girl's colored every dark corner of my universe, her existence the very reason for mine. Though I'm the monster who caused this chaos, the filthy serpent of her confusion, I don't know what I'll do if her answer's the one I don't wanna hear, the one that'll undoubtedly trip me over the edge between semirational and absolutely homicidal if she replaces me with Ryder.

I can't lose her to him; every inch of me will surely incinerate into ashes if I do.

Amber kisses my shoulder, her sweet breath searing hot through the fabric of my sweatshirt as she whispers, "I think a part of me belongs to the *both* of you after last night."

At her words, my blood stops running as I try to digest her poisonous confession, try to wrap my head around what I've done to us. Still, I have to own her feelings, suck up to the fact that a part of me knew this could happen. Yet as I drag Amber off my lap, shoving her back into her seat, the logical side of my brain splits in half, my pulse gunning through my neck as I put the vehicle into drive, speeding onto the highway in an effort to outrace my guilt for fucking up the best thing that's ever happened to me.

"Are you . . . *mad* at me?" she asks, her voice breaking as she tries to thread her fingers through mine. "Seriously, Brock. Are you mad?"

"God help me, but yes, I'm fucking pissed, Amber." I yank my hand away from hers, aware I've further diseased the only girl I've ever loved . . . the only girl who'll ever fully own every piece of me.

Amber stills a moment, her demeanor switching from worried to vexed in under a second. "God has *nothing* to do with this. How *dare* you get mad at me, Brock. You're the one who wanted this. The one who *begged* me to let us experience the multitude of pleasures this could bring. Not me!"

"Do you *love* him?" I ask, ignoring the truth behind her words, their sting, though one of the most brutal torments I've ever endured, not enough to shut me the fuck up. With images of them together branded in my mind, their undeniable chemistry is a flame I couldn't put out even if I wanted to. "Is that what's going on in that head of yours, Ber? Are you in love with him?"

She blinks, another breath-evaporating moment of silence encasing the rapid beating of my heart. "Do I . . . *love* him?"

"Yeah," I croak out, a fear so dark, so overbearing, knifing through my muscles as I wait, with wired nerves, for her to reply. "That's what I said, baby girl. Do. You. Love. Him?"

Eyes locked on mine, she shakes her head, her trembling voice so tiny—almost unrecognizable. "I don't know how to answer that. I honestly don't." She touches tentative fingers to mine, the fear I thought I had seconds ago paling in comparison to the storm of dread ripping absolute devastation through me as she pulls her hand away, nervously knotting her fingers together in her lap. "All I know is I liked being with the two of you at the same time. Liked the way it made me feel. It was as if I was the only star existing in your universes, the last sun burning in your skies. The way you both broke me down, mentally and physically, was all you'd promised it'd be and so much more. I said it last night: there's no way I can adequately express what it did to me." She sucks in a slow breath, her gaze misting. "With all of that came . . . intense feelings for Ryder. Ones I can't fully explain or even *begin* to understand."

I attempt to form a coherent thought, but I can't. The only thing I can do is pull to the side of the road, guilt for putting her in this position pressing up from my stomach, its toxicity surrounding me in a haze of uncertainty as I stare at her, trying not to lose my shit.

What kind of man does this to his girl, to the only person who welcomes, understands, and accepts every twisted corner of his mind? This asshole does, that's who, not a single fucking disgusting inch of me deserving of the purity that *was* Amber's love for me before last night.

"All I'm truly sure of is I want him again," she says with unshakable conviction, a fresh round of tears pricking her yellow orbs as she meets my stare head-on. "Need to experience both of your touches at the same time for an array of reasons." She sniffles and slithers back onto my lap, mercy coloring every crevice of her beautiful face as she presses her lips to mine.

I want to touch her. Christ, I want to touch her so fucking bad but I can't get my limbs to move, my arms cemented to my side as she slides her lips to my neck, leaving them there. "Please don't be mad at me for wanting him again, for wanting you *both* again. Like you, I expected this to be something I could handle. An emotion I could switch off the same way I have my entire life when it came to numbing my feelings." Body molded to mine, she moves her mouth to my ear, her words spoken soft. "But after last night, after experiencing what it felt like to be broken down by two amazing men, I know I *can't* switch them off. Not fully, at least. Even so, I can curb my feelings for Ryder. I swear I can. I know it may not seem like it, but I love you to the moon and back, Brock. I honestly do. I need you to understand this. More than anything, I need you to *believe* it." She seizes my lobe between her teeth and softly bites down, the caressing tempo of her tone a balm to my nerves as she loops her arms around my neck. Fingers tracing figure eights along my nape, she continues, a hint of desperation cloaking her whisper as she squeezes me as though it's the last time she'll ever get to. "Please don't take away this tiny sliver of sanity from me. I promise, from this point on, I'll tame my emotions for Ryder, keep them in check for the sake of everything you and I are. I just need to feel the way I felt last night at least once more. Just one more time, baby, please." She rears back, her hands capturing my cheeks as another tear slips down her face. "I need to let it all go, banish every second of hurt, pain, and confusion I've carried with me through the years. That's what being with you and Ryder did for me. It made me forget—even if just for a few blissful hours—that hideous day. The cold look in my father's eyes, the sound of the gunshots, their blood splattered all over the sundress my mother bought me the day before. I'd never owned a new dress, Brock. Never. They were always hand-me-downs from one of the neighbor's kids, or something my mother lifted from the Goodwill because we barely had money to pay the rent, let alone deck out my closet with new clothing. It was so beautiful, the entire thing covered in sparkly polka dots, flowers, and . . ."

She trails off, silence swooping in like a hungry vulture as her gaze turns distant, void. Although she's sporting a small smile—evidence of a happy memory dancing along the sharp, jagged edge of her worst—the fear hijacking her expression can be spotted a mile away from those who can no longer see, felt from those who haven't felt in years.

In physical pain—every muscle in my body aching for the torment continuing to rip mayhem through her soul—I swallow, fighting back my own tears from falling, my father's bullshit spiel about how a *real* man never cries ping-ponging through my brain as I clear my throat instead.

Amber drops her trembling hands to my chest, their nervous rattle in sync with the furious pounding of my heart as she burrows her face in the crook of my neck. Unable not to—my concern regarding her feelings for Ryder temporarily vanishing—I pull her into my embrace, my arms caging her in my hold as the core of who I am soaks up the warmth of her tears burning her hurt across my flesh.

"The loneliness of the room," she continues, the shakiness of her voice mimicking that of her limbs. "God, it was so quiet and still after they took their final breaths. The controlled panic in the operator's tone when, after the sun set four hours later, I'd finally picked myself up off the blood-soaked carpet to call the cops. It all just . . . disappeared when you and Ryder shared me. It was as if that horrible day never happened, like it was nothing but a simple nightmare I'd woken up from—a dark tale my mind conjured up to write about in my journal. I wasn't the Amber Moretti who was whisked away, kicking and screaming, from the only home she'd ever known. I wasn't the eight-year-old little girl who knew why heroin addicts wrapped leather belts around their arms better than I understood the math my teacher was trying to explain to me in class. I just—"

"Wait," I interrupt, her words sinking in. "What do you mean you understood why heroin addicts used leather belts, Ber? Were your parents . . . *junkies?*"

After what seems like forever, she nods. "The worst kind. But I didn't want you to know that about them."

"*Why?*" I press, feeling sick to my stomach, images of the night I'd slipped into the serpentine flesh of the devil—all but shoving my bong down her throat—exploding in my head as everything starts to click into place. It all makes sense now, every twisted fucking second of it. Her hesitancy. The anxiety clouding her beautiful eyes. Her overdramatized response to something as innocent as weed. Christ. While my girl was trying to avoid the mistakes of her parents, attempting to do right by her future, my concern was wrapped around being the first asshole to get her lit up.

Guilt makes a speedy resurgence, sinking a cannonball's worth of weight onto my shoulders as my breathing dulls to a slow shock. Confused, I prod again, trying to understand why she'd hide something so important from me. "Why didn't you tell me about them? Hell, baby. Had I known this, I would've *never* asked you to hit that bong. Dammit, Ber," I whisper, praying to God I can get her to believe me, "it would've never crossed my mind. Sure, I'd just assumed you'd already smoked it—I explained that to you that night—but had you told me your parents were strung out, I would've never laid that kind of pressure on you. *Never.*"

She remains quiet for a moment, hesitation hindering her response. "Embarrassment," she finally says through a stuttered gulp of air, her body continuing to tremble like a scared child as she fists the collar of my T-shirt. "I was embarrassed. It was hard enough telling you that he killed her, but I couldn't bring myself to tell you that my parents, the two most important people in my life, the ones who should've held my hand along this confusing journey, wanted their dope more than they wanted ... *me*."

"You're not unwanted by me, baby girl. You'll *never* be unwanted by me. It's impossible." Though I'm scared beyond comprehension that allowing her to be with Ryder again will drag her further away from me, I cave to Amber's request, her need to slay the demons from her past—no matter what the emotional cost to me might be—my top priority. "You can be with Ryder again too. I'll do whatever it is you want in order to keep you happy, to keep you mentally healthy. For now, that is. I can't promise you this will be a long term thing, though, Ber. I just can't."

"Are you ... *sure?*" she asks, aware that she's backing me into a corner.

I'm just not sure if she knows how much doing so is killing me.

Unsure if my decision makes any sense at all, I nod, resigned to the fact that I'm the asshole who caused the torment bulldozing its way through her mind. The asshole who needs to fix this, fix her. "Yeah, I'm sure." I stroke my fingers through her hair, my voice thin as I move my hands to her thighs, squeezing them. "But I also can't promise you it'll go as smoothly as it did last night."

She cracks a small grin. "You think last night went ... smoothly?"

"You *don't?*" I press, unable to contain my shock. "How's that even possible? I watched—without ripping his balls off—Ryder fuck the shit outta you." A tight chuckle ticks from my mouth as I lift her from my lap, setting her back in her seat, my attention focused on the road as I ease back into traffic. "I know I'm a little psychotic but, in my book, that's as smooth as it gets." Not about to tell her I'd changed my mind about letting them be together, I keep it light, brushing over my true feelings instead of telling her what's really burning a hole in my gut.

"Seeing you with him affected me differently than I thought it would. Still, for your sake, I'm cool with giving it another go."

Amber studies me, her eyes harboring a question.

"*What?*" I prod after several agonizing minutes, curiosity biting at my skin as I head toward my condo. "There's something you wanna say, so just say it."

"Did you love Hailey?" she asks, her words spoken with mild hesitation.

I dart a glance her way. "You already know the answer to that. I told you she meant shit to me." I bring my attention back to the road, confusion setting in as I merge onto an exit ramp. "Why would you even ask me that again?"

A pause, her silence driving me fucking crazy as I tiresomely maneuver my way through the out-of-control weekend traffic swamping the downtown Annapolis bay area.

Another moment of silence before she whispers, "You love me, right, Brock?"

"A million times more than I do myself," I answer automatically, every fiber of me telling the truth. "Till the day death steps in, stealing the very last breath from my lungs, the single last beat of my heart."

Amber blinks, a weary smile pulling at her lips. "That's the difference this time around, baby."

"What's that supposed to mean?" I ask, feeling like an asshole for not getting the point she's trying to make. "Are you analyzing me, Miss Psychology Major? Is that what you're doing? Am I your muse for an upcoming term paper regarding deviant personalities? If so, I'm the *perfect* case study."

She casts me another weary smile as she brushes her knuckles against my cheek, the soft, sensual act causing my cock to jerk awake in response. "You went into this thinking you'd be able to handle the situation with ease in the same way you did with Hailey." She shrugs, her fingers playing with my hair as I kill the engine in front of my complex. "But you couldn't because you *love* me. You never loved her. I didn't know it till I met you, but love . . . changes us—changes the dynamics of everything we ever believed in. Love's pure and selfish. It can make us want things we shouldn't and hate what it's turned us into. It's giving, greedy, indecisive, vindictive, and magical all at once. It makes us jump from one delusional emotion to the next, all the while patiently keeping us dangling in its malicious yet euphoric web. A web that's laced with beautiful lies and horrible truths."

Amber opens the passenger-side door, her head craned back to look at me before stepping out. "But one thing love remains constant at—the most important feeling it controls in us—is jealousy. When we love someone wholeheartedly, truly can't imagine getting through a single day without them, that's when love can show her rage. Once released, love's jealousy can never be taken back, her desire to forget her pain breaking all the rules, uncaring of every obstacle she destroys in her path. It's unlike any God-given emotion we're born with."

Amber slings her duffel bag over her shoulder, something akin to her own regret dimming her eyes. "But it's okay, baby. I'm just as much to blame as you are for the mess we created by doing this. We all are, Ryder included. But no matter what, I'll always love you, Brock. Even if my love changes along the way, it'll forever remain pure. You were the first man to emotionally open me up, the first to teach me that love isn't always ugly. And you might think I can't see it, but I can. You're beating yourself up for allowing me and Ryder to be together. From the second I lay next to you in bed last night, you haven't stopped."

She closes the door and circles the Hummer, her chin jutted out for me to open my window as she approaches the driver's side. "So stop, Brock." She pokes her head into the vehicle, her lips landing on my cheek softly. "Stop beating yourself up. I forgive you for betraying the trust you should've had for our love, and now I just need you to forgive me for doing the same."

She doesn't wait for me to respond. No. Instead, she turns and heads for the elevators, her statement leaving my heart scattered with nothing but the skeletal remains of my regret as she walks away. I step out into the bitter air of late November, the wind lashing at my skin as I watch the leaves chase one another across the parking lot. By the time I reach the elevators I'm at a loss for words, the ride up to my floor silent, chilling.

As the elevator doors part, I reach for Amber's hand and pull her to my chest, my arms swallowing her in my embrace like it's the last time I'll ever get to. I need this girl. Need her more than my next breath, my next heartbeat. I need her as much as a dying man needs his meds, her very being the chemo to the cancer that's infested who I used to be. With Amber, I'm whole again, a man who feels as complete as he's ever known himself to be, a king worthy of the throne his queen's set him upon.

Though not a single word is uttered between us as we make our way down my hall, I can tell Amber feels me, knows how much I love her. The only thing I fear as we round the corner to my condo is she'll stop loving me, my allowing her to be with Ryder again no different from signing her over to him.

Trying to push those diseased thoughts from my mind, I fish my keys from my pocket but stop short the second I lift my hand to the doorknob. The lock's been tampered with, the door frame bent, nearly cracked to pieces. Someone's forced their way in. I immediately reach for my gun, only to realize I left the fucking thing in the glove compartment of my Hummer.

Amber lets out a gasp as I rest my hand on her waist, moving her behind me. "Holy shit. Someone's broken in, Brock. We have to get out of here and call the cops."

"No," I say through a whisper, gently pushing her farther back. If someone's still in my place, I'm catching the dick, dead set on letting him know I was the *last* motherfucker he should've played this game with. I listen intently for any sounds of movement before I nudge my boot against the door. It creaks open, a piece of molding clanking onto the wood floor as I peer into the eerie silence of the entryway. "We're not calling the cops. I'm going in and you're waiting downstairs."

"What do you *mean* we're not calling the cops?" she asks, her tone bordering on hysteria. "And if you're going in there, I'm coming with you."

I spin on her and grasp her shoulders, giving her a light shake. "The hell you are," I spit, almost losing it. Her eyes dilate with fear. A fear not caused by the dire situation but instead born of my asshole move. I swallow back bile, a grenade exploding my heart with regret from the petrified look on her face. Trying with everything I am to keep my cool, I temper down, loosening my grip on her shoulders as I drop a kiss onto the crown of her head. "I'm so sorry, Ber. You know I'd never intentionally hurt you, but I need you to listen to me, okay?"

She nods, a noticeable chill running up her spine as her gaze whips between me and the doorway.

"You're my only concern right now. The *only* fucking one. For that, you *are* going downstairs to wait in my Hummer until I call for you. Otherwise, you're not allowed to move, you hear me?"

She goes to speak, but I cut her off before she can say a word.

"The answer's no." I seize her cheeks and press a kiss to her forehead. "Don't argue with me, because it's not gonna work. No matter what you say, you're not winning this one, Amber. You're just not. There's no way in *hell* I'm letting you go in there with me, understand?"

Another nod, this one reluctant as I shove my keys in her hand. She stares at me a second then turns, disappearing around the corner, her soft cries echoing in her wake as I try to get my head together for what might await me inside.

With Amber safe, I enter my condo and instinctively pull open the hallway coat closet, reaching for my twelve-gauge that's Velcroed to the wall. I press the gun, already cocked and loaded, to my shoulder and inch forward, moving quietly from room to room, closet to closet, eventually ending up out on the balcony. I have yet to find anything disturbed. I recover my tracks and hit each room a second and third time, the tension bleeding from my muscles ebbing some as I make my way back into the living room, scanning the space for anything I might've missed. Nothing's been touched, broken, or stolen. Not even the few grand I keep in my safe. Right down to the imprints in the carpet—save for my own footsteps—my place is in the same pristine condition it was in when we'd left for Atlantic City.

I fall into a bar chair at the kitchen island and set the shotgun on top of the counter, trying to figure out who the fuck might've done this. Considering I keep my business far away from campus, never selling to a single prick attending Hadley U, I know it couldn't have been any of those douchebags. Going into this shit, I was all too aware that was the last problem I needed—some sophomore cokehead getting picked up for some stupid shit, only to turn around and pin me to a wall with the pigs.

Yeah, no thanks.

Other than Ryder and Lee, not even my teammates know it's my blow they're most likely getting hemmed up on the night of a huge win. I took the safe route, limiting my clientele to a few street dealers and the uppity elite of Annapolis and DC, who have something to lose, those whom I could turn around and easily fuck if need be. Leverage: that's all you have in this business, the one thing that can keep you afloat. Your local congressman jacked up in a hotel, wired on the best nose-candy around, partying it out with not one, not two, but *three* of Washington's finest call girls, can make for some interesting evening news.

Especially to his wife and family.

After eliminating the young couple with a baby to my right and some one-foot-in-the-grave retired Marine neighbor to my left as possibilities, I'm at a loss for who it could've been. However, that only lasts a second. As my gaze skids across the kitchen I spot a CD leaning against the coffeemaker, chicken-scratch writing scribbled in black marker on the front of the plastic case. Alert, I yank up the shotgun and cross the room to approach the foreign object. The foreign object that *wasn't* here when I left for the weekend. Before picking it up I look around, making sure some psychopath isn't aiming his gun at the back of my skull. All clear, I bring my attention back to the CD, catching the name written on the case.

> Cindy Lewis
> 483 Culvert Road, Apartment B
> Matoaka, West Virginia
> 24736

Face, name, and address burned into my memory like acid on flesh, I know exactly who's broken into my condo. Who's attempting to blackmail the fuck outta me for the shit she knows. The shit she was a witness to. The whore from the warehouse the night I killed Dom. The whore Ryder talked me into letting go unscathed. The whore who's about to flip my whole world upside down, taking me for everything I've got. Everything I've worked my ass off for.

"Goddamnit!" I bellow, nausea roiling my stomach as I slam a fist into a column that separates the kitchen from the open dining area. Pissed, a migraine sawing through my skull, I stomp over to the entertainment center. With blood dripping from my knuckles, I shove the CD into the player, scoop up the remote from the coffee table, and stab the play button, my nerves mounting as I sink onto the couch, preparing myself for the demands the cunt's gonna make.

As the video begins, it takes me a second to recognize my own voice calling out, "*Cindy Lewis, Four eighty-three Culvert Road, apartment B, Matoaka, West Virginia, two four seven three six.*"

I blink, confused as shit, as both Ryder and I come into focus. "*Repeat what he said,*" Ryder chimes in, clenching the whore's hair. "*Now.*"

"*Cin-Cindy Lewis,*" she cries, her body shaking, "*Fo . . . four eighty-three Culvert Road, apartment B, Matoaka, West Virginia, two four seven three six.*"

"*Very good, Cindy. You wanna live?*" Ryder questions. "*Wanna wake up to your kid tomorrow? See him grow up?*"

Continuing to cry, the chick nods but doesn't say a word.

"*Answer me!*" Ryder spits, his voice going hoarse as the back of his hand connects with her cheek. She stumbles into the wall, but Ryder catches her before she hits the ground, pulling her to his chest. "*Don't just fucking nod! This is serious! Do. You. Want. To. Live?*"

"*Yes!*" she sobs, her unclothed body falling against his. "*I want to live!*"

This is a video from Dom's warehouse. But how did the whore, who left before us, get it? More so, how the fuck is it even in her possession when Ryder *swore* he cleared everything from Dom's office?

Before I can dwell on my unanswered questions, the video transitions to a darkened hallway, the claustrophobically narrow space strewn with boxes, clothing, books, and empty Chinese takeout containers, I'm convinced I'm watching the worst-ever episode of *Hoarders.* A deep, annoyed whisper breaks me from my reverie, my eyes landing on a hooded figure leading the cameraman through the less-than-stellar living conditions. The silence is deafening, my whole world reduced to what's happening on the video as the pair makes it down the hall to their final destination, stopping in front of a partially closed door. Seconds decrease to milliseconds, my heartbeat lasts a lifetime as they slip into a dimly lit bedroom. Save for an aged dresser, the space is relatively empty—a twin mattress centered dead in the middle of the room, additional heaps of dirty laundry haphazardly tossed across a multistained brown carpet.

I direct my attention to the bed where the hooded figure is standing above it, a sleeping body blissfully unaware of the evil presence. Without a word, the hooded intruder lifts his hand, displaying for the first time a pistol and—lacking even a second's hesitation—fires three shots into the huddled mass on the bed. I shoot to standing, adrenaline causing my fists to clench of their own accord as my focus remains locked on the screen. Soon after the gunshots, a child's scream reverberates in the near distance, his fear palpable. The gunman methodically moves toward the sound of the child's crying, his ogre-like stature barely fitting through the doorway. As the monster disappears into the hallway, the cameraman pans in on the bloody, unmoving mass on the bed, revealing an all-too-familiar face: Cindy Lewis, 483 Culvert Road, Apartment B, Matoaka, West Virginia, 24736.

My jaw hits the floor as her kid's cries increase, my need to stop what the psychopath's inevitably about to do to him unleashing fury across my skin with every nerve catapulting to life in my body. Helpless to do a fucking thing, I yell out into space, swinging my fists at a phantom recipient, sweat spilling from my pores as the chatter of the universe eats away at my pleas. Silence, long and menacing, chills me down to my bones before one final shot splices through the air, the child's tiny cries fading into nothing as the bloodcurdling sound of his last, mangled breath pierces me straight to the hollow of my soul. A ball of grief tightens my chest, its potency wiping out the strength from my muscles, as I watch, tears hindering my vision, the cameraman produce a small canister of gasoline. An entertained chuckle strums from his mouth as he drenches Cindy's bed in the hazardous liquid, a calculated strike of a match following the premeditated movement. Flames scream through the room, the screen shaking in sync with the cameraman's quickened footsteps as he and the hooded figure bolt out of the apartment.

The picture fades to black and I slump onto the couch, mentally disturbed beyond repair from what I've witnessed. From what I know will consume my every waking thought. I've seen the destruction man can do, experienced its brutality firsthand. But there's no doubt in my mind that this heinous crime, this horrifying, inhumane act of cruelty done to a mother and her child, trumps it all. Visions of Cindy's unsuspecting face, the wretched sound of her innocent kid's screams, will forever haunt the rest of my days spent on the gutless spine of this earth, the core of who I am stained by the vileness of humanity as a whole.

As the video restarts, my gaze widens on the mayhem unfolding before me. Hordes of families jumping from second-story windows, a father shielding his newborn daughter from a tidal wave of flames, and an array of household pets littering the streets blackens my line of sight. Limbs frozen, I watch a block of suburban row houses melt away into a skeleton of what they once were, the memories held within them spurring into the air in the form of ashes.

Shot taken from afar, the cameraman zooms in on the frenzied neighborhood below, laughter mixing with the howling screams from women and children. Blocking out stars for miles, flames lick the angry sky red, towers of smoke billowing into the frigid night air as though the devil's fingers were reaching up from hell, painting the small town with his fury.

Helpless onlookers cry out as fire engines, cops, and EMTs descend upon the scene. Another cut to black and I'm left speechless as I bury my face between my hands in an attempt to keep myself from hurling. It's no use as my stomach gives out. Knees hitting the carpet, I hunch over a wrought iron magazine rack and upchuck this morning's breakfast onto a stack of *Playboys*, my body continuing to shake as I compose myself.

After a few seconds of blank white screen, the video begins again, my heart lurching up my parched throat as I glimpse Derick, Dom's older brother, sitting at his desk. Calmly smoking a cigarette, an emotionless stare pinned onto his half-skeletal-tattooed face, Derick looks into the video camera, his deadened eyes crinkling at the corners as he screws his mouth into a slow sneer. Transfixed on the devil before me, I barely notice a woman massaging his shoulders, only her slender hands visible as Derick lifts a snifter of pale brown liquid to his mouth.

"Goddamn, I fucking love this shit!" Derick slams the empty glass onto the desk, his expression contorted with equal parts disgust and delight as another pair of female hands appears, refilling his snifter with Jack Daniel's. "But I'm not making this video to tell ya how much I love me some whiskey, Brock." A sardonic smile spreads his lips as he nods his head toward the doorway, dismissing the woman behind him. She, along with the second chick, obeys his unspoken command, the door clicking closed with their departure as he chuckles. "Of course I'm not." Sobering, his eyes darken as he leans forward, resting his elbows on the desk. "But I'm pretty damn sure you figured that much out by now. Even if you are a fucking murderer, a coldhearted pig like me, I'm sure your IQ is capable of registering what exactly the purpose of this home movie is."

Without pulling his attention from the camera, Derick takes a long drag from his cigarette, followed by a quick swallow of his drink, his voice eerily calm as he relaxes back into his chair. "Though I have to give ya credit for one thing, Cunningham. You were right when ya said the whore should've been disposed of. After ya killed my brother you remembered the cardinal rule for when the shit hits the fan for us dealers. Never. Leave. A. Loose. End."

Out of nowhere, he explodes, all calm forgotten as he jumps to his feet. "*Ever*, motherfucker! You never leave a witness alive! But you did and *I* had to clean up *your* mess, had to make sure the little cunt didn't spill details about what'd happened *or* the empire I run! You should've shoved your gun up her diseased pussy and made her pay for being there!"

As though he didn't trip the fuck out, he calmly reclaims his seat and takes a casual sip of his drink, his demeanor all business. "What Cindy did was just plain wrong, Brock. Wrong, wrong, wrong. I mean, she *knew* who killed my brother, yet she never said a *word* to me. I gave her enough time to confess her sins against my brother, the man who saved her from her abusive father and dusthead whore of a mother. I kept waiting, patiently, which is *terribly* hard for me—though I already knew it was you—for her to reveal your name. But she gave me nothin', kept her blow job–mastering mouth shut." He stubs out his cigarette in an ashtray, and pushes off his chair to stretch, his eyes devoid of human emotion. "And her kid? Well, what can I say? Had *you* taken care of her the way you *initially* planned to, maybe, just fucking maybe, his three-year-old little ass would still be alive. Though I *probably* would've put a bullet in his skull anyway—I don't need some cracked-out teenager seeking revenge on his mother's killer fifteen or so years down the road—I'll let his demise burn *your* conscience for a while." He pauses, his grin returning. "But, man oh man, you sure as *fuck* missed one helluva show. There's an epic difference between the complexities of how an adult's skull explodes under the pressure of a bullet versus a kid's. I won't get into the details of it all, but it's definitely something you'll have to try out for yourself one day."

Shotgun rattling in my nervous grip, I stare at the screen, visions of what the sick fuck did to that innocent child appearing unbidden as Derick stares back at me. I clench my jaw, refusing to take blame for his death. I can't. Still, as Derick starts to pace the office, I have a feeling the kid's short life will stay with me until the moment I take my final breath. Maybe even after.

Derick lurches at the camera, a wild look in his eyes as he shoves his face into the lens. "You fucked up, Cunningham! You should've *never* let that pussy friend of yours Ryder talk you into saving the dirty whore and her brat!" He scratches at the stubble lining his jaw, a broken-toothed smile curling his mouth as he backs away. "Shit happens, though. Everyone's allowed a moment of weakness, right? But I digress."

Taking his seat yet again and rocking back and forth in his chair, Derick produces a dagger out of the thick, smoke-filled air. Wooden handle intricately carved with what appears to be Chinese lettering, the thing makes my forearm look like it belongs to a dwarf, its length a good twelve inches or so. Its surgical steel blade catches the domed lighting at a perfect angle, momentarily blinding me, my eyes squinting in response as he runs it along his shaved head. Continuing to stare at me intently, the dick smiles and drags the tip of the weapon down the side of his cheek, producing a trickle of blood. His smile spreads from ear to ear, his eyes tumbling into the back of his head as his tongue sneaks out, collecting his blood from the blade in one slow, calculated sweep.

The cocksucker's a monster. The kind children imagine lurk in the shadows of their bedrooms but have never seen. The Boogeyman brought to life, he's what haunts nightmares.

"Did ya know I couldn't even give Dom a proper burial?" he announces, breaking the silence shrouding the airwaves between us. "My baby brother, my last goddamn living relative, is buried right here on our property. I turned his stupid-as-fuck sidekick friend into pig feed too, so there's no chance in hell he's ever gonna be found. His family thinks he took off to California with his mistress." He lets out a condescending cackle, a smile lighting up his eyes as he finishes the last of his whiskey. "I always hated that dumb fuck, but Dom? Nah, Dom loved the dick like a brother." He pauses, an icy emotion—one I can't decipher, but if I had to guess, it'd be jealousy—coating his face, as he sparks up another cigarette. "Getting back to Dom: I couldn't chance the DEA sniffing all over the warehouse here. I'm sure they wouldn't have taken well to a drug lord calling in the murder of his brother. Well, maybe they would've, but that's neither here nor there. Either way, I wasn't about to hand them over my business or my life. Not *even* for my family."

Before I can blink, he leaps from his chair yet again, his nose inches from the screen. "You killed my brother!" he growls, spittle flying from his mouth as he grabs hold of the camera, shaking it to near destruction. "Now I have nothing! Nothing, Brock! No family, just hatred! I'm going to kill you, motherfucker, make no mistake about that! Before I'm finished with you, I'm gonna make ya wish your mother swallowed you instead!"

A certified Jekyll and Hyde, Derick dips back into his cool-cat character, not a beat missed between the eerie transition as he shoves his hands into his camo pockets. "You're probably wondering how I found out about all of this. Am I right? Hell, if I were you, my head would be all over the fucking place." Attention aimed at the ground, he leisurely strolls back and forth in front of a swastika hanging on the wall behind him. "It's pretty simple, actually, but stay with me here if ya can. The video from our warehouse feeds back to a low-key apartment I keep a few miles from here. *Bamo!* Your buddy figured he had everything covered when he tore apart the camera system, but the asshole never thought about that one, did he? So much for his *supposed* genius status. Dumb fuck. Ya might wanna think about getting a different partner to head your operation."

Laughter punches from his chest, his thumbs running up and down the slim black fibers of his wifebeater as he continues to pace. "Oh yeah, revisiting the loose ends we were discussing earlier. You've left a fuckload of them for me to handle. I'm not talking about you, your useless counterpart, Ryder, or Lee, but *so* very much more. Unlike what my brother said, this is *not* a game, nor is it an empty threat. There's gonna be a reckoning, Brock. A reckoning of biblical proportions not seen since Moses destroyed the pharaoh." He stops moving, a crooked grin hiking up the corner of his mouth as he faces the camera. "I'm gonna kill every single person you hold dear to your filthy heart, your two prick friends included. To make things even *more* excitin', I'm making sure you're the *last* bastard to die. Nothing personal, buddy, but I really gotta make sure ya suffer as much as, if not more than, I have. Just knowing I took everyone ya love, slowly, one by one, from your waste of a life, will make the day I cross through the gates of hell that much more . . . special, if you will."

Derick's half-skeletal-tattooed face swallows the screen, his countenance every bit the rabid animal he is—foam flowing from his mouth, his words nothing but mere growls, none of which I can decipher as he continues to scream out a list of threats. However, before the camera fades to black, I'm able to make out one sentence—one sentence that has my heart tripping: "I plan on startin' with that brunette Barbie of yours first."

Anger, hatred, and fear pound through my muscles with every uneven breath I take. "Bet I've *really* got your attention now, Cunningham, eh? Ah yes. *Yes. I. Fucking. Do.*" A fit of laughter rockets from his mouth, his hollow stare clamped to mine as he continues to verbally rape my universe. "She'll be the first to go, the first to feel what the rip of my blade is gonna do to her slender neck. The way it's gonna expose her delicate veins. The first to beg for her life when I drag my magical steel wand down her chest and slowly rip her open, her tears hardening my cock as I slide it into her ass, fucking her better than you *ever* have."

Licking his lips, his eyes drift closed, a sigh of contentment following the movement as he releases a groan. "I'm gonna fuck each and every single one of her holes until she's so crazed, she's not gonna know which pain to concentrate on more: my cock brutalizing her inner flesh, or my blade sawing through her outer. And *right* about the same time she's strugglin' through her last breath, I'm gonna shoot my load all over that pretty little face of hers. Mind ya, this'll take place *after* I've whispered your name into her ear, letting her know *you're* the reason why she's dying. I figure it'll add a bit more torture to her final experience on this here earth. Can't deny I'm one creative bastard."

His smile slips away as he leans forward, resting his elbows on his desk. "I'll tell ya what, Brockster. Though your girl's death will be anything *but* slow, when I cut off her perky nipples, I'll make sure to send ya one, gift-wrapped and all." Folding his arms over his chest, he palms his chin and scratches at his stubble, his gaze squinting in mock thought. "You know what? Considering the circumstances, I'm gonna be a nice guy. I'll pay the extra few bucks to ship it overnight, so as to ensure its freshness for you before it starts to rot away." He rises, takes a bow, and steps in front of the camera, his face covering up the entire screen as he shakes his head. "Please, please. No need to thank me, bud. I figured it's the least I can do. Besides, what are enemies for? I want ya to have *something* to remember her by before I zip through my list of your loved ones." He sucks in a slow breath, his eyes hardening before he screams out, "Until then, no one, not a single soul around ya, can be too safe! Keep your eyes and ears open, fucker, because I'm comin' your way. If not today, next week, next month, or next year, you're gonna feel my wrath! One way or another, I'm 'bout to make the rest of your living days hell on earth!"

The screen fuzzes out, all traces of Derick disappearing as I try to breathe, try to think. Head fucked sideways, I swallow what feels like a bucket of nails, revenge roped around my muscles as a familiar voice whispers, "You know we have to kill him first, right?"

I spin and catch Ryder's eyes, his filled with as much venom as mine as he approaches, cautiously taking the shotgun from my grip. He sets it on the coffee table, his face hardened into stone as he meets my stare. Though he's on my shit list, his presence is welcomed, his visible need to take Derick down a filter of light to the darkness shrouding my entire being as I nod in response.

"How much of the video did you . . . see?" I ask.

"All of it," he answers as he lifts his weary gaze to the television. "And it's *my* fault that kid's dead, not yours. The cocksucker was right. Had I let you get rid of the girl like you wanted, he'd still be alive."

"*Motherless*," I point out. "Don't let what that asshole said *or* did fuck with you, Ashcroft. You hear me? *Neither* of us is responsible for that kid's death. Derick is, got it?"

Though he nods in agreement, I can tell it's eating at him as much as it is me, our stares locked on each other as we share a moment of grief for the kid. The kid whom we've never met, his face a mystery to us, but whose death is linked to my sins, the temporary moment of insanity that'll forever change my world.

Lost as to why he would just show up out of nowhere, especially after the way we left off—not having spoken a word to each other on the way back home—I cock my head in question, already knowing the answer. "Amber called you, didn't she?"

"Yeah." A pause, hesitancy slowing his words. "She was a mess, bro, in absolute hysterics. I could barely make out what she was sayin'."

Figures.

Still, I can't blame her. The fear in her eyes when I told her to wait in my ride was unlike anything I've ever seen . . . unlike anything I ever want to see again. Set on making sure she's never afraid like that another day in her life, I head into the kitchen, my brain exploding with thoughts of my next move to ensure her safety as Ryder leans his hip against the kitchen island.

"Madeline and Lee are downstairs with her," he adds, placing his gun on the counter. "I was in the shower when Amber's calls came in. By the time I got out, she'd hit my phone close to ten times. They knew something was up, so they insisted on taking a ride over here with me. I told them to wait with her until I knew everything was cool."

I shoot him a look. "Did you—"

"No," he interrupts, his hands held up in mock surrender. "I didn't say shit to him, *boss*. Though he keeps prodding around, asking me tons of questions every goddamn chance he gets, he still has no clue what's up."

I nod, my gut churning with confusion. After I killed Dom and Bobby, Ryder and I discussed whether or not we should let Lee in on what happened. Though it was a tough decision, I'd decided it was a no-go. I didn't want anyone knowing what I'd done, how I'd killed two men in an instant, not even Lee. Still, this shit changes everything.

Not telling Lee what happened, keeping him from what's sure to go down, can put him and Madeline in danger, their lives at risk from this second forward.

Either way I'm screwed, royally fucked with no easy way out of this mess. If I tell him about Dom, I have a potential loose cannon on my hands, someone who can turn around and use that shit against me somewhere down the road. Not that I think Lee would ever do that to me—the thought a vague, annoying whisper at best. But time and life's brutal hand can change a person, their loyalty to friends and family tossed out the window when shit hits the fan. In the same breath, if I don't let Lee in on every detail, I have a potential dead friend on my conscience, a buddy who's risked his life for me chilling in the morgue as his, and possibly Madeline's, demise rests on my shoulders.

Again, royally fucked.

As I contemplate what to do, footsteps sound down the hall outside of my place. Alert, Ryder and I reach for our guns as the footsteps become heavier, closer. With our attentions pinned on the entryway, we aim our weapons at the front door, silent, ready, as the hinge creaks open.

"Whoa!" Lee's arms shoot heavenward as he cautiously steps through the doorway. "What the *fuck?*"

"Speak of the devil," I mumble, setting my shotgun back down.

"Ever hear of *knocking*, asshole?" Ryder pockets his weapon as he approaches Lee, yanking him into my condo by the collar of his sweatshirt. "You know shit's hot right now. You should've called before you came up."

"Fuck you, bro," Lee spits. "I didn't *call* because I have no idea *how* hot shit is. No one tells me *dick.* All I was told was to wait downstairs with the girls. So let me repeat it for you in case you missed it the first time: fuck you, Ashcroft." He straightens his collar, his expression no less heated as he pushes past Ryder, making himself comfortable on the bar stool next to me.

Ryder grits his teeth, but I shake my head, warning him not to take it any further. "You left the girls alone downstairs?"

"No, I told them to take your Hummer back to their dorm and stay put until one of us says otherwise." A pause followed by an agitated sigh as his attention shifts between me and Ryder. "Now, would either of you douchebags like to let me know what the fuck's going on?" He concentrates his attention on me, something akin to begging in his tone. "I'm being serious, man. You might think I'm some dumbass surfer from the West Coast, but I'm not. I've been in this game as long as you have, and I knew, just *knew*, something was up from the second you two got back from your last pickup. If I'm in this with you guys, *really* in it, then I need to be told everything. Not be the asshole you hide serious shit from. It's not right."

I contemplate his words. Still, I can't bring myself to tell him. If I do, I leave him wide open to fuck me down the road. I decide to tell him the bare minimum, enough to let him know to stay alert, enough to keep him and Madeline out of danger.

"All I can say is some crazy shit went down," I start, feeling somewhat bad for not telling him the whole truth, but not bad enough to let him in on everything. "And because of it, heat's about to come our way. Bad heat, the worst kind. We need to keep our eyes open, watch our backs. More importantly, the girls'." I take a breath, my demeanor collected though I'm anything but. I hate doing this, keeping him in the dark, but trust can only go so far under circumstances such as this. "Don't ask me anything more about what happened, because I have no intention of telling you about it. You know all you need to know, bro. Ryder and I will take care of the rest. I need you to trust me on that. Cool?"

Lee stares blankly at me, the fight in his eyes flickering out as he rises. Expression a bed of betrayal, he nods, his shoulders slumped as he nears my front door. He grabs the knob, the fire in his eyes making a resurgence as he casts me a glare from over his shoulder. "I'll trust you for now, Cunningham. Even though you've always treated me second-best to Ryder, you've never failed at taking care of me when shit's gotten crazy, always made sure I was okay. But I'm warning you, if *anything* happens to Madeline because of some stupid shit you fucked up playing this game, I swear to my fucking life, I'll..." He trails off, his words dying on his tongue as he shakes his head in defeat and walks out of my condo.

He doesn't need to finish his sentence. I get him, hear him loud and clear. No matter how any of this ends, everyone's blood is on my hands, my split-second decision to kill a man coming back to haunt me in more ways than I could've ever imagined. Feeling emotionally vacant, a sellout at his finest, I pull in a deep breath, my main concern transitioning to the most important person in my life.

Amber.

I lift my chin to Ryder, looking to get out of here and over to her dorm as soon as possible. "Can you give me a ride to the girls' place?"

* * *

The lie I told the maintenance man about losing my keys and having to jimmy my door open was easy. However, the ride over to the girls' dorm has been the exact opposite. Ryder and I have barely talked, the unrelenting awkwardness between us a jackhammer to my head. I take that back. We've talked, having gone over our plan of attack concerning Derick and what measures we're going to take as far as making sure Amber's out of harm's way. We even agreed to keep what's really going on from her in an effort to keep her from bugging the fuck out with worry.

But we haven't tackled what's really hanging in the air above us—the elephant in the room, if you will.

Last night. The way he stepped over invisible boundaries. Boundaries I should've set but didn't. I shake my head, pissed off for letting it go as far as I did, for not stopping it the second it started. Not knowing who to blame, I turn to him, my eyes trained on his as he kills the engine in front of Hadley's main building. He knows where I'm about to go, can see the anger on my face.

"Just say it," Ryder lets out through a heavy sigh. "There's more bothering you than what went down today. Obviously it has to do with me and Amber, so just get it the fuck over with."

"You're correct," I answer, my tone matching his aggravation. "It *is* about you and Amber. It's not happening again, bro. Ever. I should have never let it happen in the first place."

"But you did." Ryder chuckles, though there's not a shred of happiness behind it. Only sarcasm and, almost imperceptibly . . . jealousy? "We all did!" He looks out the driver's-side window, his shoulders stiff as he shakes his head. "So now what? Is your plan to bury your head in the sand like a fucking ostrich and hide from it?" He whips his eyes to mine, fury igniting them. "Huh? Is that your fucking game plan, Cunningham? Got what ya wanted, didn't like what you saw, and now you're just gonna run from it?"

I take a deep breath, slowly letting it out in an effort to contain the growing anger his accusation triggered. "What I'm saying is I *love* her. I loved her last night, the day before that, and the month before that. I just got . . . Fuck, bro, I got lost in the moment the same way you and Amber did. My vision's clearer today and I know what needs to be done, and allowing you two to be together again *isn't* it."

Another chuckle, this one as he sparks up a cigarette. "Ah, you see *clearer* today. Of course. Why the fuck didn't I think about that?" He takes a long drag off his cancer stick, a grunt pushing from his mouth as the smoke skates through the car. "How does Amber feel about your *epiphany*? And do you even *care* what she thinks about it? 'Cause right about now, I'm thinking *all* you care about is that *you* couldn't deal as you watched her and me—like *you* wanted to, mind ya— together. Couldn't handle seeing her in my arms, wrapped around my dick. Couldn't stand watching me bring her the same pleasure you do, if not more. In case you were curious, *that's* what I'm thinking is the problem right now. You couldn't give a fuck less how anyone else here feels because, let's face it, you were the one calling the shots from the beginning. Kudos to you, man. You got your cake and ate the fuck out of it too."

I'm about to strangle the air from his lungs.

Again, I suck in a deep breath, holding it in for a second as I try not to jump over the console to do just that. Sure, I might've been the one who initiated last night's twisted events, but this asshole's about to cross a fine line between being able to use his dick ever again or not. "First, I know how she feels about everything," I answer through gritted teeth. "We talked about it on the way back from Atlantic City. Second, the hard truth is I mentally *can't* do it again. *Won't* do it again. I wasn't strong enough last night to tell her no, that I wanted to stop everything in its tracks, nor was I this morning when she brought it up. And for that, I'm paying the goddamn price for it today! Probably will for the rest of my life!" Losing it, my fist connects with the dashboard, further damaging the same knuckles that left their stamp on my wall earlier. "Whatever the case, you're not laying your fucking hands on her ever again! Do you understand me? Last night was the last time!"

"I'm guessing *Amber* wants to do it again?" he asks after a few, tense minutes, his brow arched as if to accentuate the question as he flicks his cigarette out the window. "And don't forget, I told you this would be different than it was with Hailey. But, hey. You didn't want to listen."

"Yeah, she does wanna do it again," I answer, my voice hoarse. "And yeah, I know what you said. But I don't need you or anyone fucking reminding me of it either."

"So how do you propose *we* tell her it's over? Do we call her a bad girl and hit her with a rolled-up newspaper? Put her in a corner?" He thrusts his hands through his hair, an air of mockery surrounding him. "Perhaps I'll just bounce out of the picture, playing the classic Ryder Ashcroft womanizing dick as I haul my ass down to the sunny beaches of Florida?"

I crack a smirk at his last proposition. No doubt it'd make things easier. Still, I wouldn't know what to do without him. Having spent my entire childhood up until now with the asshole by my side, the man's my only living brother. "I need you to tell her no if she asks about hanging out again. That you're busy. Anything to deter the situation."

"You really just want me to walk away from her, don't you? Want me to act like nothing happened?" He picks his head up, his narrowed gaze filled with a slew of emotions I don't like. "You want me to . . . break her heart."

I clench my fists, the reality of his words causing my stomach to bottom out as I tear my glare away from his.

"Say it, asshole!" he thunders, his fist taking a shot at the dashboard this time around. "Say it! That's what you want me to do! Break the girl's heart, make her feel like trash because *you* thought it'd be *cool* to share her with another guy!"

Knowing he's right, fully owning up to the fact that I'm the culprit of Amber's mental destruction—hell, even his destruction—I break, desperation filling my voice as I bring my attention back to him. "Do you know what it's like to care for someone, love them so much you're willing to do *anything* for them, regardless of the outcome to yourself? Do you?"

"Yeah," he says, his voice weary as he steps out of the Mustang. He slams the door, pokes his head through the window, his body taut with anger. "Yeah, bro. Thanks to you, now I do. I appreciate the lesson." He straightens, lights another cigarette, and heads toward the football field as he calls over his shoulder, "I'll help ya with what needs to be done with Derick, that I give you my word on. But just know I'll *never* forgive you for making me do this to her."

As dusk settles over the parking lot, I watch him disappear through the fog squatting heavy over the field. The field we celebrated so many wins in. The field where our unbreakable friendship was formed. I get out of the car and look up to the sky, knowing nothing will ever be the same between us.

Again, the mind can change what the heart thought it wanted—both unrelenting in their battle of wills—and right now, it's my heart that's winning the war, even as visions of a broken friendship swallow my thoughts.

As I head into Amber's building I push through, knowing in the end she's all that matters. All that's ever mattered.

Fuck the heart, mind, and friends . . .

CHAPTER 21

Amber

I'S BEEN TWO weeks, three days, and four hours since Ryder's answered my calls, returned a single text. Two weeks, three days, and four hours since my heart started to beat with a sorrow I can't begin to describe. I feel used, a piece of driftwood washed up on a beach. I trusted him, felt like we had a true connection. I couldn't have been more wrong. I wound up being nothing but another Hailey on his list, the clichéd notch on his bedpost.

I hate clichés, hate everything they stand for, and now I'm one of them.

To make things worse, Brock's become possessive to the point of near insanity, making sure either he, Lee, or one of his several counter-parts—none of whom happen to be Ryder—escort me everywhere I go. Be it school, work, food shopping, or a visit to the local book-store, someone's attached to my side, their presence but a car's length away from me as I try to live a seminormal life under my new routine. Caught in the undertow of something I know I'm being lied to about, the truth of what *really* happened that day at Brock's condo hidden from me, I feel like I'm about to lose it, my sanity hanging by the thin-nest of threads with every passing second.

"You have to snap out of this," Madeline insists, her eyes a deep brown ocean of concern as she flops onto my bed, tapping my nose with a pack of Twizzlers. "I'm a little tipsy, so not only are you a *serious* buzzkill right now, but you're starting to worry me." She tears into the pack of Twizzlers hungrily, nipping one out with her teeth as she shoves one into my mouth. "No joke, I've never seen you like this, Amber. You're depressed. Not your usual depressed either. It must be said that if we're going to continue our friendship, I have to know what happened. For reals, chick. I want the deets on everything that went on. The deets I'm pretty sure *specifically* happened the weekend we were in Atlantic City. Anything ringing a bell here?" A grin quirks her lips, her Captain Morgan–tainted breath inches from my face as she rolls onto her stomach. "I'm no fool, Moretti. I know Ryder, I know Brock, and I know you. The three of you walking sexpots woke up the next morning looking properly fucked. I also know Ashcroft *didn't* take anyone up to his suite because he left the casino to go running after you and never returned. Add a thick layer of awkward glances, sweaty foreheads, and Ryder unable to keep his eyes off you the next morning at breakfast, and *whamo!* You've got yourself the perfect recipe for one hell of a ménage à trois. Again, the deets, *now*, biotch."

"You don't think something's up with the guys?" I ask, ignoring her inquisition. Taking a bite of the Twizzler, I stare at Jared Leto, who's staring back at me from the ceiling. I bet he knows the answers to what the hell's going on. "I mean, considering you and I have basically been put on house arrest the last few weeks, unofficial security guards glued to our hips everywhere we go, you're not the *slightest* bit concerned that something's going on? Something the boys are lying to us about?"

Madeline shrugs, her toe tapping the bed to the beat of Nicki Minaj's "Pills N Potions" as she steals another Twizzler from the pack. "I'm aware they're lying to us about *something*, Amber. But you know the rules. *No questions asked.*" Another shrug as she gets to her knees.

Ass swaying to the rhythm, she dips her head, plopping a drunk, wet kiss on my cheek. "Besides, whatever lie they're keeping from us is probably beneficial to our well-being. Why else would they take such extreme measures to ensure we're cool?"

I dip my brows, shocked at her nonchalance. "Are you kidding me?"

"No. Why would I kid about that?" She slides off the bed, stumbles to her feet, and tosses her crimson hair into a ponytail as she crosses our dorm room, rummaging through her drawers. "You and I started dating our boys knowing what was up the whole time. We knew what they did for a living, how they made their cash flow, and the risks they took to acquire their dough. Why all of a sudden now would we worry or question *anything* they're doing? Makes no sense. They've got us. They'd never let anything *bad* happen to either of us, so why drive ourselves nuts over it?" She pulls on a Hadley sweatshirt and slams back her fifth shot of Captain Morgan, her nose scrunched in disgust as she sinks back onto my bed, handing me the half-empty bottle. "Am I making any sense right now?"

"No, none," I answer flatly.

She sighs, annoyed. "It's obvious *something's* up based on our newly appointed bodyguards, but that just means the guys are playing whatever's going on safe. You should be happy, not worried."

"You're crazy. Absolutely bat-shit crazy." I sit up and bring the bottle of Captain to my lips, the memory eraser sizzling my throat as I down at least three shots' worth. "I'm not worried about *us*, Mad." A fourth, then fifth shot as I shake my head, trying to catch up with her. "I'm worried about *them*. Whatever's going on has to be bad enough that they have a bunch of idiots following us around. Don't you see that? *They're* in danger, not us."

"Fine. Wanna know what I *really* think's up?"

"Yes," I answer, curious if she knows more than I do.

"Okay, I'll tell you." She pinches my nose as she wets my cheek with yet another one of her Captain Morgan kisses. "But *all* great things come at an expense. In order to gain entry into my psyche, you have to tell me what went down in Atlantic City. It's that or nothing. Take it or leave it."

I roll my eyes, aggravated that the little blackmailer's backed me into a corner. "You win. The three of us fucked like animals. End of story."

"OhmyGod!" Eyes nearly popping out of their sockets, she tackles me, shackling my hands behind my head as she straddles my waist. "I knew it! *Kneeeew* it!"

"Mad, get off of—"

"Wait!" she squeaks, pressing a silencing finger to my lips.

I roll my eyes again, knowing the *real* questions are about to begin.

"Everything makes sense now," she says, tapping her chin as though she's a detective working a case. "Your extreme bouts of depression. The way you've closed yourself off to everyone. You calling out of work or skipping class so you can crash in bed all day. The insane amount of crying you've been doing." A frown shadows her face, all traces of excitement gone as she squishes her nose against mine. "Amber Moretti, I want the absolute truth from you right now. You need to answer me three questions before I can go on living. My life *and* sanity depend on it." A pause, the shine of her teeth blinding me as a smirk encompasses her mouth. "How delicious was Ashcroft in bed? Was his cock as monstrous as rumors have it? And can the man eat a mean pussy like he's about to fry in the electric chair?"

"Get off of me, you psycho lush!" I half snap, half giggle as I summon the strength to throw her to my side. Sadly, she's tipsy enough that she rolls off the bed, her tiny frame hitting the wood floor with a thump loud enough to cause our neighbor below to bang on the ceiling in response. Feeling bad, I peek over the edge of the bed. "I didn't mean to do that! You okay?"

I'm greeted with a wiseass, knowing smile. "You're in love with him, aren't you? Got it bad for Ashcroft."

"*What?*" I question through a gasp, my heart pounding anew with a fresh round of pain the asshole's left me with. "No, I'm not in *love* with him. What would even make you think that? I love Brock."

Brock . . .

She climbs back onto the bed, cradling me in her arms like a mother would her newborn. And she thinks *I'm* dramatic? "Amber, I say that because of the list of emotional unpleasantries I just went through *so* conveniently for you, that you've made me endure over the last several weeks. Suck it up, you lucky slut. You have two of the hottest dudes on campus pining over you and you're depressed, crying like it's the end of the world because of your confusion about loving Ryder." She takes a swig from the bottle and blows her hair away from her forehead, a huff leaving her mouth as she hands me back the liquid bliss. "Pfft, more than half the chicks at Hadley, at least the ones who aren't carpet-munchers, would *die* to be in your position."

"No, they wouldn't," I whisper, fighting back tears. "Ryder . . . disappeared. Hasn't returned my calls or texts. Plain and simple: he used me the way he has every other girl he's messed around with." I slide from the bed and stomp across the room, wishing he were here so I could rip his balls off and feed them to him. "God! I should've known better!"

"Wait, stop!" Madeline hops to her feet and catches me by the arm, spinning me around. "That doesn't seem right. What I mean is, he's looked just as shitty as you every time I've seen him lately. And that's hard for him considering he's a walking god. Seriously, it's like he lost someone, Amber. He looks bad enough that I actually asked him if everything was okay with Casey."

"What are you trying to say?" I ask, confused as to where she's taking this conversation. The Captain's definitely drowning me in his sea. "I'm telling you he wants nothing to do with me, Madeline. *Nothing.*" Now I can't help it. The tears come, falling fast, falling hard—Mr.

Morgan aiding in their rapidness—as Ryder's touch, taste, words, and face shroud my vision, every stolen and unstolen moment we shared spiraling through my memory.

Madeline's eyes soften, her fingers stroking my tears away. "He's missing . . . *you*, Amber. You have to believe me. Again, so much makes sense now. We went to Atlantic City and after that, both of you changed for the worse. He's miserable right now and not seeing you, not calling, is the reason for it. I know it, can feel it."

"Why are you doing this to me?" I question through a sloppy, hic-cupped gulp of air as I try to compose myself. I want her to shut up. Her words are making me second-guess myself, second-guess what's really going on with Ryder. "He's not *missing* me." I chuckle through my tears, pacing the room as I simultaneously hit the bottle again and gnaw on my thumbnail. I get talented when I drink. "He's getting off on the fact that he was able to fuck me and then get the perks of *not* having to deal with me and my stained past."

She shakes her head, her hand capturing mine in a death grip. I halt, my face inches from hers. "Do you trust me?" she asks, her voice soft, soothing.

Trust. Something I've never felt. Though I've wanted to, it's not an emotion that's come easily for me, if at all. It's foreign to my bones, a rite of passage to those who've walked the clear path of a normal life, not one planted with minefields polar opposite of what it stands for.

Still, I nod, hoping I can trust Madeline, praying whatever she says will lead me in the right direction.

"Go to him now, Amber. Find him and tell him that you need him, that you're in love with him."

"I'm not in love with—"

"You are," she interrupts, pulling me closer, her hands squeezing mine harder. "For whatever reasons you have, ones I won't ask you about because they're yours to keep, you're denying your feelings for him." She sighs and wraps me in her arms. "It's written all over your face. Has been for a while. That fine piece of ass owned your heart the second you laid eyes on him, and you his."

I rear back, my heart thumping out of control as the truth in her words brush over my limbs like a raging wildfire, burning me down to the core. Who am I kidding? I *do* love Ryder. I love him in more ways than I thought was ever possible. Love him so badly it hurts. Love him the way the earth does the warmth of the sun. My unconditional match, he's whispered his love into my soul, my entire being lost without its calming presence.

Yet how do I call it love for Ryder when my feelings for Brock remain the same, untouched in all they are? There was a time in my life when I couldn't rustle up a crumb's worth of feelings, let alone love, for anyone, my heart locked off to the notion as I stood alone, afraid to death of it. I've seen what love turns into, the emotion the deadliest disease to the human race. But here I am, my heart bleeding out for two different men, the organ split down the middle between who it truly belongs to and who it truly loves and needs in order to produce another beat.

Confused, but determined to find and tell Ryder how I feel, I swallow my fear of love, my fear of trusting others. Hands shaky, I nod as Madeline hoots out in excitement. "You're right. I do love him," I confess, unable to believe I actually said it out loud. "God, I love him so much, Mad."

"I know you do!" She gathers me in her arms, squeezing me as though I'm *her* lifeline. She has no idea. "That's why this is a *good* thing, Amber."

"But it's not," I say, working myself out of her hold. I stare into her eyes, mine filling with tears again. *So weak.* "It's *not* good. Brock. I . . . I have to tell him. I can't lie to him or myself anymore. I refuse." I rush a hand through my hair and sway over to the window, peering down into the parking lot. My vision blurs on the asshole parked outside, who's there to make sure neither I nor Madeline leave the building without him following us. "Maybe he'll understand. Let the three of us go on as we are. He's the one who wanted this to begin with. Begged to see me and Ryder together."

"Hold up," Madeline says, joining me. "Okay, that's some kinky shit we'll have to hit another time, but do you honestly think you're going to be able to keep them ... *both?*" She hooks her finger under my chin, dragging my attention to her confusion-swamped face. "Amber, you have to choose *one* of them. Not both. Surely you can't expect that either guy will be *cool* with you loving the other? Come on. You're noticeably out of it, but that's just irrational thinking, chicky."

"Mo, I ... uh, mean, no. I'm not out of it," I insist through a slur. I've always sucked at lying, plus I'm half tanked. "Well, I am a *little* tipsy, but yes, I think Brock will understand. He has to. Like I said, *he's* the one who wanted this." I open the window, sticking my head out into the frigid, early evening Friday night air. "Hey, asshole!" I yell, catching the attention of the moron three stories below us, sitting in a beat-up Chevy Trailblazer, his eyes narrowed on mine as he waits, alert, for either me or Madeline to try to get past him. Gotta love my paranoid boyfriend for keeping me hostage. "Go. The. Fuck. Away." I kick him a wink, wondering if he caught it. I turn to Madeline, urgency thick in my tone. "Will you help me get out of here without numb-nuts seeing me? I have to find Ryder, Mad. Have to tell him how I feel. I'll deal with Brock afterward, but right now, I need out of here without daffy-dick down there following me."

"Yeah, I got you," she says, helping me squirm into my pea coat as I pluck my car keys off my desk and gulp back the last few ounces of Captain Cool. She shoves a white winter cap onto my head, a green cashmere scarf following her motherly act as she spins me in the direction of the closet mirror. "I don't think this whole *I can have them both and be fine* thing's gonna work in your favor, but I have to ask on a serious note: Are you really going to see Ryder Ashcroft looking like *this?*"

Through mascara-streaked eyes, I glimpse my sweatpants-sporting, vintage-Metallica-donning getup and scowl, a sigh dropping from my mouth as I rip the cap off and attempt to pat my hair down from its just-fucked, demon-clown arrangement. It's no use, but to hell with it. I'm going to see him looking like a deranged psycho stalker, my need to tell him I love him taking precedence over vanity any day.

Nodding, I slip the cap back on. "I don't care what I look like. Now, how am I getting out of here unnoticed?"

Madeline kneels down, a giggle bursting from her chest as she helps me into a pair of purple, spongey snow boots. My appearance is getting worse by the second, but I have to keep my main goal in sight . . . the man I can picture spending the rest of my life with. The man who, if not by my side, I can see dying without in my darkened universe.

Madeline gets to her feet, a smirk creeping across her face as she pats my back. "Have no fear, my dear. Momma Maddie's got a fool-proof plan."

·   ·   ·

Okay. So maybe Madeline's plan wasn't *foolproof*, but it's working.

Despite wanting to watch her put on the worst-ever alcohol-induced, embarrassing version of the belly dance, I turn away from her diversion show. Better for me, the sandy-brown-haired, unsuspecting twentysomething dumbass who's sitting in his Trailblazer—enthralled with her twisting capabilities—is buying into her less-than-stellar Marilyn Monroe award-worthy bullshit.

Score!

At a speed that'd surpass Superwoman's, I round Fifth and Washington, my panicked gaze snagging my golden-horse-driven ride. I cross over State Street, still within earshot of Momma Maddie as she continues to flirt her way through my escape. I grab the handle to the taxi and swing open the door. Nerves skyrocketing, I lunge into the backseat, my sporadic breathing trumping that of a burglar who's committed armed robbery as I tell the overly confused, and somewhat scared, driver my destination: Ryder's apartment.

No questions asked, Bin Laden's ghostly doppelgänger takes off, the vehicle slipping in and out of traffic like a centipede as we head toward Ryder's casa. I have to hand it to Middle Eastern men. They might scare me a bit, but they sure as hell know how to navigate the busy streets of Baltimore on a frantic Friday night. Before I can blink, we're in front of Ryder's apartment. However, he's not. My heart sinks some as my sluggish vision lands on his empty parking spot. Knowing this was a possibility, I tell the driver plan B, directing him to Glen Burnie, where, hopefully, Ryder's hanging at his mother's house with Casey, possibly in the midst of a game of Hedbanz.

Fifteen minutes later and no such luck, another piece of my heart bruised as I try to think of where he'd be. The only other place is Ram's Head Tavern, down in the heart of Annapolis, where Lee's sure to be the man of the night tending bar. Going with an unexpected plan C, we're off and running again, my nerves mounting as we hit West Street, tear through the roundabout, and land on Main Street, smack-dab in front of Ram's Head. I ask the driver to hang on a second before jumping from the cab to see if Ryder's Mustang's parked around the back.

Touchdown!

The orgasm-producing muscle machine is sitting pretty under a streetlamp, its black-cherry glow a condescending balm to my nerves as I pull in a shuddered breath, worried. Scared that Madeline's spiel was just that—a drunken spiel, filling me with false hope—I clear my throat, a snowflake hitting my nose as I scurry, like the desperate woman I am, through the alleyway and back over to the taxi.

"I'm going to stay here." I pluck a twenty from my purse, eager to get inside as I hand it to the driver. "Thanks."

"It taking you long enough to decide," he answers, shaking his head. "And it *fifty* for the ride, *not* twenty." He sticks his wiry hair—

smothered hand out and, with his unibrow scrunched up—its angry wave staring me straight in the face—he huffs. "You think I going to go all the way to the jungle, stop in the semijungle, and come down here into wasteful-wealth land for *only* twenty dollars?" Another huff, this one as he sticks his nasty hand out farther. "If this is truth, then you Americans are crazier than us."

And to think I was gonna slip the undercover terrorist an extra twenty for his speediness.

Shame. On. Me.

Keeping my narrowed eyes on his, I dig another thirty bucks from my purse, Mr. Captain Morgan himself—another bastard contender in tonight's Hunger Games—kicking the shit out of my brain as I slam the correct fare into the driver's palm.

He smirks.

I smirk in return, but decide a proper dose of patriotism's due. With my middle finger saluting the asshole like a true-blooded American, I spin on my heel, my feet nearly coming out from beneath me as my boots slosh through a few centimeters of freshly dropped snow.

Paying no mind to the dickhead driver's tires grinding through the white blanket of slush, I approach the crazed bar, my heart imploding as I witness Hailey Jacobs, a she-devil in the flesh, place a long, lingering kiss on Ryder's cheek from beyond the frosted window.

"You've *got* to be kidding me." My muscles tense, the hot strands of emotionally fueled gas lines reacting of their own accord as they send a signal to my hand, causing it to grab hold of the door. Yanking open the door like Hercules' long-lost daughter would if she were stuck in my mental state of WTF, my teeth skid across my lip in an angry attack, my pulse trying to fight its way out of my veins as I . . . swoop into a vacant booth like a petrified coward?

God. I can't do this. Can't approach Ryder as his cheek enjoys a second, then third Hailey-diseased kiss. I might've fooled myself into thinking I didn't love Ryder, didn't need him in my life. But as I watch him rest his hand on the porcelain curve of Hailey's neck—a smooth-as-they-come grin curling his mouth in the process—I'm convinced he's the magician who's fooled me, his talent blinding me to the truth in more ways than my liquor-fueled brain can comprehend.

He doesn't need or want me, our connection a figment of my desperate imagination.

On that horrifying note, I unsuspiciously wave down a waitress, my body twisted in the fetal position in the corner of the booth as she approaches somewhat cautiously.

"Are you . . . *okay?*" she asks, setting a napkin in front of me.

"I will be after I murder one of the patrons across the bar." I laugh maniacally.

Mute, she stares at me, appearing marginally scared.

I shake my head, spitting out an order for three tall shots of tequila.

I need to switch things up. Along with my credit card I hand her a hundred-dollar tip, asking her to add a full glass of Captain to my request.

I hate change.

I also note to keep the drinks coming, my goal set on getting as hemmed up as humanly possible as I continue to spy on the man I thought I had a future with.

The hefty tip must've satisfied her fear of me going postal, because the waitress smiles and skirts off, her Christmas tree–dotted tie swinging cheerfully in tune with the bounce in her step as her disappearing act allows me an unobstructed view of Ryder and *Hell*-ey.

It's getting worse. At least from my vantage point it is. The skank's sitting on his lap, her arm dangling over his shoulder as she whispers something in his ear.

She giggles, he chuckles, and I . . . go postal.

Hail Mary, there *is* a God, my waitress's return timed perfectly as I stumble to my feet, whip the glass of Captain from her bar tray, and chug back the entire drink, less what I spilled while bringing it to my lips, of course. I nod my thanks to her and fly into the throng of equally wasted patrons, determined to end Ryder and his little whore's life as I round the bar, purposely crashing into his side.

Not only does the impact gain his immediate attention—his baby blues the width of Saturn and its rings as his gaze hits mine—but it also sends Hailey flying from his lap.

Aww . . .

The unpaid blonde call girl rockets to the liquor-slimed wood floor, a wheeze of pain pelting from her mouth as—if at all possible—Ryder's eyes go wider.

Hot damn! Another touchdown for me tonight.

Figuring I'm on a roll, I don't say a word to Ryder. Nope. I stick to simple, yet black widow–ish. I keep my mouth shut, finding a sliver of peace in watching him shit his pants as an, *oh, I'm so very NOT sorry for knocking your sleazy date off your lap* smirk oozes across my face.

"What are you doing here?" he asks, the shock in his voice palpable over the thumping bass of the live band's drums. "And *why* are you out, noticeably fucked up, and *alone?*" He growls the last part into my ear, his hand gripping my waist as he hops from his bar stool. The dominant set of his jaw commands an answer, his eyes narrowing on mine.

Yes, I'm pissed, sober Amber counting the many ways she plans on making Ryder sterile for the rest of his remaining days as she narrows her eyes right back at him. Still, though my heart might be in the midst of bursting at the seams from witnessing his deceitful acts, and the asshole's dimpled cheek deserves *nothing* but another strike of my hand against it, I can't help it, I'm human—a poisonous concoction of strong and weak, its main ingredients made to test our every move.

With a quick intake of air, human weakness winning the battle by a long shot, my body reacts to Ryder's touch as searing streams of needing to feel his cock inside me one last time lick uncontrolled desire over every muscle and bone holding me up. Remaining tactfully mute, I shove his hand off my waist and reach for a pinkish-colored shot winking at me from the bar to my left.

Its rightful owner? Go figure. A dude who'd—undoubtedly—kick Ryder's ass if need be.

Ooops . . .

"Answer me, *now*, peach," Ryder insists through another growl, his hand recapturing the right side of my waist *right* about the same time Jolly the Green Giant loops his arm around my shoulder.

"What are you doing in public without a lookout?" Before he lets me answer, Ryder cranes his head over the bar, his eyes flaming red as he taps the linebacker's forearm. "Hey, asshole! Get your fucking hands off her before I break that neckless skull of yours in half." Ryder sends him a wink, his infamous cocky smirk front and center as he juts that beautiful square jaw of his out like the true wiseass he is. "She's taken, buddy. Go sniff somewhere else."

It could be the Master Morgan clogging my arteries, the wire of nerves rattling my rib cage, or quite possibly my newly appointed, nameless boyfriend's shot—at what I believe was a lame version of a fuzzy nipple—which slows the motion reels of my brain. Who knows the reason? But at this point, brain slow or not, I'm positive the tension-filled air's about to thicken, a dense fog of ass-kicking swallowing the oxygen from my lungs as Bibbidi-bobbidi-Bimbo climbs up from her minute-long affair with the ground. The tap from her finger on Ryder's shoulder momentarily steals his attention from the insanely pissed-off-looking ogre, who's currently rising like *The Empire* from his bar stool.

"Oh, fuck," a familiar voice croaks.

Lee!

Yep, that was Lee, his boyish physique swooping over the bar a millisecond before my nameless friend's fist leaves a decent-sized dent in the back of Ryder's skull.

The next several minutes include my brain *really* fucking off: spots of bar stools sailing through the air, bone-cracking testosterone-filled grunts, and random gasps from onlookers filling my ears and vision as I'm tossed—mosh-pit-style—against the wall. With my view of the main event clogged by a horde of amped-up college students, I don't see the rest of the show. Even if I could, I wouldn't want to, couldn't bear it. As I completely black out—my brain taking its final, fizzed shit—I know when I wake up that I'll remember one thing . . .

Remember nothing, this moment sure to tattoo its wickedness across my heart.

＊　＊　＊

I wake with a start, my senses strumming back to life as soft fingertips trace figure eight patterns across my forehead. I open my eyes and look straight up into Ryder's, my head resting cozily in his lap as I try to figure out if I'm dead or not. With a hesitant grin, he moves a piece of hair away from my face, his free hand holding an ice pack against his bloodied bottom lip as I realize I'm not dead.

Nope. I'm in heaven, Ryder my welcoming angel.

"Where are we?" I ask, liquor dominating my confused thoughts as I press a featherlight palm to my cheekbone. Shooting pain—the kind that makes the heavens burst into star-spangled colors behind your eyes—jerks me back to life. "Ahh, God! And who or *what* hit me with a brick?"

"You, *my* sweet peach, are in the backseat of my car." Winking a baby blue at me, he tackles my heart to the ground by placing a soft, lingering kiss on my lips. The heavenly copper taste of his blood stains my tongue, my heart pouncing from my chest as I try to pull myself from the euphoric fog his touch has draped me in. "That shit was some of the best . . . straight-up . . . animalistic *fucking* we've *ever* done." He pauses, a smirk lifting his mouth. "*Tell* me it was as good for you as it was me."

"I, uh, we," I stutter, watching him raise a wounded, disapproving brow. "I don't remem—"

"Just kidding," he says flatly as he lifts my head from his lap. He climbs over into the front seat, his voice not so sexually merry as he guns the car to life. "Well, I *wasn't* kidding about the backseat part. Hopefully you're sober enough now to realize you are, *indeed*, in the backseat of my car." He shoots me a look from the rearview mirror. "Wanna know where we are? What *really* fucking happened?"

"Yes!" I blurt, equally as hurt as he apparently is, but growing pissed off about him withholding information from me. Who does he think he is? A goddamn FBI agent? "Of *course* I wanna know where we are and what really happened, you asshole!"

He chuckles, I think. It could've been a growl. I'm not sure. Either way, I'd welcome anything at this heated stage. "We're in the back parking lot of Ram's Head because you and I got kicked the fuck out after getting into a fistfight. You stole some guy's drink, he tried to beat the shit out of me after I threatened him about touching you, then *you* decided the girl sitting on my lap was Hailey. The chick had no idea what was going on when you attacked her."

It all comes rushing back to me, less the part where I romped on Hailey.

Madeline's pom-pom-driven speech about going after him.

The desperate escape from my dorm.

The agonizing pain of seeing Ryder suck face with that bitch.

I sober some as anger possesses every cell in my body.

Switching gears, my hand connects with Ryder's dimpled cheek—*whack!*—as I climb over into the passenger seat.

"You asshole!" I hiss, vexed. "I've been calling you, texting you, leaving you message after message, and I catch you helping yourself to that *whore*?"

Whack!

"That . . . that, sorry excuse for wasted *oxygen*?" I cry, growing angrier.

Whack!

"You left me hanging to go back to *her?*"

"Goddamnit, peach! That girl *wasn't* Hailey!" Before I know it, the bastard pulls me over the console and into his lap, my heart whipping out of control as his eyes flare wider. "So help me, Amber, if you try to fucking move *or* smack me again, I'm gonna—"

"You're gonna what?" I lift my chin in defiance as the first half of his statement, the one he revealed before he so eloquently pulled me into his lap, finally hits me.

Wasn't Hailey . . .

Wasn't Hailey . . .

Wasn't Hailey . . .

I can tell he sees the realization smeared across my face, because a slow grin consumes his. "Are you ready to listen?" he whispers, the tension hardening his shoulders easing some as he presses his lips to the wound, continuing to hammer nails of unforgettable pain into my cheekbone. "Because, if so, I'm ready to talk."

Whack!

My right hand snags the corner of his bloodied lip in an Oscar-worthy smack, the back of my skull pouncing off the driver's-side window as I squirm out of his hold. I blink, my shock mirroring his, as fear sets in. Reacting like any normal, drunk, underage college freshman would, I catapult to the passenger side, where I swing open the door, landing face-first into a heap of snow as I dive out of the vehicle.

The sounds of Ryder opening his door, his trunk being popped ajar, and his footsteps crunching toward me have me convinced that my final smack pushed him a little too far. Just a guess, but I'm pretty sure he's about to tie me up and toss me into his trunk, a double layer of duct tape sealed across my mouth ensuring my screams go unheard as he dumps me into the icy waters of the Chesapeake Bay.

On that note, I decide getting to my feet is my best form of escape from Ryder's wrath. As I attempt to stand, alcohol hindering the usually simple act, Ryder's footsteps become heavier, faster.

Shit. This is it. Death by love.

Again, the deadliest disease to the human race.

Before I can flip onto my back, I'm lifted from the ground and wrapped in a wool blanket that reeks of gasoline and cherry-flavored cigars as Ryder spins me in his direction. I crane my head back, my eyes roving over his beautifully bruised face as he lets out a sigh.

"Now, *why* would you go do that?" He cups my cheeks, the warmth of his hands a reprieve to my frozen flesh. A grin flitters across his mouth, his head ticking back and forth in mock disappointment as he adjusts my snow cap. "I had ya pinned for being *slightly* smarter than what you've displayed tonight. Guess I was wrong, eh?"

"I did it because I needed to get away from you, asshole," I scoff, my heart shredding into tiny puzzle-sized pieces. "Because I . . . I hate you."

"No, you don't," he insists through a growl, his hands coming around the small of my back.

"Yes, I do," I toss back over a *fuck you* huff as I try to ignore how good it feels being pressed to his chest again. "Try" being the operative word. I can't ignore it, my body responding to his touch the same way a child responds to candy. I'm mentally high, euphoria exhausting every excitement-masked breath I take. "I honestly do."

"Impossible." He kisses the crown of my head, pulling me closer. "If that were true, then why'd you come looking for me?"

"Because I . . . I . . ." I freeze up, the thought of telling him I love him, after witnessing what he did with Hailey's evil lookalike, after leaving me to gulp back antidepressants like Pfizer was going out of business the last few weeks, sending a chain of icicles up my spine as my confession crystallizes on my tongue.

"Say it, peach," he insists again, his voice softer, calmer. Oh God. He's using that *I'm about to fuck you-straight into next year* bedroom tone. The tone that had me panting the second I heard it, my panties instantly soaked. The tone that's whispered beautiful words, devastating stories, and lethal threats into my ears. "I want you to say it."

"Say what?" I ask, playing stupid. There's no *way* he's on to me. How could he be? He doesn't love or need me, his earlier escapade the perfect candidate for that example. If he loved me, tonight would've never happened. He wouldn't have had that chick on his lap, wouldn't have allowed her to kiss him. Cheek or not, no. That's not how love works. I think . . . "What the *hell* do you want me to say, Ryder?"

"What I know you *need* to." If at all possible, he pulls me closer, our bodies a single, beating organ as he dips his head. Nose to nose, his eyes hold mild warning, his breath wafting over my cheeks before he touches his lips to mine, attempting to entice the words from my mouth. "Say it or else I *am* gonna hurt you."

"*Hurt* me?" I question through a maniacal burst of laughter, losing my shit as I give him an incredulous once-over. I don't lose it like I did earlier, though. Not in the physical sense, at least. Nope. I lose it worse this time, tears dumping from my eyes as my messy emotions bleed out, pouring in thick, sloppy sheets of confusion onto the snow below us. "You couldn't hurt me any more than you *already* have! I saw you with that girl. Watched you all but let her *rape* you on the bar stool!"

"And *why* would seeing that hurt you, Amber?" he snarls, re-pinning me to his chest, his fingers kneading my hips with nervous urgency as I try to push him away. No luck. His grip around me tightens, his eyes fire-blue as his lips reclaim their position, hovering just above mine in a vengeful tease. "Fucking say it, already! Say it! Why did that bother you?"

"Because I'm in love with you, goddamnit!" I cry out, relief, panic, and shock all playing a dirty game of cat and mouse with my heart, sending my emotions straight into a meat grinder as Ryder stares at me a beat before crushing his mouth to mine. Without hesitation I fall in step with his hungry kiss, our lips searing the specks of snow dusting them into heated droplets of water as we attack each other. My hands make a boxing bag out of him as I punch my fists against his chest, pissed at what he's put me through. Still, in the middle of a growing snowstorm, I devour his touch, taste, and scent. "I love you, Ryder 'King of Assholes' Ashcroft, and you *murdered* me! Murdered my love by ignoring me for close to three weeks after you fucked me!"

He slows the kiss, his whisper hoarse, desperate, as he tucks his face in the crook of my neck. "Say it again, momma. I *need* to hear you say it again."

"That you ripped my world apart, dick?" I moan, my fingers tangled in his hair as he works his mouth down the curve of my collarbone. "You hurt me, bled me dry. How many more metaphors concerning my pain would you like?"

"No, sweets." He breaks the kiss, his thumbs skidding across the chunks of mascara sledding down my face as his eyes make contact with mine. "Tell me you *love* me again."

"I love you." It comes out breathlessly, automatically, no questions as to where it's born from or where it'll end up worrying my mind.

It's said as though it's been said a million times before, the confession tingling familiar on my tongue as though the three words know who their rightful keeper is. It's said with everything I am, with all I have yet to become, my heart aching for our lost past, still—pounding anew with curiosity for what the future holds for us.

"I love you, Ryder."

"Again," he commands, his gaze locked on mine as he drags his thumbs along my lips. "Say it again, peach."

"I love you," I repeat, trying to keep my voice even despite my racing heart.

That all goes to shit as his lips seize mine, his arms draping the blanket over our heads, sheltering us from the blowing snow. The kiss starts off slow and tentative, a pang of ache—the deepest form of loss—in each soft stroke of our tongues as we reacquaint ourselves with each other. But it doesn't take long for the kiss to implode as our bodies reunite, fierce passion lighting us up with every moan and breath. Hands grappling at each other, we fall into what's defined us from the first look, the first touch: a combustible ball of sexual attraction. My ass hits the hood of his car as he whips the blanket off our heads, splaying it out over the running vehicle behind me.

Before I know it I'm on my back, Ryder's hardened body nestled between my legs as I wrap them around his waist. Oh God. He's going to fuck me right here on the hood of his car and I'm gonna let him. I need him that badly, my heart aching to feel him inside me.

"I'm so in love with you, Amber Moretti," he says against my skin, his sincerity causing me to shudder. A swell of hope crashes over me as he cradles the back of my head, bringing my face to his. "So fucking in love with you, I don't think you'll ever understand it." A deep kiss, his lips nourishment to my starving soul as he slides his hand up under my T-shirt, exposing my breast. A flick of his tongue against my nipple and I'm drowning, lost to his pleasure, my back bowed, arching into him as the heat coming from the running vehicle beneath me, and Ryder's heat from above, surround me, keeping me warm. "I thought I was dying the last few weeks," he snarls, his mouth revisiting mine in a ravenous kiss filled with greed and, almost imperceptibly, hostility. "Not seeing your beautiful face, not hearing your sweet voice. Christ. I wasn't gonna be able to hold off another day without breaking, without coming to get you. I tried to drink you away, snort you away, and sleep you away, but none of it worked." Another kiss, this one softening its angry rhythm, but still potent, destructive to my heart as he whispers, "I was losing it without you near me, momma. You're stuck in my head like a memory, everything about you making up every stained, dark piece of who I am. Again, you're . . . *mine.*"

"Wait a second." I rear up, confusion riffling through my brain as I push a willpower-forced hand against his chest. "You tried to drink me away, snort me away, and sleep me away, but you never *called* me, didn't answer a fucking *text?"* Pissed as hell, I gather myself and head into the middle of the street to hail a cab, ignoring Ryder's pleas for me to stop.

He snags me by my elbow, but I cut him off, my hand darting up to smack his beautiful face for the very last time. *Whack!* "You claim to *love* me, *swear* I make up every piece of who you are, but you—for reasons I *better* know within the next ten seconds, or else I'm aiming for your *football* this time—decided, out of nowhere, to just up and clear yourself from my *life?* I'm not a chalkboard, Ryder! You can't just erase your stamp from my skin." Tears, pure in everything broken within me, scurry down my face, humiliation eating away at my insides as I flag down an approaching cab. "And don't *even* get me started on the girls? What number did Hailey's twin make for you? Five, ten, a hundred?!"

"Zero!" he bellows, curling an ironclad arm around the small of my back. Pressed chest to chest, our hearts thumping in furious unison, his words drop from his mouth like an atom bomb. "Yes, I picked up girls! Picked up tons of them! Hell, I brought every single one of them back to my place, dead set on fucking the living *shit* outta them! But I never went through with any of it! Couldn't because how much I love and need you in my life, Amber!" Turning from Hyde straight into Jekyll, his eyes soften with an apology, his voice dimming to a whisper as the same sincerity from earlier oils his tone. "Like it or not, you own every mangled piece of this pussy-whipped maniac, peach." He touches his lips to mine, soft, teasing, as he brings my hand to his chest, splaying it across his heart. "I can't blink, eat, sleep, or breathe without thinking of you, without thinking of us and what we were meant to be from the start."

My breath evaporates into a chilled puff of smoke as I temper down, trying with everything in me to weed through the confusion continuing to layer my skin. "Then why run away from me, Ryder?" I whisper, hoping to understand his reasoning. "I'm lost. Why . . . *hurt* me the way you have?"

"It's hard to explain," he mumbles, waving the cabbie away as his vehicle all but crashes into the curb.

"*Enlighten* me." I whip around, shaking my head at, none other than the terrorist driver from earlier. "No, you stay! I don't know if I'm going home with this one yet."

Bin Laden smirks and mirrors the patriotic, departing salute I'd left him with a few hours ago, a chuckle blaring from his mouth as he speeds off down the road.

Ryder's attention hones in on the cab's fading lights as it disappears around the corner. "What the hell was that about?"

"Don't worry." I grab hold of his jaw, my eyes narrowed as I direct his attention back to me. "I don't care how hard it is to explain. Explain everything to me ... *now*."

"Brock," he rumbles through gritted teeth, his jaw hardened. Shoulders squared slabs of concrete, he starts for his car, leaving me alone, beyond confused, and pissed off in the middle of the street. "Fuuuuck!" He swings his fists through the air, curse after curse tumbling from his mouth as he picks up an empty bottle of champagne from the ground, rocketing it against the exterior brick wall of the pub. The thing explodes into dust, tiny green particles glittering like diamonds in the wind as it mixes with the slowing beads of snow.

I jump, his sudden anger flashing across my chilled bones. Scared but growing angrier, I follow after him, determined to find out what the hell's going on. None of this makes any sense. Brock—though not as amped by the idea as he was when he first brought it up—said he's cool with the three of us giving it another go. As I jerk open the passenger-side door—Ryder's eyes capturing mine the second I slip into the seat—nothing can prepare me for what he says.

"Brock told me to stay away from you," he admits through a shame-filled whisper, regret surfacing over his face as he stares at me, defeated.

I stare back, equally defeated, my emotions one huge, tangled ball of hurt and confusion as his confession sinks its lethal fangs into my heart, obliterating what's left of it. Silence wraps itself around us, a moment of calm before Ryder loses it, punching the steering wheel. He hisses in pain, blood seeping from his knuckles as he guns the engine and pulls out of the parking lot. "And I fucking listened to the dick, agreed to hurt you in whatever way necessary as long as it meant never seeing you again, never . . . feeling you again."

Dazed, I pull in a shocked breath, his words shredding me wide open as the truth behind them morphs Brock into a deceitful liar in the back of my mind. Still, how *dare* I feel this way about the only man I've ever loved up until this point, the man who unselfishly allowed me to touch, taste, and live out a fantasy most girls could only dream about, let alone experience in the flesh?

I can't, every supercilious ounce of me screaming that it's wrong.

Yet, that doesn't change the tangled emotions spurring through my head. Brock tricked me into believing he was cool with all of us doing it again, his lie a punch to my gut as Ryder maneuvers through the winter wonderland of downtown Annapolis and onto an exit ramp. Body aching with the confusion Brock's caused it, my heart hurts, the organ smothered with regret. Not so much because he lied to me, but more so because the man I've loved for what feels like an eternity is caught up in his own pain, my insisting on being with Ryder again bruising him to the point that he couldn't even tell me about it.

I've broken him, my hands filthier than his in this sinking boat's demise.

Anxiety grows, a steady mounting of unease greasing the pit of my stomach as my greatest fear blooms to life . . . I'm never going to be able to share these two men ever again. That beautiful night was a onetime thing, its powerful emotions never to be revisited. Both of my boys are hurt, their hostility toward each other a clear indication that I'm going to have to choose one of them.

But how do you pick your right arm over your left, your ability to walk versus sight? How do you choose night versus day, water versus food?

You can't. Your natural instinct is to hold on to everything that helps you live.

"You belong with me, not him, peach," Ryder says, his voice soft, a balm, but for a fleeting second, to my nerves. "Have since the day you landed, whether my fault or not, in *my* lap."

I hear him. Hear every word he's saying, but when I think about Brock finding out about my feelings for Ryder I freeze up, my muscles encased in a tomb of icicles as my head spits out the what-ifs.

What if I lose Brock?

What if I lose Ryder?

What if I never paid either of them any mind the day we all met?

None of us would be here, stuck in the unforgiving purgatory that is love.

"I came here to tell you I love you, Ryder," I start, panic re-inundating my nerves to new heights as my voice cracks, fearing the outcome. "Because I honestly do. I love you so much, I don't know who I am, if I ever did, without you. Can't picture my life with you erased from it."

He drags his eyes from the road and rests them on mine, a glitter of hope cascading over them as he reaches for my hand. "Then you'll tell Brock? Let him know you wanna be with me instead of him?"

"That's the point," I whisper, chills prickling my skin despite the heat warming it. "I—I don't know if I can pick just one of you. I need you both for different reasons. The truth is harsh, hurtful, but I can't picture going on without *either* of you by my side."

I know it's selfish, know it's most likely not an option. But I still need to try, my soul unable to choose between one part of my heart versus the other. Both men make up what's vital to my well-being, each a necessity to my sanity, my survival.

Ryder veers off onto a shoulder, nearly losing control of the vehicle as he brings the car to a slippery stop. Hands gripping the steering wheel, he focuses straight ahead. "So you don't need me the way you *claim* to?" he asks, his voice shaking with heartbreak, betrayal, as he yanks his hand away, choosing to crush it into the dashboard instead of the steering wheel this time. "I *refuse* to share you again with him, and if you think I ever will, you're crazier than I thought!" Chest heaving, he drops his hands to the side, his head hung in regret as his tone simmers down. "Christ, peach, I need you to myself. Can't you *see* that? *Feel* that? I loved you from the instant I set eyes on you, from the second you walked into that goddamn cafeteria—slash—dining hall, and nothing will ever change that. I need you. *All* of you. Your hurt, your wiseass mouth, your magic, your nightmares, your dreams, your happiness, your . . . future. I can live without the sun, but I can't exist without you. That's *my* point. *My* harsh fucking truth." He brings his weary gaze to mine, fury resurfacing on his face as he stabs a finger against his temple. "Whether I was prepared for it or not, regardless if I wanted it, you're here, stuck in my mind. Brock shared something so precious, so goddamn sweet and sacred, with someone else, auctioned it off for cheap because he figured that's what he needed, what you needed! You didn't need that. All you needed was me, and the asshole knew that, took advantage of it! If you were mine, someone'd have to fucking *kill* me before I *ever* shared you with anyone else! Jesus! You can't have the both of us! Don't you get that?"

"I know I can't!" I blurt, recapturing his hand, tears falling from my eyes as his vicious words concerning Brock nearly crack my skull wide open. "And it's not that at all! I need you more than anything!" I take a calming breath, hoping I can make him understand what I can't even begin to. "I didn't think my heart was capable of loving *one* man, let alone *two*, Ryder. There was never any room for love because it was beaten into my brain early on that it was something you fought to keep out, battled to ward off your heart from to keep it unharmed by the pain it inevitably causes in the end. God, I feared love. Feared what it would do to me. Feared I'd . . . turn it into the same thing my parents did." I drop my head in shame, my attention honed in on our interlocked fingers.

Without a word, he unropes his hand from mine and gently touches my jaw, his expression a jigsaw puzzle of hurt, desperation, and confusion as I lift my watery eyes to his.

My heart splits, my tears falling faster as I try to grab a breath.

I want to take his pain away, demolish his confusion, and cure his desperation. But I can't even help myself, the disease I am, the incurable cancer I'll forever remain, simply created to kill off the hopes of all around me, wipe out the dreams of anyone who gets too close.

"I just need a little time, that's all." I sniffle, the look of despair coloring his face a noose around my neck as I pray that he'll wait for me. "Time to make a clear decision. One I know is the right one for me, for *all* of us. I know choosing who I need and love the most should come simple, an automatic click in my brain. But it's not for me. Before Brock, I'd never been in love, never felt what it was to need someone so badly you can't think straight." I lean over the console and seal my lips to his cheek, the sound of our heartbeats echoing through the car as I pull back, ashamed of what I'm asking of him. "Not only am I scared to death, but I'm confused, Ryder. I know I shouldn't be, know that putting both of you in this position isn't right, but I don't know what else to do. So please, if you can, just give me a couple of days to get my head straight."

He nods tightly, his face wounded beyond the scars I created, beyond anything I ever want to see again.

So selfish, toxic.

As he puts the car in drive, slowly easing onto the highway, I can't help but wonder if I've already killed off his hopes, wiped out his dreams.

Unsure if I have, there's one undeniable truth I can't run from, one petrifying fact that's about to change all of our lives: the hourglass is on the table, two beautiful hearts awaiting my decision . . .

CHAPTER 22

Brock

Walls closing in around me, I feel like I'm gonna hurl, my entire universe crashing to pieces as I belt down 695 toward Ryder's place, doing at least thirty over the speed limit.

Fuck the cops. Fuck Ryder. Fuck my parents. Fuck Brandon being gone.

Fuck . . . everything.

Hands curled tight around the steering wheel, Amber's voice haunts my head, nausea roiling through me as our conversation from earlier sparks to life.

"We need to talk." The panicked wariness in Amber's tone causes my heart to jump as I claim a seat on my couch, already knowing what she's about to say, able to feel it with every hesitant move she makes across my living room. She snatches a spot next to me, fear dilating her pupils as she takes my hand in hers. "It's . . . important."

"What's important is me not knowing where the hell you've been all night," I bite out, my anger seeping through my serpentine skin more than my relief that she's okay, her beautiful face unharmed by Derick's threats. "Why you decided to sneak past the guy I have watching after your safety. That's what's important to me right now."

"You know you sound like a wannabe Don Corleone, right?" Amber

ridicules through an exhausted sigh, her eyes puffed out like deep red bags of cotton candy as she hits me with one of her soft, caring smiles, gently guiding my head down onto her lap in her magical process.

She wins. I do sound like an overprotective douchebag, but that's not the case in point. Amber chose to disobey my strict orders of not going anywhere without me or her lookout, without someone making sure Derick can't get near her.

But, God, why do I feel so safe here, staring up into my angel's eyes from below her? That's because when I'm with Amber, I'm fucking Superman, sitting on top of the world, the ultimate untouchable force.

Still, for making me worry for several hours while I sat here calling and texting her, Amber not only deserves a punishing yet unforgettable fuck from yours truly, but the dick who was supposed to keep his eyes latched on hers is more than deserving of a severe ass-kicking, also courtesy of yours truly.

Whoever said I was a complete asshole was wrong. Less driving myself crazy over what Amber's about to admit to, I'm feeling more than generous tonight.

Before I can crack a grin at her somewhat entertaining joke, Amber's smile fades, transforming into something no boyfriend ever wants to witness . . .

. . . One huge I'm about to ream you a new ass frown, thick with a heavy dose of heart-damaging crying. Fuck me . . .

"Why'd you tell Ryder to stay away from me?" she questions over a hiccupped gulp of grief, tears pouncing from her eyes as she pets my hair. Considering she looks like she's about to eat my balls for breakfast, the notion's confusing. "I know everything, because Ryder admitted to everything. Admitted to loving me. Needing me. Wanting to be with me." Crying surpassing the hysterically dangerous point, she lifts my head from her lap and inches away from me, her back hitting the corner of the couch, her arms hugging her knees as she stares at me, almost appearing . . . scared to death? Christ, what have I done to this girl? "You made him purposely . . . hurt

me by telling him to ignore my calls and texts. Why? Why, baby? I don't understand. You said you were okay with the three of us being together again. Why lie to me while telling him to back off?"

She said a lot, but the only words my brain pick up on is the part about Ryder admitting to . . . loving her. My heart explodes right there on the spot, regret for ever opening this can of worms crawling all over me.

I spark up a joint, praying a little green will help calm me down as I pull into Ryder's neighborhood, seeking the asshole's blood. The high does fuck all to chill me out, my best friend's deception hitting bone-deep as I slide into a parking spot in front of his and Lee's apartment. Boundaries. I never set them, leaving Ryder to step over what should've kept him and his feelings for Amber in check.

I pop open my glove compartment, reach for my pistol, and load it, ready to set all kinds of fucking boundaries as I kill the engine. Another rip from the joint and my head starts spinning with Amber's confession, her final blow to my heart sending me over a cliff as she continued.

"But before you answer anything," she chokes out, wiping her nose with the back of her hand, "you need to know that I . . . Brock . . . God, Brock, I . . . love Ryder just as much as he does me, if not . . . more. But I don't love him any more or less than I do you. I don't . . . think, at least."

"What the fuck do you mean you don't think you love him any more or less than you do me, Ber?" I shoot to standing, *rage, hurt, and confusion attacking me from the inside out despite having known this was coming. Her barely answering my calls the last couple of weeks, not wanting to fuck around when we did see each other, skipping class, work, and her therapy sessions told me all I needed to know, warned me of what the future was about to upchuck in my face . . . her finally admitting to loving Ryder.*

I knew it.

Knew she loved him the day I asked her if she did.

The day she lied about how she really felt about him.

I yank a glass-framed picture of her and me on the weekend that ru-

ined my life, knowing she's not to blame for the mess that's become of us as I bullet it across my living room. It explodes against my fireplace, its jagged edges some kind of you deserve this, asshole sick, twisted representation of the universe's way of slicing my heart open. Loud and destructive to everything evil, self-centered, and fucked up I've become since Brandon's kidnapping, since the angel before me stepped into my life, its insidious whisper keeps asking, "Are you happy now?" It's laughing, screaming to me, "Don't forget. You were the architect of this structure, the almighty creator of the smoky ash it's now burned into."

Even so, I buck against it, my world splintering on its axis as I make a duplicate glass-framed picture of us—the first time I met her foster parents—the fireplace's next victim. The memory crystallizes into thin air, all it meant melting into what remains of a dream—a dead dream I let slip through my fingers. "How do you not know who you love and need more?" I snarl, seething to punch something. I refrain, the fear in Amber's eyes halting me on a needle as she stands to her feet, slowly backing away from me like a scared animal would a hunter.

Christ.

No. Never. Fucking never. I'm not that guy, that sorry fuck of an excuse of a man who takes pride in petrifying the woman who makes up the glue that holds his universe together, the essential piece to his life force.

Feeling like the ultimate dick, I step toward her, my hands tentatively coming up to cup her cheeks. She allows me to touch her dampened skin— thank God—the fear trickling over her face drying some as the anger on mine calms. "I don't understand, baby girl." I shake my head, unshed tears born from not grieving Brandon like I should've been allowed to, unseen tears created by turning my girl into something she's not, coming as close as they ever came from dripping from my eyes as I move my hands into the silk of her hair, bringing her lips to mine. "How can you not know it's me you love more?" I ask, my voice shaking like a certified pussy, fear that I've lost this gem forever cracking my words. "You're my world, Ber, not his. I know I messed up by sharing you with him. And, fuck, baby. If I could *take it back I would. But you can't leave me like this. You just can't. You gotta give me another chance to make things right, the way they should've been from the second we met."*

"I love you with all my heart, Brock. I always have, and I'm pretty sure I always will. But I'm lost, confused, broken, nearing . . . hopeless," she says through a self-deprecating whisper, her gaze begging for forgiveness before her lips land gently on my jaw. Her expression a smorgasbord of pain, she says one final thing. One final thing that has me painfully aware that the time I've spent with the girl who's served as a painkiller to my past, a ray of light to my future, is almost up, my love for her lost upon my best friend's love for her as she pulls back. "So I know a decision needs to be made. One that'll kill off a piece of each of us," she continues, numbly, an emotionless flower on autopilot as she turns toward my bedroom. "One I hope to make by the end of the week."

My bedroom door clicks shut, my heart, sanity, and fear caving into my soul, speeding my breathing, swallowing whole everything I'd had planned for us in one, slick your life's over, dick gulp.

I yank my Hummer keys off the entryway table, and it dawns on me that I'm cool, as good as any other heartbroken motherfucker. Temporary insanity will be the key player in my defense concerning the murder of my best friend . . .

As I slip behind the wheel, I'm pretty sure I've got a solid game plan . . .

CHAPTER 23

Ryder

I HAVE JUST ENOUGH time to shower and slide on a pair of sweat-pants when I hear a loud *crack-crack-crack* on my door, the sound breaking me from the temporary bliss of Amber's confession.

The girl loves me . . .

Christ. When she told me that, I knew she was mine, knew I'd won her heart. The undeniable want in her kiss, the unhidden truth swirling in her eyes, and the unmistakable need for me in her every touch couldn't tell me otherwise.

It's me whom she'll pick, me whom she'll spend the rest of her life with.

Still, I shouldn't get ahead of myself. Though she loves me, there's still a good chance she'll pick Brock, leaving me to rot away without her because of her confusion as the fucker sucks the life out of her, using her weaknesses in his favor.

I exit my bedroom, ready for what's to come, for what I've been waiting for over the last forty-five minutes or so. Absolute mayhem. I know it's Brock behind my door, Amber's truth propelling him straight to me. When I dropped her off at his condo she told me she was telling him about her feelings for me, letting him know she plans on making a decision during the week.

457

If I know Brock as well as I think I do, the sick fuck's in the midst of losing his mind, my head on display in a trophy case the only thing running through his thoughts as he waits for me to open the door. Taking proper precautions, I pop the back cover off the surround-sound subwoofer and grab my Smith & Wesson, loading it as I peek out the window from behind the closed blinds.

Well, fuck me. It looks like me and my buddy have a lot more in common than I thought, the both of us holding guns in our hands, his aimed at my front door—straight for my head—mine hanging loosely at my side as I unlatch the lock.

I turn the dead bolt and swing open the door as I lift my gun to his head, getting off on our mirrored poses.

"Come here to kill me, bro?" I question, a smirk on my face as Brock's glassy eyes shoot open. "Such a shame too. I thought we had a pretty good thing goin' for us the last couple years." I step forward, jabbing the barrel of my gun against his right temple as he does the same to mine. "Mm, feels good, doesn't it? The taste of death so close, so . . . *here*, it makes ya hard." My expression goes placid, his turning white as I cock my weapon. "The only things I was ever really sure of were pussy's wet and life's a bitch. Plain and simple, that's all I knew was solid, something that'd never change on me. But *never* in a million fucking years—ultimate pussy up for grabs or not—did I think my *best friend*, my partner in crime, would show up to my apartment looking to . . . do me in."

"You *love* her, asshole?" he hisses, sweat caking his forehead despite winter's brutal bite. Body shaking like a roller coaster, Brock moves the barrel of his gun beneath my chin, betrayal possessing his expression as his free hand attacks his pistol in a paranoid grip.

I hold my stance, fear not an option as I simply stare into his eyes.

"Answer me!" he demands, impatience causing him to twitch with anxiety. "Like, *really* love her?"

"I love her with every breath I breathe," I answer, the calmness, the undying finality in my tone, a whisper of freedom to my senses as revenge takes over Brock's.

Surprisingly enough, he doesn't shoot me, but the dick makes sure I feel him pistol-whip my cheekbone before he charges at me, his bull-like rage knocking me flat on my back as he tackles me to the ground. He chucks his gun across the room, deciding to use his fists as his weapons as they leave a few reminders of his hostility against my stomach, head, and ribs. I show him the same courtesy, pitching my gun onto the linoleum entryway as I clone his reminders. Unleashing all of my frustration for Amber's past pain, present confusion, and future hurt, I dig into every crevice of his body, letting him know he's playing with the wrong man, has fucked with the wrong girl's emotions.

Rolling around on the floor, we beat on each other like rabid gorillas, two strangers in a bar fight, our fists swinging wildly until exhaustion slows us. Before I can blink through another bloodstained blur, we're both on our backs, staring up at the ceiling, our breathing a battered mess as we drop our arms to the side, physically and emotionally spent.

Silence reigns a second before Brock whispers, "This wasn't supposed to happen."

"What wasn't supposed to happen?" I ask over a cough, blood dripping from my nose as I sit up, backing myself against the couch. "Us beating the *fuck* outta each other, or us trying to *kill* each other?" I yank my old football jersey off the entertainment center, using the thing as a towel to soak up my blood. "There's a few variables here, so why don't ya enlighten me, bud. Again, what wasn't supposed to happen?"

I know what he's referring to, what's eating him alive. Still, I want to hear him acknowledge it, *need* to see the regret seep down his face as he says the words.

Brock gets to his knees and backs himself against the wall across from me, his hand reaching out for my jersey as he shakes his head. "You and her falling in love. *That's* what wasn't supposed to happen." Another whisper, his face pained beyond the damage I caused it as he, too, uses my jersey to sop up the blood pouring from his brow, nose, and bottom lip. "What the fuck was I thinking?" He drops my jersey to the floor, his hands buried in his hair as he starts rocking back and forth. "Goddamnit! What the fuck was I *thinking?*" Brock grits out, his misty, narrowed eyes pinned to mine as he punches at his chest like Kong himself. "I knew you wanted each other. Knew the two of you had some freakish chemistry I couldn't compete with! Yet I *still* shoved her into your arms, all but begging to have my heart demolished in the end."

Remaining silent, I stare at my friend. Though she has yet to pick either of us, Brock's already grieving the loss of Amber, hating himself for it, wishing he could take back that one decision as he tugs at his hair like a madman.

And just like that, I don't wanna witness Brock's pain, feel his anguish, or step into his terrifying reality. Like me, he could lose the girl he loves, the girl he needs to complete his next breath. A minute ago I wanted to see the asshole suffer. Now the fucker's got me feeling bad for him, my mind warring over who's *really* the dick who dragged us into where we are now.

I knew how dirty shit could get, was more than aware of where this could lead all of us. Still, my heart roared for what it wanted, for what was so close in physical reach yet so mentally far away. Unable to ignore Amber's pull, I went along with it, hoping like an imbecile that everything would even out, that neither I nor Amber would develop feelings for each other.

Head clear, it's fucking simple: I loved the girl before that night ever happened, loved her with everything I was and will ever be before I even knew I did.

I stand up, my body aching from head to toe as I stare down into the eyes of a depleted man. Despite feeling bad for him, I need to say one thing to Brock. The one thing he should've known the second Amber opened her darkened world to him. "She's not a robot," I mumble, reaching for his hand. "She never was."

He accepts my aid in getting to his feet, his hand clasped around mine as his gaze skirts around the room, lost, desperate for answers to something people have questioned for millions of years . . .

Fate.

Not knowing where either of our fates lie, I pick up my gun from the floor, unloading the bullets from it as I not so gracefully make my way to the front door. Between the bar fight with Amber and Brock's ambush, I'm positive I'm gonna wake up hurtin' tomorrow morning, every muscle in my body telling me to fuck off as I wait for the ghost of Amber's decision to come haunt me.

Shoulders slumped, and spirit visibly fighting the same battle I am, Brock locates his gun, his face disturbed as he approaches me. "You actually had the goddamn thing loaded?"

I spring a brow, unsure if the asshole's fucking with me. "Like you didn't."

"I did at first," he admits, a guilty grin peeling across his face, "but after I got out of my ride I rethought what I was doing. I figured you'd do the same. Guess I was wrong." He sobers, his eyes swimming in a pool of questions as he tucks his gun into the waistband of his jeans. "I've already killed for Amber. I wonder, *really* wonder, if you would've been able to kill for her love as well . . . friend."

I don't answer him. I don't have to. If the *wanna test me out?* look burning through my glare doesn't tell him the answer he's seeking, then the dick never deserved Amber to begin with.

He nods, accepting my unspoken words, knowing—friend or not—I'd kill him in a heartbeat for her if it came down to it. "So where do we stand after she's picked her leading man?" he asks, his voice calm, eerily monotone as he leans against the doorjamb. "We're just . . . finished?"

"How can there be any trust between us after what went down tonight?" I'll live out the rest of my life wondering, hour by hour, minute by minute, and second by second if he's gonna change his mind and leave the bullets in the gun next time. Trust is impossible for us now. We're nothing but a shell of what was once solid, tight. "Yeah. That ain't happening."

Arms crossed over his chest, he tilts his head. "Really, bud? It's just that simple for you? After everything you and I've been through, the countless times we had each other's backs, our friendship's done?"

"Yeah. It's as simple as that." I nod tightly, knowing there's no going back but hating the fact that there's not.

"Fine," he says, his tone teetering between hurt and pissed. "After we take Derick out, which needs to happen soon, we'll go our separate ways."

And just like that, something else happens. Something that, just a couple of months back, I would've never seen coming, couldn't even picture it . . . The man who's claimed the title of my best friend for as far back as I can remember, the only true brother I've ever known, walks out of my life, the love we have for a rare diamond amid cavernous rocks heavy enough to crash our unbreakable mountain of friendship down.

He knows it. I know it. So what the fuck is the use in lying, denying what'll inevitably happen?

One of us killing the other somewhere down the road . . .

CHAPTER 24

Amber

Broken.

My heart's literally broken, the very organ that keeps me alive slowing its beat as I write the final words of my parting letter to the man whose heart I'm equally going to break tonight.

One hour.

A single hour remains before I have to look him in his eyes—those beautiful eyes that captured my soul from the second they stomped into my life—and tell him the reasons why I chose his best friend over him.

Feeling sick to my stomach, I seal the envelope, my gaze sweeping over the name written on the front of it one last time before shoving it into the front pocket of my satchel. Words can heal, words can bruise, and tonight mine will do both to two worthy contenders, the two most amazing men to have ever stepped foot into the chaos of my life. Into the chaos of . . . me. Born from all I've torn apart, all I've poisoned, a friendship is in ruins, its once indestructible loyalty a casualty of my love for them.

I stand, fearing with everything in me what his face will look like when I try to explain that even though we're a perfect match in so many ways, we're not meant to be. Never were. Our coming together was fleeting, a shooting star barely seen from Earth, still beautiful, magical, as it slips past your eyes. Though a blip on the road map of my life, he'll forever remain with me through every unsteady step I take without him over the roots of my future.

All I have, all I need, has been right here next to me the whole time, the man who's always loved me, having taken the backseat to my heart so many times when I ignored his love, discounting it for something else . . . someone else. The light emanating from the man who makes up my past, present, and future—burning brighter than a billion shooting stars ever could—has seared his name into my soul, his presence the air I'd kill to breathe.

Emotions hanging from a slippery tight wire covered with excitement and sorrow, I pull open my dresser drawer, plucking out a replica of the notebook I've kept since the day my parents died. Everything's there. Every good, bad, and scared day I lived through copied onto the once blank pages. Every confused, frightened minute I wished away into the whisper of the darkened moment. Every second of questioning and requestioning my parents' love for me while feeling the absence of it from those who were . . . *caring* for me. Thoughts stained in black ink, every thought I've had over the last decade resides in this notebook, this offering of my complete truth to the man I know will hold it in his hands, taking care of it the way it needs to be . . . the way he always has. The first page, my letter to him. The reasons why I chose him, why I can't take another step forward without his love guiding me.

Still, I can barely think straight, my memory twisting with the sound of Brock and Ryder's worried voices when I'd called them to let them know I'd made a decision, that tonight was the night I'd be leaving the diner with one of them. Time and place set, this is it. I'm about to wreak havoc on one of their lives, leaving him to pick up the pieces of the carnage I've left behind.

With everything in place, I glimpse my reflection in the mirror, sickened by the girl who's staring back at me as I slip on my coat and scarf. Who does this to someone, plays their heart like a game of chess? I do, that's who. A black widow in the flesh, I'm about to eat a man alive, killing off every dream he had for us. On the verge of not going through with it, coming close to choosing neither guy so as to save all of our hearts from splitting in two, I take a calming breath.

The man I love and need is here with me in spirit, his face consuming my thoughts as I grab my keys off my desk and head out of my dorm room.

As I make my way down the stairwell and out into the icy hold of Old Man Winter's arms, to my surprise, there's no one waiting for me to flee campus, not a single Brock- or Ryder-imposed bodyguard awaiting my escape. Considering Brock insisted on picking me up to drive me to the diner, where we'll meet Ryder for this . . . this final good-bye of sorts, I guess the lack of a lookout shouldn't come as a surprise. For reasons that still remain a mystery to me, it looks like they didn't place anyone here because they figured they wouldn't need to. Brock will be here in fifteen minutes.

I shoot him a text, letting him know to go on ahead to the diner without me. I'm driving myself there. I shut off my cell, not wanting to see the texts that he and Ryder will undoubtedly send, warning me not to step foot out of my dorm without one of them here.

Satchel flung over my shoulder and notebook tucked under my arm, I fumble for my keys halfway across the parking lot. Fingers half frozen, my key chain slips from my grasp, landing with a hush in the recently dropped snow. Before I can reach for them, a swastika-tattooed hand crosses my vision, lifting them for me.

"Let me get those for ya, darlin'," he offers in a raspy drawl, its dark tone raising the hairs on my neck.

His voice reminds me of a predator's. A viper coiled, ready to strike.

With my keys in his possession, he rises, a crooked grin scarring his face.

A half-skeleton-tattooed face.

Death's mask.

"Sorry I startled ya, but you seemed . . . faraway." Grin unwavering, he dangles my keys from his index finger. "So you want these or not?"

"I—I do. Thank you." My words are spoken through a halting whisper, the faux smile tightening my lips betraying my surprise and sudden fear as I tentatively reach toward his upturned palm.

I gasp as his hand swallows mine, my keys stabbing into my skin with the tightening of his grip. Before I can produce another thought, he yanks me into his chest, his nose buried in my hair as he sniffs at the snow-dampened strands. All of my words come undone, my fight-or-flight instinct pumping its juices through my veins as a voice from within screams for me to run. Frozen, my limbs don't receive the urgent message, my entire body an icicle stuck to the pavement as he slowly backs away.

Eyes as dark as crow's wings, a smirk etches his mouth, the towering set of his body leaning against my driver's-side door, blocking me from getting in my car as he crosses his arms over his chest. "Sorry about that. I couldn't help myself." A pause, the intent in his deadly stare showing nothing but harm. "I've spent the last several weeks wondering what you . . . smelled like, what Brock gets to wake up to every morning."

It hits me all at once. He's the reason my boyfriend's begged me not to make a move off campus without telling him beforehand.

The reason Ryder and Brock have kept someone watching after me the last few weeks.

The reason I may never see either of their beautiful faces again after tonight.

Here to take my life, camouflaged before me, the Grim Reaper's eyes never leave mine as he scratches at the stubble along his jaw. "You *are* Amber Moretti, correct? The cunt who's been fucking Brock? The cunt I've been *dying* to get my hands on?"

I don't respond. Instead, my gaze instinctively drops to a quarter-sized blot of blood staining his camel-hued bomber jacket, its cuff gleaming ruby red with the fresh stain as everything starts to click into place. Not only is he here to take my life, but he's already taken my lookout's. My attention shoots out into the parking lot, my breathing picking up as I scour my surroundings. Nothing. Not a single soul's here with us, finals and the wintry mix keeping most students in for the night.

"Ain't ya gonna answer me?" he growls, impatient.

Remaining frozen with fear, my eyes meet his for a brief moment before slipping back down to the blood on his cuff.

He catches me in the act, his eyes flicking down to the blood, then back up to mine. Head cocked to the side, his expression turns void, no signs that a human soul resides within this man, this devil's serpent, as his fist connects with the side of my head.

Skull splintering in pain, my keys slip from my jellified fingers, the notebook following in its wake.

Now I lay me down to sleep . . .

I hit the ground, my nails clawing at the cold pavement beneath me as I try to regain my bearings, try to get to my feet.

I pray the Lord my soul to keep . . .

Starting to blank out, he rolls me onto my back with the tip of his boot, his evil face inches from mine as he crouches down, hovering above me.

If I die before I wake . . .

As my surroundings fade to black, my eyes drifting closed as the warmth of my blood pools around my head, comforting me in some sick way, the only thing I can think of is my two boys. If my two shooting stars—though one brighter than the other in my sky—are going to be okay without me, able to make amends without their weakness blocking their way.

I pray the Lord my soul to take . . .

A Round of Applause, Otherwise Known as
My Acknowledgments

Fɪʀsᴛ ᴀɴᴅ ꜰᴏʀᴇᴍᴏsᴛ I'd like to thank God. Though I'm not what most would consider an insanely religious woman, I'm aware a force more powerful than myself swept me under his care, making sure I stayed (somewhat) sane the last few years. There's no question I've been blessed, and for this, religious or not, I'm eternally grateful to whoever, whatever, was responsible for making my success—both outwardly and mentally—possible.

To my rug rats, Joseph, Matthew, and Ava. I love you kids more than you'll ever know, more than my fluffy words could ever express. Not until you have your own children will you come close to understanding how deeply my unconditional love for you all runs. Mommy apologizes for so many things I've missed, so many precious moments of your lives I can never get back. Not that anything I write here can replace our lost time, but please know this has *all* been done so your futures are easier, the weight on your shoulders lighter.

To my better half, my kickass husband, Joe. Aka "Big Daddy." You've always been, and will forever remain, my rock. You might feel that staying home the last couple of years to watch our children turned you into less of a man, a Mr. Mom, as you call yourself. But this, my love, isn't true. Not even close. In the eyes of both the kids and I, you're not only our savior, but the strongest man to have ever walked the earth. While I chased after a dream, you held our family together, became the concrete keeping our unit from crumbling apart. From the teenage wild boy I fell in love with nearly twenty years ago to the incredible, supportive husband and father you've turned into, you're all man, baby. A man whom no one in this family could go on without having by their side. Your dad would be proud of you, Joe. Nothing but love, babe. Nothing but love.

To my kid sister, Patricia. Aka "Titty." Thank you for the daily texts and phone calls filled with encouragement. When I thought I couldn't go on writing *Amber to Ashes*—scared to absolute death while revisiting the ghosts of my past with each resurrected dirty memory, my fear exploding as I faced the ones continuing to haunt my present with each tortured page I got through—your words centered me, the truth behind them a balm to my nerves. Coming from someone who's trudged through so much shit in her young lifetime, a beautiful soul who had her closest friends turn their judgmental backs on her before they could see how sparkling clean she came out on the other side of her battle, your words meant the world to me. It's not *me* who's amazing, not me who anyone should be proud of. It's *you*, my little "Sing Noel" star. Never forget that, kiddo. GNSDILY, forever.

To the second strongest man to have ever walked the earth. My brother, Sal. Just watching you achieve so many things, climb so many mountains, kept me in a constant state of awe. You're a kind and caring person, my brother. Never let anyone tell you different. I think Mommy is finally proud of us all.

To Lisa Pantano-Kane, Cara Arthur, and Angie McKeon. There was no limit to the amount time and help you each lent in the creation of *Amber to Ashes*. Hours spent on the phone talking plot, days spent emailing scenes back and forth, right down to catching me when I was falling; you gals were my anchor, your no-nonsense attitudes my lifeboat when I was drowning. Thank you for always keeping it real. All my love and gratitude.

Tina Reber, Gretchen de la O, and my mate from across the pond, Julie Watson. You ladies know me through and through, every tortured cell in my body never once going unnoticed by any of you gems—my wingless angels. Still, you each accepted, and continue to accept me, for what I've turned into . . . a woman whose skin was being scratched by the devil's razor-sharp fingernails, a woman who currently is never allowing that other diseased mind back into her soul ever again. You've each witnessed me at my very best and have carried me through my absolute worst, your unyielding concern for where I was mentally, physically, and spiritually, depthless. While I was in Atlantic City, gambling against the angry winds of time, miles upon miles separating us, each of you helped me roll those winning dice, aided me in flipping over a set of rockets. Just know that with every still-slightly wrangled piece of who I am, I'll be forever grateful for what each of you walked me through. All, all, all my love. Thank you. XO.

To those of you who'd pop up in my Facebook messenger window (you know who you are), checking to see if I was okay. Thank you. Your constant, streaming words of encouragement kept me driving forward.

To my editor, Jhanteigh Kupihea, for putting up with my fits, quick change of mind, and daily mood swings for the past year and a half. I wish I had your patience, your grace, when handling a person such as myself. Maybe that's why I'm the writer and you're the editor? I heard our breed is a . . . special kind to deal with. After it was all said and done, you made my words soar, and for this, I thank you a gazillion times over.

To my beast of an agent, Jane Dystel, from Dystel & Goderich Literary Management. From the second I'd heard your thick New York accent, way back when I'd just dipped the tip of my toe into the raging waters of this industry, I knew we'd make a good match. How could we not? I might have you by a few feet, but we're both strikingly good-looking women who are as tough—if not tougher—as nails. Thank you for taking a chance on me, the past two years spent under your wing was everything I imagined it would be ... a spectacular burst of knowledge surrounding this "writing world." Thank you for dealing with the psychotic nutter I tend to turn into roughly twice a month for one reason or another. Even when I'm well aware that I'm in the midst of being overly dramatic concerning something petty, just as Jhanteigh does you handle me with practiced grace. No wonder you two meet up for lunch every so often. I'm betting you're both trying to talk the other out of not kicking me upside the head. ☺ Cut and dry: Thank you for teaching me the ins and outs to all of this whilst still keeping me in check.

To my cover artist, Regina Wamba, from Mae I Design and Photography. You pulled it off again, love. As I'd said with the first set of *Collide* and *Pulse* ever created: I'll never write a book without your stamp of originality on it. All my love.

To Ashley Farrow Padgett for helping come up with *ATA*'s name during a giveaway of mine. It hooked me right away and fits the story beautifully. Thank you.

To any and all blogs participating in spreading the word about *Amber to Ashes* (whether a favorable mention or not), thank you for always helping us authors. Without your cheerleading and unwavering support, our jobs would be a tad bit harder. You all amaze me. Nothing but love.

To anyone else I may have forgotten to mention. These things are hard to write, no joke ☹.

Last but certainly so very important: my readers. Thank you for waiting for me to bang out another tale. It's been a long ride. Considering *Amber to Ashes* is 90 percent true-life pieces of myself, made up of fragments of my past and present (the other 10 percent thrown in to make you wonder what it is I've *really* gone through ☺), it was a doozy to write. Standing in the mirror, really seeing who you've become, is a scary thing. Having to face your rights and wrongs, your good and bad, is even scarier. If I've learned one thing from getting through the first part of *Amber to Ashes* is to forgive the ghosts of your past. Sure, they're going to pop their ugly heads into the life you currently lead, but never allow them to force you into becoming scared to death of your future.

It's yours, not theirs.